PRAISE FOR ROBERT BAILEY

Rich Waters

"Small town, big story—*Rich Waters* works like magic as a mystery and a legal thriller, but what I loved best was Robert Bailey's attention to the details of character and place. I'd ride with Jason Rich to a courthouse anywhere!"

—Michael Connelly, #1 *New York Times* bestselling author

Rich Blood

An Amazon Best Book of the Month: Mystery, Thriller, and Suspense

"Well-drawn characters match the surprise-filled plot. Phillip Margolin fans will be enthralled."

—*Publishers Weekly* (starred review)

"*Rich Blood* is a deliciously clever legal thriller that keeps you turning pages fast and furious. Robert Bailey's latest is wildly entertaining."

—Patricia Cornwell, #1 *New York Times* bestselling author

The Wrong Side

"Bailey expertly ratchets up the suspense as the plot builds to a surprise punch ending. Readers will impatiently await the next in the series."

—*Publishers Weekly* (starred review)

"Soc̶ ensify a workmanlike mystery."

—*Kirkus Reviews*

T0026892

Previous Praise for Robert Bailey

"*The Professor* is that rare combination of thrills, chills, and heart. Gripping from the first page to the last."
— Winston Groom, author of *Forrest Gump*

"Robert Bailey is a thriller writer to reckon with. His debut novel has a tight and twisty plot, vivid characters, and a pleasantly down-home sensibility that will remind some readers of adventures in Grisham-land. Luckily, Robert Bailey is an original, and his skill as a writer makes the Alabama setting all his own. *The Professor* marks the beginning of a very promising career."
— Mark Childress, author of *Georgia Bottoms* and *Crazy in Alabama*

"Taut, page turning, and smart, *The Professor* is a legal thriller that will keep readers up late as the twists and turns keep coming. Set in Alabama, it also includes that state's greatest icon, one Coach Bear Bryant. In fact, the Bear gets things going with the energy of an Alabama kickoff to Auburn. Robert Bailey knows his state, and he knows his law. He also knows how to write characters that are real, sympathetic, and surprising. If he keeps writing novels this good, he's got quite a literary career before him."
— Homer Hickam, author of *Rocket Boys / October Sky*, a *New York Times* #1 bestseller

"Bailey's solid second McMurtrie and Drake legal thriller (after 2014's *The Professor*) . . . provides enough twists and surprises to keep readers turning the pages."
— *Publishers Weekly*

RICH
WATERS

ALSO BY ROBERT BAILEY

JASON RICH SERIES

Rich Blood

BOCEPHUS HAYNES SERIES

The Wrong Side

Legacy of Lies

MCMURTRIE AND DRAKE LEGAL THRILLERS

The Final Reckoning

The Last Trial

Between Black and White

The Professor

OTHER BOOKS

The Golfer's Carol

RICH WATERS

ROBERT BAILEY

THOMAS & MERCER

Published by Thomas & Mercer, Seattle

www.apub.com

Amazon, the Amazon logo, and Thomas & Mercer are trademarks of Amazon.com, Inc., or its affiliates.

ISBN-13: 9781542037297 (paperback)
ISBN-13: 9781542037280 (digital)

Cover design by Jarrod Taylor
Cover image: © tcsworkshop / Shutterstock

Printed in the United States of America

For my brother, Bo Randall Bailey

PART ONE

1

Trey Cowan blinked at his half-empty mug and pressed it to his lips. He breathed in the scent of cheap draft beer and felt the stares that always accompanied him everywhere he went in Marshall County. He didn't have to imagine their thoughts and muffled conversations. They were the soundtrack of his life.

Do you remember when Trey threw for five hundred against Scottsboro?

Or when he ran for sixty against Albertville in the mud?

He was a right-handed Snake Stabler.

He would have started at Bama as a freshman.

Could have been a first-round draft choice.

Trey drank from his glass, the beer tasting as bitter as his thoughts. He glared at the mirror above the bar and saw the patrons of the Brick Grill & Bar enjoying their food and themselves. Then he stared at his own glazed, bloodshot eyes in the reflection.

He pressed his forehead to the cold mug and closed his eyes. Why had he come here? He could get drunk by himself at home. Was it some kind of sick torture he enjoyed putting himself through? Were the folks in the Brick really talking about him? Or thinking about him at all? Hell, did they even see him? Or was he simply invisible, like a piece of worn-out furniture or a neon beer sign on the wall?

When he felt a hand squeeze his shoulder, his whole body tensed.

"Hitting it pretty hard, aren't you, champ?"

Trey opened his eyes but kept his gaze fixed on the mirror. "Leave me alone, Kelly," he said, his teeth clenched.

"Well, now, that's no way to talk to your favorite former receiver." Kelly Flowers took a seat in the empty stool next to Trey and waved the bartender over. "Diet Coke, Teresa."

A woman with long black hair walked over. She wore a white tank top and tight jeans. "Coming right up," she said. "You on duty or rolling off?"

Kelly ran a hand through his hair, and Trey glared at the deputy's reflection in the glass. He was wearing his khaki uniform, complete with gun belt.

"That depends on my friend here," he said, leaning his right elbow on the bar and peering at Trey.

Teresa placed a glass of soda in front of Kelly and shot Trey a concerned glance. Trey sighed and took a sip from his mug. Finally, he turned and looked at the officer. "What do you want?"

"Nothing big," Kelly said, his voice low but not quite a whisper.

"*What?*"

"Tyson needs you to make a delivery tomorrow."

Trey felt a ripple of adrenaline combined with hate scour through him. He drank another sip of beer but tasted nothing. "No."

Kelly chuckled. "What do you mean, 'no'?"

Trey leaned forward. He was almost nose to nose with the officer. "I mean . . . *no.*"

Kelly grinned as Teresa ambled over. "Need a menu?" she asked.

"No, I'm good, but my friend here probably needs some nourishment."

"I'm not hungry," Trey said, shifting back in his seat and taking another drink from his mug.

"Bring us some cheese fries," Kelly said, winking at the barmaid.

"Yes, sir," Teresa said.

Kelly covered his mouth and coughed. When he spoke again, there was an edge to his tone. "Do you really want to risk getting on Tyson's bad side?"

Trey downed the rest of his beer and held up his mug. When Teresa came over, Kelly waved at her. "This one's on me."

"OK," she said, placing the empty glass in the sink and taking another cold one out of the mini freezer below her. She put it under the tap and angled it to get the perfect pour. When she handed it to Trey, she leaned forward and whispered, "That's the last one, OK?"

Trey nodded.

"You have been hitting it hard," Kelly said, his voice matter of fact. "I take it your tryout with Birmingham failed."

Trey glared at the deputy. How in the hell could he know that?

As if sensing the question in his eyes, Kelly shrugged. "I eat at Top O' the River once a week. If you were hoping to keep your aspirations on the down low, you probably shouldn't have told Ms. Trudy. She's a wonderful woman and the best waitress in the place. But . . . she's got some loose lips on her."

Trey sipped his beer, gazing down at the bar. He knew Kelly was lying.

"Momma wouldn't spit on you if you were on fire. Try again."

"You know, come to think of it, I may have heard something from your ex-girlfriend. She's an awful friendly sort."

Trey squeezed his fists together until his knuckles cracked. An image of Colleen popped into his mind. She wore a sundress and lay across his bed, looking up at him with her seductive brown eyes. Then, grinding his teeth again, he saw her as he'd seen her last. In the cab of Kelly Flowers's off-duty truck. Riding with him to do God knows what. Trey felt his face turning red. His mind and heart were racing.

"And sure appreciative of the product I've delivered to her." The deputy's voice was like a knife slowly cutting across his chest. Trey reminded himself to breathe. He knew it would be foolish to attack a police officer in a public place, but Kelly Flowers was pushing all his buttons.

"Why don't you give football another try?" the officer continued. "That was your best sport. Five-star quarterback, pride of the Guntersville Wildcats. Offers to every school in the country, including Bama. If your leg has healed well enough to take a run at baseball, why not the pigskin?"

Trey took a long gulp of beer. He wouldn't be explaining his life choices to this prick. Flowers's condescending tone continued to fuel the fire now raging within him. Pictures of Colleen consumed his thoughts and combined with the helplessness that had come over him since he'd entered the bar. He was broke. He thought about Flowers's proposition. A delivery for Tyson, while dangerous, would help him keep his apartment and pay the bills and might even fund another tryout. How could he say no?

Nobody turns down Tyson Cade . . .

Trey squeezed his left hand into a fist and then relaxed it. Again, he forced himself to breathe.

As Teresa placed the plate of cheese fries between them, Kelly stretched his arms behind him. "It's no wonder that Colleen left you."

Trey lifted off his seat. He felt his feet hit the floor, and he grabbed hold of the side of the bar. He turned toward his former friend, who was now cackling.

"You're stupid all day long, ain't you, Trey?"

That was it.

Trey grabbed Kelly under the collar and picked him up off his stool, heaving him to the floor. He tried to kick the officer in the head, but Kelly rolled and shot to his feet, showing the nimble quickness that had made him a good slot receiver in their days together on the football team.

They circled each other for a couple of seconds, as a rustling of sounds rang out from the restaurant. "*I'll kill you,*" Trey hissed. "I swear to God, I will."

Trey lunged forward, throwing a wild punch that missed. All the beer he'd consumed had made him slow and sluggish. The deputy stepped to the side and elbowed Trey in the back, causing him to lose his balance. He would have fallen down if he hadn't run into one of the bar tables. When he turned around, Kelly was pointing a pistol at his head.

There was a scream from out in the restaurant, and Trey saw several patrons heading for the exit. He also noticed a few folks holding up their cell phones, capturing every moment for posterity's sake.

"I guess you answered my question," Kelly said. "You're as dumb as a box of hammers. Turn around and put your hands behind your back."

Trey held his ground, fists clenched, and glared at the officer. Then, feeling dizzy, he blinked and looked around the restaurant. He saw a family seated in one of the booths. There were two kids, a teenage girl and a young boy. The girl was wearing a Guntersville High letter jacket. Trey couldn't tell the sport. She was looking right at him, her eyes wide. Scared. The boy, who was towheaded with a ketchup stain on his Auburn T-shirt, was hiding behind his sister's shoulder and peeking out to look at Trey. When Trey met his eye, the boy ducked down in the booth. On the other side of the booth, a middle-aged woman, presumably the children's mother, had her hand covering her mouth. Finally, there was the dad, arms crossed, eyes narrowed, shaking his head. He looked familiar. Guntersville was a small town, but Trey couldn't place the face. Trey moved his eyes around the restaurant and saw similar expressions of fear, curiosity, disappointment, and anger. The room seemed frozen, the only sound coming from the television set above the bar.

"Hey, dipshit," Kelly said. "Turn around now or I'm going to call for backup."

Trey swallowed, feeling sweat on his cheeks and forehead. Shame engulfed him, and he glanced back at the family in the booth. They were still looking at him. Everyone was looking at him. *They all hate me. I . . . hate me.*

"Do what he says, Trey." It was Teresa's voice, and Trey turned toward her. "Please," she added. "You're scaring everyone."

Trey breathed in the scent of beer, burgers, and wings. He unclenched his fists and squeezed his eyes shut before opening them. Then, slowly, he turned around and put his hands behind his back. He felt the cold steel of handcuffs close around his wrists and then a rough hand on his back.

"Now, walk ahead of me real slow," Kelly said, the officer smelling of cheap cologne. Again, Trey swallowed and tried to breathe. His heart was racing, and he felt as if he might hyperventilate. "Move your feet," Kelly ordered.

Trey shuffled toward the exit, keeping his head down. There were murmurs from the patrons, and Trey thought he heard the word *loser*. Perhaps he was hearing things. *Doesn't matter,* he thought. *I am a loser.*

"Sorry for the commotion, folks," Kelly yelled as the murmurs grew louder. Finally, Kelly pushed Trey out the front door and slung him up against the exterior of the building.

Trey let his shoulder blades slide down the brick wall until his backside hit the concrete pavement. The alcohol combined with the altercation had made him woozy, and he thought he might be sick.

"I ought to arrest you," Kelly said, spitting on the sidewalk and glaring at him. "You're drunk. You assaulted a police officer. I could probably put you in jail for a while. Might do you some good."

"Assaulting a police officer." Trey spat the words up at him. *"You?* Tyson Cade's inside man in the sheriff's department. Double agent Kelly Flowers." Trey was talking loudly, and he didn't care.

Kelly took out his gun again, leaned down, and placed the barrel up under Trey's neck. "Now there's no one around, and you just threw me off a stool inside the restaurant and threatened to kill me. I could pull this trigger, and not a soul would ever say a word. I probably wouldn't even be investigated."

"Then *do it,*" Trey said, hearing the desperation in his voice. "Do it."

As he felt the weapon dig into his throat until he coughed, Trey closed his eyes. Then, his neck loosened, the pressure gone. Trey opened his eyes, and Kelly Flowers was standing over him. The officer was looking up and down the sidewalk, having put the gun back in his holster. "What's up with you, man?" Kelly finally asked.

Trey scoffed and shook his head. Then, using all the strength he had left, he rocked forward onto his knees, planted one foot on the ground, and stood up. His arms, which were locked behind his back, were throbbing from the effort. "Are you r-r-really going to take me in?" Trey asked, slurring his words.

Kelly took a key out of his pocket. "I'll let you go under one condition."

"What's that?"

"That you show up at the Alder Springs Grocery at eight a.m. tomorrow ready to drive."

"I told you—"

"And now I'm telling you. You're going to jail, or you're going to drive for Tyson tomorrow."

Trey tried to gather his thoughts. He leaned against the wall. The world had begun to spin. "How much?"

"Twenty-five hundred," Kelly said.

Trey bit his lip and gazed down at the sidewalk.

"Well?" the deputy asked. "Isn't that more than you make in a month cleaning toilets for the city?" He paused. "For a half day of driving."

"Where?"

Kelly spat on the ground. "You'll find out when you get there, but you should be back in Guntersville by early afternoon."

Trey let out a ragged breath. He looked past Kelly down the sidewalk, where the young family in the restaurant was now leaving. The little boy was holding his mother's hand, peering over his shoulder at him. The dad glanced in Trey and Kelly's direction, but only for a second. *Nothing to see here. Just a high school loser getting arrested.* Trey ground his teeth together. Part of him wanted to lunge at the officer and force Kelly to put him down like a sick dog.

I'd be doing everyone a favor . . .

"How about it, champ?" Kelly asked, taking a step closer.

Trey continued to watch the kid, wondering if he played any sports. Was he good? Was he fast? Did he have a strong arm? Trey hoped, for the boy's sake, that he was an average athlete. Being great at football in a small southern town was a curse.

"All right then," Kelly said. "Guess I'll be taking you to jail. Tyson is going to be very disappointed."

"Eight in the morning?" Trey asked, seeing the boy and his sister hop in the back seat of their family's SUV. Seconds later, the car was gone. The street, empty.

"Yep," Kelly said. "Don't tell me that you're starting to smarten up."

Trey finally gazed at Kelly Flowers, whose smug expression sent a rumble of nausea through Trey's stomach.

"Well?" the deputy asked.

"I'll be there."

2

Trey collapsed on a bench outside of Fant's Department Store about a hundred feet from where he'd almost been arrested. He watched Kelly Flowers's squad car disappear down Gunter Avenue and extended his middle finger toward it. His feet felt like blocks of concrete, and when he swallowed, he tasted acid. His arms, wrists, and hands ached from the handcuffs, which Kelly had removed after Trey had agreed to make the delivery.

I'm a puppet, he thought, going over the scene that had unfolded inside the bar and out on the sidewalk, envisioning Kelly Flowers's cocky face.

And that sonofabitch is pulling the strings.

For a long time, he sat on the hard surface and watched the town he'd spent his whole life in. More patrons left the Brick, and Trey figured the only ones left were at the bar. Which is probably where he'd still be if Kelly hadn't decided to harass him. *Twenty-five hundred dollars,* he thought, sighing and looking up at the sky. Clouds covered the stars, and all he saw was darkness. The only light came from the two traffic signals in either direction on Gunter and the glow from a few streetlamps.

Finally, forcing his feet to move, Trey trudged down the sidewalk and then up Scott Street toward his apartment. As he crested the top of the hill, his right leg buckled, and he fell forward onto the asphalt, scraping his hands but managing not to face-plant. He screamed, rolling to his side and looking over his shoulder for any oncoming cars. Then he laughed, the sound as bitter as the taste in his mouth.

It had to be past ten on a Monday night. With the exception of the Brick, everything was closed in downtown Guntersville, and there was hardly a car in sight. He could probably lie here all night without any worry of being run over. Trey peered up at the sky, feeling hate burning through his body.

He and Kelly had grown up a stone's throw from each other in Alder Springs. Kelly was two years older than Trey, and Trey had always viewed him as almost an older brother. They had done everything together as kids and had been good friends in high school. When Trey had suffered his leg injury, Kelly had been there for him and his mom. Getting groceries for them and helping out after Trey's dad had split town. Kelly had gone to Jacksonville State for a couple years. Then he'd come home and joined the sheriff's department.

But everything had changed when Kelly got mixed up with Tyson Cade.

Trey ground his teeth together. "Sellout," he whispered. Then he shook his head, knowing that he was now doing exactly what he'd written off Kelly for engaging in.

Dealing with the devil.

I have no choice, Trey thought.

But that wasn't true, was it? There was always a choice. Trey didn't want to live in poverty. He would not ask his mother for money, nor would he move out of his apartment and crawl back home. If he had any chance to ever break in with a Minor League club, he needed money and time.

And he was out of both. He was twenty-four years old. Not getting any younger. And sure as hell not getting any faster. His leg had healed enough for him to run, but he was nowhere near the speed demon he'd been six years ago. But he could still hit. He could play first base. Surely some club would give him a chance.

But so far, no team had.

Trey sighed and rolled over on his side. He again glanced down the hill and saw no cars. Finally, he pushed himself to his feet. He spat on the ground and began to walk. His pace was slower, his leg aching after the fall. Ever the glutton for punishment, he pulled out his phone again and sneered at the one-sentence rejection he'd received from the scout for the Birmingham Barons earlier in the day.

Sorry, Trey, but the team is looking for someone with more speed and versatility.

How many versions of that exact same message had he received in the last few months? It was now early April. The season had already started. Any aspirations of playing this year were gone. And if he were honest with himself . . .

"*I'm done*," he whispered.

As his apartment came into view, he thought about the deal that Kelly had shoved down his throat. "Twenty-five hundred dollars," he said out loud. The officer was right. That was more than a full month's pay from the city for a few hours of work. More money than he'd ever made in his four previous deliveries for Tyson. Would he go through with it?

I have no choice, he thought again.

When Trey entered his apartment, he limped to the couch and plopped down. He was exhausted. Drunk. And he didn't have a clue what he was going to do.

He gazed at the barren walls of his home. There were no paintings. No family pictures. The fridge in the kitchen contained no reminders. No magnets of ball teams' schedules. The only things on the counter were a few empty beer cans and a couple of unopened bills.

His apartment was as empty as his soul.

Hanging his head, Trey walked into the bedroom. He dropped to his knees and looked under the bed.

For a long time, he stared at the gun safe.

He was so tired. Exhausted with waking up and going through the motions of a life that had essentially ended the second his leg had broken on the thirty-seven-yard line of Chorba-Lee Stadium on the campus of Guntersville High School six years ago.

And worn out with the regret of buckling under the demands of Kelly Flowers and, by extension, Tyson Cade. Of being their puppet. Of feeling trapped. And of having the only good thing left in his life spoiled by his decision to do Cade's bidding.

"Colleen," he whispered, grinding his teeth as he remembered hearing her name coming out of Kelly's mouth.

Trey slid the safe across the floor and undid the latch.

He'd purchased the shotgun last year. Trey wasn't much of a hunter, but he'd gone to a few dove shoots with his dad and knew how to use the weapon. Sucking in a deep breath, he grabbed the twelve gauge and a couple rounds of buckshot from the bottom drawer of his dresser.

What am I doing? he thought, closing his eyes and feeling the room begin to spin.

Then, forcing his lids open, he exhaled and headed for the door.

3

At a little past midnight, Deputy Kelly Flowers pulled into the Alder Springs Grocery. The store had long since closed, and the only light was from a lone streetlamp and the cloud-covered quarter moon above. Though the convenience store had video cameras at the entrance, Kelly was far enough away that he could not be seen on the lens.

He was now driving an unmarked black pickup but was still in his uniform. He climbed out of the truck and glanced at his phone. 12:15 a.m. The meetup was just down the road at an abandoned barn. He grabbed the bag he'd picked up thirty minutes ago and began to walk down Hustleville Road.

He whistled a Luke Combs song and thought about his encounter with Trey Cowan at the Brick a few hours earlier. Trey was a lost cause. He'd told Tyson as much. He was also ungrateful. Where would the former five-star quarterback be without Kelly's benevolence? Because of Kelly, Trey had earned close to $7,000 over the past six months. Making easy deliveries for Tyson. Was it big money? No. Had it kept Trey out of bankruptcy and from living in his momma's shack? Hell, yes.

He owes me, Kelly thought, shaking his head and rubbing his back, which was still sore from being pushed off the stool at the bar.

If he doesn't show some gratitude soon, he's going to end up in a ditch.

Kelly reached the barn at exactly 12:29 p.m. One minute early. He took a pack of gum out of his pocket and stuck two pieces in his mouth. Then, nodding, he saw headlights approaching from the north, and a truck pulled up to him.

Kelly felt a tingle of unease as he approached and saw the passenger-side window rolling down. The truck looked vaguely familiar, but something wasn't right.

When he noticed who was inside, he cocked his head. "What the . . ."

He stopped talking when he saw the barrel of the shotgun pointed at him.

"Now hold—"

But the blast from the weapon drowned out his words.

4

"Alexa . . . play 'I Wanna Be Rich,' by Calloway."

As the familiar drumbeat opening blared across the speakers in his bedroom, Jason Rich smiled into the mirror and tightened his tie. Then he winked. Another smile. He turned around, moved his pelvis in a circle, and then sang the lyrics he knew by heart. Then he broke into his favorite silly dance. The one he'd pull out at parties when he really wanted to break things up. He made a fist with his right hand and lowered it to his left knee and then back up. Then he did it again. And again.

"Are you for frickin' real?"

Jason turned toward the unhappy voice. "Nola!" he yelled, smiling from ear to ear.

His seventeen-year-old niece gazed at him through the door that opened to the den. Her hands were on her hips, and her face registered a look of pure and unadulterated annoyance. She had strawberry-blonde hair, blue eyes, and the world's most deliberate and devastating eye roll, which she gave him now, followed by an impatient sigh. "We're gonna be late," she said.

"Come on," he said, lowering his fist back to his knee and jerking it back. "It's the lawn mower, baby." Then he danced over to her and did it again. "This is my signature move."

"Sorry. I wasn't born in the Stone Age."

He ignored her and sang the chorus as he moved in a circle round her and bounced his left hip into her right. "Come on, it's the first day of trial. It's tradition."

"But you've only tried one case."

He pointed at her and then danced back to the mirror. "True, but before mediations, I always play this song, and I want the same positive vibe for this trial."

"The only vibe I'm getting is the sudden urge to vomit."

He looked at her. "Have you read the copy of *The Secret* I gave you?"

Another eye roll.

"Well, if you had read it, you would know that people attract what they are thinking about." He held out his palms. "I'm thinking and even singing about wanting money. Lots and lots of money. And by doing so, I'm sending out a transmission to the universe, which will bring me . . ."

He paused, waiting for her to fill in the blank.

"A bowl of puke?" she guessed.

"A big verdict," Jason said. "A huge settlement during the trial after the defendants see the writing on the wall. Something that brings . . . lots and lots of money."

"And if it doesn't work?"

"It will," Jason said, turning and looking at her. "You just have to believe."

Eye roll number three. "I liked you so much better when you were a drunk."

He stared at his reflection again and grabbed a comb, shrugged, put the comb down, and then ran his hands through his hair to tousle it.

"You are the ultimate narcissist," Nola said, using her new word. She seemed to have a different negative description of him every week. But, at least for this one, Jason figured she might be right.

"Got to look good for the jury," Jason said. "But not too good," he said, running his fingers along his stubble.

"You have no worries there," she said, her voice monotone as she turned and walked to the door. "You're not going to make me listen to that mess on the way to school, are you?"

He shook his head. "Of course not. Once we're in the car, we have to listen to my theme music."

For a second, she looked confused. Then her eyebrows creased. "No. Please, Uncle Jason. Please don't do that—"

"I'm sorry, Noles. Tradition is tradition."

———

Five minutes later, they were in his Porsche. It was a midnight-black 911 with his brand advertised on the plate.

GETRICH

He pulled out of the driveway and felt her eyes boring into him. "Is it your mission in life to embarrass me?" she finally asked.

"No, just a fringe benefit of having a bunch of billboards and being your guardian."

As they turned from Mill Creek Road onto Highway 79, Jason looked at her and raised his eyebrows. "You ready?"

She must have been tired of rolling her eyes because all she did was shrug. "Why couldn't we have taken my car?"

"Because I'm going to court right after our meeting. And because you're grounded."

She sucked air through her clenched teeth.

"So . . . are you ready?" Jason repeated.

She looked away, but Jason thought he saw the tiniest hint of an annoyed smile. "Siri, play my theme music," he said.

As the opening guitar riff of "Highway to Hell," by AC/DC, exploded out of his sound system, Jason Rich let the roof down on the sports car and howled up in the air.

"Uncle Jason, it's freezing!" Nola screamed, folding her arms across her chest.

But he ignored her, thinking about Nate Shuttle and the army of defense lawyers waiting for him in Florence and trying not to worry about the conference they were about to attend. "Nah, it's good," he screamed back. "The cold will get the blood flowing."

He brought his attention back to the road as his niece turned away from him.

"Mr. Rich, I'm glad you could be here," said Shawna Carter, the counselor at Guntersville High School. She wore dark slacks and a beige sweater and had an open manila folder on her desk. She looked at a couple of pieces of paper in the folder before eyeing Jason. "Your niece asked for this joint meeting, and I think it's an excellent idea."

Jason glanced at Nola, who was sitting with her hands in her lap and gazing at the desk. She had on her customary faded jeans, a gray Guntersville High hoodie, and tennis shoes. She'd placed her backpack on the floor. "Well . . . me too," he said, returning his focus to the counselor.

"As I'm sure you are aware, Nola is struggling in her studies."

Jason looked at his niece out of the corner of his eye. Was he aware of a problem? Every time he asked her about school, she said things were fine. Nola didn't look back at him, but she did begin to squeeze her hands together.

"You *are* aware that she is currently failing three of her classes. English, math analysis, and history, and she has a D in Spanish."

Jason took in a deep breath. Trying to keep things positive, he asked, "Is there anything she's passing?"

Ms. Carter gave him a stern look. "She has a B plus in stagecraft."

"Well, that's good, right?"

"Everyone else in the class has an A," Nola offered, her voice distant, still staring at the desk. As with almost every conversation he'd tried to have with her since Christmas, she seemed completely checked out. Not ignoring him or Ms. Carter, but not engaged. A prisoner to this conversation . . .

. . . *and her whole life,* Jason thought. He peered from his niece to the counselor.

Ms. Carter, her expression softer, nodded to confirm what Nola had said was true.

"OK," Jason said, rubbing his hands together and thinking on the fly. "It's the beginning of April. There's still a month and a half left before graduation. There's time to turn this thing around, right?"

Carter gazed at Nola and then down at her folder. "Yes, that's possible . . . but not if a few critical things don't change."

"Like what?" Jason asked.

"Nola hasn't been going to class, Mr. Rich. She's missed eleven days of school, and when she is here in the morning, she's skipped her afternoon classes on many occasions." Carter paused. "She was also sent home last week for being under the influence of alcohol . . . or something else . . . during school hours."

Jason felt heat on his cheeks as he fumbled for the right response.

"You didn't know, did you?" Carter asked.

Jason kept his eyes on the floor and shook his head.

"I didn't think so. She was sent home with a note, and we attempted to contact you. An email was left on the address that we have in the directory and a voice mail on your cell phone."

Jason gritted his teeth. How many emails did he get a day? Did this one get blocked by spam? Or had he just missed it? He never listened to his voice mails because they were almost always spammers. *Good grief . . .*

He turned to Nola. "Why didn't you give me the note?"

"Why didn't you check your voice messages?" Her blue eyes pierced him. "Or your emails?" When Jason didn't answer, Nola crossed her arms and looked away in disgust.

"Look," Carter continued. "As a school counselor, my qualifications only go so far. I help kids having problems at home, with their friends . . ." She paused. ". . . with drugs. But most of that assistance comes in the form of making referrals to specialists."

"Nola is seeing a psychologist," Jason said. He gave a sheepish smile. "I am too. It's been a trying year with her mother's . . . my sister's . . . death as well as her dad's, and I'm new to this whole guardian thing."

Carter returned a warm smile. "I know that. Nola has told me about the efforts you've made. She also informed me that prior to this year, she hadn't seen you in years and that you're coming off your own stint at a rehabilitation center."

Jason tensed. "That's right. I'm an alcoholic." He said the words like he'd done in a hundred AA sessions since returning to Guntersville last year. There was no embarrassment or shame anymore. That's what he was. He said it the way he might tell someone that his sign was Scorpio. Or that he was right handed.

Carter looked at Nola, and Jason followed her eyes. His niece was peering at the floor. Her arms were crossed tight to her chest. Jason got the odd sense that if he tried to touch her on the shoulder or the hand, she might scratch at him like an angry cat or that his fingers might burn from the hate oozing from her. He sat back in his chair and took a deep breath, noticing that the desk had a family picture of Carter with a man and two boys who appeared to be in their teens. The photograph was at the beach, and they all had tans and wore big smiles. "You have teenagers?" Jason asked.

The counselor gave a knowing smile, glancing at Nola and then back at Jason. "Yes, I do."

Jason again fumbled for words. He was a few hours from picking a jury, and he figured he was more nervous right now than he would be then. He'd prepared to try the case. He'd read depositions. He'd looked at medical records. He was trained as a lawyer.

He had no training on being a parent. There was no way to prepare. "I'm doing the best I can," Jason finally offered, his voice weak.

"Mr. Rich, I didn't bring you in here to scold you. I know that you and Nola and Niecy have been through hell this past year. I just wanted us all to be on the same page. Nola is having problems, and if something doesn't change, she isn't going to graduate."

Jason rubbed his pant legs. "I grounded her last week because she missed curfew." If anything, his voice and this comment made him feel weaker. He glanced at Nola, who was still looking at the floor.

"She told me," Carter said. "She . . ." There was a pause, and Carter leaned across the desk and spoke in a gentle voice. "Nola, why don't you tell your uncle what you told me."

Silence. Nola looked up from the floor and now gazed at the ceiling. She sighed but said nothing. Still checked out. Still a prisoner.

Carter clasped her hands together and looked at Jason, who braced for whatever was coming. "Nola said you had a girlfriend . . . your neighbor . . . who's been gone for a few months. Chase is her name, right, honey?"

Jason felt a lump in his throat and looked at Nola, who nodded while still staring at the ceiling.

"Nola had become close with Chase," Carter continued. "But she said that there was a . . . breakup?"

Now Jason gazed at the ceiling, feeling his heartbeat quicken. Seeing images of Chase in his mind that he had been trying to banish. Her short hair. Her laugh. Her fruity perfume. The smell of her sweat.

He swallowed. "Chase and I are old friends, and she is our neighbor. We were dating . . . and then Chase left a couple months ago."

"Right after Christmas," Carter said, her voice soft.

"Yes," Jason said. *Christmas* . . . for most, a mention of the holiday would provide happy memories, but for Jason, hearing the word out loud made his heart flutter and spirit sink. "Chase and I . . . uh . . . had a . . ." He stopped just short of saying *fight* and glared up at Carter. "Look, I don't see how my love life is relevant to this conference. I'm here because I want what's best for Nola, and I care about her very much."

"Nola says that you've been gone from home a lot since the breakup."

Jason sucked air through his teeth. "I'm a personal injury lawyer with cases pending throughout the Southeast. I can't always pick when I have a hearing or a trial, and I have to do my job." He held out his hands. "I'm home as much as I can be, and I always arrange for a responsible adult to be at the house when I'm gone."

"Are you calling the Tonidandel brothers *responsible adults*?" Nola hissed the question, again piercing Jason with her glare. When she looked at him this way, she reminded him so much of her mother, who'd had the same crystal-blue eyes. Jason swallowed at the memory, bittersweet.

"They're decorated soldiers, and you love Satch," he said, keeping his tone measured.

"They're batshit crazy," Nola challenged.

Jason looked at Carter, both for help and also to see if Nola's use of profanity had any effect.

The counselor placed both her hands in the air, palms facing them. "Let's stay on point, shall we?" Her voice was firm. "Mr. Rich . . ." She turned to Jason. "Nola says that she's tried to talk with you about Chase, but you always blow her off."

Jason felt a twinge of anger mixed with frustration. "What do you want me to say here? The split with Chase wasn't my idea. I loved . . ."

He bit his lip and looked past the counselor to the wall behind her. "I've had a hard time dealing with losing Chase. I haven't wanted to talk about it with Nola, because if I dwell on the loss, then it becomes a trigger for my own problems with alcohol." He met Carter's eye. "Recovery isn't something that happens and then it's over. It is a twenty-four-seven, three-sixty-five-days-of-the-year thing. I'm doing well, but my health is fragile."

"And what about Nola's health?"

Jason saw movement out of the corner of his eye and turned. Nola, her arms still crossed, mouthed the word *"Hello."*

Jason rubbed his hands along his pant legs. It felt like the conversation was moving in a circle. "What's the deal here?"

"Mr. Rich, would you be open to talking with Nola about Chase now."

"Like . . . right this moment?" he asked.

"That's one of the reasons why we're here. Are you amenable?"

He shrugged. "I guess."

"Not good enough," Carter snapped. "Are you open to hearing your niece's concerns about Chase?"

"Concerns?" Jason looked at Nola. "What's going on here?"

"See." Nola's voice, firm and resentful, rang out again in the small office. She was looking at Carter. "He won't talk about it."

"Won't talk about what?" Jason asked. "I'll talk about anything."

For a moment, none of them spoke. The room felt stuffy. Sweat beads had broken out on Jason's forehead. If there was an open window, he might have jumped out of it.

Carter leaned back in her chair and crossed her arms. She gazed at Jason, then Nola, and then back to Jason. "Mr. Rich . . . Nola . . . I called this meeting because we're in a critical time, and I'd hoped for an open and frank discussion. That doesn't appear to be possible today, but I hope you'll continue to pursue an open line of communication. You're going to need it." She paused to clear her throat. "Mr. Rich, I understand that you have a busy job, but the situation with Nola is what it is. If something doesn't change with her and change soon, she's looking at repeating her senior year at best."

Jason felt a flutter of anxiety. "And at worst?"

"Suspension . . . possibly even expulsion."

"For missing a few classes? Are you kidding?"

"For missing the majority of her classes. For being under the influence of drugs or alcohol at school. There've also been rumblings from some of the teachers and a few of her classmates that she's bringing methamphetamine to school."

Jason couldn't believe his ears. *"What?"* He gazed at his niece. "Where—"

"Mr. Rich." She clasped her hands together. It appeared as if she was trying to choose her words very carefully. "As I said, we are in a critical time. Nola really needs you to be present, now more than ever." She glanced at Nola and then back at him. "I'd hoped this meeting would be more productive, but it was really intended to be a beginning."

"To what?" Jason asked, feeling as if he were the kid being scolded more so than his niece.

"To something different," she said, standing and extending her hand.

Jason rose and shook it. "OK," he said.

He tried to pull away, but she held on. "Now more than ever, Mr. Rich." She finally let go, and Jason took a step backward. His legs felt wobbly, and one foot had fallen half-asleep. "I understand," was all he could manage.

———

Once outside the office, Jason turned to Nola, but she kept walking. "Nola?" he called out, but she didn't stop.

"Going to class," she yelled, but she didn't turn around or slow her pace.

He started to call after her but stopped himself. What was he going to say? There was so much to unpack that he wasn't sure where to begin.

"She's a good kid."

Jason turned toward the voice and saw that Shawna Carter was now standing beside him.

"I know," Jason said. "She deserves better."

"Well . . ." She patted his shoulder as she started to walk away. "She's got you."

That ain't much, Jason thought, saying goodbye to the counselor and heading for the exit. Once he was outside, Jason took in a deep breath of the cool spring air and slowly exhaled. He counted to ten and did it again. And then again.

He took out his phone. It was now almost nine, and he was due in Florence by noon. Jury selection would start at one. He checked his email. Forty-one new messages. He sighed and put the phone in his pocket. He trudged toward the Porsche and collapsed into the front seat.

He needed to be present. *Now more than ever . . .*

But instead, he was about to be gone for at least a week. Jason punched the steering wheel and gazed around the packed parking lot. He was struck with a tremendous urge to have a drink. He could feel the sensation in his bones. The instant buzz that a bourbon and water would provide. The refreshing taste of a cold beer. Hell, anything. The syrupy awfulness of Mad Dog 20/20. Jason didn't care.

Inject it in my veins.

He squeezed the wheel and punched it three more times. Then he slapped himself in the face. Once. Twice. Three times. He looked around to see if anyone was watching him. If they were, they'd think he was a lunatic.

I . . . am . . . doing . . . the best . . . I can. And then he said the words out loud. "I am doing the best I can."

He forced himself to put the car in drive. Despite the cool temperature—fifty-seven degrees—he left the top down and felt the chilly air run through his hair. He breathed deep and exhaled as he turned left onto Highway 431. He practiced observing everything he passed. An office building, Total Dental Care, on the left. *That's my dentist.* The fork in the road at the McDonald's where Blount Avenue circled to the right and Gunter and Blount became one-way streets. Then the restaurants, storefronts, and businesses of downtown Guntersville. There were police cars everywhere, and the blare of sirens was loud and constant. Jason wondered what was going on. Had there been a robbery? A shooting?

Something worse?

Two miles later, the cold air and the distractions had done the trick. The urge to have a drink had passed. Jason breathed a deep sigh of relief.

"Siri," he said, sticking out his jaw. He glanced at himself in the mirror and then back at the road. "Play my theme music."

The opening guitar chord sent a shiver of adrenaline through him. He cranked the volume. *AC by God DC,* he thought.

Jason screamed as he ascended the Veterans Memorial Bridge and gazed at Lake Guntersville on both sides of him. As he neared the bottom, he saw his own billboard. One of a hundred he'd pass on the way to the Shoals.

IN AN ACCIDENT? GET RICH!

Jason shook his fist at the highway poster of himself and took in another breath of cold air.

I'm doing the best I can.

5

Inside one of the stalls of the girls' restroom on the second floor of Guntersville High School, Nola Waters sat on the commode and unzipped her purse. She opened a small package and carefully spread a line of crystal meth over the top of her spiral notebook, which rested on her knees. She took a straw from her purse and snorted the drug. She thought of her clueless dumbass uncle and Shawna Carter. And her mother, who'd gaslighted her at every turn before she'd been killed last year.

Finally, she closed her eyes and envisioned her dad, who'd been the only stable influence in her life. She saw his Gunter's Landing cap floating on top of the water and then the rescue team bringing his corpse up from the bottom . . .

Nola opened her eyes and wiped fresh tears. She reached in her purse and snatched a Smirnoff vodka miniature. She unscrewed the top and kicked it back. Then she wrapped it in toilet paper and opened the stall. She threw the wad away and took out some mouthwash. She gargled, spat, and looked at herself in the mirror, feeling hate burning alongside the alcohol through her veins.

Nola Waters hated school. She hated her uncle. She hated Shawna Carter.

She hated . . . *anything and everything.*

Nola extended her middle finger at her reflection.

Then she wiped her eyes and headed to class.

6

Trey Cowan woke up on the floor of his mother's kitchen. When he opened his eyes, his cheek was stuck to the grimy tile surface. He pushed himself onto his knees and tried to get his bearings. He blinked, and his temples began to pulse with pain. He glanced at the small wooden kitchen table in the bay window where he'd eaten breakfast every day of his life from birth to age eighteen. He saw a half-empty fifth of Jim Beam and a couple of shot glasses on the table. Nothing else.

"Mom?" he asked, pressing his hands against the floor and rising to his feet. His cell phone was still in his pocket, and he pulled it out. The screen showed two missed calls from a number he didn't recognize. The time was 8:47 a.m.

"Shit," Trey whispered, leaning against the counter by the sink to steady himself. He ran cold water and put his hands under the faucet. He splashed his face several times and wiped it with his T-shirt. "Shit," he repeated.

He was late. He glanced at his phone again, knowing it would be unwise to call the number back. You didn't call Tyson Cade. He called you. And when he did, it usually was never a good thing.

Trey walked over to the table and grabbed the fifth of whiskey. Not bothering with the shot glass, he unscrewed the top and took a long sip, wincing as the liquid burned his throat. He moved his eyes around the tiny two-bedroom shack he'd grown up in. He tried to piece together what had brought him here, but the events of last night were a jumbled mess in his mind. The altercation with Kelly Flowers at the Brick. Stumbling home. Grabbing his shotgun . . .

Trey closed his eyes and ground his teeth together. He took another sip of whiskey.

"*Shit*," he said out loud again, hearing the fear in his voice as his hands began to tremble. He gripped the bottle with both hands and brought it to his lips, spilling some down his neck. Then, wiping his mouth, he headed for the door, taking what was left of the fifth with him.

His mother's driveway was made of gravel, and there was room for only one car. Trey had parked his truck in the grass. He climbed inside and thought about calling his mom. She worked the front desk at Sand Mountain Used Auto during the day and then as a waitress at Top O' the River at night. For as long as he could remember, Trudy Cowan had worked two jobs to provide for their family. Trey's father, Walt Cowan, was a drunk who went from one construction crew to another. He now worked on the panhandle of Florida, his dreams of early retirement dashed by Trey's leg injury.

Trey started the vehicle and grabbed the wheel with both hands. What had brought him to Alder Springs . . . to his mother's house . . . last night?

He sipped from the bottle and shook his head. Then he put the car in gear and eased out of the grass and onto the gravel.

A minute later, he turned left onto Hustleville Road.

———

Trey drove in a trancelike state down the lonesome stretch of asphalt that he'd spent most of his life going back and forth on. He blinked as he saw the police cars at the Alder Springs Grocery and felt his pulse quicken as he noticed more patrol vehicles up the road at Branner's

Place, an old barn that had been a hangout after football games in high school.

When he reached Lusk Drive, his phone began to ring again. It was the same number as before. Trey glanced at the screen but didn't answer. He turned left and headed toward Blount Avenue. When he got within reach, his cell dinged with a text message. He picked up the device, and the name on the screen caused his heart to flutter.

"Colleen," he said, opening the text.

There are cop cars surrounding your apartment complex. Everything ok?

Trey pulled off at a gas station before he reached Blount. He texted back:

Why are you at my place?

He saw the three dots immediately pop up. But then they went away, and there was nothing.

Trey banged his fist on the wheel. In the absurdity of the moment, he was almost more disappointed by Colleen's failure to respond than the fact that there were policemen at his home.

Trey put the car back in gear, but he didn't turn right on Blount Avenue. Instead, he continued straight and hung a left on Gunter. Two miles later, after passing the Paul Stockton Causeway, he saw the placard indicating GUNTERSVILLE HIGH SCHOOL.

As if on autopilot, Trey drove around the school to the football stadium and parked his truck. He grabbed the fifth of bourbon and walked toward the field where he'd thrown over a hundred touchdowns in three years as starting quarterback.

He strode toward the fifty-yard line with purpose. At 9:15 a.m., though school was in session, there was no one at the football complex.

He stopped at midfield and looked around the gridiron. He took another sip of Jim Beam and trotted toward the south end zone. He stopped on the thirty-seven-yard line. Remembering the play as if it happened a few seconds ago, he went through it again. It had been a bootleg to his right. Option to run or pass. The blindside defensive end got a great jump, and he could feel his footsteps behind him. Trey saw Justin Crigger, his tight end, dragging across the middle. Could still see his jersey. Number 87. He was open. Trey had slowed his step and brought his arm back, planting on his right leg, forgetting about the defender. Just as he was about to release the ball, he felt his jersey being yanked from behind. The ball slipped from his fingers, and then his right leg exploded in pain. He heard a crunching sound, and he fell to the turf.

He'd never seen the linebacker coming in low. He'd been so focused on getting the ball to Crigger that he'd ignored everything else. He should've thrown the ball away and lived to play another down, but he'd tried to be a hero. As he lay on the ground, staring up at the lights, he knew his leg was broken. His season over. But all he could think about then was how stupid he'd been. Selfish even.

But he had thought he'd play again. Known he would. He'd even managed a smile as he was carted off the field to a standing ovation. A doctor would be able to fix it. No problem. He'd still be playing college ball next year. And in the NFL three years after that. Right?

Trey brought the bottle to his lips and managed another sip. His headache was gone, but he felt slow. Lethargic. *Stupid all day long . . .*

He winced as he heard Kelly's voice in his mind. Then he heard something else.

"Trey?"

He looked up from the grass and saw a figure walking toward him. The man wore a red golf shirt with the Wildcat logo over the heart. Khaki pants. White tennis shoes. The man was tall and thin. He still had a light-gray beard and similarly colored scraggly locks. He was just as Trey remembered him. Hell, Trey wondered if Ronnie Kirk had popped out of the womb wearing khakis and tennis shoes.

"Coach," Trey said, his voice hoarse.

"What are you doing, son? It's school hours. I just got a call from our security guard, who saw you on the cameras."

Trey chuckled and took a knee, just as he'd done hundreds of times before and after football practices for this man. He took another sip of bourbon. "Haven't heard much from you since my surgery." He looked across the field to the home stands, focusing on the spot around the forty-yard line ten rows up, where his parents always used to sit. He smiled. "Come to think of it, I haven't heard from anyone at the high school since then."

"Trey, Harv had to call the police. They're on their way. You can't be at school . . . in the state you're in."

Harv was the security guard. He'd been there longer than Coach Kirk. Trey had once signed a football for his son. Trey took another sip of whiskey, tears welling in his eyes.

"Trey, what's going on?"

"What's going on?" Trey repeated the coach's question, finally peering up at him. This man, who he'd looked up to as a father figure in school. Who'd always been a run-first coach until Trey had showed up as a freshman. Then, quite reluctantly, Kirk had opened up the offense, and Trey had set the state on fire. "I'm about to be arrested, Coach."

"I'll talk to the officers," Kirk said. "There's no need for an arrest. You were a great player and student at this school. We just can't have you here drinking during school hours. You understand, don't you?"

Trey heard the sound of police sirens in the distance. Faint at first but getting closer. "None of that'll matter, Coach. They'll lock me up anyway."

Trey took a final sip from the bottle, turned it upside down to make sure there was nothing left, and then pushed himself off the ground.

He turned and heaved the glass up in the air as hard as he could toward the north end zone.

He watched it fall to the grass just short of the goal line. "That was sixty yards, Coach," Trey said, wiping the tears from his eyes. "The arm still feels great."

"And the leg?" Kirk asked.

The sirens were loud, and Trey looked past his old coach to the parking lot, where at least six sheriff's cruisers had come to a stop.

"It's better," Trey said. "I can run straight ahead pretty fast. Clocked a four point nine last week." Trey had run a 4.4 before the injury. "But I still can't move side to side."

"Trey Cowan!" a voice said through an airhorn.

Trey and Coach Kirk both turned toward the voice. A uniformed officer was about forty yards away. Behind her were five more officers. Outside the stadium, the number of police cars had grown to ten.

"That's an awful lot of cops for a trespassing call," Coach Kirk said, a trace of fear in his tone.

"That's not why they're here, Coach."

They looked at each other, and Kirk blinked. "What did you do, son?"

Trey swallowed. His throat was so dry. He saw Kelly Flowers's cocky grin in his mind. "Something I can't take back."

"Trey Cowan, I want you to get down on your knees and put your hands behind your head!" The officer had gotten closer now. Maybe twenty yards.

"Is this really necessary?" Kirk asked, taking a step toward the officer.

"Get out of the way, Coach."

When Kirk hesitated, the officer glared at him. "Now, sir!" Kirk moved backward as the officer closed in.

Trey fell to his knees as two deputies converged on him at the same time and turned him over on the ground. As his arms were being handcuffed behind him, Trey smelled the freshly mowed grass and began to chuckle. A tackle on this spot had ended his football career and ruined his life.

Now he was being arrested in the exact same place. *Fitting,* he thought.

"You think this is funny?" one of the officers on top of him whispered into his ear. Trey could feel spittle on his lobe. As he was jerked to a standing position, he saw a number of uniformed men and women. Behind them, Coach Ronnie Kirk stood with his arms folded. Eyes wide. An expression of utter bewilderment on his face. Principal Gary Ferguson, still sporting his signature mustache, had joined him.

"Coach?" Trey said, his voice a whimper, as Kirk looked down at the ground. "Mr. Ferguson?"

The longtime Guntersville High principal, who had once driven Trey to Scottsboro for a game when the quarterback had missed the team bus and who had sat between Trey's parents and Nick Saban the night the Alabama coach came to watch Trey play, looking as proud as a peacock, now carried an expression of pure contempt on his red, puffy face.

"Trey Cowan." A female officer stepped forward, her eyes narrowing into slits. "You are under arrest for assaulting a sheriff's deputy." She paused. "And you're being investigated in connection with the murder of Deputy Kelly Flowers."

Trey's eyes widened. *"What?"*

"You have the right to remain silent."

7

Outside the Marshall County Sheriff's Office, the American flag was lowered to half-staff. There were television news vans from all over north Alabama and print and digital news media from the entire state surrounding the building. Every few minutes, one of the TV broadcasters would report on the "murder," the "shooting," or the "gruesome tragedy" that had left a young officer dead.

Locals placed flowers against the front door, and what had started as a few bouquets had grown to quite a display. There were also photographs of Kelly Flowers being passed around outside and plastered on the television screens each time a report was given. Most of the pictures showed Flowers in his police uniform, but there were others in his Guntersville Wildcats football jersey and graduation photos from Guntersville High and the Northeast Alabama Law Enforcement Academy.

"A decorated officer with a bright future," Kisha Roe, editor of the *Advertiser-Gleam*, Guntersville's local paper, called him in her story on the murder.

If the mood outside the building was like a carnival, inside the brick exterior, the vibe was somber and, at times, hysterical.

Kelly Flowers had died at twenty-six years old. He was unmarried and had little in the way of family. A sister in Huntsville. A cousin God knows where.

He'd been with the department for four years, and every employee knew him. Kelly was good with names, remembered birthdays, and always seemed to have a joke or a quip. In a world of no-nonsense lawmen, Kelly Flowers had been a ray of sunshine.

And now he was gone. The desk clerks fought back tears as they answered the phones, repeating "The sheriff has set a press conference for eight in the morning" until their voices were hoarse. In the bowels of the building, the guards, deputies, and higher-ranking officers tried to keep things professional and go about their business, but it was impossible.

Kelly's death hit harder than most due to his youth and his jovial personality. The young officer's demise was also a reminder to every one of them that they might not come home from a shift.

Calls had come in from law enforcement agencies across the country. The governor of Alabama had even phoned in, offering the sheriff her condolences and demanding that justice be done for the fallen Flowers.

In his corner office on the third floor, Sheriff Richard Griffith sat behind his large desk. A laptop computer was in front of him, and he clicked through the crime scene photographs taken that morning. He had turned his overhead fluorescent bulb off so that the only illumination in the room came from the sunlight shining through the blinds in his lone window and the glow from the computer screen. Gazing at yet another picture of the dead body of one of his youngest officers, Griff rubbed his eyes and stood. He closed the blinds and leaned his elbow against the window frame. "Walk me through it again."

Detective Hatty Daniels cleared her throat. "Flowers's body was found at seven twenty-eight a.m. yesterday morning outside of an abandoned barn on Hustleville Road in Alder Springs. Lynn Branner, the owner of the property, discovered it. Branner, who goes by 'Bull,' lives in a house behind the barn, and his driveway goes right past the structure. He got out of his truck, recognized Flowers, and called 911."

Griff sighed. "I've known Bull forever. He's not a model citizen, and there was a time he used that barn to sell alcohol to high school kids. Hell, he probably sold beer to Kelly back when he was in high school." Griff scratched the back of his neck and closed his eyes. "Trey, too, I'd imagine." He turned toward his chief investigator. "Is there anything linking Bull to the killing other than the location?"

"Not that we've been able to find."

Griff glanced down at the screen, gazing at the body of Kelly Flowers. The lifeless eyes. The bloody hole in his deputy's chest that made a trail down his abdomen and spilled over his belt buckle and down his leg. The sheriff's right hand began to shake, and it was all he could do to keep his voice from doing the same.

"You OK, Griff?"

"No, Hatty. I'm not. But go on."

"There was a shotgun shell casing found near Flowers's body. Three-inch buckshot. There was another found in the passenger-side floorboard of Trey Cowan's truck." She paused, and Griff looked at her. "Three-inch buckshot," she finished.

"Exact same?" he asked.

"Looks almost certain, but the ballistics expert at the crime lab will confirm."

"Have we heard back from Clem yet?"

"No, but we should any minute. He did say, upon first inspection, that the wounds appeared to be from multiple shotgun blasts."

"Upon inspection," Griff said, spitting his words. "Talking about Kelly like he's a piece of spoiled meat. What else?"

"Dispatch received several calls from the Brick the night of April 8 about an altercation between Flowers and Cowan. I'm sure you've seen the videos we've gathered from a couple of the phones."

Griff nodded. "I called Kelly after those calls came in, and he said he thought he had things under control. He didn't sound all that concerned."

"Trey picked him up off a stool and threw him to the ground. He threatened to kill him, Griff. If that's not a strong motive for murder, I don't know what is."

"I agree," the sheriff said, and his hand began to shake again as he looked down at the body on his screen. "I should've done something. A word of warning. Something."

"No one knew Trey better than Kelly," Hatty said. "You can't blame yourself."

"He was murdered on my watch, Hatty. One of my officers. You understand, don't you?" His voice was shaking now. "I'm the captain of this ship, and Kelly was my responsibility." He bit his lip. "What else?"

"A twelve-gauge shotgun was found in Trey's truck. Remington model. Fingerprints on the handle were identified as Trey's. His clothes are currently being checked for gunshot residue, but the results aren't back yet. Ballistics is also going to compare the casings to the barrel."

"I'm no firearm expert, but my understanding is that it is difficult to trace a shell casing back to a shotgun."

"That's my understanding too," Hatty said. "Shotgun ballistics are more complicated than handguns, but let's see what the crime-lab guys say."

Griff sat on the edge of his desk, again looking at the screen. "Ronnie Kirk and I went to high school together. Been friends forever. I've never seen him so shook up."

"One of his former players has been brutally murdered, and the prime suspect is probably his most famous former player," Hatty said, her voice matter of fact. "Flowers and Cowan were teammates. I'm sure Coach Kirk probably feels some responsibility."

"It's a crazy world," the sheriff said, his voice distant. "I doubt anyone really knows anyone. It's not Ronnie's fault."

"And it's not yours either."

Griff stared at his desk as her phone began to ring. She answered and then placed the device on the sheriff's desk. "OK, Clem, I've got you on speaker phone."

Dr. Clem Carton was the longtime coroner for Marshall County and investigated all homicides and suspicious deaths in the area. When he spoke, his voice sounded tired and stressed. "Sheriff, you there?"

"I'm here, Clem. What's the verdict?"

"Cause of death is two gunshot wounds to the chest. Based on the size of the wounds and the fragments and pellets located in the chest cavity, there doesn't appear to be any doubt that the weapon used was a twelve-gauge shotgun."

Griff and Hatty shared a look. "Approximate time of death?" the sheriff asked.

"Between midnight and two yesterday morning, April 9."

Several seconds of silence followed. The only sound was the coroner's shallow breaths on the other end of the line. "Thanks, Clem," Griff finally said.

"I'll have my report to you in a couple of days."

"Good work, Clem," Hatty added and ended the call.

Griff walked to his window and cracked the blinds. It was 5:30 p.m., but the parking lot was still a circus below. "How are the witness statements coming?"

"Sergeant Mitchell is gathering them as we speak. At least twenty people saw the altercation at the Brick, so there're quite a few."

"And Coach Kirk?"

Hatty gestured to his laptop. "His statement's in the file."

"Does it read like a confession?"

"Pretty much. Trey never actually told him he killed Flowers, but the implication is there."

Griff rubbed the back of his neck. "And Trey's mother says he spent the night at her house."

41

"Yes, sir. Trudy Cowan's residence is less than a mile from the barn where Kelly was murdered."

Griff finally sat down and placed his chin on his fists. He looked at the screen again and closed his eyes. "Do you think we have enough?"

"After Clem's report, I'm not sure how we could have much more. At this point, it's just a matter of when we do it."

Griff let his hands fall to his desk, and he gripped the wood, thinking things through. Finally, he gazed up at his investigator. "I agree. I want you to call the district attorney and run through the facts with her. Assuming Shay approves, I'd like to make the arrest first thing in the morning."

"Before the press conference?" Hatty asked.

"Yes," Griff said. "And I want you, Officer Mitchell, and Shay present when we make the announcement. If Shay's available, that is."

"Yes, sir," Hatty said, turning for the door.

"Hatty?"

She turned toward him.

"Is there anything we're missing here?"

She blinked her eyes. "Why do you ask that? You heard me run down the evidence. It's overwhelming."

"Do we know why Kelly was at Branner's Place in his uniform?"

Hatty sucked in a breath. "Not exactly."

"What does that mean? You're his direct supervisor, Hatty." His tone carried a challenge.

"And you spoke with Kelly an hour and a half before he was killed." She fired her response back like she was spiking a volleyball. "It's only been thirty-four hours. We are working through all of his active files, but we both know that we may not figure this out. Kelly lived in that area, and he may have been following a lead. He'd been investigating Tyson Cade's operation, and I assume his presence at Branner's Place had something to do with that angle."

"You know where assumptions get us."

"It's the best we have for now." Hatty grabbed the door handle. "We'll figure it out, OK? Trust me."

"I do," Griff said. "Hatty . . ." His voice was shaky again. "I'm sorry. I just . . . want justice for Kelly."

"I know," she said. "Me too."

———

Back in her own office, Detective Hatty Daniels shut the door and locked it. She pulled out her computer and accessed her private files, which were found only on the hard drive of her laptop. She opened a folder entitled "MISC" and then clicked on a subfolder, "IA." In addition to being the department's chief investigator, Hatty Daniels was also its internal affairs officer.

Inside the subfolder, there were a number of still photographs, one video, and a lone Word document saved as "KFI." She clicked on the document and scanned the title for the umpteenth time.

Kelly Flowers Investigation.

She let out a deep breath and perused her summary, which was a running timeline beginning on March 1. The last entry was April 8 at 4:00 p.m.

Approximately eight to ten hours before Flowers's murder.

Hatty clicked out of the report. Only one other person in the department knew about her investigation of Flowers. She'd wanted to be sure before she accused a fellow officer, especially one of her direct subordinates, of a serious offense.

I should've told Griff . . .

But she hadn't. Kelly Flowers was one of the sheriff's favorites. She knew she couldn't go to Griff with accusations and innuendo. She'd needed cold, hard facts.

But now Flowers was dead.

She squeezed her hands together and thought through her conversation a few moments ago with the sheriff. *I didn't lie,* she thought. *My investigation of Flowers doesn't appear to have anything to do with his murder . . .*

With a shaky finger, she clicked on one of the photographs. It wasn't the best image, but the faces depicted were unmistakable. The same two people were in each of the thirty-two photographs as well as the sole video, which lasted fifteen seconds.

Kelly Flowers . . . and Tyson Cade.

Doesn't prove anything. Hatty could hear the sheriff's defensive voice in her thoughts. *Kelly was investigating Cade. Stands to reason they might have been seen together.*

Hatty's thoughts drifted to her timeline, the last entry in particular. Then she clicked out of the photograph and closed her laptop.

She covered her face with her hands and finally admitted the truth. *I'm scared.*

8

On Thursday nights, closing time at Top O' the River was 9:00 p.m.

If this was a normal night, Trudy Cowan would be chomping at the bit to get home and crack open a cold PBR. Maybe drink a few on her neighbor Paul's front porch and watch the cars whistle by on Hustleville Road. Sometimes she liked to bring home a couple of catfish fillets, fries, and hush puppies, and she'd take the food over to Paul's. They'd eat, drink, and enjoy the fruits of a "friends with benefits" relationship.

But this wasn't a normal night. Hell, nothing had been the slightest bit normal since Trey had been arrested at Guntersville High School two days earlier.

And the crazy had really ratcheted up yesterday when her only child had been charged with the murder of Sergeant Kelly Flowers. Last night, a brick had been thrown through the front bay window of Trudy's house, and she'd been getting dirty looks at the restaurant. So much so that the manager had asked her to work cleanup in the back.

I'll be fired soon, Trudy knew. She'd already lost her job at the used-auto place. The owner, Jeb Mullins, had terminated Trudy a few hours after Trey had been brought in for questioning.

Trudy washed her last dish at 10:30 p.m. She walked out of the restaurant with her head down, not wishing for any small talk with any of the other employees. She almost laughed at the ridiculousness of the thought. It wasn't as if anyone wanted to be caught dead in her presence right now.

Trudy sighed and spat on the ground. She unlocked her dusty sedan and collapsed into the front seat. She gazed out over the steering wheel at Lake Guntersville, which was lit by a half moon. Trudy could see the Paul Stockton Causeway and the lights of the Hampton Inn behind it. Finally, she leaned her head against the wheel and began to cry.

"Oh, good grief, Trudy."

She jerked her head toward the sound and felt a strong hand close down over her neck and cover her mouth.

"No screams. You know who this is. I'm going to remove my hand, but you need to calm down."

Trudy's breath came out in gasps, and she struggled to regain her senses. She closed her eyes and opened them.

"That's it," the man said.

"Jesus, you scared me," Trudy said, looking at him through the rearview mirror. The inside of the car was so dark that all she could make out were his eyes. "You can't sneak up on an old woman like that. I about had a heart attack."

The man snorted. "You'll outlive us all, Miss Trudy."

For several seconds, the car was silent. The only sound was Trudy's breathing. "What am I going to do?" she finally asked. "My boy is innocent. He needs a lawyer, and I don't have enough money to pay for one. And I'm afraid someone's going to hurt him before he ever gets to trial. I got a brick thrown in my front window last night. What's going to happen to Trey in that jail? With all those police officers hating him because they think he killed one of their own." She peered hard into the mirror. "My boy isn't a murderer."

Again, there was silence, and Trudy finally turned all the way around and looked at the man face to face. "I ain't never asked nothing of you, but I've always been good to you. When you was a kid and even now that you're doing what you do."

"I know, Miss Trudy. That's why I'm here." He leaned forward and kissed her cheek. "To help."

Trudy fought back tears as she exhaled with relief. "Thank you," she whimpered. She closed her eyes and began to cry, barely hearing the back door open and close. When she had gathered herself, she saw him walking away. Trudy flung open the door and began to run toward him. "Wait," she hissed.

A black Chevy Tahoe pulled to a stop in front of the man. He grabbed the passenger-side door handle. He turned around as Trudy caught up to him.

"What are you going to do?" she asked as a soft rain began to fall.

Tyson Cade grabbed both of Trudy's hands and squeezed. "You won't be having any more bricks thrown into your home. I run Sand Mountain, and no one attacks my people. No one . . . except me."

Trudy felt a shiver of cold run up her arms that had nothing to do with the rain. "Thank you, Tyson. I hate to ask for more, but Trey needs a lawyer," she pled as the rain began to pick up its pace. "A good one."

"Don't you worry, Miss Trudy. I know a great attorney. Probably the most famous in the state." He paused. "Or infamous . . ."

Trudy wrinkled up her face as Tyson climbed inside the SUV. Before he closed the door, he winked at her. "And this particular lawyer owes me a favor."

PART TWO

9

Inside the bowels of the Lauderdale County Courthouse in Florence, Jason Rich sat on a hard bench and waited.

And waited.

And waited.

By 4:30 p.m. on Friday, April 12, 2019, the jury had been out almost the entire day. Closing arguments had finished up at 9:30 a.m., so they were going on seven hours. Jason figured that was a good sign for him. His friend and mentor Knox Rogers, a brilliant medical malpractice defense attorney in Huntsville, had told him that juries normally came back with a defense verdict in civil cases pretty soon. Two hours was a good go by. Anything more than that, and Knox said he would begin to get nervous. Staring across the hallway at opposing counsel, Nate Shuttle, Jason hoped that was the case.

Shuttle was a fourth-generation lawyer from Birmingham who defended trucking cases for a living. He had thick salt-and-pepper hair and a similarly colored goatee. He always wore a dark suit, white shirt, and some version of a striped power tie. Shuttle was a good lawyer, but he had a temper, and Jason had a way of pushing the man's buttons. After a hearing in Jasper a few years ago, the two had gotten into a fistfight after Jason called Shuttle a prick. Though both men had been investigated by the Alabama State Bar, it was Shuttle who'd walked away with a fine.

Of course, Jason's problems with the Alabama State Bar predated his scuffle on the Walker County Courthouse steps with Nate Shuttle and had reached a head last year when the board issued an emergency suspension of Jason's license after he showed up drunk to a deposition. After a ninety-day stint at the Perdido Addiction Center on the Gulf Coast, Jason returned to practice under a strict zero-tolerance policy. According to his friend Tony Dixon, the bar's general counsel, this was his last chance.

Sitting next to Shuttle was his cocounsel, Winthrop Brooks, who just so happened to be the chairman of the Alabama State Bar Disciplinary Commission. It was a cheap shot for Shuttle to involve Brooks, Jason thought, as Brooks did mostly commercial litigation. He had no business trying a trucking case, but Shuttle was now in the same firm as Brooks, having joined Faulk & Stephens, one of the largest law firms in the state, earlier in the year. Jason figured that Shuttle, being the prick he was, couldn't resist providing Jason a reminder of the bar's watchful eye as the lawsuit had sledded downhill toward trial.

Jason caught Brooks staring at him and winked. Then he smiled wide at Shuttle, who scowled back stone faced at Jason. Jason, in turn, gave Shuttle a mock glare and then chuckled.

Shuttle shook his head. "Win, I'm going to go get a Coke from the vending machine. You want one?"

"I'll go with you. I may get some crackers." They both stood and walked down the hall.

"I'll take some peanuts and a Fresca, boys," Jason said, calling after them, but they both ignored him.

That left the third member of the defense team. Holly Trimble was a twenty-eight-year-old associate attorney from the small town of Fayette, Alabama. She'd been with Faulk & Stephens since graduating law school and was Shuttle's primary assistant on all of his cases. For Jason's money, Holly was easily the smartest lawyer for the defense, and he thought her opening statement in this case had been brilliant.

She was giggling. "Peanuts and a Fresca?" Her soft southern twang was pleasant, and she had a cute way of squinching up her nose when she laughed.

"It's a winning combo," Jason said, glancing at Brooks and Shuttle as they strode down the hallway and then back at Holly. "I love giving those two a hard time."

"I can tell." Holly gave him a weary smile, looking like she might want to say more, and then peered down at her phone.

"Your opening statement was fantastic," Jason said. "I'm glad those guys hogged the rest of the trial. I'd be a lot more nervous if you had done the closing."

"Thank you," she said, her face turning a slight shade of red. Her eyes rose to meet his. "You did a good job too. You . . . weren't what I was expecting."

"And what was that?"

She creased her eyebrows and laughed. "An asshole."

Jason held out his palms and gave a dramatic nod of his head. *"Thank you!"*

He said it loud enough to where Holly covered her mouth and turned her head.

"I swear," Jason continued, shaking his head. "You put up a few tacky billboards, and *everyone* thinks you're an asshole."

She giggled again. Her cheeks were now scarlet, and it again seemed like she wanted to say something else. But then, just like that, the moment passed. Her eyes darted back down to her device.

A tad disappointed that the flirting was over—he much preferred the banter with Holly Trimble to the testosterone-fueled stare downs with Brooks and Shuttle—Jason decided to do the same. He'd been getting texts from his partner, Izzy Montaigne, about every thirty minutes asking for an update. He also had check-ins from his lead investigator, Harry Davenport. His neighbor, Colonel Satch Tonidandel, had texted, asking nothing about the trial. Instead, Satch asked him to bring Mickey some Singin' River IPA home and he and his other brother, Chuck, some orange-pineapple ice cream from Trowbridge's. Make sure you keep that shit cold, Satch had ordered.

Yes sir, Colonel, Jason replied, letting out a nervous laugh. He missed home and was hoping to be back tonight.

Finally, Jason looked at all of his texts to Nola since Tuesday morning. She hadn't responded to a single one of them. The only way he knew she was OK was his check-ins with Satch each night. The Tonidandel brothers had alternated staying at the house while he was gone. *Like Ozzie and Harriet,* Jason thought, shaking his head. With Chase gone, the only help he had were the three retired army veterans, each of whom suffered from some form of PTSD, and, while perhaps not "batshit crazy," as Nola had so eloquently described them during the meeting with counselor Shawna Carter, the brothers were getting more eccentric by the day.

Things have to change, he thought to himself. He needed to be present in Nola's life.

Now more than ever. He heard Ms. Carter's voice in his mind.

Jason leaned his head back, thinking again of his and Nola's meeting with the school counselor. During breaks from the trial, he'd done little else. Nola had wanted to talk about Chase, and Jason had blown her off, according to the counselor.

Chase . . .

Jason closed his eyes. He'd tried so hard not to think about her this week.

Now, though, all of the waiting and the angst were making it impossible. He took in a deep breath . . . and let his mind wander back to last Christmas.

———

Jason squeezed the handlebar throttle on the Sea-Doo, and the watercraft's front end went straight up into the air. He howled as it landed back down on the smooth water and hurtled forward. He watched the speedometer as it hit thirty miles per hour. Then forty. Fifty. Sixty.

"Are you trying to kill us?" Chase yelled, but Jason could barely hear her over the sound of the engine.

When he reached seventy miles per hour, he finally eased his hand off the accelerator and waved at the cars passing above on the Veterans Memorial Bridge.

"Shouldn't we be turning around? It's getting late. Not to mention it's Christmas Day, and we are the only fools on the water."

"Just be patient," Jason said, turning his head. "We'll be there in ten minutes. And what are you talking about? It's seventy-five degrees."

"Be where?"

Jason cranked the Bluetooth radio full blast, and out of the speakers came Randy Travis's "Deeper Than the Holler."

He gazed up at the sky, and there wasn't a cloud in it. He glanced at the time on the console. It was 4:20 p.m. Perfect, he thought. Sunset was in about twenty minutes, their destination fifteen. He felt again for the tiny box in his swimsuit pocket. How many times had he checked already?

As Randy crooned the last verse, Jason readied the next song. "Wonderful Tonight," by Eric Clapton. As the familiar chords opened the tune, he felt hot breath in his ear. "Are you trying to get laid?"

Better than that, Jason thought, staying quiet.

At 4:40 p.m., Jason pulled the Sea-Doo to a stop fifty yards from shore. In front of them was a mountain with a cliff top. High above it was the moon, which was half-full. Not quite perfect, but close enough. Jason cut the engine and then the music. In an instant, the only sounds were the breeze whistling through the treetops in front of them and the water pooling around them in the wake left from their voyage.

"The cliffs at Goat Island?" Chase asked. "We aren't going to jump, are we? It's way too cold for that. And, if memory serves, you're a bit of *a fraidy-cat." She wrapped her arms around his waist and kissed his ear. Then his cheek. He breathed in her fruity perfume and her natural earthy scent. It was an intoxicating combination. He savored the feeling and then turned around to face her.*

Chase Wittschen's light-brown hair was cut short. When she wore it this way, which was quite often, it always made Jason think of Mary Stuart Masterson in the old John Hughes classic, Some Kind of Wonderful. *He'd kidded her about that one summer in high school, when they'd discovered the movie during eighties week on the Superstation. Her eyes were brown, her skin olive, and her smile contained a tease in it. She wore a light-gray sweatshirt over her bathing suit, and she squinted against the fading sunlight.*

"Earth to J. R.," she said. "What are we doing here? And why are you staring at me with that goofy grin. You look like one of your damn billboards."

Jason continued to peer at her, feeling the box in his pocket and growing tense. Nervous. His heart was pounding. He looked up to the high spot on the edge of the cliff where kids would jump. Chase was right. He'd never been brave enough to leap from the top. Perhaps that's why he'd chosen this location. He might not have the courage to jump off a cliff from sixty feet up.

But he did have the stones to ask the woman he loved to marry him.

He glanced to the west and saw the sun beginning to set, flashing a golden light over the dark-brown water. Perfect, *he thought.* Now or never . . .

He pulled the case out of his pocket and opened it. The solitaire diamond was 1.5 carats. Impressive, but not gaudy. Jason knew that Chase would never go for anything too showy. He cleared his throat and looked at her.

Chase had brought her hands to her cheeks and was gawking at the ring.

"I've loved you since I was fourteen years old," Jason began, pausing as a gust of wind blew through his hair and rocked the Sea-Doo. He gripped tight to the ring case and gathered himself. "Savannah Chase Wittschen . . . will you marry me?"

For a few seconds, her eyes moved from the ring to Jason and then back to the diamond. Her face was tense, and Jason couldn't read it. Finally, she stood . . .

. . . and dived into the water.

"Chase?" Jason didn't know what to do. He stood and looked around. The sun was sliding below the mountain. It would be dark soon. "Chase!"

She still hadn't come up for air.

He put the ring box in the security compartment in the front console. "Chase!"

Still nothing.

Finally, he jumped in, feeling an instant sensation of incredible cold. He shot to the surface and slung his head from side to side. "Holy crap!" he screamed. Then he heard loud cackles.

"Chase?"

He saw her swimming toward him. When she was within a few feet, she splashed him in the face.

"Are you crazy?" he yelled, wiping the water from his eyes.

"Me?" Chase hissed. "What about you? Have you lost your ever-loving mind?"

Jason was dumbfounded. "Chase . . . didn't you hear what I said?"

"Yeah, I heard you. Jason, have you been paying attention at all to what's been going on these last few months? Or hell, the last week?"

He treaded water, beginning to get used to the cold. Despite his shivers, his face was growing hot. "What are you talking about?"

She splashed him again. "You want to get married? Jason, I love you, but we have nothing in common. I'm a homebody. A lake rat. I'm not comfortable around a lot of people, and you . . . you're the pied piper. Your billboards. Your commercials. Your firm airplane. I mean, you're always going. Depositions. Hearings. Meetings. Alabama. Tennessee. Florida. I hardly ever see you, and when you are around, you're making me go to parties like Knox Rogers's shindig two nights ago."

Jason frowned. "You didn't have fun?"

Another splash. "*Are you kidding? I spent the whole night trying not to have a drink, while you butterflied around like the prom queen, backslapping with all of the good ole boys and flirting with the women.*"

Jason continued to tread water, feeling his energy dissipate. "*Chase, I'm sorry. You're my girlfriend. I want you to go to parties with me. Knox is my friend. And his clients and friends are all possible referral sources. My job is to attract cases. I am who I am.*" *He paused.* "*But I'm here now. Out on the lake with you. On a Sea-Doo on Christmas Day, asking you to marry me. I don't care if we are different. When I'm with you, I feel alive. I always have.*"

For a moment, she just stared at him as they floated in the water. "*You would be miserable with me.*"

"*You're wrong,*" *Jason said, growing angry.*

She shook her head. "*You're only seeing what you want to see. It's the same problem you're having with Nola. When you're here, which isn't very often, have you noticed she's never home?*"

"*She's a high school senior. She has her friends. Her life . . .*"

"*And it's falling apart.*" *Chase swam toward the Sea-Doo and climbed on. Jason followed, feeling as if he'd been kicked in the groin. Once he was back on his seat, he spoke while looking at the water.* "*I've noticed that she's been drunk a few times. But, you know, she's a teenager.*"

"*And you're her guardian. You're all she's got.*"

"*I've tried to talk with her, but she won't listen. We don't really know each other. I had hoped she'd come to you.*"

"*Me? I'm barely hanging on myself, J. R. I'm an addict just like you. And you know damn well what my biggest trigger is.*" *She punched his shoulder.* "*How could you do this?*" *Her lip began to tremble, and she looked away.* "*Look, it's almost dark. We need to get back.*"

Jason patted his pocket, which was now empty. The ring was now in the compartment under the console. Not on Chase's finger. He peered toward the west, but the sun was gone. He looked at her, tears streaking her face. "*Chase, what's going on?*"

"*I'm sorry, Jason. Please . . .*" *Her voice cracked.* "*. . . just go.*"

10

"Counsel, they've reached a verdict."

Jason's eyes popped open, and he shot to his feet, staring toward the voice. The bailiff stood in front of the double doors, beckoning them to come in. Jason blinked his eyes, returning to the present. He could feel the energy and nerves coming from Nate Shuttle, Winthrop Brooks, and Holly Trimble as they brushed past him. Jason took out his cell phone and dialed his client, who had gone to have coffee with his sons across the street. "Reg," Jason said, his voice parched. "It's time." Jason sent Izzy and Harry the same text—The jury's back—and then he entered the courtroom.

———

Ten minutes later, Judge Warren Elliott gestured to a woman in the front row of the jury box. "Mrs. Foreman, has the jury reached a decision?"

"Yes, we have, Your Honor." The foreman was a woman named Michelle Hurd. A nurse at North Alabama Medical Center. Thirty-seven years old. Jason had thought she looked sympathetic, and that's why he hadn't struck her during jury selection. Now, she held in her hand a single sheet of paper that would decide the future of his client, Reginald Jackson.

Reg was an assistant football coach at the University of North Alabama. He and his wife, Leah, had two adult sons, Antonio and Marquee, both of whom also worked in the Shoals area. Leah had been driving to a UNA football game two Octobers ago. The traffic on Highway 72 had been thick, as usual. She passed through an intersection on a yellow light. An eyewitness, Charles Russell, who was in the right-hand lane but behind her, testified that the light was yellow when she entered the intersection of 72 and Cox Creek Parkway.

The eighteen-wheeler driven by Bernard Scheer, a sixteen-year veteran of Fisk Oil, was trying to time the light. The rig never slowed as it began to cross 72, T-boning the Toyota Corolla driven by Leah Jackson and crushing the driver's side.

Leah was dead on impact. She had been a wonderful wife and mother. A career homemaker who was looking forward to being a grandmother. Now gone, because Bernard Scheer was late for a delivery.

The defense had gotten mobile phone records that showed that Leah had sent a text just seconds prior to the accident. She'd been texting and driving, which was a crime, Nate Shuttle had argued in his closing. And she'd entered the intersection on yellow. If that wasn't contributory negligence, what was?

The courtroom was dead silent as Michelle Hurd rose to her feet. Jason was struck by the loneliness of the spectacle. Unlike the packed house for his sister Jana's murder trial in Guntersville last year, this case had garnered no spectators save for his client's sons, Antonio and Marquee, who sat in the row directly behind them.

Jason watched as Mrs. Hurd turned to read. Then he closed his eyes and held his breath.

"We, the jury, find for the plaintiff and award as damages the sum of . . . $25 million."

———

Jason exhaled as Reginald Jackson collapsed into his arms. Then Marquee and Antonio were on him in a bear hug. There were huge sobs and shouts of, "Thank you, Mr. Rich. Thank you."

Jason felt dizzy as he walked across the courtroom to shake hands with the enemy. *"Win, lose, or draw, you always act like the verdict is what you expected,"* Knox Rogers had advised him. *"That's what Professor McMurtrie taught us in trial advocacy, and that's what winners do. Act like you've been there before even if you haven't."*

Nate Shuttle and Winthrop Brooks both had pale faces as they began to pack up their briefcases. "Good job," Jason said. To their credit, both turned and shook Jason's hand, but neither said a word as they shuffled for the door.

"Congratulations," Holly Trimble whispered as she walked past.

"Thanks," Jason said.

"You know we're going to appeal," she added.

Jason grinned wide. "I'll worry about that tomorrow."

———

Jason waited for twenty-five minutes until the courtroom was empty save for him.

Reginald Jackson and his two sons had gone home, all three of them dog tired from the anxiety and grind of the trial. They were happy, but no amount of money was going to bring Leah Jackson back. Jason knew that the loss of Leah was what they were thinking about now. Not the money, but the matriarch of their family. Antonio and Marquee's mom. Reg's wife. A beautiful soul taken from the world.

Jason had cried real tears with them. As a personal injury attorney, he'd been able to have many special moments with clients where he had settled cases for a lot of money. The emotions for the clients were the same then as they were today. Happiness. Relief. But, most of all, a bittersweet sadness.

But for him, as a lawyer . . . as a human being . . . this feeling was different. He had just hit one of the largest verdicts in Lauderdale

County history. He'd won. The defense hadn't agreed to give his client money. Jason had taken it from them.

He'd won his first jury trial last year when he'd successfully defended his sister, Jana, on charges of capital murder. But he hadn't been able to enjoy that victory. It was too personal, and too much had happened in the aftermath.

Jason took a deep breath, vowing to savor this one for as long as he could. He got up and walked around to the railing facing the jury box, which was now empty, and then looked up at the judge's bench. His father, Lucas Rich, had tried many cases. He had called Jason a carnival act with his billboards and his racket of settling cases.

Jason felt his eyes moisten, and he managed a smile. Lucas Rich had never cared much for any display of emotion. He had thought a lawyer should be like Atticus Finch. Stoic. Professional. Somber.

Jason Rich was none of those things. He'd never been able to please his father, and once he gave up on the endeavor, he'd gone out of his way to do his job differently, to prove his father wrong.

He gazed upward. "How do you like me now, Dad?"

Jason wanted to enjoy the moment, but he couldn't help but feel sad. *Why couldn't he have just been proud of me?*

Jason leaned against the jury railing, thinking of his dad and sister. Both gone, but never far from his thoughts. He had won today, but he was losing at home. Chase had left him. Nola might not graduate high school. And his sobriety was hanging on by a thread, as evidenced by his near relapse after the meeting with the school counselor.

He sucked in a deep breath and shook his head from side to side. *I'll worry about that tomorrow,* he thought, echoing what he had told Holly Trimble. Then, forcing an exaggerated grin, he turned in a circle, holding his arms out like he was the "Macho Man" Randy Savage entering the squared circle for a wrestling match. As a kid, while Lucas Rich had spent weekends billing hours at the office and Jana was hanging out with friends, Jason had been glued to the television set watching WWF,

WCW, and NWA wrestling. He had loved the good guys, the villains, the theme music, the costumes.

The sheer spectacle of it all.

Sticking out his jaw, he held his right pinky finger up in the air and moved it horizontally in front of his face. Then he screamed the Macho Man's catchphrase and a line from one of the icon's most famous promos.

"Ohhhhhhhhh! Yeahhhhhhhhh! The cream will rise to the top!"

Jason walked over to the plaintiff's table, grabbed his briefcase, and headed for the door. As he turned off the lights in the vacant courtroom, he looked back and thought of one more thing Randy Savage might say.

"Can you dig it?"

11

Jason arrived home at 8:00 p.m. As expected, the lights of his home on Mill Creek Road were off. He'd texted and tried to call Nola to no avail. All he'd gotten in response was a cryptic text: Congrats. I'm spending the night at Harley's.

Jason sighed and looked across the street, where the Tonidandels' shack was lit up like Christmas. As Trace Adkins liked to sing, every light in the house was on. He reached inside his Porsche and pulled out a six-pack of Singin' River IPA and a tub of Trowbridge's pineapple-orange ice cream, both of which he'd iced down in a cheap Styrofoam container he'd gotten at a convenience store. Then he trudged across the street, not bothering to knock. He knew the door would be open.

As he crossed the threshold, he saw movement out of the corner of his eye. It was a huge old-school Igloo cooler, and it was being lifted up and on top of Jason's head.

Jason screamed as ice-cold lime Gatorade drenched his hair and suit. He blinked his eyes, tasting the thirst quencher, and then he started to laugh as he took in the crowd in the tiny den.

His partner, Isabel "Izzy" Montaigne, wearing jeans and a number 2 Derrick Henry Alabama football jersey, her dark-black hair up in a ponytail, ran to him and jumped in his arms, getting herself wet in the process. "You did it, Jason Rich!" she squealed, and then another icy Gatorade bath came down on both of them, this time fruit punch flavored and coming from the other side.

Now saturated with the sticky sports drink and snorting, as some of it had gotten in his nose, Jason looked to his left and saw Chuck Tonidandel, the middle brother. Chuck's bald head was covered by a straw cowboy hat, and he wore jeans, shitkicker boots, and a blue tank top that showed off his enormous arms. He pulled on his long, scruffy beard and dropped the cooler he was holding, reaching one of his huge hands toward Jason, who latched on. Then he closed his eyes. "Thank you, Lord, for blessing brother Jason with sweet victory."

"Amen!" was the collective response of the rest of the group, all of whom knew that Chuck Tonidandel spoke seldom, and when he did, he was either quoting a Bible verse or praying.

Jason wheeled to his right, where Mickey Tonidandel, the youngest brother, held the other cooler. Mickey had a thinning blond mullet, a Fu Manchu mustache, and an infectious high-pitched laugh, which he delivered now. Whether it was five degrees outside or a hundred, Mickey always wore shorts because he hated "static cling," as he called it. He typically wore some kind of rock concert T-shirt, and tonight's entry was Whitesnake from 1997. Mickey looked like he could have been in that band. "Did you bring my beer?"

Jason held up the six-pack, which was now covered in equal parts ice and Gatorade.

Mickey snatched it and walked away, yelling "Thank you!" as he made his way to the back of the house.

Jason felt his hands being squeezed and lowered his eyes to Izzy.

"Twenty-five million," she let out in a loud whisper, and Jason smelled champagne on her breath.

"Not bad, J. R." Harry Davenport, the firm's chief investigator, patted Jason's shoulder. He wore his customary black T-shirt and faded jeans and spoke in a low drawl. "I doubt there have been many verdicts in the Shoals any bigger than that."

"Thank you, both," Jason said, feeling his cheeks growing hot. "We're a team, and we won big tonight." He paused and then smiled.

"I was hoping there might be a Gatorade bath but wasn't sure how you'd pull it off."

Izzy punched his arm. "It's tradition."

Jason brought them both in for a group hug, feeling as good as he'd felt in a long time. "Hey, where's Satch?"

Izzy hiccuped and covered her mouth. Then she giggled. "He's in the back watching . . ." She giggled again. ". . . TV."

"What?" Jason asked, looking to Harry, who rolled his eyes.

"You'll see," he said, slapping Jason on the back. "J. R., I'm going to take this one into Huntsville for some R&R. Got us a room at that Bridge Street Westin."

"Sounds good," Jason said. Harry and Izzy had been an on-again, off-again couple for years, and it appeared that they were back on.

"Congrats, amigo."

"Thanks, Harry," Jason said. "Take care of our girl." He nodded in Izzy's direction. His partner had just tipped a bottle of champagne up and then hiccuped. "Twenty-five million buckeroos!" She squealed, and Jason and Harry both shook their head. "She'll be passed out before we get to New Hope," Harry said as he walked over, picked her up in his arms, and carried her past the threshold. "I'll call you in the morning," Izzy hollered as the door slammed shut.

Jason looked around the room, the floor now covered with Gatorade and ice. If Chuck and Mickey were worried about the mess, they weren't showing it. Jason picked his way through the puddles and trudged to the back den. The flooring was rickety plywood, and there were only a few rugs. As Jason entered, he saw that Chuck and Mickey were both sprawled on an old leather couch against the wall.

On the other side of the room, Colonel Satchel Shames Tonidandel sat in a tattered La-Z-Boy recliner that was a tad too small for his six-foot, three-inch, 250-pound frame. With the footrest out and the chair fully reclined, Jason wondered how it could withstand the weight and leverage Satch was applying.

Satch didn't look up, his eyes glued to the television set. The colonel had curly brown hair and a salt-and-pepper beard that he was pulling on at present. He was tense. Locked in. Jason followed his eyes, blinked, and then looked at Mickey and Chuck, who were also staring at the screen.

"Hey, this part here is good," Chuck said.

Satch held up a finger. "If you ruin it for me, I will wipe my ass with your toothbrush."

"God, forgive him," Chuck said. "How many times you seen this, Colonel?"

"It gets better every time," Satch said. "Now shut the hell up. Jock's about to whup some ass." He pointed at the screen, and Chuck and Mickey both stifled laughs.

"*Dallas*?" Jason whispered, looking to each of the brothers and then back at the screen, where Jock Ewing, the Ewing patriarch of the famous soap opera, played by the legendary character actor Jim Davis, was getting into a fistfight with another man. Jock's sons Bobby and Ray—Jason couldn't remember if Jock knew that Ray was his son yet—were also fighting off the other man's friends, and the eldest son, J. R., ended the fight by taking a beer bottle to a man's head.

Mickey nodded, whispering, "He watches *Dallas* and *Falcon Crest* every Friday night like he's stuck in 1984. And he'll only watch one episode a night." He giggled and shook his head.

On the screen, Jock, Ray, Bobby, and J. R. were now walking out of the bar together arm in arm after winning the brawl.

"Thank you, guys," Jason whispered. "I'll clean up." He backed away, but Satch's gravelly voice stopped him. He turned and noticed that the television had been paused.

"You done good, Jason. I'm proud of you."

"Thank you."

"You bring my ice cream?"

"Yes, sir. Right here." He held it up for the big man to see.

"Thank you. Put it in the freezer, would you?" Satch asked, his eyes glued again to the tube.

Jason fired off a salute and walked back to the front of the house. He put the carton in the freezer and then found a mop from the utility room.

He ran a hand through his sticky hair and chuckled. It was good to be home.

———

Thirty minutes later, Jason was sitting in the screened-in sunroom of his empty home. He gazed out at Lake Guntersville. He had showered and put his soaked suit in the dry cleaner's box. He looked at his boathouse, thinking it would be lake weather soon. Time to get the Sea-Doo out.

The 1.5-carat diamond that Jason had bought Chase Wittschen, unless it had been stolen, should still be in the front console compartment of the watercraft. In his disappointment in the aftermath of coming home after his and Chase's ill-fated voyage to Goat Island on Christmas Day, Jason had forgotten to remove the ring case before putting the cover back on the Sea-Doo. He'd realized his gaffe once he was inside the house, not having the energy to go get it.

So it had stayed behind.

Meanwhile, Chase had left the next morning, December 26. Jason had brought coffee over to her, hoping to patch things up. He'd found a note instead. *Need some space. I'm sorry.*

That's all it had said.

And Jason hadn't seen or spoken to her since. He knew she had been back a few times, but never when he was around. Always when he was out of town for travel.

Nola had mentioned seeing her. As had Satch. But she hadn't called, texted, or left anything for Jason other than her original note.

None of it made sense, but Jason didn't have the time or the wisdom to unravel what was going on. He couldn't control Chase any more than he could control Nola. Or his deceased sister, Jana. Letting go of those things was one of the teachings of AA. The serenity prayer.

Jason said it every morning, but he still had a hard time abiding by it.

Since Chase's departure, Jason had put a twin bed out on the sunporch, and this was where he slept best. Breathing the clean natural air as the sounds of nocturnal insects and the occasional breeze through the trees mixed with the whirring of cars passing over the Mill Creek overpass on Highway 79.

He lay back on his pillow and gazed again at the dark water. A few hours earlier, he had won for his client a $25 million verdict. An hour ago, he was being drenched with Gatorade by good friends who cared about him.

Now, though, Jason Rich felt completely alone.

12

Not drinking had become Jason's "superpower."

At least, that's how he liked to think of it. He'd relapsed nine months ago after his reprimand in front of the Alabama State Bar. His fall off the wagon had been precipitated more by events in Jana's murder case than the blowhards at the bar who'd given him his public shaming. Regardless, since then and especially in the six months after Jana's trial, as his schedule had returned to normal, Jason had noticed that the simple act of not drinking alcohol had given him something that he'd chased his whole career.

Time.

Instead of drinking four or five beers starting at 6:00 p.m., he was able to use that time to make a few extra phone calls, read over a deposition, reply to emails, and assist Izzy with the screening of new cases. Likewise, he went to bed earlier and got up clearheaded. In the lead-up to big mediations and especially in the month prior to the Reginald Jackson trial, Jason felt that he was as good a lawyer as he'd ever been. Since he couldn't drink to burn off steam, he'd done other things to combat the stress of practicing law. He almost always listened to music now. Something . . . anything . . . was better than nothing. He also read books, both fiction and nonfiction—self-help entries like *The Secret* and *The Power of Positive Thinking*. He got eight hours of sleep most nights. Finally, with an assist from Chuck Tonidandel, he'd started doing something he'd never done before in his life.

Jason Rich, whose only brand of working out prior to sobriety was lifting twelve-ounce longnecks, had started a strength-training program.

Relishing these positive thoughts, Jason grasped the bar with both hands. Then he adjusted and readjusted his grip. He sucked in a deep breath and lifted the bar off the rack, exhaling just before bringing the weight down to his chest and pressing it back up. "One," he said out loud, lowering the weight again. "Two." This time, he held the bar up for a split second. On the loudspeakers, he could hear AC/DC's "Shoot to Thrill" drop into the chorus. His goal was three reps, which he had never done before with 205 pounds. He exhaled again and lowered the weight, then thrust the bar up with all his strength. "Three!" he screamed and reracked the bar.

He sat up on the bench and gazed out the open door of the garage. At this time of morning, the rays of bright sunshine made the water of Lake Guntersville glisten.

Jason stood up from the bench and flexed like he might be Hulk Hogan after winning a match. Then he screamed out his best Ric Flair "Wooooo!" as the AC/DC track switched to "Hells Bells."

A fisherman in a bass boat who had parked for a few minutes by his boathouse glanced his way with a startled expression on his face.

Jason waved, but the man didn't return the gesture. He backed his boat up and drifted down the line to the next boathouse.

Bad form to yell while a person is fishing, Jason thought, his face turning serious for a second. Then, another thought popped into his mind. *Fuck it.*

"Wooooo!" he screamed again, arching his back and tilting his head to the sky. Then he strutted toward the front of the garage like the Nature Boy did after taking off his robe to start a match. The boat continued to move past the next boathouse and began to speed away. The fisherman looked over his shoulder and extended his middle finger to Jason.

Jason guffawed and turned up his right thumb. His universal retort after receiving the bird. The fisherman shook his head and swatted at him like he might be a fly.

"What?" Jason asked out loud, holding out his palms and grinning. "Hey, Alexa," he said, turning to the small cylinder. He tried to think of an appropriate song, and then snapped his fingers, thinking of something that Holly Trimble had said yesterday: "Play 'Asshole,' by Denis Leary."

Jason moved the bench from underneath the rack and cranked out a set of twelve pull-ups. Then he loaded a trap bar with forty-five-pound plates and did a set of ten dead lifts. Sweat streamed down his forehead, and Jason wiped at it with his T-shirt. It was 9:30 a.m. on Saturday, and Jason, fresh off a huge verdict and almost ten hours of decent sleep, was feeling good.

Alive. Which was why he enjoyed lifting weights so much.

Jason hung two more forty-fives on the trap bar. He walked out of the garage and spat on the grass. Then, after taking a long sip of Gatorade, he walked with purpose back to the bar. Stepping inside the opening in the middle, Jason grabbed the handles, squatted, and pulled upward with his glutes, hamstrings, and back. He did five reps and then let the weight fall to the ground.

But this time, he didn't scream. Instead, he put his hands on his knees as Denis Leary ranted about the virtues of being an asshole.

Jason had made a fortune settling personal injury cases. But since he'd shown his chops in the courtroom by obtaining a not-guilty verdict for his sister in her murder trial, the dam had broken. And yesterday's win solidified that he was here to stay. Not just a billboard attorney. *A trial lawyer . . .*

Jason and Izzy had added two associates to help with the caseload, and they were still having to turn good files away due to the volume. Jason ought to be happy. Ecstatic even. He was thirty-seven years old. He was a multimillionaire several times over. He was a hot commodity.

But one overpowering thought kept him restless and on edge. Waiting for karma or God or some other cosmic force to strike him down.

I represented a guilty client.

His sister, Jana, had killed her husband, Braxton Waters, on July 4, 2018. She'd hired a handyman named Waylon Pike to do the deed, all part of her master plan. Jason had learned the truth a week after the trial.

He closed his eyes and placed his sweaty face into his T-shirt. Then, shaking his head hard, he stood and walked back to the trap bar. But before he could add any more weight, a figure appeared in the opening to the garage.

Satch Tonidandel's eyes had a permanent reptilian narrowness to them, and they were creased even farther than usual.

"What's up, Colonel?" Jason asked.

"Nothing good," the big man said, his voice grave. "He wants another meeting."

"Who?"

Satch frowned. "You know who."

———

Tyson Cade.

Just hearing the name in his thoughts sent a shiver of cold through Jason's body. He finished his workout in a daze, going through the motions in an effort to steady himself. Satch said the meeting would be at 10:00 p.m. on the third hole of the Goose Pond Colony golf course. Jason was to arrive by water and come alone.

"I guess proposing that he drop by the office on Monday was out of the question?" Jason had asked.

"You know how Cade operates," Satch had fired back.

73

Jason did. He had made the acquaintance of the methamphetamine czar of Sand Mountain last year during Jana's case, and the young drug lord had initiated several surprise visits and clandestine meetings.

What now? Jason wondered, as he backed his Sea-Doo out of its space in the boathouse. He'd spent the last twelve hours pondering that very question, and he was still at a loss.

He had no one outside of the Tonidandel brothers he could confide in, and they hadn't offered much in the way of assurances. "Can't be a good thing," Satch had said, as they had come up with their plan a few hours earlier. "No shit," Jason had fired back, causing Mickey to guffaw and Chuck to bow his head for a silent prayer. The Tonidandels were all a little off, but Jason felt fortunate to have some protection, and he'd leaned on the brothers, especially Satch, in the months after his sister's death.

Tonight, he would rely on them again. Jason flipped the lights on the watercraft and did a loop around the cove at Mill Creek. At 9:00 p.m., the lights were on in most of the houses on both sides of the slough. Jason steered the Sea-Doo toward the back of the cove, idling where the water began to shallow out and become marshy. Beyond this point, the lake narrowed into a creek, and a cold spring percolated. Jason had enjoyed two of the best times of his life at that spring, which could only be reached with a canoe or a kayak. He peered past the grassy marsh toward the back of the cove, taking in the sounds of crickets and the occasional frog. For mid-April, the night was uncharacteristically sticky, and Jason felt his neck beginning to sweat. Jason wondered if it was the humidity in the air or the anxiety that had engulfed his being that was making him perspire.

He took in a deep breath and clicked open the console where he had put his driver's license and phone. Tonight, he had also placed a small handgun inside, courtesy of Satch Tonidandel. "Probably won't do you no good, but it's better than nothing," Satch had said. "Just in case you need more cover than what we're providing."

Jason touched the gun and then removed his hand as if he'd had it on a hot iron. Satch and Chase had both taken him shooting since his return to Guntersville, but he was a terrible shot. He smirked at the tiny pistol, figuring some garlic and holy water would provide better protection. Up above the main compartment, there was a smaller pouch to keep valuables. After hesitating, he clicked it open and gazed at the black felt case that held Chase's engagement ring. For a long moment, he glared at the object, which seemed to embody all of his failures.

Finally, taking in another breath and slamming the pouch and console shut, he squeezed down on the throttle, and the Sea-Doo took off toward the bridge. As he approached the tunnel, he glanced toward his own house, where all the lights were off but the upstairs kitchen lamp. He'd left it on for Nola, who still hadn't come home from Harley's house. He hadn't bothered to tell her about Cade's request, because he didn't want to upset her. Things were already volatile enough. Before Christmas, Jason had turned to Chase for help with Nola. But then Chase had gone AWOL.

Jason glanced at the dark and empty home of Chase Wittschen and gave his head a jerk. If Chase had gone off on a drinking binge, he hoped it wasn't because of him.

But it probably is, he thought. She'd so much as told him last year that he was a trigger for her alcoholism. Then, in their last conversation on Christmas Day under the cliffs at Goat Island, she'd said she was barely hanging on. He had pushed too hard for her to be a part of his life, and she hadn't been ready. Like the Tonidandels, Chase had to deal with nightmares and anxiety from her time in the service as a helicopter pilot. As a kid, she'd always been quiet and unassuming. Jason had never had a relationship with her beyond the waters of Mill Creek and, truth be known, didn't know a lot about Chase's life outside of their time together. She'd told him little snippets about her experience in the army, but nothing about the time period between high school graduation and enlisting. She'd gone out West for a time to work on a ranch—he remembered hearing that from his mother. She had no brothers or sisters, and she never talked much about her parents. To Jason, Chase was similar to the swamp girl from the book *Where the Crawdads Sing*, one of his favorite reads of the past year. His knowledge of her was almost solely limited to seeing her in this tiny pocket of Lake Guntersville.

But she's more than that, Jason thought. *That's just all I've cared to know. That's what she was trying to tell me at the cliffs.* He spat in the water and shook his head. What had Chase said last year as they were reconnecting as friends?

"It's always about you, Jason."

He pressed the throttle down with his right hand, and the Sea-Doo plunged forward. Regrets about Chase and Nola weren't going to help him tonight. He needed to be alert and focused. *And lucky,* his subconscious added.

Jason tapped the ceiling of the concrete overpass as he crossed under the bridge into the main channel. As always, the view of the water took his breath away. That was why he loved Mill Creek so much. The cove had its own private slough of water, but if a person were to venture under the bridge, all of Lake Guntersville and the Tennessee River awaited. The feeling of seeing the channel open up normally gave him a thrill, but tonight it only added to his increasing angst. He hardly ever got out on the water after dark, and he wasn't too keen on making the trip to Goose Pond regardless of how beautiful it was.

Jason engaged the throttle and took off down the lake, his hair blowing in the breeze. At this time of night, there were no other watercraft in sight, and the water looked like a sheet of glass. As he watched the speedometer climb—thirty-five, forty-five, fifty-five, sixty—he sucked the air into his lungs and prayed that whatever lay ahead on the third hole of Goose Pond Colony golf course was a small inconvenience.

But, as he passed the Docks restaurant and rounded toward the marina, Jason had a sinking feeling. As if he were being pulled back down into quicksand after having finally extricated himself from the mire.

He parked his watercraft and hopped onto the dock. Cade's instructions were to go to the marina via Sea-Doo and walk the rest of the way.

The golf course was about a mile away. Jason glanced at his phone. 9:30 p.m. The Sea-Doo trip had been quicker than he'd expected, but he still had at least a mile and a half walk in front of him. Jason glanced down at his feet. He'd worn Tevas for the ride but wished he had thought to bring tennis shoes for the walk.

Good grief, he thought, as he forced his feet to start moving. *I obtained a $25 million verdict yesterday . . .*

But here he was. Meeting with the meth king of Sand Mountain in the middle of a public golf course in the dark of night to talk about God knows what.

The sad part was that he hadn't even considered not going. Hadn't even bothered to ask Satch if he could blow it off.

He knew he had to go. When it came to Tyson Cade, free will and choice flew out the window.

Feeling his heart thudding in his chest, Jason picked up his pace.

———

Twenty-two minutes later, at 9:52 p.m., Jason arrived at the tee box of the third hole at Goose Pond Colony golf course. Had he not been as nervous as a long-tailed cat in a room full of rocking chairs, he might have enjoyed the nostalgia of walking one of his favorite local courses under the moonlight. Jason had played on the golf team at Davidson College and, for a New York minute, considered playing professionally. He'd always loved playing "the Pond," as he and his high school teammates had called the lakeside golf course. The first hole was a straightaway par four that went slightly downhill. Even in the near darkness, Jason had been able to picture the thousands of tee shots he'd hit on the hole, which usually left a short iron to the green. Jason had walked from the first fairway to the second tee box and gazed up the hill at the quirky par five, which was a sharp dogleg right that went up a steep hill and then down to the right. As Jason trudged up the hill, he almost ran into a gaggle of geese, and the momma goose had hissed at him, causing him to yell out loud and then curse under his breath.

When he had finally reached the third hole, which was a par three that abutted Lake Guntersville, he put his hands on his knees and tried to catch his breath. Though he was a lot stronger since he'd started lifting weights, he hadn't put much cardio work in, and his lungs were repaying him for this omission now.

"Need some oxygen, Counselor?"

Jason raised his head while still keeping his hands on his knees. Tyson Cade sat on a bench along the cart path. He was holding what looked to be a small golf club in his hand. Maybe a wedge? He wore black pants and a black T-shirt, and his hair was longer than the last time Jason had seen him and slicked back in a cut reminiscent of former Lakers coach Pat Riley.

"You need a haircut," Jason said, straightening his body and ambling toward the younger man.

"Oh, I'm always changing my look. I'm kinda like Keyser Söze. You seen the movie?"

"*The Usual Suspects*," Jason said.

Cade snapped his fingers. "Bingo." Cade stood from the bench, and Jason noticed he was chewing on a toothpick. "I try not to let anyone get too good a look."

"So to what do I owe the pleasure?" Jason asked. "I thought all our business was done. All accounts settled." He hesitated. "Even stephen."

Cade took a package out of his pocket and opened the wrapper. It was a Little Debbie oatmeal creme pie. He took a big bite of the treat and grunted. "Damn, that shit's good. I can see why Coach Saban likes them so much." He winked at Jason. "Yet another reason why he's the GOAT."

Jason took another cautious step forward. He squinted at the drug lord. "Tyson—"

"You know I saw Saban up close once." He took another bite from the pastry. "Six years ago. Guntersville versus Boaz. Saban was in town to see Guntersville's quarterback." Cade paused a half second. "Trey Cowan."

A tiny chill tickled Jason's heart.

"I think you are familiar with Trey," Cade said. "He testified in your sister's trial, didn't he?"

Jason said nothing. Cowan had been arrested earlier in the week for murdering a police officer. Jason had seen the story on the nightly news in Florence and had read a few articles online yesterday while he was waiting on the Jackson verdict. Trey Cowan had been a can't-miss football prospect who had broken his leg his senior season. Dr. Braxton Waters had done the surgery, and there had been complications; Trey had never been able to play football again. That history had made Trey a potential alternative suspect in Jana's trial last year. Jason had called him to the stand, and though Trey had initially hurt Jana's case, he'd eventually provided key assistance that had no doubt helped them notch a not-guilty verdict.

"Cat got your tongue?" Cade asked.

"I know him."

"He's in a lot of trouble," Cade said, sucking on the toothpick and letting out a low whistle. "And he could sure use a good lawyer." His lips curved into a crooked grin.

Jason's stomach clenched as the reason for the meeting became obvious. "Not only no, but hell no," he said, keeping his voice steady but firm.

The grin remained plastered to the drug dealer's face. "Well, that's not very nice. Especially seeing how Trey helped you out last year. And you kinda jumped the gun, didn't you? I haven't even asked you yet."

"I don't owe Trey . . . *or you* . . . anything," Jason said. "All Trey did was tell the truth when he was put on the stand in Jana's case. You don't get a medal for that. And as for you—"

"Let's stop with the attitude, Counselor." Cade's voice cut through Jason's like a sharp steak knife. "I'm not exactly asking you for a favor. I'm telling you what I want."

Jason stared back at him. "And I'm telling you that the answer is no." Jason couldn't imagine a more impossible case than representing a cop killer in a venue as conservative as Marshall County. *Especially if the defendant was also linked with the region's meth king . . .*

Cade snatched the toothpick out of his mouth and flung it on the ground. Then he shook his head. "Well . . . that's a crying shame," he said. "I mean, your niece, what is she, seventeen? She'll probably only get juvie, but buying and consuming meth at school is still pretty bad. Will hurt her chances at getting into the college she wants."

Jason felt heat rise within him, remembering how Shawna Carter had said there were rumors that Nola had been bringing meth to school. "What are you talking about?"

"I have a high school kid who works for me. He's been selling all manner of drugs to the little girl. Xanax, Klonopin, meth, weed, and even a gram of coke." He whistled. "Just like her momma, ain't she?" He placed his hand on his chin and looked down at the pavement. "Course, she ain't near as stealthy as Jana, and though I'm no drug counselor, I'm pretty sure she's addicted to the Xanax." He glanced up at Jason. "Would be a shame if a little birdie told the police all of this, wouldn't it?"

Jason put his hands on his hips. "Wouldn't you be implicating yourself?"

Cade cackled. "Naw, son. All it would take is an anonymous call to a deputy and a routine traffic stop. If she tipped them on my high school dealer, the boy wouldn't say a word, or I'd make sure his cock and balls ended up in a jar on his momma's kitchen counter."

Jason ground his teeth together, again thinking back to his and Nola's visit with the school counselor. Things were much worse than even Shawna Carter knew. *And I've been utterly clueless . . .*

"Don't beat yourself up, Counselor," Cade said. "Teenagers have been pulling the rug over their parents and guardians for eons."

"Are you blackmailing me?" Jason finally asked.

"Call it what you want," Cade said. "But that's not all." He sighed and peered at Jason. There was a glint in his eye. "Have you seen your girlfriend lately?"

The blood drained from Jason's face.

"Didn't think so," Cade said, putting the rest of the oatmeal creme pie in his mouth and chewing while he talked. "I have." He wiped his mouth and slung the wrapper toward a trash can adjacent to the bench, missing badly. "I've actually seen quite a bit of Miss Chase Wittschen."

Jason balled his hands up into fists.

"Don't be a hero, Jason," Tyson said. "I've got guns aimed at you from the water, and if you lay a hand on me, you're gonna be shot up worse than Sonny Corleone."

Jason loosened his hands. "Where is she?" he asked.

Cade walked over to the bench and sat down. "Don't you worry about that, Counselor. She's fine." His gaze narrowed. "Well, maybe that's pushing it. She's alive."

"Where is she?" Jason asked. "What the hell is this, Cade?"

He crossed his legs. "This is me playing hardball. Chase Wittschen is an addict, Jason. Just like you. And she's taken a mighty hard fall off the wagon. If the wrong person gets wind of it . . . say, the sheriff . . . then she'll likely go to jail for a while. Course, in her current condition, she's just as likely to kill herself . . . or others."

Jason sucked in a ragged breath and blinked his eyes. His heart was pounding, his body drenched with sweat. "Tyson, I can't take on a case like this. I'm not a criminal lawyer."

"You did a hell of a job for your sister."

"That was a miracle," Jason said. "My first-ever jury trial. I was lucky and made a ton of mistakes."

"You won. And, as I hear it, you won big yesterday over in Florence. You've become quite the trial lawyer, Captain Billboard."

Jason rubbed his face with his hands. "Why? What is your connection to Trey Cowan? Does he work for you or something? I tried to make that association in the lead-up to trial last year and couldn't do it. Trey seemed clean. Has something changed?"

Cade shrugged his shoulders. "My reasons aren't for you to know."

"Wouldn't he be better off with someone with more experience? I can refer him to a seasoned criminal defense lawyer."

Cade snorted. "Nope. I want you, Jason. You're good. You may have screwed up a few things in Jana's trial, but you have excellent instincts." He grinned. "And you're lucky. I'll take talent and luck over experience any old day. Look at me. I'm barely thirty years old, and I'm the most powerful person in Marshall County." He began to walk backward toward the dark water. "Experience is overrated."

Jason glanced past him and saw a small runabout boat motoring toward the shore. Before stepping onto it, Cade turned back to Jason. "There is a hearing on Monday morning at nine a.m. My sources tell me that if Trey doesn't have a lawyer, the court will appoint him one before anything starts." Cade paused a beat. "I expect you to be there."

"And if I'm not."

Cade raised an eyebrow. "Do you care about your niece and girlfriend?"

Jason opened his mouth, but no words came.

"Have a nice night," Cade said, saluting Jason before climbing onto the boat.

As the watercraft sped away and then disappeared, Jason collapsed onto the bench where the drug lord had been sitting. He didn't look up as footsteps approached.

"Bad?" Satch asked, taking a seat next to him.

Jason continued to stare at the dark water. "Worse," he finally said.

13

At 8:45 a.m. on Monday, Jason stood in the foyer to his office and gazed at himself in the mirror. He was wearing a navy suit, white shirt, and red tie.

Jason scowled at his reflection, thinking of a new billboard slogan.

Accused of murdering a cop and have an in with the local drug kingpin . . .

". . . get Rich," he whispered.

"Damn straight," a woman's voice belted out. The tone was strong, aggressive, and confident and could only belong to his partner, Isabel Montaigne.

"Izzy, tell me that this isn't the dumbest thing I've ever done in my life."

"Can't do it," she said, walking over and putting her hands on his tie. She adjusted and tightened the knot, and Jason grimaced. "The stupidest thing you've ever done, Jason Rich, was represent your crazy sister. That will always take the cake." She patted his shoulders. "Everything else is icing. But . . . this is damn sure the craziest."

"If I had any choice at all, you know I wouldn't do it."

Izzy frowned. "You seem to never have any choices when it comes to cases you take in Marshall County. As I recollect, you had no choice but to take Jana's case."

"That actually was a choice. This . . ." He trailed off.

For a moment, there was silence, and finally he felt his partner's hands grabbing his own. "I know," she said. "Nola denies the drug use?"

He groaned. "Yep. And since I challenged her, she's tuned me out even worse. Just sits in her room with her earbuds in when she's home, which isn't often."

"And Chase?"

He hung his head. "Nothing. I've sent Harry and Satch out to find her, and still no leads."

Jason glanced out the window of the front door and saw Harry standing by Jason's Porsche. Beyond him, toward the courthouse, Jason could see people lining both sides of the street outside the courthouse. Some were holding posters with Deputy Kelly Flowers, in full uniform, on them. Others held **BLUE LIVES MATTER** signs. There were at least ten deputies guarding the front of the courthouse. If Trey Cowan had any supporters, he didn't see them.

Jason had heard that the home of Trey's mother, Trudy Cowan, had been vandalized a few days after his arrest. He'd told Nola to stay home from school today and had assigned her a security guard who was to watch her every movement.

She was none too pleased at being watched but had no problem with skipping class for the day.

Jason took in a slow breath and exhaled, keeping his eyes on the crowd in front of the courthouse, wishing he had an escape hatch. Taking this case was not in his best interests as a lawyer and could hurt his practice. The Deep South, for the most part, was a conservative region that revered police officers. Jason took cases in an area that comprised almost the entire Southeastern Conference: Alabama, Florida, Georgia, Tennessee, Arkansas, and Mississippi were strongholds. His representation of a man accused of brutally murdering a sheriff's deputy was bad for business and could result in fewer calls and fewer referrals. As Izzy liked to say, you were only as good as your last case.

Right now, his last case was obtaining a multimillion-dollar verdict for a deserving widower whose wife was killed by an eighteen-wheeler. But, in a few short minutes, the narrative would flip-flop. His most recent matter would become defending a criminal accused of killing a community hero.

From the penthouse to the outhouse, Jason thought.

And, as far as he could see, he had no social cards he could pull. Since the defendant, Trey Cowan, and the victim, Kelly Flowers, were both white, there was no racial component to this trial, no way to position Trey as being discriminated against. And there'd be no corresponding protests or upheaval at the brutality that Trey's mother had already endured.

The deck was stacked.

"It's time," Izzy said, interrupting his thoughts. "You sure you want to go in the front. The sheriff offered a back way in if the rumors turned out to be true."

Jason shook his head. The plan was for Harry to drop Jason off at the front door of the courthouse at 8:55 a.m. so that he could enter the courtroom at 9:00. No use getting there any earlier than need be, and besides . . .

"I'm Jason motherfucking Rich," he said out loud, straightening his arms and trying to clear his head of everything but the task at hand. Then he gazed at his partner.

"You know it," Izzy said.

Ten minutes later, Jason hopped out of the passenger side of the Porsche as flashbulbs went off in every direction and a smattering of boos and yells came from the mob outside.

"Mr. Rich, are the rumors true?" a familiar voice asked. "Are you about to make an appearance as counsel of record for Trey Cowan, the former quarterback of the Guntersville Wildcats who's been charged with the murder of Sergeant Kelly Flowers?"

Jason turned toward the voice and gave a toothy grin to Kisha Roe, his old high school classmate and the lead reporter for the *Advertiser-Gleam*, Guntersville's flagship newspaper, who'd pushed her way through the crowd to him. "Happy to discuss the case with you after the hearing, Ms. Roe," he said, and she nodded back. As more questions were thrown his way, Jason was swarmed by the police officers and led through the doors of the courthouse. He flashed his attorney badge to the security guards and made a beeline for the steps that would take him to the circuit courtroom. As expected based on the madhouse outside, the courthouse was also packed, and Jason kept his eyes ahead of him. A few moments later, he opened the double doors to the courtroom and stood for a second in the opening.

Every seat in the gallery was taken. Despite his anxiety, adrenaline surged through Jason's veins. He hadn't stepped inside this room since a jury had come back with a not-guilty verdict for his sister, Jana, some six months ago. The reading of that decision was perhaps the most exciting, thrilling moment of his life.

As Jason glided down the aisle toward the defense table, he saw Trey Cowan standing by two officers. The defendant wore an orange prison jumpsuit, and his hands and feet were shackled.

Am I about to represent a guilty client again? Jason wondered.

He approached Trey and touched his arm. "I assume you know why I'm here."

"You're my attorney?"

Jason bowed. "Expecting someone different?"

"Momma told me she had gotten me someone good, but . . . *how?*"

"Don't worry about it right now," Jason said. "Let's just get through this hearing, OK?"

Trey opened his mouth to say something, but his words were drowned out by the bailiff's announcement that His Honor had entered the courtroom.

"ALL RISE!"

Jason faced the bench, feeling butterflies in his stomach and tasting acid in his throat, as Judge Terry Barber sat down and adjusted his robe. Of the two circuit court judges in Marshall County, Barber was considered a bit more plaintiff friendly in civil cases and defense leaning in criminal cases. This conclusion was by virtue of Barber's career prior to donning the robe, which consisted mostly of criminal defense assignments and the occasional car wreck case. The other judge, Virgil Carlton, a former prosecutor, was viewed as more conservative. For Jason, who had never tried a case in front of either one, he wasn't sure who he would have preferred. This was yet another example of why his victory in his sister's case was an anomaly more than a harbinger of future success. In Jana's case, an out-of-town judge from Tuscaloosa County, Powell Conrad, was brought in, which leveled the playing field, as the district attorney had no prior experience with Conrad.

Here, district attorney Shay Lankford had tried dozens of cases in front of Terry Barber and would have a clear comfort level despite His Honor's leanings. Jason glanced across the courtroom to where Shay was standing only to notice the prosecutor peering back at him with a scowl. She wore a burgundy suit and matching heels and held a yellow notepad under her arm. She shook her head at Jason as if she couldn't believe he was actually in her courtroom again, and Jason winked at her.

"Please be seated."

After waiting for everyone to comply with his command, Barber looked out over the courtroom and cleared his throat. "We are here this morning on the case of the State of Alabama versus Trey Jerome Cowan." Barber spoke with a nasally southern voice that wasn't the most pleasing to the ear. He had blond hair that was graying on the sides and thinning at the temples. "The purpose of this hearing is to advise the defendant of the charge against him in this case. It had also been my intent to appoint counsel for the defendant." Barber peered over the bench at Jason. "But it seems that may not be necessary. Mr. Rich, are you here on behalf of the defendant?"

Jason straightened his posture. "Yes, Your Honor. I am."

A smattering of murmurs spread through the gallery. Jason glanced at Shay Lankford, but she was staring at her notepad as if Jason's appearance contained not even the slightest curiosity for her. It was a good act, because Jason knew that Shay had to be shocked and probably a little pissed off. Her only defeat in trial since becoming lead prosecutor was courtesy of Jason, and he figured she was none too pleased to see him dabbling in criminal law again, especially on a case of this magnitude.

"Very well then. Will the defendant please rise?"

Trey Cowan stood on shaky legs next to Jason.

"Trey Jerome Cowan, it is my duty as the circuit court judge of Marshall County, Alabama, to advise you that the State of Alabama has brought a charge of capital murder against you. If you are found guilty of this charge, then you will be put to death by lethal injection." Judge Barber stopped and stared at Trey with an expression as stern as his words.

Jason knew it was coming, but the gravity of the stakes still made him queasy. In the state of Alabama, if an officer was killed in the line of duty or while engaging in an activity related to his official capacity, then the murder was a capital offense punishable by death. Izzy had confirmed this fact with Professor Pamela Adams, the dean of criminal law at Cumberland School of Law in Birmingham. Also, according to Harry's very preliminary investigation, Deputy Kelly Flowers had been killed at just past midnight while wearing his uniform. Jason took in a deep breath and exhaled. *Second criminal case, second capital murder charge,* he thought. It was absurd but true.

"Does the defendant understand the charge being brought by the state and the sentence sought?" Judge Barber asked, after a good five-second pause.

Trey glanced at Jason and then back at Barber. "Yes, sir."

"Good. There are a couple more matters to address. Mr. Rich, before your appearance, your client filed a pro se motion to lower bond, which I had originally set at $10 million. Do you have anything to add to the defendant's motion?"

Jason blinked, trying to think of something quick or smart to say. Nothing came to mind. "No, Your Honor."

"Good, because there's nothing that you could possibly say or argue that would make me change my mind in this case. The defendant's motion is denied. All right, last thing. Will the defendant be seeking a preliminary hearing?"

For a minute, Jason's mind clouded. Jana had refused the prelim in her case to expedite the trial. There, the facts were simple. A handyman named Waylon Pike had confessed that Jana paid him to kill Dr. Braxton Waters. A prelim likely would have accomplished nothing.

Here, though . . .

"Your Honor, may I have a moment to confer with my client?" Jason asked.

Barber squinted at Jason. "A brief moment, Mr. Rich."

"Yes, sir." Jason leaned toward Trey and whispered into his ear. "A preliminary hearing gives us a sneak preview of the state's evidence against you. My advice is to request one. Are you good with that?"

Jason leaned back and looked into his new client's eyes, seeing a mixture of doubt and confusion.

"I guess that's OK," Trey managed.

Jason turned back to the bench. "Yes, Your Honor. The defendant does request a preliminary hearing."

"All right then," Barber said, glancing down and beginning to flip some pages in front of him. "Let's set it a couple weeks from today. April 30 at 9:00 a.m."

"Thank you, Judge," Jason said.

Barber stood and leaned over the bench. "One more thing," he said, raising his voice, which only made the tone higher and more nasally. "I'm imposing a gag order in this case. No discussions, comments, or communications whatsoever with the press, is that understood?"

"Yes, Your Honor," Shay said, standing and pressing down her pant legs.

"Mr. Rich?" Barber snapped.

"I understand, sir," Jason said.

"You better," Barber said. "I will not stand for any shenanigans from you like in the Waters trial. Do you hear me?"

Jason bit his lip. It was all he could do not to fire back, *What shenanigans do you mean?* Jason might have been aggressive in speaking with the press prior to the gag order in Waters, but after Judge Conrad had imposed one, he'd played by the rules the same as the prosecution. He knew Barber's attitude was more a product of the professional jealousy and curiosity that Jason garnered due to his in-your-face advertising strategy. He'd received similar call downs in other courtrooms across the state. It was as if his aggressive marketing campaign somehow made him a scoundrel that needed a stern rebuke before every case.

Jason stared up at Terry Barber and forced a smile. He knew it wouldn't help his client if he lost his temper. He'd only be feeding His Honor's preconceived negative opinion of him. "I hear you, Judge. No shenanigans." He held up three fingers. "Scout's honor."

Barber's eyebrows wrinkled. "Were you a Scout, Mr. Rich?"

At this, Jason's mouth loosened, and he didn't have to force his smile anymore. "No, sir, I wasn't."

14

Fifteen minutes later, Jason sat across from his new client in the attorney consultation room of the Marshall County Jail. The tiny area had a folding table and two aluminum chairs and was enclosed by four cinder block walls. The floor was a dusty tile. Jason peered around the room and breathed in the stale scent that seemed to envelop the jail like sweat in a locker room. The last time he'd been in here was with Jana on the morning of the last day of her trial. To say that the room brought back good memories would be a lie.

Despite his victory in Jana's case, Jason still felt like an impostor. He wasn't a criminal defense attorney. He'd had one high-profile case, but that was it. Why in the hell would Tyson Cade want him as Trey Cowan's lawyer? But Cade had explained the deal at Goose Pond. Jason had represented a guilty client and won. *Is that what I'm tasked with here?* he thought, sizing up the shackled man sitting across from him.

"How you been?" Jason finally asked. "I mean, other than the whole being-arrested-for-murder thing." Jason forced a smile, but Trey didn't return the gesture. His gaze was blank. He seemed to still be a little numb from the hearing and the shock of seeing his new attorney.

"I've had better days," Trey finally said.

"I haven't seen you since my sister's trial."

"That's because you haven't been back to the Brick since then." He waved a hand at a fly that was buzzing by his nose. "I'm there every night."

"I don't drink," Jason said. Then, figuring it was best to try to develop some trust, he added, "I'm an alcoholic. Went to rehab for ninety days last year. When I got out, I almost had a drink the day of discharge, but I got a frantic call from this jail by my sister."

Trey smirked. "And the rest is history. Local boy makes good."

Jason crossed his legs. "Not exactly. I fell off the wagon during the trial pretty bad, and I've had a couple near screwups since Jana's death." He sighed. "And while we won the case, Jana's murder in the aftermath of the verdict made it a hollow victory."

At this, Trey nodded, and Jason saw the first hint of something going on behind the man's eyes. "I felt bad about that too," Trey said. "Seems like my testimony may have sent Burns over the edge." He glanced up at Jason. "I should have come forward sooner."

Jason glanced down at the floor, remembering the powerful moment during the trial when Trey Cowan had said he'd overheard Waylon Pike bragging about a deal he'd been offered to kill Dr. Braxton Waters. The only person besides Trey who heard him was Jackson Burns, whose wife had been having an affair with Braxton. Jason had utilized Trey's testimony to set up Burns as an alternative suspect for Braxton's killing. Burns, who'd been battling severe depression since the breakup of his marriage, snapped after Jason challenged him on the stand. After the not-guilty verdict came down, Jackson Burns lay in wait behind the Brick restaurant while Jason and Jana headed to his Porsche. He came off the sidewalk with a gun and tried to kill Jason, but Jana stepped in front of her brother and took the bullets.

She was dead before the ambulance arrived.

"Why didn't you say something sooner?" Jason finally asked, raising his gaze to meet his client's.

Trey rubbed the inside of his left wrist with the steel handcuff that encircled his right hand. "Didn't want to get involved. I like to stay under the radar around town. When I see people I grew up with . . ." He trailed off.

"What?"

"Nothing," Trey said. "Look, I'm sorry about Ms. Waters."

Jason crossed his arms. "That makes two of us."

For a few long seconds, the room was silent. Finally, Jason took a yellow notepad and a pen out of the briefcase he'd laid on the floor and scooted his chair closer to his client.

"All right, Trey. I've been on this case exactly an hour. If I'm going to be able to help you, I need you to tell me everything you can remember about the night of April 8 and morning of April 9. But first things first. What's your connection to Tyson Cade?"

Trey raised his eyebrows. "Why do you ask that?"

"Because your mother didn't hire me. Cade did. And he didn't exactly ask nicely."

Trey gripped the table and leaned toward Jason. Their faces were only a few inches apart. "What are you saying?"

"He's blackmailing me, Trey. And he's putting my family at risk."

Trey glanced down at the table. "That doesn't make sense," he whispered.

Jason pushed his chair back from the table and crossed his legs. "I need you to answer the question. What is your connection to Cade?"

Trey gazed up at the ceiling. He took in a deep breath and exhaled. Finally, he chuckled, and the sound had a palpable bitterness. "It's complicated."

15

An hour later, Jason left the consultation room frustrated and famished. Trey Cowan was holding back, and he figured his new client's hesitancy was caused by the same Sand Mountain pariah who had gotten Jason into this mess. About all Trey had given up about his relationship with Cade was that he had done a few deliveries for the drug lord. As for the night and morning that Kelly Flowers was murdered, Trey said he got into an argument at the Brick with Flowers that ended in a shoving match. He couldn't remember much else after that except that he'd gotten very drunk. He'd walked home, grabbed his shotgun, and gone to his mother's house in Alder Springs. The next thing he remembered was waking up on the floor of his mom's house.

His answers to critical questions seemed disingenuous or, worse, downright untruthful. Why had he retrieved the shotgun? *"I can't remember. Anytime I go to Mom's, I like to have a gun. Sand Mountain is a rough place."* All of his words were generally true, but they rang hollow to Jason, and he figured a jury would call BS too. *"What was the argument between you and Flowers about?"* For this, Trey couldn't make eye contact with Jason. *"He was giving me a hard time because I failed my tryout with the Barons. Kelly liked to needle me, and I wasn't having it that night."*

As for the trip to the Guntersville High School football stadium, Trey said he had nowhere else to go. The last time he'd felt happy in his life was as a quarterback on that field. He also admitted to suffering from depression since his injury. He'd stopped taking his antidepressants because he thought they made him weaker and slower on the baseball field, but the absence of the medication had caused his thoughts to spiral out of control. Jason asked where Trey filled his prescriptions and the name of his doctor, figuring this was a positive fact for the defense, especially if they ended up having to plead insanity.

After sixty minutes of back-and-forth, Jason surmised that, outside of his new client's admission to battling depression, the rest of his story was pure-grain horseshit.

When Jason had finally heard enough, he knocked three times on the door and glared at Trey. "You aren't doing yourself any favors by keeping things from me. You're only making the jury's job easier. You saw all of the spectators in that courtroom today. Outside of your mom, none of them will be rooting for you, and I'm not sure we could get a fair and impartial jury in any state in the South. We're the road team in this one, Trey. If this were the Iron Bowl and we were Alabama, then this trial is going to be worse than going into Jordan-Hare Stadium and facing ninety thousand fans all screaming 'War Eagle,' you understand?" He paused, hoping his message was sinking in. "I expect our next meeting to be more productive."

Trey said nothing. Instead, he stared at the table as a female guard swung open the door and escorted Jason out.

How in the hell am I supposed to represent someone who won't talk to me and, when he does talk, sounds like he's lying? Jason thought as he strode down the hall and toward the elevator. He was starving, but before he could leave the jail, there was one more thing he had to do.

Pull the Band-Aid off, he thought, as he stepped inside the elevator and clicked the button for the top floor.

———

At the reception desk, a young woman with blonde hair held a phone tight to her ear. "District attorney's office, can you hold?" Then she glanced at Jason. "Can I help you?" She looked down at the phone, and then her eyes shot back up at him.

"Is Shay around?" he asked. "I'm—"

"I know who you are," the woman said. But before she could buzz the prosecutor, Jason saw Shay coming his way.

"In my office," she said, walking past him without another word. Jason saluted the receptionist and followed Shay down the hall and into a room. Jason was barely a foot inside the door when she slammed it behind him.

"Mind telling me *what in the living hell* you are doing representing Trey Cowan?" Her tone was equal parts anger and exasperation, and it startled Jason. Though he'd had a few intense encounters with the district attorney, they had all been civil and professional.

"He is a client who needed a lawyer." Jason fumbled for more words. "And he's a . . . friend."

"Oh, whatever. Have you seen him since your sister's trial? What? Do you think you owe him for helping you obtain a not-guilty verdict for a murderer?"

Jason crossed his arms tight across his chest and glared at her. Most of the law enforcement officials in the sheriff's office as well as the local media had bought Jason's alternative theory that Jackson Burns had killed Dr. Braxton Waters. And since Burns was shot and killed by Harry Davenport and the Tonidandel brothers shortly after the car dealer opened fire on Jason and Jana, the case was closed. But, based on the look in Shay Lankford's eyes, it was still very much at the forefront of her mind.

"I'm sorry that you lost your sister, Jason, and I will begrudgingly admit that you did a good job for her in the trial, but you were also lucky as hell. Do you really think that you can be that fortunate twice in a row?"

Jason shrugged. "What's the old saying? I'd rather be lucky than good. And . . . I had a pretty good day in Florence last week."

"That was a personal injury case. Why don't you stick . . ." Shay's face had reddened to match her burgundy suit, but she gritted back whatever she was about to say. She took in a deep breath and smoothed out her pant legs. "There won't be any plea deal in this one. With an officer down, it is the death penalty or bust." She took a step toward him, and Jason smelled a pleasant raspberry scent emanating from her. When she spoke, her breath smelled of peppermint. "I have to win this case, Jason." Her voice didn't waver, but Jason thought he saw a flicker of fear in her eyes.

"You up for reelection soon?"

"November," she said. "And I can't have two capital murder losses on my scorecard leading into it." Her eyes narrowed, and any hint of timidity was gone. "I *will* get a conviction."

"Well . . . good luck to you," Jason said. "But first, I need some discovery. It would be great to see what y'all have before the prelim."

Shay walked over to the top of her desk and grabbed a brown file jacket. "We had copied this off to give to Mr. Cowan's court-appointed lawyer." She scowled. "Guess it's yours now."

"Thank you," Jason said.

She gave an ever-so-slight bow. "I'd suggest watching the fifteen video recordings from the Brick the night of April 8 showing your client attacking Sergeant Flowers and threatening to kill him. I'd also highlight the coroner's report demonstrating that Officer Flowers was killed with two blasts from a twelve-gauge shotgun in the chest at close range. And guess what? That exact weapon was found in the cab of Trey Cowan's truck with only his prints on it." She placed both hands on her cheeks in mock surprise. "I think you'll find a Thanksgiving feast worth of motive, opportunity, and means in those materials."

Jason put the file jacket under his arm and turned for the door. When he grabbed the knob, Shay's voice stopped him. "I understood why you took Jana's case. Blood is thicker than water and all that jazz. But Trey Cowan? As a favor for him being a good witness? He and his mother can't have enough money to pay you, and you don't need any more damn publicity." She walked toward him and sniffed the air. "Something about this whole thing reeks, Jason, and you've got it all over you."

Jason gazed down at the prosecutor's heels and then let out a mock sigh before grinning up at her. "Well . . . I guess I'm going to go home and take a shower."

Shay hesitated for a beat. Then she laughed.

Jason was dumbfounded. He had never heard the no-nonsense district attorney laugh before, and the sound of it was loud, hearty, and full of pent-up energy. He couldn't help but join in.

After a moment, she crossed her arms and rolled her eyes at him. "Get the hell out of here."

Jason held up the folder. "Thank you."

16

The Porsche was idling on the curb when Jason exited the jail. It had been over two hours since the hearing, and the crowd had dispersed. He flung his briefcase and the file jacket in the trunk and hopped in the passenger seat, looking at Harry. He intended to instruct his investigator to head straight to Charburger, as Jason was craving a grease fix.

But the concerned look on Harry's face stopped him cold.

"What?"

"Satch just called."

"And?"

"Chase is back."

Jason's heart fluttered, and he bit his lip. "How bad?"

Harry put the car in gear, and the Porsche sprang forward. "It's a mess, J. R."

———

Fifteen minutes later, Jason stood in the family room of his house. Chase lay on the couch, curled up in a ball with her knees tucked tight to her chin. She was shivering and had a blanket wrapped around her. Sweat poured from her face, which was pasty pale. Her short hair was matted down with perspiration. She stared across the room at the fireplace, but her eyes were blank.

"Chase?" Jason asked.

She didn't acknowledge him.

Jason looked around the room. Satch and Harry were standing against the wall leading out to the sunroom. Arms folded. Grave expressions on their face. Jason focused on the older Tonidandel. "When did you hear from Cade?"

Satch scratched the back of his neck. He wore a pair of blue jean overalls with no shirt. "Hour ago. Wasn't him. A minion. Said they'd be dropping Chase off on her boathouse dock in five minutes. I walked down to the dock and helped them get her out of the boat." He pulled at his salt-and-pepper beard and grunted. "Then I carried her up here."

"What do you want to do, J. R.?" Harry asked. "She's in withdrawal pretty bad. Don't you think we should take her to the hospital?"

"Yes," Jason said. "But not here. She's liable to get out and go straight back to Cade." He glanced again at Satch. "You know she was using?"

"No. Did you?" He fired the question back harsh, as was his way. Bullshit was a foreign commodity in the Tonidandel universe. The meaning was obvious. Jason had been Chase's boyfriend up until last Christmas. Then Chase had broken things off, and no one had seen her since.

It's my fault, Jason thought. He shouldn't have let her go. He should have handled things better. Been more mature. She'd said she was barely hanging on, but Jason had been more worried about himself. He had been angry at being rejected. Concerned about his own alcoholism. Disappointed that his dream engagement scenario had been doused.

It's always about me . . .

"No," Jason finally said. "I knew she'd bought meth from Cade in the past. But she'd gone to rehab for it and been clean for over a year. I knew she was an alcoholic like me, and she'd fallen off the wagon at least once. But I haven't spoken to her since Christmas." He looked around the room, and no one would meet his eye. Satch and Harry had both known about his surprise plans for an engagement on Christmas Day, as had Izzy. They knew she'd left him, and each had questioned him about the breakup, but Jason's standard response was, "I don't want to talk about it."

Jason sighed and stared up at the ceiling, finally closing his eyes. After a few moments, he felt a hand on his shoulder.

"J. R.?" Harry's voice was soft but firm. "We have to do something."

Jason opened his eyes. He started to speak, but then he heard the front door jar open. "I'm home," Nola yelled. She stopped dead still when she noticed the men standing in the family room. Her hand went to her mouth when her eyes lowered to Chase. "What's going on?" she asked, looking at her uncle.

Jason peered at her. She wore a pair of khaki shorts and a white-and-blue Sea N Suds T-shirt. She'd gotten it during their spring break jaunt to the coast last month. The trip seemed a lifetime ago. Jason and Nola had stayed at the Turquoise Place resort. Nola's sister, Niecy, had left Birmingham-Southern for the weekend and joined them. They'd eaten good food and soaked up the sun and fun on the Redneck Riviera. Nola had mostly hung out with Niecy and their collective friends, but at least for several days, there had been no arguments. For a few precious moments, even with Chase's departure, Jason had felt like he had a family. Little had he known that the wheels on his new life were about to completely come off.

Jason stared at Nola, processing the crisis and then making his decision. "Do you have any meth?"

She opened her mouth. "What? Is that what she told you?" Her tone was defensive, and she glared at Chase, who continued to convulse on the couch, and then back at Jason. Her expression changed from anger to confusion. "Why would you . . . ?"

"Tyson Cade is blackmailing me with your and Chase's drug use. That's why I had a guard follow you today, and that's why I wanted you to skip school." He pointed at the couch. "Chase is going through withdrawal from methamphetamine, and I need to take her to a detox facility." Jason took a couple of steps toward his niece, and she gazed at the floor. Her lip had begun to tremble. "Nola, I need to give Chase something to ease her symptoms so that I can take her to a place that will help her."

"Why don't you take her to Marshall Medical?" Nola snapped.

"Because that's a temporary fix, and it's too close. Nola, if you care about Chase at all—"

"No," she said.

"What do you mean, *no*?" Jason felt anger boiling within him.

"I mean, no, I don't have any meth." She paused. "I'm out. I can get some more, but—"

"Damnit!" Jason yelled, turning away from her. "I could get some more. We all could get some more. Everyone in here knows Tyson Cade."

"Don't yell at me," Nola said. "You asked me a question, and I answered it." She wiped fresh tears from her cheeks and crossed her arms, staring down at the floor.

"Jason, how long is it going to take you to get where you're going?" Satch asked.

"Two hours. Maybe three. Depends on the pilot and whether the plane is ready."

Satch squinted. "The plane? You're gonna fly somewhere?"

"Yes," Jason said.

"Well . . . why don't we give her a little Jack Daniel's," Satch said. "That should calm her down."

"And I've got some Xanax," Nola said, peering up at him, her arms still crossed.

Jason turned to her, raising his eyebrows. He knew he shouldn't be surprised, but he was anyway.

"You wanted my help, didn't you?"

"Yes. Get whatever you have." He looked at Satch. "Whiskey is a good idea." Then he pointed at Harry, but he was already on the phone.

"The jet," Harry said. "On it." He stepped into the sunroom to finish his call.

Jason walked over to the couch and sat next to Chase, who continued to shake. He touched her shoulder, but she pulled away. Jason fought back his emotions and gritted his teeth. He looked up and Satch was gone, having left out the front door to retrieve the Jack Daniel's.

Nola sat on the couch next to him. "Has she said anything?" she asked, her voice a whisper.

Jason shook his head. Then he put his arm around his niece, and she didn't lean away. "I'm going to call the school and get you excused for a couple of days."

She pulled back. "What? Why?"

Jason let out a deep breath. "Because I want you to see where we're going."

17

Tyson Cade walked into the Alder Springs Grocery on Tuesday afternoon around 2:00 p.m. He grabbed his usual—a twenty-ounce Sun Drop and two Twinkies—and ambled up to the counter.

"Dooby, you are looking as fine as ever. Whatcha know good?"

"Same old," she said, and her tone was cold.

"Something wrong?"

Marcia "Dooby" Darnell had dark-red hair that flowed down her back almost to her bottom. She wore a frayed white tank top and cutoff jeans. At almost forty years old, Dooby had a sexy toughness that Tyson had always liked, and as the primary checkout clerk at Sand Mountain's go-to convenience store, she had provided a wealth of information to Tyson over the years.

Dooby frowned as she rang up the junk food. "Folks in the Sprangs seems to think that you might have had something to do with Kelly Flowers's murder."

Tyson chuckled at the local pronunciation for Alder Springs. "Well . . . what do folks in the Sprangs say?"

"That you had gotten cross with Kelly and that Trey is a patsy."

Tyson tossed a twenty-dollar bill down. Dooby started to make change, but he grabbed her hand. "Keep it," he said. "What else do they say?"

She squinched up her face. "There's a lot of talk about the billboard lawyer taking Trey's case. No one quite gets it."

Tyson guffawed. "Well, I do. Jason Rich is a publicity hound. Why else would he need all those highway spectacles?"

Dooby shrugged and then peered at him with her green eyes. "Tyson, what are you up to?"

Tyson was a good ten years younger than Dooby Darnell, but he'd had some fun with her in the cab of a truck a few times. He leaned in and bit her on her earlobe. "Wouldn't you like to know?"

She giggled and pulled away from him. "Seriously. Folks around here are worried about Trudy. With Walt gone, Kelly dead, and Trey in jail, she's got no one."

"She a tough old bird," Tyson said, grinning at her and feeling a tingle in his loins.

"You're going to take care of her, aren't you?"

He leaned toward her again, whispering into her other ear. "I always take care of my own, Dooby girl. You know that." He let his nose run down her neck and then pulled away. "Let me know if you hear anything else about the case."

"I will."

"Tyson?"

He stared at her, and she curled the index finger of her right hand toward the palm in a "come here" gesture.

He approached, and she leaned over the counter. "Did you do it?" she whispered.

"Do what?"

She looked around and glanced outside the store. It was barren, which wasn't all that surprising for this time of day. "Did you kill Kelly?"

Tyson gritted his teeth and figured it was time to teach the desk clerk a lesson. "What's in it for me?" he asked.

She narrowed her eyes and cocked her head toward the back of the store. He followed her down an aisle of potato chips, batteries, and assorted other conveniences and into a storage closet. Once inside, she pulled her shorts and panties down. She started to turn around, but he pressed into her and bent her over a cart.

He didn't last long. Tyson's life was a stress fest, and he hadn't enjoyed a woman in at least two weeks.

"Was it good?" Dooby asked as Tyson groaned into her ear. When he didn't answer, she added, "Will you tell me?"

He turned her and grabbed her around the waist.

"Did you kill—?"

Tyson clutched her neck, cutting off her words. Then he began to squeeze. "Do you really think I'd ever give you information like that, Dooby? Do you believe I'm that stupid?"

She grasped at his arms. "I'm sorry," she whined. "Please don't . . ."

"You give me information, Dooby. And in exchange, I provide protection and money." He took his right hand off her neck and let it drift down to her groin. "And occasionally . . . pleasure. Do you understand?"

She nodded as a tear slid down her cheek.

Five minutes later, Tyson walked toward the front of the store and grabbed his goodies. Dooby had gone from the storage closet to the bathroom to freshen up and to apply a new coat of makeup over her bruises. Once outside, Tyson ate both Twinkies in three bites each and drank most of the Sun Drop in one long gulp. He belched once and then again. A woman was filling up her SUV at one of the pumps, and she frowned at him. He shot her the bird.

Seconds later, a dark sedan pulled into the parking lot, and Tyson hopped into the passenger side. Once out on Hustleville Road, Tyson spoke without looking at the driver. "What's the status?"

"Rich took off in a private jet from the Guntersville airport a few minutes ago with the Wittschen woman and his niece."

"Any idea where they're headed?"

"No, but the best bet is medical treatment for Wittschen."

"Stop here," Tyson said. The car pulled onto the shoulder of the road in front of a gravel parking lot containing a large barn.

Branner's Place had been run by Lynn "Bull" Branner from the early nineties until Bull finally ran out of money in 2014. When open, above the table, it had been a sawdust-floor, jukebox-in-the-corner dance place for the good folks of Sand Mountain. Under the table, it had been a great place for adults to buy alcohol in a dry county and for the underaged to get their hands on some booze. Now, it was nothing more than an abandoned shack.

And the scene of a murder.

Tyson scanned the area. The yellow crime scene tape was still up. Kelly Flowers, his inside source in the sheriff's office, had met his maker right here.

"So . . . do you know why Kelly was out here when he was killed?" the driver asked.

Tyson glared at the driver, a newbie named Sanderson. Then he reached into his pocket and pulled out a container of toothpicks. He took one out and stuck it in his mouth. *So many questions,* he thought, his mind drifting back to Dooby Darnell. The brazenness of her inquiries. Tyson bristled and chewed hard on the toothpick until it snapped in his mouth.

Tyson Cade was thirty years old. He'd been the methamphetamine king of Sand Mountain for almost five years. He was a young man, but he felt twice his age. *It ain't the years, it's the miles,* his best friend and most trusted adviser, Matthew "Matty" Dean, liked to say. He had a lot of miles on his wiry frame, and he figured he'd be lucky to live to fifty. He hoped that when the devil called him home, he went out like Marcellus "Bully" Calhoun, the famous Jasper drug lord, had a few years back. Shot dead on a golf course at the ripe old age of sixty something. No illness. No suffering. Just double tapped and put down.

Tyson had grown up poor. He'd never known his father. His mother, Ruthie, worked several jobs before turning to prostitution to put food on the table for her only child. Ruthie Cade had been a beautiful woman. Tall with an hourglass figure and large breasts. She hadn't been ashamed of her choice. *"I can make $800 a week hooking,"* she'd told him when he came home early from school and caught her with one of her clients. *"That's over three grand a month. Twice what I can make working two honest jobs."* Still in shock by what he had seen, Tyson had gone out and sat down by a tree in the field behind their mobile home. Eventually, he'd felt his mother's hand on his neck and heard her whisper words that he would never forget.

"Tyson, when you have money, you have power. It's more important than oxygen, you hear me, son?" She'd made him turn to face her. *"What I do is for money and money only. I do it so that we . . . and you mainly . . . can have a life."* She had ground her teeth together, forcing back the tears. *"Don't you ever cry for me, son. I'm not going to. I want you to take the money I make for you and make more of it. Make a pile of it. Make so much of it that no one can hurt you or touch you. Make enough, and people will do what you say."*

The lesson had stuck. Tyson had made his first meth sale when he was sixteen years old. His first grand by the time he was seventeen. For a while, he balanced school and being a meth dealer. He made straight As at Guntersville High School and got a partial scholarship to Snead State for baseball. But when his mother died of viral meningitis at the beginning of his sophomore year, he dropped out of college to sell drugs full time.

Because of his youth and his lack of any baggage—no wife, kids, or family of any kind and no prior crimes—Johnny "King" Hanson had considered him expendable and had given him tasks that were dangerous. Late-night boat deliveries to out-of-state dealers. Solo meetings with volatile distributors. Pop ins on cooks who were taking too long. Tyson could have been killed, and King wouldn't have cared. But, instead of wilting under the pressure, Tyson had thrived on it. Before long, he'd worked his way up to being King's enforcer. The one called to do the dirty work that had to be done.

When King was finally busted and sent to the Saint Clair Correctional Facility, Tyson Cade, at twenty-five years old, ascended to the throne of the Sand Mountain drug empire. There was no passing of the guard. When King was arrested, Tyson, with the help of Matty Dean, killed the two dealers who were expected to compete for the job. Then he began to give the orders, and no one challenged him. By the time King Hanson was convicted and sentenced to prison, Tyson was in full command.

Now, some five years later, the demands and challenges of his job never slowed down. If he got tired . . . if he got lazy . . . if he let his constituents ask questions that they had no business asking, he knew where he'd find himself.

In jail.

Or dead.

"Let me tell you something," Tyson said, taking a part of the broken-off toothpick and sticking it into the side of the driver's neck.

Sanderson yelped and started to say something, but Tyson held up a finger.

"I know you're new to my operation," the meth dealer said. "But there's one rather large rule." He hesitated and then fired off a right cross that caught Sanderson right under the jaw. "I ask the questions. And everyone else does the answering. Got it?"

But Sanderson had slumped over. Knocked out cold.

"Crap," Tyson said, opening his door, walking around to the driver's side, and elbowing his subordinate onto the passenger seat. He put the car in gear and sighed.

"I guess I have to do everything around here."

18

The jet landed at a private airfield in Pensacola, Florida, around 5:30 p.m. They rented a car and drove the remaining twenty miles.

Chase had stopped shaking, but she hadn't said a word on the flight. She'd stared out the window of the jet and curled her legs up against her chest like a child. The combination of Xanax and Jack Daniel's had calmed her, but she was still numb from whatever Tyson Cade and his team of drug dealers had done to her.

Nola had also been quiet, though her teenage curiosity couldn't help but ask a few questions about the plane, which Jason had bought in December at Izzy's urging. With cases active in six different states now, the firm needed to be more mobile. Izzy had researched their options and gotten them a good deal on a seven-seater Cessna with GET RICH branding.

Jason pulled his rental—an older-model Toyota Camry—into the Sacred Heart Health Center at 5:55 p.m. Before leaving Mill Creek, Nola had walked over to Chase's house and packed her a small duffel with a few changes of clothes and a bathroom kit. She wouldn't be needing anything else.

He had called ahead, and there was a space for her in the detox unit. The plan was for her to spend as long as it took getting over the withdrawal symptoms, and then she'd be transferred to the Perdido Addiction Center, which was commonly referred to as the PAC by those who worked there or were patients.

Jason had spent ninety days in the PAC last year at this same time. But, though addicted, he hadn't had to check into detox. Now, he was a helpless spectator as two female nurses led them down a hallway and proceeded to help Chase out of her clothes and into a gown. Then they looked through her bag to make sure there was nothing sharp. Some fingernail clippers were removed from the bathroom pouch as well as a pair of tweezers. The hair dryer was also taken out. Jason and Nola were to bring these home with them. Chase would be supervised while using anything sharp until out of the detoxification unit.

Jason turned away for most of it, unable to watch. He had signed Chase up for a six-month stay at the PAC. That was the maximum, and, based on her condition and the fact that she'd already been to rehab once, he figured she needed it. Plus, there was the whole issue of what she had been doing with Tyson Cade. Why had he had control over her whereabouts? How was it that she was "delivered" to Jason's house earlier today?

Jason shuddered at the questions, knowing that a meth addiction was one of the worst a person could have. People completely lost themselves in their dependence on the drug.

Stealing a glance at his old friend and sometime love, he knew that she was lost.

"We're going to take her now," one of the nurses said, her voice containing no frills and only a hint of compassion. When you spent all day long dealing with addicts, you probably became jaded by it all, Jason figured.

"Chase?" Jason asked.

She looked at him with blank eyes.

"I'm sorry, honey, but I know these people will help you." He glanced at Nola, but she was staring at the tile floor, arms folded tight across her chest. She hadn't put up much protest at being asked to come here, but to say she was a willing participant would be an exaggeration. "Nola, do you want to say anything?" Jason pressed.

"Get better, OK?" Nola reached a hand toward Chase's arm, but her fingers didn't quite touch. Then the teenager snatched her arm back and turned away from both of them.

Jason sighed. Then he hugged Chase and kissed her on the cheek.

Chase bit her lip, and it started to shake as she looked at Jason. Finally, she spoke for the first time. Her voice was dry and just above a whisper. "I'm sorry."

Jason touched her cheek, and she closed her eyes.

Then the nurses whisked her out of the room and down the hallway.

———

Jason sat down on the cot in the tiny triage room and placed his head in his hands.

After a few minutes, he felt the tiny bed give as Nola joined him. "It is so cold in here," she finally said. "Not the temperature. Just the people. The nurses. The receptionist. Everyone's so cold."

Jason patted her knee. "They have to be that way. This is a place where you're stripped of everything. Your clothes. Your pride. Everything you have." He paused. "Gone. It all has to go. You set it down along with your addiction, and hopefully . . ." His voice began to quiver, and he gritted his teeth, thinking of the day he got out of rehab. Of going to the Flora-Bama Lounge and Package Store. Of ordering a Corona and looking at the bottle. Bringing the beer to his forehead and smelling it. He even remembered the cute waitress with the Auburn cap. He had so badly wanted to drink the beer. To get drunk and then to find a woman for the night.

But he hadn't. He'd gotten a call from Nola's mother that had brought him home to Guntersville. Back to the practice of law. To his family, what little he had left. And to Chase.

"And hopefully what, Uncle Jason?"

He peered at her, feeling tears welling in his own eyes. "A new life."

19

By 8:00 p.m., the Marshall County Sheriff's Office had long since closed for the day. But the light in the main conference area—or "the war room," as the officers referred to it—was still on. Inside it, Detective Hatty Daniels paced around the long rectangular table, pressing her chin tight to her chest. At the head seat, Sheriff Richard Griffith crossed his legs and watched the department's top investigator.

Hatty had dark-brown skin and short hair and was not prone to bullshit. After two trips around the table, she finally stopped and looked at the sheriff.

"Well, spit it out," he said.

"At the time of his murder, Kelly Flowers was being investigated by internal affairs." She paused. "By me."

Griff's eyes narrowed. "For what?"

"Possibly being an inside mole for Tyson Cade."

Griff blinked his eyes and gazed down at his desk and then back up at her. "Hatty . . . are you trying to tell me that Kelly Flowers was working for Cade?"

Hatty gave a swift nod.

Now it was the sheriff who stood and began to pace as Hatty took a seat in the middle, crossing her arms. Finally, he stopped and placed his hands on his hips. "Give me the high points," he said. "I mean the low points. You know what I mean." He barked the words, and Hatty flinched at his tone. For the most part, Richard Griffith was a laid-back lawman, but this was the first time he'd had to deal with the murder of an officer.

And it's an election year.

"We have photographs of him meeting with Cade. Also, his phone records show calls from a number of different burner phone numbers with no calls back, and . . . we had an informant. A local who had been investigated by Flowers for DUI and possession of methamphetamine."

"Investigated? Those are 'is what it is' charges. What would he be investigating?"

"Apparently, he said he wouldn't arrest her and could also get her a lower price for meth in exchange for certain . . . favors."

"Jesus H. Christ."

"I'm sorry, Griff."

"You said you *had* an informant. What happened to her?"

"She's gone. Not at home. Not answering calls or texts. Not working." She banged on the table with her right fist. "Gone."

The sheriff put his hands in his pockets. "The photographs don't prove anything. Tyson Cade is public enemy number one around here. I would expect officers in my department to be seen with him. Hell, I would hope for that, and we asked Kelly to investigate Cade because they both grew up in Alder Springs."

"Griff—"

"Let me finish. And the calls are likewise useless. Circumstantial evidence proving nothing. But the informant . . . that's different. If there is someone out there willing to blow the whistle on Kelly Flowers, then that paints a different picture." He hesitated. "That is proof."

"Was proof," Hatty corrected.

He looked down at her with a question on his face.

"Kelly Flowers is dead. Even with proof, what do we do with it?"

Griff rubbed the back of his neck and sighed. "Does anyone else know about this?"

"Sergeant Mitchell has been assisting me. Other than George, no. I was about to talk with the district attorney about a deal for the informant, but then my witness disappeared."

Sheriff Griffith walked another circle around the table and then sat down. "Why did you sit on this for so long, Hatty?"

"I didn't sit on it. George and I both wanted to be sure what we had . . . we didn't want to accuse an officer of that type of wrongdoing unless we were certain, and like you just mentioned, we didn't have any real proof. Only a lot of smoke."

"What do we do with this, Hatty? Flowers was murdered. He's a hero around here now. A martyr. You saw how the initial appearance went. It was crazy. We're planning a funeral for him next week with a procession through town and a twenty-one-gun salute."

"I know," she said. "I don't have the solutions."

"Damnit," he said, leaning his meaty forearms on the table and placing his chin on top of his fists. "If Flowers was mixed up with Cade, then that makes Cade a possible avenue of investigation for Trey Cowan's defense lawyer. Is there any indication that Cade could possibly have been involved with Flowers's murder?"

Hatty crossed her arms. "All the evidence points to Cowan. There are videos of him threatening to kill Flowers. He had owned a shotgun that appears almost certainly to be the murder weapon. And his antics after the murder at the Guntersville High football field indicate guilt." She paused.

"But?"

"But we still haven't answered one question. What was Flowers doing at Branner's Place in Alder Springs at midnight? Was he investigating someone for us? If so, I have found nothing on his phone, in his desk, or in any of his files that would indicate so, and the folks he worked most closely with in the department are likewise clueless. And if he wasn't working for us . . ."

"Was he working for Cade?" the sheriff chimed in. Then he added, "Good freakin' grief."

"It's a mess," Hatty finally said, flinging up her hands and walking down to the end of the table. "What makes matters worse is Cowan's lawyer."

The sheriff grunted. "Jason Rich. This case was already a circus without him joining in."

"That's not the half of it," Hatty said. "He knows our informant."

"What?" Griff's eyes widened as he stared at the detective. "Who?"

Hatty looked at him over her shoulder. "His ex-girlfriend . . . Chase Wittschen."

20

As the sun began its ascent over the Gulf of Mexico, Jason sat on the sand and gazed out at the emerald-green water. He'd barely slept a wink all night. They'd gotten a room at the Hampton Inn at Orange Beach and then eaten dinner at Sea N Suds. The mood had been somber, and Nola had picked over her seafood while Jason forced himself to wolf down a fried shrimp basket. Once back in the room, Nola said she had some homework, and Jason fought the urge to buy a six-pack from the cooler at the front desk. He had known he could also hop in the rental and be at the Flora-Bama in five minutes in one direction or the Pink Pony Pub in the same amount of time the opposite way. He felt completely strung out and on edge after having witnessed Chase, who was one of the strongest people he knew, be reduced to nothing more than another addict on the detox unit.

Her helplessness went against everything he knew about her. Chase had flown attack helicopters in the army and had faced serious combat in Afghanistan. Now out of the service for over five years, she taught men and women alike to fly airplanes as a flight instructor. She also knew more about kayaking, fishing, and the lake than anyone he'd been around.

It was depressing seeing her wilt against the power of addiction, and Jason felt a powerful urge to join her. And he might've given in to that impulse if it hadn't been for Nola. If he fell off the wagon, especially now, what would that signal to her? She was already skating around the boundary line of addiction herself.

So he'd gone to the hotel's fitness center, where he'd torn into multiple sets of bench press, shoulder press, dead lift, squats, dumbbell curls, triceps kickbacks, and pull-ups. When his arms felt like jelly, he got on the treadmill and ran for twenty minutes until his lungs felt as if they would pop out of his chest. Then, sufficiently exhausted, he went outside and breathed in the fresh salt air. He walked on the beach until his desire to have a drink finally left him. Then he plopped onto the sand and gazed up at the stars. At some point, he must have fallen asleep.

He awoke to the rays of the sun on his face and the sound of the waves crashing in front of him. His mouth was dry, and his arms, shoulders, and back were stiff and sore.

But his head was clear.

Jason looked out at the water and said a silent prayer of gratitude. He was tired but sober.

And he knew what he had to do.

"Hey," Nola's voice came from behind, and then she sat on the sand next to him. "How long you been out here?"

"Awhile," Jason said, his voice scratchy.

"So what now?" she asked.

"We're going to take a walk, and you're going to tell me everything." He took in a breath of the ocean air and exhaled. Then he looked at her. "Every drug you've taken. Each person you've bought from. Any place you've been to buy." He hesitated. "And any direct contact you've had with Tyson Cade."

She didn't look at him, but she managed a nod.

"It's going to be OK," Jason said.

"You don't know that." Her tone was sad. "Nothing is OK right now. Chase . . ." She started to cry.

Jason put his arm around her neck and gave it a gentle squeeze before letting go. "It's OK," Jason said, rising to his feet and brushing the sand off his legs. "I'm sad too." He took in a deep breath of the refreshing salt air and let it fill his lungs. "We've been through a lot together, wouldn't you say?"

Nola stood and looked at him, her eyes squinting against the sun. "Yes."

"We'll get through this too," he said. "But to do so, you have to be honest with me."

"OK . . . but."

"But what?"

"You're going to be so disappointed in me."

Jason chuckled and began to walk down the beach. "Oh, Nola. For me to be disappointed in anyone would be the ultimate pot-and-kettle moment. Whatever you've done, I promise you that I've done the same or worse."

"Will you tell me some of your worst moments?" Nola had a timid smile on her face.

"Yes, I will," he said, squeezing her shoulder once she caught up with him. "But you first."

21

Nola's gateway drug had been Xanax.

She'd first tried it at the urging of, who else, her mother. Jana had been hooked on Xanax and a number of other antidepressants, and she had frequently offered the medication to Nola whenever she was stressed or had any outburst of anger or irritation. Without telling Jason, Nola had taken Xanax throughout Jana's trial, and Niecy had filled a couple prescriptions for herself and given them to Nola. When the pills had run out, Nola had found a source closer to home.

Kevin Martin was called K-Mart by all the kids at Guntersville High. K-Mart threw the best parties. Drove a nice car. Wore designer clothes. And yes, had an in on pretty much any drug a high school student or, hell, anyone of any age could ever want. Nola was able to purchase Xanax pretty cheap—about $100 for thirty pills. Of course, Nola and Niecy had both inherited sizable trust funds established by their father, which paid her a nice stipend each month. Nola was easily able to afford the Xanax, and when she grew more depressed, she sought an upper to take to give her a rise.

In Marshall County, the upper of choice was methamphetamine. "Sand Mountain SlimFast," as the locals called it. K-Mart had a source for meth as well, and he started selling it to Nola along with the Xanax.

"I did a half gram of meth before school to keep me going during the day and then Xanax in the afternoon to chill."

"Did you take anything else?"

She looked out at the ocean then.

"I have to know everything, honey. Tyson Cade is a dangerous man. I need to know what you've done to be able to better protect you."

"Pot," she finally said, not looking at him. "A few times at parties when a joint was being passed around. And the gummies laced with THC. K-Mart gave those out as party favors when he would throw something big at his house. And I did coke a couple times but didn't like it."

"Anything else?"

"I drink. I mean . . . you know, alcohol. Vodka mainly. Trulys or some other seltzer." She paused. "All my friends drink."

"Did K-Mart get the alcohol too?"

She gave a sheepish smile and shook her head. "I can get that myself. I have Niecy's old ID."

Jason couldn't help but smile despite his concern. "Smart," he said.

"Easy," she corrected.

Jason kicked at the incoming waves, his mind racing with more questions.

"Who was K-Mart's source?" he asked, knowing that whoever the middleman was, the chain would end with Tyson Cade.

"He never told me that. K-Mart was pretty tight lipped about where he got his drugs. He would ask what we wanted, and he'd have it in a few days."

"Sounds like a cool customer," Jason said, sarcasm easing into his tone.

"He's really popular."

"Are you and he more than friends?"

She shrugged and looked at the ocean. "Friends . . . with occasional benefits."

Jason tried to keep any judgment out of his face or tone. Teenagers had to make mistakes if they were going to grow. God knows, Jason had made enough of them when he was her age and had continued to do so. Dating and doing business with a drug dealer was a pretty big lapse in judgment, but what was done was done. Jason had learned that himself in rehab. If you kept your eyes behind you too long, you could never move forward. You had to set your burdens down. You had to release everything that was bringing you down. He was through eight of the twelve steps of AA now, moving at his own pace so as not to have any setbacks. Listening to Nola's story made him glad he was taking it slow.

"Is that everything?" Jason asked. They had walked over two miles and could now see Perdido Pass in the distance. The sun was full in the sky, and he was sweating. They sat down on an outdoor swing and gazed at the ocean.

"Yes, sir."

"Have you had any direct contact with Tyson Cade?"

"No, sir. Only K-Mart."

"What about Chase? Have you ever done meth with her?"

"No. I never saw Chase doing any drugs. I was shocked that she was involved in anything."

Jason leaned his head back on the swing and stared up at the sky. "Me too."

For a long moment, neither of them said anything. Finally, Jason asked the question that he'd wanted to ask since they'd started their trek down the beach. He'd held it back because he didn't want her to be defensive. He figured he'd have a better chance of getting the truth if he let her tell her story first.

"Have you taken anything since we left Guntersville?"

Nola didn't hesitate. "No, sir."

"Meth?"

"No."

"Xanax?"

"No."

"Anything at all?"

"You don't believe me, do you?" She got up from the swing and started walking fast back toward the hotel. Jason followed, having to jog to keep up.

"It's not that I don't believe you, honey. It's just . . . I've been there. And I've lied to people. Addicts are the best liars."

"I'm not lying, and I'm not an addict," Nola said, her tone fierce.

"OK," Jason said, holding up his palms.

"I want to go home," Nola said. "I have a test on Friday, and I need to study for it."

"Stop," Jason said.

When she kept walking, Jason raised his voice. "Stop!"

Nola did as instructed this time. She turned and put her hands on her hips. "What?"

"Nola, the PAC has a spot for you. I've arranged for it, and I know I can talk the school into giving you thirty days to get yourself right. Especially after all you've been through."

"No," she said.

"It was the best thing I ever did."

"Well, I'm not you. I'm not Mom. I'm not Chase. I'm *me*." She crossed her arms. "And I'm not going to rehab. I don't need it. All I need is for you to take me home." She started walking again, and Jason let her go.

For a moment, he gazed out at the gulf. His plan had been to leave them both at the PAC. That had been the main reason he'd asked Nola to come. Sure, he'd wanted her to witness Chase's admission, as he thought it would be good for her to see just how bad being sent to detox was.

But he'd also wanted her to attend the PAC at least for a month. To nip in the bud whatever issue she might be having with drugs and alcohol before it grabbed ahold of her and didn't let go.

It wasn't surprising that Nola was resistant. If anything, that proved to him the wisdom of his plan. But he wouldn't force her to go. He knew that at the end of the day, it was up to the patient to realize that he or she needed help. You had to own up to the problem before you could ever get better.

And Nola wasn't there yet.

Was she telling the truth? Had she told him everything about her experiences buying drugs?

Or had she left out a key detail?

Was Nola a true addict? Or just a user who could walk away from meth and Xanax without any ill effects?

Jason looked down at the sand and then out at the ocean. "*I don't know*," he whispered. Jason took in a deep breath of salt air and cleared his lungs. That seemed to be his answer to everything right now. What had happened to Chase? Why had Cade leaned on him to represent Trey Cowan? Was Nola lying to him? And finally . . .

What in the hell am I doing?

Jason gritted his teeth and forced his feet to move forward down the beach.

22

Nola got to the hotel room before Jason. She took out her key card, but she dropped it before reaching the knob. "Shoot," she said, bending over and looking back at the elevator. She saw and heard nothing. Nola snatched the card off the floor and tried again, gaining entry and heading straight to her room. She walked into the bathroom and locked the door. She took off her clothes and turned on the shower.

Then she unzipped her toiletry kit. She took out the small bottle of Advil and reached inside. But instead of a brown ibuprofen tablet, she pulled out a white pill. She popped it into her mouth and kicked her neck back to swallow it down.

I'm a liar, she thought. *A liar, an addict, and a loser.* She took a deep breath and grabbed the sink. She had told her uncle most of it, but she'd left out some things.

And not just about taking Xanax on this trip.

If only that was all. If only . . .

She looked at herself in the mirror and then, unable to bear the sight of herself, stepped into the shower.

As the water cascaded over her face, she began to cry.

23

Jason slept during the flight home. It felt like only five minutes, but it was something. Once the wheels on the plane hit the ground in Guntersville, he felt refreshed, focused. Harry met them at the tarmac to help with their bags, and Jason didn't even let him get his hello out before he started in with the plan.

"I need you to do a full profile on the victim. And I'm talking everything. Family history. Education. Work experiences. Friends. Enemies. Criminal background, if any. I want to know everything about Sergeant Kelly Flowers. If there was a skeleton in his closet, I want you to find it."

"Isn't it risky putting the victim on trial, J. R.?" Harry asked.

Jason stopped at the SUV, a five-year-old Ford Explorer that was Jason's more practical vehicle. Harry opened the back seat door for Nola, and she climbed inside. Once her door was shut, Jason stared at his investigator. "Yes, Harry, it is risky and probably foolish to put the victim on trial in a murder case, but that's not what I'm after."

Harry rubbed his chin. "You want to know what Flowers was doing at the barn at midnight. Was he meeting someone? Investigating a lead for the sheriff's department or . . . perhaps something personal for himself." Harry nodded as he spoke.

"Exactly," Jason said. "If we figure out why Flowers was out at that barn, then perhaps another suspect will emerge."

"Or we will confirm that our client is guilty."

"That too," Jason agreed.

Harry started to walk around the driver's side, but Jason grabbed his arm. "Wait."

"What?" Harry asked.

Jason leaned close to his investigator. "I need you to do something else."

"Spit it out."

Jason glanced inside the SUV, where Nola was immersed in her phone. "I want you to investigate a kid at Guntersville High School named Kevin Martin. The kids call him K-Mart. According to Nola, he's who she bought her meth from."

Harry's eyes wandered toward Nola. "All right . . . I'm on it." The hesitation in his words was the only indication that he might be surprised. Harry Davenport had worked as a bouncer at Sammy's strip club in Birmingham and done his own tour in Afghanistan. When he said he had seen it all, he was telling the truth. "So this K-Mart kid is hooked up with Tyson Cade." A statement, not a question.

"Has to be. Maybe not directly. Perhaps there's a middleman. But all meth in Marshall County—"

"Begins and ends with Cade," Harry chimed in.

Jason stole a glance at Nola as he grabbed the passenger-side door handle. "Exactly."

"What does this have to do with the case, boss?" Harry asked, moving around the front of the Explorer while holding Jason's eye.

"I'm tired of this prick, Harry. You should've seen Chase. I'm not sure if she's ever gonna be the same, and I'm betting Cade targeted them both. Once we get a read on this K-Mart clown, I want to know if he was instructed to go after Nola."

"You think Cade wanted to have something on you?"

Jason scowled at him. "My girlfriend and my niece. You think that's a coincidence?"

Harry looked away and scratched his neck. "Well, Chase had a prior drug problem and is also an alcoholic." He moved his eyes to Jason. "And Nola is a teenager who just lost both her parents."

"Harry—"

"All's I'm saying is he could have simply seized on an opportunity. I'm not thinking that Cade is some kind of criminal mastermind. He can't be much more than thirty years old."

"And he's been in the Sand Mountain drug game his whole life. You told me that last year."

"He has, but why would he want to hurt you?"

Jason thought it through out loud. "Maybe he knew that he, or one of his associates, was going to need a lawyer. He knows I'd never volunteer to represent him or an employee of his, so he had to have something on me."

"Listen to yourself, J. R. You're reaching. Tyson Cade is an opportunist and nothing more. He saw an opportunity, and he's leveraging free legal work out of it. That's it and that's all it is. Besides, no offense, but why would he purposely set you up to represent anyone in a criminal case? You've tried all of one murder case." He spat on the ground. "That ain't much experience."

"But I won," Jason said, breaking into a sheepish grin.

"And you were lucky as hell, don't you think? You gonna be that lucky again?"

Jason's smile faded. "I guess we're gonna find out."

"J. R., I want you to listen to me and pay attention. I understand what you're doing. You're trying to protect the ones you love, and you feel that representing Trey Cowan is the only way you can do that. I get it. I do." He paused.

"But."

"But don't go to war against Tyson Cade. Try the case. Win. Lose. Get a mistrial. Whatever. Do your job, stay in your lane."

"What if Cade prevents me from doing that? He almost sabotaged Jana's case, and he assaulted Niecy and me along the way. What if he does the same here, but worse? Look what he's already done to Chase."

"She did that to herself, J. R."

Jason peered at the ground. The conversation was wearing him down. He knew his friend meant well, but he wouldn't be deterred.

"I don't want to see you get hurt, man," Harry said. "You've come a long way since last year."

"I don't want to get hurt either, Harry. I don't want anyone to get hurt. But I'm not sure I'm ever going to be able to have a life in Marshall County until I deal with Tyson Cade."

Harry's face was grave, his voice firm. "There is only one way to *deal* with a person like Cade. Do you know what I mean?"

"Yes."

"Are you prepared to go that far?"

"I'll do whatever it takes to protect my family, Harry." He pulled the door open and peered at him one last time. "Whatever it takes."

24

Tyson Cade bought his usual at the Alder Springs Grocery, but he barely acknowledged Dooby Darnell. He handed her a five-dollar bill, ignored her attempt to give him change, and asked no questions. For her part, Dooby said nothing. She knew she was skating on thin ice. Tyson could tell it in her demeanor. The sweat that had gathered under her lids and on her neck was a dead giveaway, as was the way she averted her eyes and didn't look at him. She was scared, and she had every right to be after Tyson's interaction with her in the storage room.

He walked out into the cool night air and bit into the Twinkie, relishing the sweet taste. As the sedan rolled to a stop beside him, he climbed inside as the door opened for him. He shut it and watched the driver.

"So what's the good news from the sheriff's department?"

"Nothing you want to hear." There was a pause and then a grunt. "Before his murder, Flowers was being investigated for potential involvement with your . . . operation."

"Really? And what was the yield on that?"

"We have phone records and photographs."

"So what? Proves nothing."

"We also have an informant. Or we did at least. She's gone, but she was dealing with Flowers and was going to turn him in."

Tyson popped his knuckles and gazed out the window at the houses that fronted Hustleville Road. "Chase Wittschen," he said.

"You already knew?"

He took a sip of Sun Drop. "A hunch. So what? So you had an informant. Kelly's dead. Your informant has no one to inform on. Besides, she's an addict, so her credibility is nil. And she's far away from Marshall County now."

"How do you know that?"

"I know," Tyson said. "Anything else?"

"This . . . situation, if it ever was made public, could be very embarrassing for the department."

Tyson cackled. "I imagine so. That's why you shouldn't make it public."

"I'm not sure we'll have much choice. Cowan's lawyer will probably serve discovery requests that will force us to disclose the investigation of Flowers."

"Does the DA know anything?"

"Not yet, but she's asked for Flowers's records herself. We just haven't given her the internal affairs file yet." There was a pause. "But it's inevitable, Tyson."

As they reached the intersection with Highway 75, Tyson said, "Turn left and pull into the dealership."

The driver obeyed. When they came to a stop in front of Sand Mountain Used Auto, Tyson looked at his chauffeur. "The only thing inevitable in Marshall County is me. And, from my view, this investigation of Flowers is more of a problem for the sheriff's department than it is for me." He licked his lips. "How many people know?"

"Three."

"Then make it go away. Get rid of the file."

"I can't do that."

"Sure you can."

"No, Tyson, I can't. I could lose my job if anyone found out that I was withholding or destroying evidence relevant to a capital murder trial."

Now Tyson laughed out loud. "And what do you think will happen if anyone finds out you're dealing with me?"

"No one will."

Tyson grinned and leaned toward the other person. "They will if I tell them."

The driver's eyes widened. "What, you can't—"

"I can get another mole as easy as pie. Look at how simple it was to nab you."

Tyson opened the door and then knocked on the window. Once it came down, he leaned his elbows on the sill. "I don't want that file turned over to the DA, and I damn sure don't want Jason Rich to get ahold of it." He glanced over his shoulder and then back to the person behind the wheel. "Get rid of it." He narrowed his gaze and lowered his voice. "Or I'll get rid of you."

25

Once back at Mill Creek, Jason called Izzy. "We need to prepare discovery to the state," he said. "I want everything the sheriff's office has on Kelly Flowers. I've got Harry doing a deep dive on the victim, but we need all the paper they have on him. I'm looking for any clues as to what he was doing that led him to that barn in Alder Springs the night of the murder. The sheriff's office has been silent on that subject, so I'm assuming he either wasn't on police business, or they aren't sure what he was doing."

"Already on it," Izzy said. "I've drafted some broad requests, but you know we can't serve them until after the arraignment."

"That's right." Jason snapped his fingers and jerked his head. He'd forgotten the rule, which wasn't all that surprising considering the Cowan case would be his second criminal case of any nature. He walked out into the sunroom upstairs and sat down in a rocking chair. He glanced inside, but there was no sign of Nola. She'd already gone downstairs to her room. "Well, I'm glad you're on top of it. Have you looked at the documents Shay gave us?"

"Yes, I've done a comb through already. There are at least ten videos of Trey assaulting Flowers at the Brick. The audio isn't good on some of them, but, on a couple, the words come in loud and clear."

"And?"

"And our client threatened to kill the victim a few hours before the officer was murdered."

"What did he—"

"Trey's exact words were, '*I'll kill you. I swear to God, I will.*'"

Jason leaned back in the chair. "That doesn't leave much to the imagination. And what of the gun?"

"Trey owned a twelve gauge, and the sheriff's department found that exact shotgun in the cab of his truck with only his prints on it."

"Did the coroner's report conclude that the blast came from a twelve gauge?"

"Yes. Forensics are a bit tricky with shotguns. It is difficult to trace a shotgun shell to a particular gun, but Dr. Carton's preliminary conclusion was that the murder weapon was a twelve-gauge shotgun." She stopped, and it sounded like she was taking a drink of something. Probably Diet Coke, if Jason had to figure. His partner drank more Diet Cokes in a day than John Daly in a major championship.

Jason stood and peered out at Lake Guntersville. The sun was beginning to set from behind the house, and the water looked dark and mysterious, which fit his mood to a tee. "Set up a meeting with Dr. Carton," Jason said. "Maybe there's something else he can tell us." Jason stuffed his hands in his pockets. "Anything additional in the state's materials worth noting?"

"There's a statement from Ronnie Kirk, the football coach at Guntersville High. Trey was talking to him when the police arrived. Trey told Kirk that he knew he was about to be arrested. Also said that he couldn't take back what he'd done."

"Damn," Jason said. "Practically sounds like a confession."

"I know. There's also a statement from Trey's mother."

"Is there anything helpful in it?"

"No. Just says he came to her house around eleven at night, and she was already asleep. Trey was drunk and said he'd gotten into it with Kelly Flowers. He was slurring his words, and Ms. Cowan was tired. She listened for a few minutes and then went back to bed, because her job started at six in the morning. When she got up the next day, Trey was passed out on the floor of her kitchen. She didn't wake him and went to work. Said it wasn't the first time he'd passed out at her house."

Crap, Jason thought. "So she doesn't help at all."

"No. She gives him no alibi, since she went back to sleep. And she mentions that he was still angry about Flowers."

"Is there anything good for us in what Shay provided?"

"No."

"How far is Trey's mother's house from the murder scene?"

"Less than a mile."

"Is there information in there about how Trey . . . or anyone else . . . could know that Flowers was going to be at Branner's Place?"

"Branner's what?"

"I'm sorry. That's what that barn has always been called. Used to be a hangout for high school kids and ne'er-do-wells. Marshall County, outside of its four main cities, is dry, and Branner's Place served alcohol and other things under the counter."

"How did it stay open for so long?"

"Marshall County is about ninety-five percent law-abiding citizen and five percent outlaw, and the majority of that five is located in or around Sand Mountain. Branner's Place was far enough off the road that it didn't cause much disturbance."

"Is it still up and running?"

"No," Jason said, walking into the kitchen and pulling a yellow notepad out of his briefcase. "Closed about seven or eight years ago, but I think Bull Branner still owns the land."

"That is who discovered the body," Izzy said. "Lynn 'Bull' Branner."

Jason rubbed his chin, thinking that they might have finally stumbled upon something positive. "We definitely need to meet with him. Bull's a shady character." Jason jotted the man's name down on his pad. "I'll take that one."

"OK, back to your question. The answer is no. There's nothing in the district attorney's file about why Flowers was at Branner's Place."

Jason nodded to himself. "That's their soft spot then. They can prove motive out the yin-yang and means with the shotgun. But what about opportunity?"

"I'm sure that Shay will argue Trey's proximity to the murder gave him all the opportunity he needed."

"Agreed. It looks good on paper, but the question remains."

"How could Trey Cowan have known that Flowers was going to be at Branner's Place?" Izzy said it out loud. "Have you asked him?"

"He can't remember anything after getting to his mother's house but is adamant that he didn't leave."

"Too bad his mother can't confirm his alibi." Then, as if she was turning a page in her brain, she asked, "All right, what else?"

Jason stared at his notepad. "Remind me the name of Braxton's CRNA who testified in the trial last year. She was dating Trey at the time."

"Colleen Maples," Izzy said.

Jason couldn't help but smile. His partner had a photographic memory. "Yes," he said, writing her name down on the page. "We need to track her down as well."

"Do you want me to take her? I seem to recall her being a bit chilly toward you during Jana's case."

"Definitely," Jason said.

"Anything else?"

Jason rubbed the back of his head and again stared at the lake. "I can't think of anything at the moment."

There were a couple of seconds of silence. Then Izzy spoke, her voice softer. "How did it go in Perdido?"

"Terrible."

"Did Chase ever speak with you?"

"No," Jason said, hanging his head. "She barely said a word."

"Jesus . . . I'm sorry."

"Yeah, me too."

"And what about Nola?"

Jason glanced toward the kitchen, and then his eyes drifted to the den. Nola was still downstairs. "She was pretty shook up by it."

"That's why you brought her, wasn't it?"

"Yes."

"Did you get her drug source?"

"Yes. A guy named Kevin Martin. Kids call him K-Mart."

"That's original."

"Harry's going to look into him."

"Isn't that kind of dangerous?" Izzy asked, her tone amped up now. "I'm sure he's hooked up with Cade. And how does Nola's supplier help us defend Trey Cowan?"

Jason forced himself to take a deep breath and then exhaled. "Just circling the wagons, Iz. Trying to protect my family from any more issues."

Another break in the conversation, and Jason knew his partner's mental wheels were turning. "OK then. I understand. Do you think Nola is still using?"

"She says no."

"Do you believe her?"

Jason didn't immediately answer.

"Jason?"

"I don't know. That's one of the reasons I've asked Harry to look into K-Mart."

"OK," she said. "Hey, Jason Rich."

He smiled. Occasionally, when his partner was trying to emphasize a point, she used both his first and last name. "What?"

"Hang in there."

26

Trey Cowan gazed through the plexiglass at the woman, feeling a weird combination of guilt, anger, and lust.

"How are you?" Colleen asked. She had her brown hair up in a ponytail and wore green surgery scrubs.

"I'm fine," he lied.

She rolled her eyes. "Same old Trey. Stuck in jail for two weeks. Charged with murdering a police officer. 'How am I? Oh, I'm good. No worries.'"

He managed a genuine smile. "It's good to see you." He glanced down at the floor and then back up at her. "Why did you come by my apartment the morning I was arrested?"

Her eyes flickered. "I saw the police cars. They were everywhere. I was . . . worried."

"About me?"

She gave him another eye roll. The gesture had always been sexy the way Colleen did it, and Trey felt a tremor of excitement. "Yes, about you."

For a few seconds, they just looked at each other. Their romance had never made much sense. She was a good ten years older than Trey, and she had been the CRNA for Dr. Waters's surgical repair of his broken tibia. She and Waters were having an affair at the time, and witnesses said they'd had an argument during Trey's operation. Though the evidence was not conclusive, Colleen believed that her personal relationship with Dr. Waters had affected the doctor's response time to the infection that Trey developed after the procedure. After the lawsuit was over—Dr. Waters obtained a defense verdict—Colleen had sought Trey out to offer an apology. He had invited her for a beer, and one drink turned into four, which turned into them rolling around in his bed the rest of the day.

His own relationship with Colleen had affectively ended last October when it became evidence in the Jana Waters murder trial. The fling had been fun when it was under the radar, but once everyone knew about it, the shine had worn off for Colleen. At least that was Trey's assumption.

There was also the matter of her burgeoning drug use . . . and a new man in her life.

Kelly Flowers . . .

"Why are you here, Colleen?" Trey finally asked. He couldn't hide the hurt in his tone.

"I'm just . . . worried about you."

"Me? I figured you would be angry with me. Given who I'm charged with killing." He glared at her, and she gazed down at the floor.

"Look," Trey finally said. "We had our fun. *You* had your fun, and you moved on. You don't owe me anything."

She peered up at him. "I'm not here because I feel guilty."

"Then why the hell are you here?"

"I guess I'm curious. What is Jason Rich doing representing you?"

Trey frowned. "He's who my mother got."

"How? No offense, but you don't have the kind of money to afford an attorney like Jason Rich. And neither does Trudy."

"Then you'll have to ask Mr. Rich. All I know is that he's my lawyer."

"Cade's paying him, isn't he? That's the only thing that makes sense."

Now Trey gazed down at the floor, not answering her.

"Trey, for all you know, that bastard killed Kelly himself or had someone do it at his bequest, and you're his patsy. He's hired Rich to represent you to make it look good, but he fully expects you to go down for it."

"Give me a break, Colleen. That's some kind of conspiracy theory." He cocked his head at her. "Is there something you're not telling me?"

She put her hand to the glass. "Trey, I know about Kelly's association with Tyson Cade. I know firsthand." Her lip started to tremble, and Trey again envisioned her in the back of Kelly's truck. "It makes me sick how the whole town is treating Kelly like he was some kind of a hero. He was a sick sonofabitch who used his badge and his association with Cade for his own personal benefit." She wiped her eyes. "He hurt a lot of people."

Trey kept his gaze on the concrete floor. It was all true. "How long did you date him?"

She scoffed. "We didn't date. I used him for drugs, and he used me . . ."

Trey looked up from the table and wasn't sure what he saw in her eyes. Hurt? Regret? Shame? He'd never been able to read people.

"Eventually," Colleen continued, "he got bored with me and found someone else's life to ruin."

"Who?"

"I don't know."

"Well . . . I guess I'm sorry," Trey said, his voice edged with sarcasm.

She leaned toward him, her eyes narrowing. "Have you told your lawyer about how you . . . and Kelly . . . worked for Cade?"

Trey shook his head.

"Then how is Mr. Rich going to be able to effectively represent you?"

"I don't know."

"Trey, this is your life. You're being charged with capital murder. You understand that, don't you?"

"Yes."

"Are you willing to sacrifice your life to keep Tyson Cade out of trouble?"

"It's not that simple," Trey said. "Tyson owns Sand Mountain. He *owns* me."

"How?" she asked. "How in here could that still be the case?"

"My mom," Trey said. "My dad too." He hesitated. "You."

"What about us?"

Trey sighed. "He'll kill all of you, Colleen. Don't you understand? No one that I care about is safe."

"But how can you win?" she asked, a trace of desperation creeping into her tone.

He gave his head a jerk and stood. "That's up to Mr. Rich."

27

The fire was raging full tilt by 8:30 p.m. Satch, Chuck, and Mickey Tonidandel sat around it in lawn chairs, each with a red Solo cup of something in their hand. Jason didn't ask. Every so often, one of the brothers threw an item on the fire, and sparks flew into the evening air.

This was what folks in Mill Creek called "taking out the trash."

"What's on your mind?" Satch finally asked, poking the fire with a stick.

"I want you to ramp up our security detail. I don't want to go with an outside group this time." Jason paused and met Satch's gaze. "Just you . . ." Jason moved his gaze to Chuck and Mickey. ". . . and your brothers. We need more manpower, and I want you to hire the additions."

"What about Niecy? Last time, Cade attacked her."

Jason bristled as he remembered the frantic trip to Birmingham after he'd received word that Nola's older sister had been attacked by one of Tyson Cade's goons. They'd roughed her up to send him a message. Would they go that route again? Jason didn't think so. He figured Cade would focus on Nola, Chase, and Jason himself, but he wasn't taking any chances. "I've hired a Birmingham group to have a guard watching her place at all times and to also follow her if she ever leaves campus."

"Did you tell her that?"

"Yes. Full disclosure."

"How'd she take it?"

"She was shaken, but she understood. She was more worried about Nola and Chase."

"And how are they?" Satch asked.

Jason peered into the fire. "Chase is in rehab. She'll be there for a while. And Nola . . . is OK."

"You don't sound convincing."

"I know."

"What do you want from us and our team?"

Jason looked up from the flames. "Full surveillance of my house by water and land." He hesitated and then nodded. "I have complete trust in you. If what I'm paying you now is not enough, just name your price."

Satch rubbed the stick with both of his hands. "That'll be fine. Anything else?"

"Yes. Do you know Bull Branner? Used to own Branner's Place out at Alder Springs?"

"Yeah, I know Bull," Satch said.

"He comes to the range just about every week," Mickey added, pulling on his mustache and throwing a trash bag into the fire.

Jason rubbed his chin. The Tonidandels owned a gun range off of Highway 431. Chase had actually been an instructor there for a while. The three brothers also trained patrons in the use of all variety of firearms. "I need a meeting with him. Even though his barn store is closed, he still owns the property, and he's the one who found Kelly Flowers's body." Jason stood and grabbed a stick. "At the murder scene."

"We'll set it up," Satch said. "Bull's crazier than a shithouse rat, but he owes us a few favors."

Jason grinned, thinking how crazy a person had to be for him to be referred to as such by Satch Tonidandel.

"What else?"

Jason walked a lap around the fire. "You boys have lived in Marshall County your whole lives. You know the players here. You're familiar with Tyson Cade and how he operates. I need some reconnaissance on what Cade is up to these days. Where's he selling? What's he distributing? Who are his buyers? Is he having any trouble?"

"Why is any of that important?" Satch asked.

Jason stopped walking and gazed across the street to his house, where Nola was downstairs studying. "The murder happened at Branner's Place. That's Cade country, right?"

Satch flung some rotting wood on the fire. "Big time. If Sand Mountain had a beating heart, it's right in the middle of Hustleville Road." He squinted at Jason. "And Sand Mountain *is* Cade."

"I need to understand what Cade's stake is in this murder trial. I knew exactly why he was interfering in Jana's case, but I don't get it with Trey Cowan. I'm assuming that Trey worked for him in some capacity, but I haven't been able to confirm that. But I think Cade's entanglement in this situation must run deeper." Jason stopped talking and moved his eyes to each of the Tonidandel brothers before gazing back into the raging fire.

"Jason, if we dive into our own investigation of Cade, that could increase the danger to you and your family."

"I think that's inevitable regardless of what we do." He threw another stick on the fire. "I'm tired of playing defense against this prick, Satch."

The colonel grinned, but there was no humor in his eyes. "We can do that, Jason, but it's going to up the buying price of our services."

"Understood," Jason said.

Satch walked around the fire and stood in front of Jason. He leaned forward and spoke just above a whisper. "You realize that there's only one way you're ever going to rid yourself and your family of that sonofabitch."

Jason held Satch's gaze. "Yes, I do. That's why I want you to do one more thing for me."

"What's that?"

Jason took a Glock 43X semiautomatic handgun out of his pocket. "I want you to teach me how to shoot."

PART THREE

28

"ALL RISE!"

Jason and Trey rose together as the bailiff bellowed his opening salvo. Judge Terry Barber strode out of his chambers and to the bench, walking with a forward lean and holding a file under his arm. He sat down and spoke without looking up.

"State of Alabama versus Trey Jerome Cowan." Then he stared down from his high perch, first focusing on the district attorney. "Madame Prosecutor, is the state ready for the preliminary hearing?"

"Yes, Your Honor," Shay said, looking both elegant and intimidating in a black pantsuit.

"And Mr. Rich. Is the defendant prepared to proceed?"

"Yes, Your Honor," Jason said, straightening his light-gray suit, which was slightly wrinkled.

"All right then. Ms. Lankford, call your first witness."

Shay glanced to the man sitting next to her and cleared her throat. "The state calls Sergeant George Mitchell."

As the officer walked to the witness stand, Jason watched with mild curiosity. He was expecting Detective Hatty Daniels to be the prosecution's only witness today. Daniels was older and more experienced. The investigative report was primarily authored by Daniels, though Mitchell was involved in the interviews. Daniels had also been the state's chief witness in Jana's trial. Mitchell was of average height and medium build with a high-and-tight military-style haircut. Jason had met the man in passing during Jana's trial but had never paid much attention to him.

Maybe Shay is mixing it up, Jason thought. *Or perhaps Daniels isn't available. Or . . .* Jason smiled to himself at his own silliness. *Or this is the damn prelim, so Shay knows all she's got to do is show probable cause, and she doesn't want to give me a free shot at cross-examining her lead investigator.* Still, though, regardless of the ease with which the state could make its showing, this particular preliminary hearing *was* a big deal. Jason peered behind him, where the gallery was, as he expected, full to capacity. Most of the spectators appeared to be reporters, and Jason nodded at his friend, Kisha Roe, the new editor in chief of the *Advertiser-Gleam.* Because of the gag order, Jason hadn't been able to participate in any interviews, but he'd already promised Kisha the full scoop after the close of the case. She winked at him, and he remembered he needed to talk to her about something else. Or rather, someone else.

Jason wrote *Teresa Roe* on his yellow notepad as Sergeant Mitchell was sworn in as a witness.

Shay was even more bare bones than Jason thought she'd be. First, she introduced one of the various videos from the Brick showing Trey assault Kelly Flowers and then threaten to kill the officer. She then went over the coroner's report, where Clem Carton opined that Kelly Flowers was killed with a blast from a twelve-gauge shotgun to the chest. Because the rules of evidence were not applicable in the preliminary hearing, Shay could have Officer Mitchell recite the key points of the report. Next came the evidence of Trey's purchase of a twelve-gauge shotgun at Guntersville Tackle and Outdoor a year earlier and the inventory of Trey's truck, proving that a twelve-gauge shotgun with a pack of buckshot shells was found in the cab. Finally, Shay had the officer detail the events of Trey's arrest and his remarks to Coach Ronnie Kirk.

"No further questions, Your Honor," Shay said.

"Cross-examination, Mr. Rich?" Judge Barber asked.

"Yes, Your Honor," Jason said, standing and taking a deep breath. He knew this part was going to be tedious, but he might as well get the most out of it. "Officer Mitchell, you aren't the lead investigator for this case, are you?"

"Objection, Your Honor," Shay said, shooting to her feet. "Irrelevant."

Jason held out his palms. "Your Honor, this is the preliminary hearing. The rules of evidence don't apply." He shot the district attorney a glance. "And even if they did, my question is very relevant."

"Overruled," Barber said. "Madame Prosecutor, Mr. Rich is correct. The defendant should be given plenty of leeway to examine the witness."

"Yes, Your Honor," Shay said, her voice seeming to emerge from behind clenched teeth.

"Sergeant, do you remember the question?" Jason asked.

"Yes, I do," Mitchell said. "No, I wasn't the lead investigator. But I was part of the investigative team."

"Who was the lead?"

"Detective Hatty Daniels."

"And where is she today?"

Mitchell glanced at the prosecution table and then back to Jason. "She's sick."

Jason turned to the gallery, where he saw that most of the spectators appeared to be watching closely. "Well . . . I hope it's nothing serious." Then he turned back to Mitchell. "Sergeant, can you tell me the names of everyone who was at the Brick on the night of April 8?"

———

For the next three hours, Jason grilled Sergeant George Mitchell on every conceivable subject he could think of that might have any relevance or significance to the case. Jason had never cross-examined a witness before at a preliminary hearing, but he'd taken hundreds of depositions, and there was very little logistic difference. Ninety-five percent of a deposition was a fishing expedition to learn every conceivable thing the deponent knew about the operative facts. The other five percent was to establish helpful facts and sound bites.

Suffice it to say, George Mitchell didn't offer much in the way of additional information beyond what was in Shay's file.

But, as his examination neared its close, there were a couple of nice sound bites.

"Officer, does the state have any witness that saw Trey Cowan shoot Sergeant Flowers."

"No."

"Are there any witnesses to the shooting at all?"

"No."

"But despite the lack of any eyewitness testimony, my client, Mr. Cowan, was charged with the murder?"

"Correct." Mitchell glanced at the prosecution table and then back at Jason. "The evidence we did obtain clearly establishes Mr. Cowan as the killer."

Jason purposely smirked. "And let's examine that, shall we? You have a video of Mr. Cowan, who is clearly drunk, pushing Sergeant Waters down and making threats."

"He assaulted the victim and threatened to kill him," Mitchell fired back.

"He was drunk, right?"

"He had been drinking, yes."

"In fact, my client is a regular at the Brick, isn't he?"

"Yes. Our investigation has determined that Mr. Cowan did frequent the Brick."

"And by frequent, you mean he went there almost every night."

"Yes."

"Let me ask you this, Sergeant. What was Kelly Flowers doing there?"

"The bartender, Ms. Roe, indicated that Sergeant Flowers approached the bar and began to speak with the defendant." Mitchell paused. "But she was unable to hear much of their conversation."

"Was Officer Flowers in uniform?"

"Yes, he was."

"Was he there on behalf of the sheriff's department?"

"Not that I'm aware of. At least not until Mr. Cowan assaulted him."

"Was the sheriff's office investigating Mr. Cowan?"

"No."

"Did the bartender, Ms. Teresa Roe, say anything else about Sergeant Flowers's demeanor?"

"She said he was teasing the defendant."

Jason raised his eyebrows in mock surprise. "Teasing him? About what?"

"Like I said, she didn't hear much, but . . . she did hear Sergeant Flowers refer to the defendant as stupid."

"And what happened after that?"

"The defendant pushed the victim off his stool and threatened to kill him."

"Wouldn't you agree that Officer Flowers provoked Mr. Cowan?"

"I wouldn't agree or disagree. Just reporting the facts."

Jason nodded. "And the facts are . . . that the Marshall County Sheriff's Office has no idea why Sergeant Kelly Flowers was dressed in full uniform and *teasing* Mr. Cowan at the Brick at approximately eight thirty p.m. on April 8."

"That is correct. But Kelly and Trey . . ." Mitchell caught himself and stopped. ". . . the victim and the defendant were old friends."

"So this was just one friend, who happens to be a police officer and who happens to be in uniform, seeking out another friend in his frequent watering hole to give him a hard time."

"We don't know what they were talking about, but that, more or less, sounds accurate."

Jason walked back to the defense table and snatched his legal pad. "Sergeant, why was Kelly Flowers in Alder Springs at midnight on April 9?"

"Well, for one, Flowers lives in that community."

Jason approached the stand. "Has your department's investigation determined what Officer Flowers was doing at a barn off Hustleville Road commonly referred to as 'Branner's Place' at midnight on April 9?" Jason licked his lips. "Just before he was murdered."

"Specifically . . . no," Mitchell said with hesitation in his tone. "However, generally, we know that Sergeant Flowers was in uniform at the time of his murder and that he had also been assigned the task of investigating the Sand Mountain drug trade. Also, since our office has received tips in the past of possible drug-related activity at this particular barn, our conclusion is that Flowers's presence there was related to his official capacities as an officer."

Mitchell testified as if he were reading directly from the death penalty statute, which required the officer to be either on duty or doing something "related to his official capacities as an officer" for capital punishment to apply. For Jason's money, the mystery of what, exactly, Flowers was doing at the time of his death was the primary weakness in the state's case, and he was not surprised that Mitchell hemmed and hawed around it.

"Detective, has the sheriff's office ever investigated Trey Cowan for being involved in the Sand Mountain drug trade?"

"No."

"Has Mr. Cowan ever been convicted or even charged with any drug-related offenses?"

"Not that I'm aware of."

Jason wanted to continue the line of questioning but decided that discretion was the better part of valor. The bottom line was that it sounded like there was no connection between the reason the department had for Flowers being at Branner's Place and Trey Cowan. That would be a significant fact in favor of the defense at trial.

Maybe the only fact on our side, Jason thought as he strode back to the defense table. "Can you think of anything else?" he asked Trey. His client shook his head. Jason was about to say "No further questions" but then realized there were a couple of background questions he'd forgotten to ask.

"Sergeant, before his death, had the sheriff's department had any issues with Officer Flowers?"

"What do you mean?"

"Had Officer Flowers ever been written up or disciplined for any violation of protocol or procedure?"

"No."

"Was he ever charged or convicted of a crime himself?"

"No." Then, with a trace of defiance in his voice, Mitchell added, "Kelly Flowers was a good cop."

Jason dropped his notepad on the defense table. He didn't want to end on Mitchell's statement, but he also didn't want to ask something he'd already asked. He nodded at the officer and peered at Judge Barber. "No further questions, Your Honor."

"Anything further, Ms. Lankford?"

"No, Your Honor."

Judge Barber leaned forward in his chair and formed a tent with his hands. "All right, if that closes the evidence, then it is the court's ruling that the State of Alabama has produced sufficient evidence to show probable cause that the defendant, Trey Jerome Cowan, is guilty of the murder of the victim, Sergeant Kelly Flowers. This case is hereby bound over to the grand jury." Barber took his gavel and banged it once on the bench. "We are adjourned."

29

Kisha Roe was waiting on Jason when he exited the courthouse. "Surprised to see you out here," Jason said, smiling at his old friend. "Figured you'd be the first one to greet me out of the courtroom."

"The great Jason Rich does need his space," Kisha said, extending her fist, which Jason nudged with his own.

"What's up?" she asked. "You know I can't interview you, and you're probably risking a tongue-lashing from Barber just being seen with me."

"I'll take that risk," Jason said, looking both ways and crossing Gunter Avenue with Kisha on his heels. "Mind if we talk at the office?" Jason asked.

"Not at all."

The Rich Law Firm's Guntersville office was located on the corner of Worth Street and Gunter Avenue about a block south of the courthouse. A familiar location to both of them.

"So how does it feel practicing law in the same building as your father?" Kisha asked as Jason trotted up the steps. He paused on the stoop and gazed out at the highway. Thirty yards away and hovering fifty feet in the air was a billboard with Jason's smiling face on it.

He was wearing a navy suit, white shirt, and red tie on the advertisement, and his face was adorned with its typical three days of dirty-blond stubble. His similarly colored hair was short but stylishly unkempt. His teeth were white, making his smile a bit toothy. Was it cheesy? Yes. Was it tacky? Hell, yes. Would his father have approved? Absolutely not. In fact, one of Jason's finest hours had been installing the billboard while his dad, venerable old Lucas Rich, was still practicing.

But did it work?

Hells to the yes, Jason thought, looking down at Kisha. "Weird," he said, finally answering her question. "It feels weird, but also . . ." He again peered at the billboard before opening the door. ". . . kinda right."

They went through the lobby area, where two twentysomethings—a man and a woman—were tasked with answering the phone. Jason had his main office in Birmingham, which had four folks who handled the constant cold calls. Somehow, his partner, Izzy, vetted every single inquiry in some way or another, filtering out the dogs and keeping only the cases with the best facts on liability and with the highest exposure to the defendant. Jason saluted his reception team and strode down the hall to the firm's conference room, which doubled as a library. He'd bought the building in November from a restaurant group and had been pleased at his restoration of the space. While the front barely resembled the office that Lucas Rich had practiced in, Jason had taken great pains to re-create the library the way his father had decorated it.

If there was ever a closeness that he had felt with his dad, it was in here. He looked at the three long rectangular tables and then the ceiling-length bookshelves that adorned all four walls. As a kid, he'd done his homework in here every day after school. Sometimes, he and Kisha had studied together.

"Wow," she said, sitting down at one of the tables. "Does this bring back old times?" She nodded toward a painting on the wall. "Have you . . . made peace with him?"

Jason followed her eyes to the framed portrait of his father. His thick silver hair and eyebrows were accentuated by light-blue eyes. The painting had been a gift from the local bar when he'd announced his retirement. Little did anyone know that Lucas Rich would last only a few months after stepping away from the law before he died of a heart attack. Like Coach Bryant with football, he just didn't seem to have anything left after leaving the practice. Kisha had been on the receiving end of many of Jason's rants about his father during their high school days at Randolph, a private college prep school in Huntsville.

"I'm not sure," Jason admitted. "I hope being here is a way of making peace, but sometimes it just feels like another act of defiance." He sighed. "You know, Dad thought a lawyer should never advertise. Word of mouth was the way an attorney should get his clients." He wrinkled up his face and made his voice sound deeper and more deliberate. "'Jason, you should be able to attract business with your reputation only. If you can't, then you need to be in another line of work.'" He made a grand gesture with his hand. "'Like selling *automobiles*.'"

Kisha laughed. "That's a pretty good impression."

Jason also chuckled. "You want to know how many times I heard that speech?"

"A few."

He scoffed. "Dad just didn't get it. You ever listen to any Waylon Jennings?" he asked.

"Uh, not much. Country music . . . especially old country . . . isn't my thing."

"Me neither, but Dad loved it. Ironic, really. He loved Waylon, and I'm the living embodiment of one of his songs."

Kisha wrinkled up her face in confusion.

"'Are You Sure Hank Done It This Way.'" Jason snorted. "That was one of Dad's favorite songs, and it is literally exactly what I'm doing. I've been successful . . ."

"I'll say."

"But I haven't done it the way Dad did." Jason gazed at the portrait of his father. "And he never could get over that."

"Have you gotten over it?"

Jason peered down at the floor and crossed his arms. "I don't know," he finally said.

For a few moments, silence filled the library. Jason breathed in the scent of old court reporter books, which were pure decoration, and walked over to his collection of fiction, spreading his hand across some of his favorite stories.

"So what's up, Jason?" Kisha repeated the first question she'd asked him outside the courthouse.

"I need your help," he finally said.

"You need to meet with Teresa again?"

"Yes," he said. "How's she doing?"

Teresa was Kisha's wife. They'd married a couple of years earlier. Both had come out around the same time, and they'd met at the beach while each were on vacation. After spending all day together, one thing had led to another, which had led to marriage. Both women had been very helpful in his defense of Jana the previous year, and now Teresa was a key witness in Trey's case.

"Fine," Kisha said. "Annoyed at all the attention she's been getting from the sheriff's office . . ." Her lips curled into a tentative smile. ". . . and from you."

"I know, and I'm sorry," Jason said. "It's just that the Brick was where Trey's confrontation with Flowers happened, and she saw the whole thing and heard some of their conversation."

"She's told you everything she knows."

"Has she?" Jason asked, rubbing his chin and sitting on the edge of one of the tables. "I know we've covered everything that happened on the night in question, but I want to go deeper than that."

Kisha crossed her arms. "OK. Well, we were planning to go out to dinner tonight. Why don't you join us?"

"Are you sure?"

"Yeah, as long as you're buying."

"Of course," Jason said. "Wait, where are we going?"

Kisha walked to the door of the library and spun around with a grin on her face. "Old Town Stock House."

"Ah," Jason said. The Stock House was a fabulous restaurant and the most expensive in town.

"That cool with you?" Kisha asked.

"I'll see you there," Jason said.

As she opened the door, Jason thought of one more question he wanted to ask her. "Hey, Kisha?"

She looked over her shoulder. "Yeah?"

"Do you know much about Detective Hatty Daniels?"

"I know she wasn't there today at the hearing, and you made a bit of a show of her absence."

"So you noticed that."

"I did."

"Didn't you think it was odd that she wasn't there?"

"Maybe a little."

Jason waited, but Kisha remained quiet.

"Is there anything else you can tell me about her?"

She looked at him, giving away nothing. Stone-cold poker face. "Let's discuss it tonight, OK?"

Jason narrowed his gaze. "Kisha?"

"Tonight."

30

Shay Lankford slammed the door to her office once she and the sheriff were both inside. "Griff, what in the hell happened today?"

Sheriff Griffith stared back at her with hard eyes. "We won is what happened. The case was bound over to the grand jury."

"That's not what I mean, and you know it. *Where is Hatty?*"

"Sick," the sheriff said.

"Bullshit. Hatty hasn't missed a day of work in three years. I saw her yesterday, and we went over the examination and the expected line of cross. I prepared her and ended up having to roll with George."

"And you and George rolled fine," the sheriff said.

"Only because it was the prelim." She took out her phone and held it out in front of him. "I've called her ten times today, and it rings and rings. Goes to voice mail every time."

"She's probably screening your calls."

"And when have you ever known Hatty to do that."

Sheriff Griffith gave his head a jerk and turned for the door. "I do it when I'm sick, Shay. Look, I've got other things to do today."

"Don't you dare blow me off, Griff. This is a capital murder case. The second one my office has filed in two years. Shall I remind you how the last one went?"

"No," he said, looking down at the floor.

"Well, we may have accomplished the objective today, but we didn't start off strong. George Mitchell is not Hatty. He's a beta, and I need a damn alpha on the stand." She paused and walked toward him, leaning forward with her hands on her hips. "I need Hatty."

"You had her for the Jana Waters case, and you still lost."

"*We* lost, Griff," Shay said. "Just like *we* will both lose in November if we don't make damn sure Trey Cowan is lethally injected for murdering one of your officers. Do you understand?"

The sheriff gritted his teeth. "Yes, ma'am, I do."

"Good," Shay said, turning and walking back to her desk. As the sheriff grabbed the door handle, she called after him, her tone as cold as ice. "Griff?"

"Yes."

"The second you hear from Hatty, you tell her that I want to speak with her."

"OK," he said.

"And Griff?"

He stopped as he was halfway out the door but didn't turn around.

"It would be nice if your department could figure out what, *specifically*, Kelly Flowers was doing at Branner's Place before he was killed."

The sheriff scratched the back of his neck and nodded his head.

"*Really nice*," Shay added.

31

The phone buzzed in the passenger seat, but Detective Hatty Daniels didn't take any notice of it. She kept her hands on the wheel, forcing herself to focus on the green road signs.

She sucked in a deep breath and felt her heart begin to pound again. She glanced at the phone, saw the name on the screen—Sheriff Griffith—and then shifted her gaze back to the highway.

How many times had Griff called her today? She'd lost count. And whatever the number, it wasn't as many as the district attorney.

"*What am I doing?*" Hatty asked out loud. Her voice sounded almost foreign to her, and she realized that she hadn't said a word all day. She looked again at her phone, which had finally stopped vibrating. The device was resting on top of a manila folder.

Inside the binding was a copy of every document in her investigative file. Keeping her left hand on the wheel, she moved her right to her pants pocket, feeling the indention created by the thumb drive. Since leaving Guntersville at three thirty this morning, she'd probably checked to make sure she had the USB stick once every hour. As if it might be an engagement ring or some family heirloom that she didn't want to lose.

I wish, Hatty thought, grinding her teeth together. As far as she knew, the folder and the USB drive were the only two copies of her investigation into Sergeant Kelly Flowers. She'd made them three weeks ago, right after notifying Griff of her conclusions. At that time, the file had been kept on the hard drive of her laptop but not on the interdepartmental network. Her partner, Sergeant George Mitchell, had felt the investigation might be compromised if the file was available to everyone, and his stance had made sense to Hatty. In fact, she had even agreed with it. If anyone had ever gotten wind of what she and George were doing, they could search her documents and find the drive saved as "KFI," which was short for "Kelly Flowers Investigation." Were they being paranoid? Maybe a little. But when you suspected one of your comrades of being in cahoots with the county's foremost drug dealer, you couldn't take any chances.

Saving the documents on a backup drive was sound police work. What if she lost her computer or someone stole it? With it also being on the USB stick and printed out, the investigation was more secure. But, if she were honest with herself, she knew those solid reasons weren't the impulse that had driven her to make copies of everything.

Had she really thought someone would delete the file from her laptop? I mean, how stupid was that? Any computer guru worth her stuff could go into the metadata of the computer and discover that the file had been destroyed. No one would do that, right?

Wrong. Three days ago, she had discovered the file folder missing on her hard drive. At first, she'd thought it was a glitch. She'd rebooted the laptop twice to make sure that her eyes weren't deceiving her.

They weren't. The file was gone.

The only times she'd ever not had the computer with her were on short lunch breaks or occasionally when she'd walk across to the courthouse to visit with the district attorney. She had always shut the door to her office when she left. Wasn't that reasonable? In a sheriff's department, no less?

Yes. Of course it was. But the fact remained. The folder had been erased. Someone, another officer or employee of the department, must have gone into her private area, booted up her laptop, typed in her personal password, found the drive containing the KFI investigation, and pushed the delete button.

Who could have done that?

Hatty could think of only one realistic possibility, and the very idea made her arms shiver with gooseflesh. How could George Mitchell, her partner for years, do that to her? And why?

What didn't she know?

She sighed and rolled down the window of her silver Honda Accord. She'd kept her civilian vehicle eight years ago when she was finally issued a black unmarked Dodge Charger. She wasn't exactly sure why other than she didn't want to go through the hassle of selling it. The small sedan was so old that the Kelley Blue Book value was next to nothing. So she'd kept the fossil of her former life, and every so often, she'd driven it to the grocery store or to the gym. She probably hadn't put more than a hundred miles on it since she'd been granted the Charger.

She'd driven over two hundred already today.

Hatty squeezed the wheel and again glanced at the manila file folder. She had worked too hard to lose her career. She wouldn't lie to protect a police officer's reputation. She wouldn't withhold evidence to ensure that her boss won reelection in November. She wouldn't compromise her values. She was forty-four years old and had spent half of her life in law enforcement.

But what could she do? Since noticing the file had been deleted, she'd also gotten the sense that she was being followed. She'd noticed the same blue Mustang behind her the last couple of days to and from work. Was she being tailed? And if so, by who? Someone in the sheriff's department? Tyson Cade?

When Hatty had left this morning, she hadn't seen anyone behind her. She'd been watching her rearview mirror like a hawk ever since, and she had seen nothing suspicious. She'd driven south toward Birmingham and made it all the way to Montgomery before she turned around and headed north.

As the sun began to set, Hatty crossed the Tennessee state line. A few minutes later, she clicked her blinker and got off on the familiar exit. Then she turned left onto Highway 31.

She was confused. She was scared. And she was exhausted.

But she knew what she needed.

A safe harbor where she could think through her next move . . .

. . . *and a damn good lawyer.*

Hatty breathed a deep sigh of relief as she passed a sign stating **PULASKI, 20 MILES**, knowing that she was going to the only place that might have both.

"*Home,*" she whispered.

32

Lynn Caldwell Branner had been called "Bull" since he was seven years old. Then, he was five feet, four inches tall and well over a hundred pounds. Huge for a first grader. Over the course of the next fifty years, Bull hadn't grown another inch, but he had packed on another 150 pounds. The man was built more like a barrel than a bull, but the nickname had stuck.

At 6:50 p.m., Bull was shooting an AR15 in one of the twenty stalls at Screaming Eagle Gun Camp, affectionately named after the unit that all three Tonidandel brothers belonged to in the army. The target was a good fifty yards away, and from Jason's standpoint, the compact man was hitting the middle of it pretty much every time.

Jason wore earplugs and goggles and stood next to Satch, who had said that Bull would speak with them after he finished his session. At this time of night, there was no one else at the range, as closing time was in just a few minutes. Jason pulled out his phone, checking the time. He needed to be back in Guntersville by 7:30 p.m. for dinner with Kisha and Teresa. He saw that he had a text from Harry and clicked on it.

Call me.

Classic Harry. As cryptic as ever, but the investigator wouldn't be texting if he didn't have something.

Jason put the phone back in his pocket and continued to watch Bull, who peppered the air with shots. Over the course of the past thirty days, Jason had spent several afternoons at the range with Satch, trying to get comfortable with the Glock handgun he'd bought after his trip to Perdido. He'd never been a gun guy. His dad had enjoyed hunting and shooting skeet, but Jason had never taken to it. Before his first session with Satch two weeks ago, he could count the times he'd shot a firearm on one hand.

Now, though being around a range was still relatively foreign, he'd at least gotten over the flinches. Even with earplugs, the sound of an AR15—or hell, just about any gun—was jolting, and it took a while for Jason not to jump out of his shoes every time he heard one fire. But eventually, the sounds became part of the background and nothing more.

Finally, Bull pushed a button on a screen to the left of him, and the target moved toward him until he ripped the paper off the background. He examined his handiwork and then wadded it up and stuffed it into a carrying case he'd brought with him. He carefully placed his rifle in the case and then approached Satch and Jason.

"Good shooting," Jason said.

Bull took off his goggles. Jason had met him years ago during high school, but he doubted Bull remembered. The man's expression was kind of a perpetual half grin, mouth slightly open and eyes glazed as if he always had a three- or four-beer buzz. He looked down, and for a moment Jason thought he might spit, but instead he peered back up at Jason. "The colonel . . ." Bull nodded at Satch. ". . . says you wanted to speak to me about Kelly Flowers's murder." He stepped forward, and his forehead was about even with Jason's chin. His massive belly protruded to where it almost touched Jason's clothes. He was close enough that Jason could smell a pinch of dip on the man's breath. Sure enough, Bull turned around and walked back to his stall, spitting into a cup he'd placed on the counter. Then he threw the cup away and picked up his carrying case. "Come on. Let's talk out by the truck."

Jason glanced at Satch, who shrugged. Then they followed Bull out of the range, into the lobby, and then outside the building. Once they had closed the door, Jason looked back and saw Chuck Tonidandel turning the **OPEN** sign around so that it now read **CLOSED**.

Bull pulled the tailgate down on his Ford F-150 and slid the case into the back. Then he spat tobacco on the ground and squinted at Jason. "Whatcha want to know?"

"Do you still own the property off Hustleville Road where Kelly Flowers was shot and killed?"

"Shore do," Bull said, spitting again. "And I'll tell you just like I told Detective Daniels. I didn't see nothing. I ain't hear nothing. I got up for work in the morning and saw a body lying on the ground. I walked over to check it out and recognized Kelly Flowers. He had his uniform on, and his chest was a bloody mess. Dead."

"How'd you know it was Kelly?"

"Kelly was from the Sprangs just like Trey." Bull pulled a can of Skoal out of the back pocket of his jeans and took another pinch out. He stuffed it under his bottom lip and squinted at Jason. "Kelly was a pretty good kid growing up. Never got in much trouble. He came to my store at night like the other teens, but never ran afoul of the law that I remember. His mom and dad were quiet folks. Mac Flowers worked at Wayne Farms, and I think Jill was a housekeeper. Both dead now too."

"Any other family?"

"Older sister named Bella. Quite the looker. She lives in Huntsville now." His half grin widened. "Rumor is she dances the pole."

Jason cocked his head.

"She's a stripper," Bull clarified, though Jason had understood his meaning the first time. "Or so I've heard."

"Where does she . . . work?" Jason asked.

"I can't remember. Either Jimmy's or Visions. Both of them are out Highway 72."

Jason pulled out his phone and brought up the notes section. He typed in *Bella Flowers*, *Visions*, and *Jimmy's* with his thumbs. "Anything else you can tell me about the family?"

"Naw," Bull said, spitting a stream of brown snuff onto the grass adjacent to the pavement.

"What about Kelly Flowers before he died?"

"What about him?"

"Did you have any contact with him? What was he like? Did he still live in Alder Springs?"

Bull rubbed his chin. "Yes, to the last one. He lived in his folks' old house, which was about a mile from my land."

"And you still live near the barn?"

"My house is right behind it, but I never go in there. Hell, I hardly use the barn anymore."

"On the night of Kelly's murder, did you—"

"I was out cold, son," Bull interrupted. "I drink a six-pack of Miller Lite every night before bed. You could say it's my version of melatonin."

"What are you doing these days for work?" Jason asked.

"I work on the assembly line at Pilgrim's Pride. Seven a.m. to three p.m. Monday through Friday. Been doing that for near about thirty years."

"Did you hear the gunshots?"

Bull smirked. "I didn't hear shit. I woke up the next morning at seven a.m. for my shift. Was going to work and saw the body. Then I called 911."

"What happened next?"

"The cavalry arrived at my barn, and Detective Daniels started in asking me if I seen anything or heard anything, just like you been doing."

All the mentions of Hatty Daniels reminded Jason that she hadn't been there this morning at the preliminary hearing. Was that strange or was it strategy? Jason snatched his phone, remembering his dinner with Kisha and Teresa. It was now ten after seven.

"What about my client, Trey Cowan? What can you tell me about him, Mr. Branner?"

"Call me Bull." He spat again. "Trey was a good kid. I hardly ever saw him at my barn because he was all about football and getting a scholarship."

"What about after the injury?"

Bull stared down at the pavement. "I've heard a few rumors."

"Like what?"

"Like him maybe getting mixed up with Tyson Cade. Needing money and such."

"What about Kelly Flowers? Any rumors about him?"

Bull blinked and again spat on the ground. "I heard he was investigating Cade for the sheriff's office."

Jason felt his pulse quicken. "Anything specific?"

"No," Bull said, but Jason felt the answer was a bit quick. Almost rehearsed.

"No?" Jason pressed.

"No," Bull repeated. "Listen, boys . . ." He glanced at Satch and then back at Jason. "I wish I could help you. I wished I coulda helped Detective Daniels. But I don't know nothing. I'm sorry." He opened the door to his truck and climbed in. When he cranked up the ignition, Jason knocked on the window. Bull rolled it down and stared at Jason.

"Let me know if you remember anything else."

"You think Trey's been set up?" Bull asked.

"Yes," Jason said, not entirely sure he believed it but wanting to give Bull a reason to come clean if he hadn't told them everything.

Bull took a cup from the center console and spat into it. Jason wondered how many spit cups the man had lying around his house and automobile. "Well . . . that's some tough shit," he finally said. Then the pickup eased forward. Seconds later, it was turning right onto Highway 431.

"I think he's hiding something," Jason said, watching the truck disappear into the distance.

"Maybe," Satch said. "But if he is, we're not ever going to find it." Satch paused. "And you know damn well why."

Jason sighed. "Cade."

33

Bull Branner bought a case of Miller Lite on the way home. He was going to need a bit more than his customary sixer tonight. He drank three cans on the way home and cracked open a fourth as he hopped out of his truck. He enjoyed shooting guns, but he might have to find a new range. The Tonidandel brothers had always been good to him, but no amount of friendship and loyalty was enough to even chance getting on the wrong side of Tyson Cade.

Bull drank his fourth beer in two swallows by the truck and then hauled the rest of the case the two hundred yards from his three-bedroom shack to the barn he and his family had operated for three decades as "Branner's Place." He unlatched the gate and stepped inside, breathing in the smell of hay. Nowadays, he leased the barn to local farmers to store hay and soybeans. It had been eight years since the store was open, but there were still a few remnants, including the long bar in the loft upstairs. Back then, you could get a drink either upstairs or down, and there was also a package store where you could take your booze home or, in the case of the local teens, just outside to their vehicles, which were always strewed across the grass in every direction. He'd gotten busted a few times for bootlegging, but not enough for the risks to outweigh the profits. And once he got on the good side of the local meth trade, the cops left him alone for good. Eventually, though, the locals got tired of the youngsters and their teenage antics and found other places to catch a buzz. Every watering hole had its expiration date, and Branner's Place got to where it was costing too much to keep open.

Though Bull didn't miss the stress of trying to make ends meet, he did sometimes pine for the excitement of those days. As the owner and sometimes bouncer, he'd mill about, occasionally having a one-night stand with a recent divorcée or getting his own private peep show from some drunk college girls. They were mostly good times, he thought, as he passed through the back of the barn to the other side.

From here, he could see Hustleville Road and, in the distance, the lights flickering from the Alder Springs Grocery. Thirty yards to his right, there was still yellow crime scene tape covering a span of about ten feet where Sergeant Kelly Flowers had been shot and killed a month earlier.

Bull grabbed a lawn chair from inside the barn and brought it to within a few steps of the yellow tape. He set the case of beer on the grass and plopped down in the seat. He let out a loud belch and snatched another can of Miller Lite. He popped the top and took a long swig as a car buzzed by on Hustleville Road.

Since Branner's Place had closed its doors, the barn and the space outside had served two additional purposes outside of storing hay and other crops. Of course, both of those uses had been suspended since Kelly Flowers's death.

Bull crushed his can after finishing the beer and flung it on the ground. He cracked open another and stared over his shoulder at the barn. The facility had made an excellent place for storing methamphetamine and any other drugs that Tyson Cade was distributing. Bull took a long sip of beer, thinking about how easy it had been to lie to the lawyer. When your life depended on discretion, it was easy to stay quiet.

But Bull knew that storing drugs wasn't the use that Tyson coveted most with his barn. He pressed against the chair, and its wobbly frame gave as he rose to his feet. He gazed up at the quarter moon and belched again. Then he stared at the yellow tape and drank down the rest of his beer.

His family's legacy had become a place where drugs were sold. A meetup spot off the beaten path where a dealer could deliver his product and get paid. And where disagreements could be discussed and worked out . . .

. . . *or not.*

Bull sighed. Did he know why Kelly Flowers was here the night he was killed?

Hell yes, he did. But would he ever tell a living soul?

Bull grunted. *Hell, no, I won't.*

34

Jason called Harry on his way back into town.

"I've got good news and bad news, J. R."

"Let's hear the good first," Jason said, stepping on the accelerator as he ascended the Veterans Memorial Bridge.

"I have a pretty good read on Kevin Martin. K-Mart, as the kids at Guntersville High call him, lives in a mansion out on Buck Island. His family moved here two years ago, and he became very popular very fast. He's a linebacker on the football team, has a four point oh grade average, and drives a black fully loaded Range Rover." Harry paused. "But that's not why he's so popular."

"Drugs?"

"Yep. The family moved in from Rochester, New York, after K-Mart was charged with a DUI and possession of marijuana. He ended up getting youthful offender status, so not on his public record."

Jason didn't even ask how Harry had discovered this information. If a kid was granted YO, then his record should've been sealed and confidential. But Harry Davenport was as resourceful as he was street smart. He was also persistent. These traits made him an outstanding investigator and a hell of a good friend. "So K-Mart moves into town; charms his classmates with his looks, smarts, and athletic ability; and then plugs into the local drug trade and becomes everyone's source for their preferred vice."

"That's pretty much it."

"Have you been able to establish a clear link with Cade?"

"No, and I don't think I will. Cade is too slippery. I can connect K-Mart with a man named Matthew Dean. Dean owns a used-auto dealership in Boaz, and K-Mart has a quote unquote 'job' there. The thing is I've never seen him stay at the place longer than an hour."

"So Dean is the link with Cade?"

"Possibly, but he'd probably cut off all his fingers and toes before he'd tell us."

"Follow him, Harry. We need to track the chain all the way to Cade."

"What's the goal here, J. R.?"

"To have something . . . anything . . . on Cade that we can use for leverage. He's blackmailing me with Chase and Nola's drug use, and I'm tired of playing defense."

"What you are playing is a dangerous game with a professional. We investigate lawsuits and criminal cases, Jason. Not drug dealers in the hopes of blackmailing them. We need to stay in our lane, or we are going to end up being run off the road. Do you feel me?"

Jason punched the steering wheel with his fist, thinking back to the meeting with Bull Branner. The barrel of a man was hiding something, and it was likely because Cade had something on him too. "Yes, Harry. I feel you. But I have to do something."

"You are doing something. You're representing Trey Cowan. You're practicing law, which you are damn good at doing. But you're not a cowboy, and no amount of shooting lessons with crazy-ass Satch Tonidandel is going to make you Wyatt Earp."

Jason sucked in a deep breath and exhaled. It was no use arguing. Besides, as usual, Harry was right. "You said you had bad news."

There was a pause, and for a moment, Jason thought he'd lost service.

"Harry?" Jason asked, looking out over Lake Guntersville as the sun made its final descent under the clouds. "Harry?"

"Still here," he finally said.

"What's the bad news?"

"I'm sorry, Jason."

"Just spit it out."

"Nola's still using," he said. "I saw her buy drugs off of K-Mart."

"Good grief," Jason said, gritting his teeth.

"It gets worse."

"How is that possible?"

Another pause. "Harry?"

"I can't be a hundred percent but . . ."

"Harry?"

". . . I think she's dating the bastard."

35

Jason was seething as he entered the Old Town Stock House. Nola had lied to him. In Perdido and every day since. She had said she was done with K-Mart. With meth. But it had all been an act. Seeing Chase's predicament had done nothing to sway her from using.

Jason saw Kisha, who waved him over to her table, which was located behind the bar in the back. As he moved through the restaurant, he glanced at the columns of liquor bottles and the draft beer taps and, not for the first time in the last thirty days, felt a craving himself. He knew he shouldn't be upset with Nola. If his niece was an addict, and it sounded like she was, then she had lost control of her ability to stop. *Just like I had,* Jason knew.

And the struggle never ended.

Jason forced a smile and tried to clear his thoughts as he sat down across from the couple. "Well . . . what are we celebrating?"

"A free dinner," Kisha said, giggling and flashing her teeth. Both women had glasses of wine in front of them, and based on their eyes and demeanor, it appeared that they might be on their second round.

Teresa opened her mouth in mock anger and lightly flicked Kisha on her shoulder. "Our anniversary," she said. "It was actually last week, but we're late celebrating."

"Congratulations," Jason said, holding out his fist, which each woman nudged with her own. "I hate to be crashing your party."

"It's . . . OK," Teresa said, shooting Kisha a glance that told Jason that it probably wasn't.

"I've been trying to set up a meeting," Jason said, holding out his palms to Teresa as a waitress came over and asked him what he wanted to drink.

"Diet Coke," he said. Then, turning back to Teresa: "This won't take a minute, I promise, and I will pay for your dinner."

"I was kidding about you buying, Jason," Kisha said.

"You didn't sound like you were joking," Jason teased, looking from his old friend to Teresa. "Just a few questions."

"Shoot," Teresa said.

"When we spoke on my sister Jana's case, you said that Trey was a regular at the Brick. I'm assuming that hadn't changed leading up to the murder."

"You assume right. If anything, Trey was coming more often and staying later." She frowned at him. "And drinking more. Much more."

"Was something bothering him?"

Teresa rolled her eyes. "Isn't this something you should be asking him?"

"He said he failed a baseball tryout with the Barons."

"I didn't know about that. All he told me about was his breakup with Colleen."

"Colleen Maples," Jason said, nodding. She had been a pivotal witness in his sister's trial. She hadn't cooperated with Jason then, and she wasn't being agreeable now. Izzy had not had any luck arranging a meeting or even a phone call with the nurse anesthetist.

"Why did they break up?"

"Trey never said much. Just that they never made sense to begin with." She shrugged. "Can't say he was wrong there."

"Does Colleen ever come into the Brick?"

"A couple of times with Trey," Teresa said. "None since the breakup."

"What about Kelly Flowers? Did he come in much?"

"Usually only when Trey was there. A few times, when Trey wasn't there, he'd ask me if I'd seen him."

Jason felt a tickle of interest. "Why would he do that?"

"I don't know. Trey and Kelly went to high school together and were teammates on the football team. I assumed they were friends."

"Had you ever seen them get into an argument before April 8?"

"Not really. A few times, I saw Kelly talking to Trey and Trey not saying a whole lot." She took a sip of wine. "But I didn't think much of that, because Trey wasn't a big talker."

Jason took out his phone and thumbed a few notes of what she had said.

"I saw Kelly only one time with someone other than Trey. It was about two weeks before he died."

"Who?"

"A woman. She looked kind of familiar, but I didn't recognize her. I'd never seen her inside the restaurant before."

"Describe her," Jason asked.

"Dirty-blonde hair. Short hair. She'd come in for a couple of beers just before closing time, and Kelly had sat down next to her."

Jason felt a rush of heat run through his body. He sucked in a quick breath and wiped his forehead.

"You OK?" Teresa asked.

"But you didn't recognize her?" Jason asked, thinking as fast as he could. Had he ever taken Chase to the Brick? Had he ever been around Kisha or Teresa with Chase? Since Jana's death, he had laid pretty low. He and Chase had normally eaten at one of their houses, or occasionally, they took the Sea-Doo to the Docks in Scottsboro. Chase was a homebody who didn't like to go out. *No,* Jason thought, answering his own question. He probably had told Kisha, his longtime friend, about Chase, but she had never met her. And he was quite certain that he'd never been around Teresa with Chase.

But the woman she just described . . . Maybe he was being silly. Short dirty-blonde hair wasn't much to go on.

"Can you tell me anything else about her?"

Teresa took another sip of wine and pressed a thumb to her chin. "Well, there's one other thing, and I'm not sure why I remember it."

"What's that?"

"I'm pretty sure her name was Savannah," Teresa said. "Like the city. I thought that was interesting."

Jason had stopped breathing. "Her first name?"

"Yeah," Teresa said. "I can't remember her last."

Jason finally exhaled. *Savannah Chase Wittschen . . .* He had always teased Chase with her first name because he knew she hated it.

"Did you tell the police about the woman with Kelly Flowers? This . . . Savannah?"

Teresa squinted. "I'm pretty sure I told Detective Daniels."

Jason looked down at the table as the waiter set a Diet Coke on a coaster next to him. He grabbed the glass and drank half of it down, grimacing to keep from burping. He'd gone through Hatty Daniels's investigative report and all of the witness interviews, including the one with Teresa, at least a dozen times, and there was no mention of a woman that Kelly Flowers had left the bar with two weeks prior to his death.

An oversight? Jason wondered. *Or maybe Daniels didn't think it was important.*

Jason took a smaller sip of his drink as Kisha and Teresa ordered their food. Old Town Stock House had the best steaks around, and both of them ordered the fillet.

"Nothing for me," Jason said to the waiter. He looked at Teresa and then Kisha. "I've already taken up too much of your time." Jason's heart was pounding. Unless Chase Wittschen had a look-alike with the same first name or Teresa was lying, neither of which seemed plausible, Chase was having drinks with Sergeant Flowers and leaving the bar with him two weeks before he was killed.

Jason felt an odd mixture of anger, jealousy, and fear coupling with shock. He needed to get out of there, but he had one more question.

"Kisha, I asked you about Sergeant Daniels not being at the prelim, and you hesitated and said you'd talk to me tonight. Do you know why she wasn't there or anything else about her?"

Kisha glanced at Teresa, who shook her head.

"What I know isn't relevant to the case."

"Kisha, no," Teresa said.

"Can you please let me decide what's relevant?" Jason asked.

Kisha looked at Teresa, and finally the bartender looked away. "Whatever," Teresa said.

"Every once in a while, T and I will go into Huntsville. We like to shop at Bridge Street and have dinner and a movie. There's a bar over there that we like to go to called Envy. Nice place." She paused. "It's not a gay bar, but it is LGBTQ+ friendly. We like the vibe. The live music is cool, and we can dance and let loose."

"That's great," Jason said. "But what does that have—"

"We've seen Sergeant Daniels there a couple times," Teresa snapped. "Once alone and once with another woman."

"Did you say hello?"

"Yes," Kisha said. "She was pretty freaked out when she saw us. She asked that we not say anything about seeing her."

"And we just broke our promise," Teresa said.

Jason leaned back in his chair. "So you saw her? So what? Haven't we moved far enough into the twenty-first century where Sergeant Daniels's sexual orientation, whatever it may be, shouldn't be relevant?"

Kisha looked at him like he might be a first grader. "Jason, this is Marshall County. It's one of the most conservative places in America. Our relationship flies under the radar. I report the news for the *Gleam*, and Teresa is a bartender. Our jobs are anything but high profile."

"But Sergeant Daniels is in the news all the time," Teresa said. "She's a public figure, and she's told us that she would love to be sheriff one day."

"I see," Jason said, feeling dumb. "So why are you telling me this?"

"Because I do think it's weird that Hatty wasn't at the hearing today," Kisha said, and she sounded genuinely concerned. "This is her case. I can't think of a reason she would leave, so . . ."

"You think she's come out to her colleagues?"

"Maybe," Teresa said, but Kisha was shaking her head.

"What do you think?" Jason asked his old friend.

Kisha leaned forward. "I think someone in the department may have seen her like we did. Except maybe in a more compromised position. Maybe they've threatened to reveal her secret? Or perhaps Hatty is scared about it and needs some time."

"It sounds like you know her pretty well," Jason said.

"I admire her a lot," Kisha said. "A smart, kick-ass Black woman in a field dominated by good ole boys. When I first joined the *Gleam*, she was always cooperative with interviews and seemed to enjoy the fact that I was so openly gay."

"Jealous, more like it," Teresa said.

"Maybe that too," Kisha admitted.

Jason rubbed his neck. His brain was scrambled. Part of him was still thinking about Chase meeting Kelly Flowers. The other part was trying to glean whether any of this information about Sergeant Hatty Daniels, however interesting it might be, was helpful. He stood from the table. "Ladies, it's been a pleasure."

Kisha stood with him. "Jason, please be discreet with what we've told you."

"I will," he said. "I promise."

He kissed Kisha's cheek and gave Teresa a wave. "Now . . . I want you to enjoy your anniversary dinner."

———

Before leaving the restaurant, Jason caught up to Kisha and Teresa's waiter and had her run his card for their meal. "Make sure they order dessert and give yourself twenty-five percent," he said.

Then he left the restaurant, walking in a daze toward his Porsche. He hopped in and fired up the sports car. After letting the engine rev for a full minute, Jason finally couldn't handle the emotions swirling inside of him.

"Fuck!" he screamed, squeezing the wheel until his wrists hurt. He had thought things couldn't get much worse after Jana's death, but they had. He was a failure. As a guardian to Nola. As a friend to Chase. About all that had gone well was his law practice, but that was mostly due to Izzy's legwork and the verdict he'd obtained for Jana. *A miracle,* Jason thought, putting the car in gear. As he turned onto Gunter Avenue, he felt frustration and hate building within him.

I'm a joke . . .

On the surface, he was a multimillionaire lawyer. But underneath, he was losing everything he still cared about in this godforsaken world. Nola and Niecy were his last connections to his family, and Niecy was in college and moving on with her life. *At least I haven't screwed her up,* Jason thought. But Nola was his responsibility, and he'd failed.

"Fuck!"

Jason pressed the accelerator down as he passed over the Paul Stockton Causeway. He wanted a drink. He wanted to get drunk and howl at the moon. He undid his tie and rolled down the windows. It was a bit cool outside for the top to be down, but he lowered it as well. Feeling the cold air whipping through his hair, Jason took in a deep breath.

"Chase," he whispered. In the wind-soaked interior of the Porsche, he couldn't hear his voice. *"What were you doing?"*

Up ahead, Jason saw the neon lights of a liquor store and pulled into the parking lot. He turned off the car and gazed at the different advertisements. Miller Lite. Jack Daniel's. Smirnoff. Bombay.

Jason leaned his head against the steering wheel. When was the last time he'd had a drink? Last August, right after his public reprimand by the Alabama State Bar. Tyson Cade had accosted him in Montgomery. Threatened his family. And he'd finally reached the end of his rope. He'd made it almost nine months.

Jason lifted his head and clicked the door handle. "Chase . . ." he whispered, stepping out of the Porsche and into the cool of the night.

. . . what were you doing?

36

"Ms. Wittschen, how can I help you if you won't talk to me?"

They sat in a tiny office with a window that overlooked the Gulf of Mexico. Chase stared past her counselor, whose name she either hadn't heard or forgotten, out to the emerald-green waters. What she really wanted right now was to walk out of this room straight into the waters. She wanted the waves to consume her and her throat to fill with salt water. She wanted to choke on the water and have the breath pulled out of her.

She wanted to die in a sandy heap at the bottom of the ocean. Where no one would ever find her. Where Jason . . .

Chase's lip began to tremble.

"Ms. Wittschen, it is obvious you are very upset. Why won't you talk about it? Let me in. Let me . . . or someone here . . . help you. Tell us what happened."

Chase wiped her eyes and continued to gaze out the window.

"I'm sorry," she said, seeing Jason in her mind and then the crooked grin of Kelly Flowers the last time she'd seen him.

"I just . . . can't."

37

Tyson Cade sat on the rocks below the Mill Creek overpass. He wore a cap, T-shirt, and jeans and cast his rod out into the water. This area was known for crappie, catfish, and bass, but Tyson didn't even have bait on his line. He gazed across the water at Jason Rich's home.

"Do you believe the kid?" Tyson asked, not looking at the man seated next to him on the rocks. His companion also held a rod and reel. It was common for folks to fish on the rocks at night, and there was another fisherman about a hundred feet away from them.

For several seconds, there was no answer. Tyson gritted his teeth. "Matty, I asked you a question."

Matthew Dean had a thick head of gray hair and a beard to match. Since he spent much of his time on the water, he had a permanently sunburned face and leathery skin. At sixty years of age, Matty had been in the meth trade his whole life, first working for Richard "Sally" Salisbury and later for Johnny "King" Hanson. Now, he worked for Tyson, and truth be known it was Matty's belief in and support of Tyson after King got busted that led to Tyson taking over.

Tyson trusted no one, but he didn't think that Matty would bullshit him.

The older man cast his line and grunted. When he spoke, his voice sounded like tires treading through deep gravel. "K-Mart is probably the savviest dealer we've ever had at the school. Calm, cool, calculated. He would be popular without his connection to us."

"You still haven't answered me. Do you believe him or not?"

A long pause. One of the reasons that Tyson liked Matty was the other man's deliberate nature. He wasn't always right, but he rarely made knee-jerk decisions. "I do," he said.

"OK, what does K-Mart say his follower looks like?"

"He hasn't seen the driver, only the vehicle. He said it's a maroon SUV."

"That's not much to go on. We at least need a picture or license plate. Preferably both."

"I told him that."

Tyson continued to gaze at the Rich home. The lights were off and had been since he got to the overpass an hour ago. The attorney was working late, and his niece did not appear to be home either. "Let's say the kid is right. It may be that Rich is having Nola followed and K-Mart is caught in the cross fire. Because he's smart and observant, he's noticed the vehicle."

"That would make sense. Especially if Rich wanted to keep tabs on his niece. But she already has a security guard watching her. Why would Rich need someone else?"

Tyson cast his line again and slowly began to reel it in. That was a good point. "Remind me the security situation again."

"One of the Tonidandel brothers watches the home each night. They split it up."

"Just one?"

"Yeah, but those guys are good. All ex-military. Whoever's on duty keeps a constant vigil on the water and the road and is packing an AR and a couple handguns. If we ever made a move, we'd be dealing with John Rambo."

Tyson bit his lip. He had grown weary of Colonel Satch Tonidandel and his two crazy brothers. They weren't afraid of him, and that bothered Tyson.

"What about the college girl?"

"Still at Birmingham-Southern. She has a guard with her at all times. To and from class and someone who watches her apartment at night."

"And Nola?"

"Like I said, a security officer follows her to and from school and pretty much wherever she goes at night."

"Pretty much?"

"She's been able to lose the officer a couple times. When she goes to K-Mart's house, he takes her out on the lake in a Jet Ski or boat, and that's when she normally buys her meth."

"Same security detail as last year?"

"No. Different. Locals."

Tyson spit into the water and cast his rod again. "What about the lawyer?"

"On his own for now . . . but he's packing a pistol."

Tyson chuckled, wondering if Jason Rich was really stupid enough to go to war with him. He reeled in his line and stood from the rocks.

"Keep me posted on K-Mart, Matty. If someone is following him and that someone is working for Jason Rich . . ." He glared one last time at the lawyer's home. ". . . they'll have to be dealt with."

"Yes, sir."

38

At 8:30 a.m. the following day, Jason stared into a steaming cup of coffee. He still wore the same gray suit he'd been wearing the day before, but he had discarded the tie. He rubbed his stubble and gazed at the steam coming off the mug. Then he grabbed the handle and took a sip, wincing as the hot liquid scalded his throat going down.

"Good?"

Jason nodded, not making eye contact with the woman sitting across from him.

"So you took me right up to the point where you walked in the liquor store last night." She paused. "What happened next, Jason? Did you buy any alcohol?" Another hesitation. "Did you drink anything?"

"No," he said, taking another sip of coffee. He reached into his pocket and dropped a pack of gum on the counter. "I used the bathroom . . . I bought this." He exhaled a deep breath. "Then I left." Jason finally looked at the woman across from him.

Ashley Sullivan had red hair with a smattering of freckles on her face. She was an attorney in Cullman, Alabama, and she was also the president of the Alabama Lawyer Assistance Program. She had become Jason's mentor last year after his stint in rehab, and he met with her once a month. Usually, these meetings were scheduled, but this morning's conference was impromptu. Jason had left the liquor store in a cold sweat and had driven straight to Cullman. He'd parked in the Cracker Barrel parking lot, checked in with Satch Tonidandel to make sure Nola was home and safe, and then stayed in his car until the sun began to rise. He'd texted Ashley at 7:00 a.m., told her it was an emergency, and now here they were.

"What kept you from falling?" Ashley asked, covering his hand with her own and giving it a gentle squeeze.

"I don't know. Nola, I guess. Chase. My career. I mean, it hasn't even been a month since I hit the twenty-five-million-dollar verdict in Florence."

She winked at him. "Heard about that one. Nice."

"Not drinking has literally been my superpower. That's what I call it, because I feel I'm so much better." He flung up his hands. "But, last night, I wanted a drink. I *still* want a drink. I want to get drunk. I want to drink a fifth of whiskey. I want to go to a bar, drink a six-pack, and then . . ."

"Then what?"

"Nothing."

"Jason, you really need to talk with your therapist. Celia is trained to ask you the right questions. I'm glad you reached out to me, and I'm here to listen. But, as your mentor, I really think professional help would serve you best right now."

"I prefer you," he said. "You're an addict. You've been through it. You know what wanting a drink feels like. I am more comfortable with you."

"I'm glad," she said. "But I can't fix it. Only you can do that."

"How?"

"I'm not a therapist, Jason, but I can tell you from experience that recovery isn't easy. You've been out for just over a year. You've had one relapse, right?"

"Yes. After my public reprimand last August."

"So that was about nine months ago. Think about all that has happened since then. The emotions of your sister's trial and then her death. Becoming Nola's guardian. Moving into your childhood home. The breakup with Chase. That's a lot. Now, you've taken on this Trey Cowan case. Isn't that a bit much? I mean, I know you won your sister's trial, but criminal law isn't your thing. Why get involved?"

"It's complicated."

"Try me."

"Cowan was a key witness for me in Jana's trial." Jason's mouth formed the words, but there was no feeling behind them.

"Oh, come on. There's got to be more to it than that."

"Like I said . . . it's complicated. I am being . . ." He looked at her and decided he couldn't burden her with this information. Perhaps he should talk with Celia Little, his psychologist. At least those conversations would be privileged. He didn't think Ashley would ever betray him, but he wasn't big on trusting other lawyers. Besides, he liked her and didn't want to tell her anything that might put her in harm's way. Perhaps he was paranoid, but such was the power of Cade.

"Being what?"

"Foolish I guess," Jason said, looking down at the table. "I want to get back in the courtroom. When I'm in the middle of a trial, it's a thrill, you know." All of what Jason said was true. He did love the action of trial work. But it was also complete bullshit. As he raised his eyes to meet Ashley's, her smirk told him how much of what he'd just said she believed.

"Really? You're a bad liar, Jason."

He chose silence this time, gazing back down at his mug.

"OK, so you won't tell me why you took the case. Can you at least talk to me about what triggered you last night? You almost fell off the wagon? Why?"

Again, Jason had to choose his words carefully. "Chase had a bad relapse." He grabbed his cup with both hands and continued to gaze at the brown liquid.

"I know. You told me on the phone, remember?"

Jason did. He had called Ashley after getting back from Perdido. He nodded.

"You were worried about Nola then too. Has anything happened?"

"Chase is still in rehab."

"That's a good thing, right?"

"Her counselor says she's not participating in any of the sessions. She went through detox and seems to physically be doing well. But she's barely said a word since she's been there."

"It takes time, Jason. You know that. There's a lot of shame involved in relapsing. Remember how you felt?"

Jason blinked, seeing an image of Chase with Sergeant Kelly Flowers in his mind. Talking at the Brick. Leaving the restaurant together. How could Teresa be right about that?

"Jason?"

"I remember," he finally said. Then, leaning back in his chair, he exhaled. "Nola is still using. Even after our visit to Perdido, she's still buying drugs and using them."

Ashley grimaced. "I'm sorry."

"I'm failing," Jason said. "As a guardian, I was probably away too much after Jana's death, and Nola spiraled out of control. As a boyfriend, same thing. I was away a lot, and when I was home, I came on too strong. Too aggressive. Pushing Chase into things she wasn't ready for. Parties. Forced social events. A marriage proposal. I guess she couldn't handle it anymore. She left me. She abandoned her home. And, at some point, she must have fallen off the wagon." He paused. "Hard."

"Why couldn't she handle it?"

Jason glanced at Ashley and then back at the coffee cup. "I'm no shrink."

"Why do you think? You said that she told you last year that you were a trigger for her. Why?"

He shrugged. "Because I'm an asshole."

"Come on. Don't blow this off. And that's not true anyway. I don't think you're an asshole."

"Thanks." He took a sip of coffee. "What I'm about to say will probably make you change your mind."

"Try me."

"OK then. I guess . . . maybe . . . my relationship with Chase has always been limited to Mill Creek, and I have a big life outside of it. I did in high school, and I do now. I think that maybe she's insecure and doesn't think she's good enough for me, which is completely not true. If anything, I'm not good enough for her."

"Have you ever tried to tell her that?"

He shook his head. "No."

"Maybe you should."

He gave his head a jerk. "Too late now."

For a long moment, there was silence. Then, Ashley touched Jason's hand. "You can't control other people. Free will is a bitch, right?" She smiled, and her eyes were warm. "I'm sorry about Chase. And Nola. But you can't help either one of them if you're teetering on the edge of a relapse. When the flight attendants are giving their preflight instructions, what do they always say about the oxygen mask?"

Jason wrinkled his face.

"Put your own mask on first. Before you try to help someone else, even your own child." She paused. "You have to be able to breathe first, Jason. Do you understand?"

"Isn't that selfish?"

"It's survival. You can't help anyone else if you are using. It's as simple as that. You have to take care of yourself first."

"How do I do that?" Jason asked, feeling the helplessness in his voice.

"By not quitting, first. You didn't have a drink last night. You drove here. You are talking to me. It's obvious that you don't want to quit."

"I'm close to the breaking point."

She slammed her hands on the table. "Why? Because your ex-girlfriend has relapsed? Or is it because she didn't accept your marriage proposal and may have hooked up with another man? Perhaps you don't know Chase as well as you think, huh?" She cocked her head, and Jason felt his face begin to warm. He again saw Kelly Flowers and Chase together in his mind.

"Jason, triggers are only successful because they make you think negative and harmful thoughts. Failure is a trigger for you, like it is with many addicts. You think you are failing, and so you escape with alcohol. But remember what I've always told you."

"Alcohol can never be a solution."

She slammed her hand on the table again. "Correct."

Jason looked at her. Ashley's eyes had a fiery intensity to them that blended well with her red hair. He was beginning to feel a tad bit better. "Thank you."

"You're welcome." Then she leaned forward and put her elbows on the table. "Jason, based on what you've told me, you've struggled with low self-esteem ever since you were a boy, right?"

"My father . . ."

"You couldn't please him."

"I never measured up. As a student. As an athlete." He chuckled. "And especially as a lawyer."

"You've worked through those feelings since going to rehab, but . . . these recent struggles have brought a lot of those feelings back." She hesitated. "Am I close?"

"Maybe." He thought about those bittersweet moments after his victory in Florence. Standing in the empty courtroom. *Why couldn't he just be proud of me?* "I . . . don't know."

"Jason, you can't always avoid your triggers. Especially the internal ones. Believe me, I know. That's why you need what I call 'defusers.' People and activities that make you feel good. That flip the script and get you to thinking positive thoughts. Lean on those people and things now." She stood and walked around the table. "I have to go. I have a meeting this morning."

"Thank you for listening."

She squeezed his shoulder. "You can do this."

39

You can do this.

Jason's thoughts were an echo of Ashley Sullivan's last comforting words as he drove straight to the Marshall County Jail. He felt better. The urge to drink had finally passed, and as he hurtled down Highway 69 in his Porsche, he realized that his mentor from Cullman was one of his best defusers.

He checked in and was escorted to the attorney consultation room. Ten minutes later, Trey was sitting across from him. He wore an orange jumpsuit, his feet and hands shackled.

"You look like hell," Trey said.

"And you look like you're trying out for a reboot of *The Longest Yard*."

Trey wrinkled his eyebrows.

"Never mind," Jason said, hearing the exasperation in his tone. "I need more from you, Trey."

"What do you mean?"

"What I mean . . ." Jason leaned his elbows onto the table. He was close enough to smell Trey's stale scent. ". . . is that we are going to lose, and you are going to be lethally injected if you don't give me something . . . *anything* . . . else."

"I can't give you what I don't have."

"So can you sit there and honestly say that you've told me everything that happened the night of Kelly Flowers's murder?"

Trey looked down at the table. "Yes."

"You're lying, Trey. I know you are lying, and I'll be damned if I understand why. This is only your life we're talking about."

Trey said nothing and continued to stare a hole into the table.

"Then let's talk about Flowers. He was your buddy, right?"

"He *was*."

"You knew him well then."

Trey shrugged.

"Was he dating anyone?" Jason asked, his teeth clenched as he thought of Chase.

"I don't know. Like I said, we were close but not so much recently."

"Did he know you were working for Tyson Cade?"

Trey didn't answer.

"Did he? You said you had made a few deliveries for Cade. Did Kelly know that? Was he holding that over your head in exchange for something else? Had he threatened to arrest you? Was he pressuring you for information about Cade?" Jason banged his fist on the table. "Is that why you killed him?"

Trey stood. "This meeting's over."

"No, sir," Jason said. "This meeting is only beginning. You've put my family, what little I have left, in peril. Your situation has resulted in me being blackmailed by the county's most dangerous person, and I'm sick and tired of it. I'm representing you for free, Trey. I'm the only friend you've got in the world. You owe me. Now I need you to tell me the whole story."

"Mr. Rich, I'm sorry. I really am. But I can't do that. If you want the whole story . . . you'll have to get it from Tyson."

Jason stood and put his hands on his hips. "Are you kidding me?"

"I wish I was joking, but I'm not. Tyson Cade owns me. I can't tell you what I know, or everyone I care about will be put at risk. I can't do that."

Jason hung his head. Anger was boiling inside him. Fueling him. He hadn't slept in over twenty-four hours. He'd left Cullman and only gotten madder by the second. "Trey, by not talking to me, you are putting everyone I care about at risk. I'm not sure why Tyson demanded that I represent you, but I know what he expects." Jason licked his lips. "Victory," Jason said. "He expects me to win, and I can't win if you don't talk to me."

Trey shuffled toward the exit. He knocked three times on the door with his shackled hands. Then he looked at Jason. "I didn't kill Kelly Flowers," he said.

Jason sighed. "Then help me defend you. Give me something. *Anything.*"

Trey leaned his head against the door. "OK." His voice was hoarse. Weak. "I can't shoot a gun for shit."

Jason wrinkled up his face. "What?"

"I can't shoot. I can't hit a bull in the ass from five yards. Dad took me dove hunting a couple times when I was little, and all I came home with was a bruised shoulder. No birds. Not even a feather." He chuckled bitterly. "Wasn't my thing."

"Then why did you bring the shotgun to your mom's house? What possible purpose could you have had for taking it?"

Trey closed his eyes. "I was drunk, Mr. Rich. And . . ." He sighed. "Depressed."

"That's not an answer to my question. Why did you—?"

"I wanted to kill myself," Trey said, lifting his head back and butting the door with it. "At least I thought I did." He opened his eyes and stared at Jason with a vacant gaze.

Jason wasn't sure what to say. This information was helpful. Combined with his drunkenness, the fact that Trey wasn't a good shot was a nice nugget for the defense. One that would have to be supported with another witness, but still. He'd asked for something, and Trey had given him a small glimmer of hope.

But it wasn't near enough. "Trey, I appreciate you telling me this. I really do. I know that was hard to admit, and it provides a plausible explanation for why you brought the gun and why you might not have been able to kill Flowers, but . . . I'm begging you. There has to be some connection between you, Flowers, and Cade. Branner's Place was used for drug deals. You heard Detective Mitchell on the stand yesterday. That's the reason they're giving for Flowers being out there. What's the link?"

Trey sighed and shook his head. As the guard opened the door, he spoke in a flat voice. "If you want to know everything . . . I told you what you have to do."

40

Jason called Satch the second he was in his car and moving forward.

"I need a meeting with Cade."

"Sure that's a good idea?"

"I don't have a choice. I can't win this case if I don't have more information, and I'm getting nowhere with my client. Trey says if I want the whole story, I have to get it from Cade." Jason gritted his teeth as his Porsche ascended the Veterans Memorial Bridge.

"All right then," Satch said. "Where do you want this meetup to take place?"

"On our turf," Jason said. "A place you and your brothers feel completely comfortable. I want all three of you there. Cade has to come alone."

"Jason, we don't give ultimatums to a man like Tyson Cade."

"Who says?" Jason asked. And then he ended the call.

41

At 4:55 p.m., Sheriff Richard Griffith knocked twice on the district attorney's door.

"Yeah."

He opened the door and stared at Shay with a grim look on his face.

"Still no word from Hatty?"

Griff shook his head. "She's ghosted me."

"Me too," Shay said. "It's so weird. Hatty's such a professional. I've always respected her."

"She's the best detective in my department."

"Can you think of any reason for her to disappear like this?"

"No."

"Come on, Griff. There's got to be something. Does it involve the Cowan case?" She lowered her voice. "Anything in her personal life?"

"I don't know, Shay," the sheriff said, collapsing into a burgundy chair in front of Shay's desk. "It boggles my mind. She's the lead investigator for every big case in our department . . . and she's disappeared."

Shay began to pace her office. "Any thoughts on where she might have gone?"

"Not really. She grew up in Pulaski, but I'm not aware of her having any family left there. I'll send out some feelers."

"Do that for sure." She scratched her chin. "Who were her closest friends? In or out of work?"

Sheriff Griffith ran his hands through his hair. "That's just it. Hatty was a bit of a loner. Forty-four. Not married. No family to speak of. No social life." He paused. "The job was her life."

"Sounds familiar," Shay said. "Except I'm thirty-two."

For a moment, there was an awkward pause. The sheriff stared at the ground. Finally, he looked up at the district attorney. "I'm sure you've . . . probably heard the rumors about Hatty."

"What? That she's a lesbian."

Griff nodded.

"I have, but so what? Folks say that about me too. We're in the twenty-first century."

"This is Marshall County, Shay. We're always running about fifty years behind."

Shay sighed and grabbed the back of her neck. "I know."

For a long moment, neither of them said a word. Then, finally, the sheriff stood. "I'm going to keep trying to reach her, and I'll send feelers out where I have contacts." He paused.

"But?"

"But if I don't hear something definitive from her by the end of the week, then we'll have to suspend her and possibly terminate her employment."

"She's the lead investigator on all of my big cases too," Shay said. "None bigger than the Trey Cowan murder trial."

"I know, and I'm doing everything I can. But it's looking more and more like she's going to need to be replaced." He paused, his expression grave. "I'd start planning for that if I were you."

42

Hatty Daniels woke up at the Comfort Inn on College Street. Two blocks from downtown Pulaski. She'd checked in with a fake name and paid in cash. Perhaps that was unnecessary, but she wasn't taking any chances.

She had two cups of coffee and took in the complimentary breakfast. Then, without further procrastination, she made the call she'd been dreading since crossing the Tennessee state line.

"Hello?" a female voice answered.

Hatty closed her eyes. She hated to involve anyone else in her mess. *There's no other way,* she told herself.

"Hatty, is that you?"

"It's me."

"Oh, my gosh. It's so good—"

"I'm in trouble," Hatty interrupted. "I'm in a mess, and I need . . . help."

"Where are you?"

Hatty told her.

"Can you hold tight for a few hours. I've got to be in court this morning, and we are making a bust this afternoon."

"Yes," Hatty said, gripping the phone with both hands to keep them from shaking. "But I need to check out of the hotel. I need to keep moving."

"Remember Hitt's Place?"

At the mention of the bar, Hatty's face broke into a faint smile. "Of course."

"Meet me there at six thirty."

"OK."

A pause and Hatty could hear the sounds of her own heavy breathing. Her heart was pounding. *No turning back,* she thought.

"Hatty, are you all right?"

"No," Hatty said. "See you soon." Then she hung up the phone and dropped to her knees by the bed. Hatty prayed every morning after breakfast. Had since she was in grade school. It was a habit, as ingrained as brushing her teeth.

Dear God, please forgive my sins. Please help me . . . Hatty tried to think of more, but she couldn't.

Please help me.

43

Crawmama's was a seafood place off Highway 431 just past the Paul Stockton Causeway. Tucked in behind Big Lots, the restaurant had been started in 1987 by a woman who thought she could sell seafood out of her van to folks in a lake town. Turns out, she was right. After a month, the reception to her concept was so good that she acquired some space for a brick-and-mortar establishment. Now, more than thirty years later, Crawmama's had gone through several additions and, to Jason, favored the Flora-Bama a bit with its relaxed vibe, sprawling patchwork of buildings, and excellent food.

The Tonidandel brothers rarely ate out, but when they did, the boys preferred Crawmama's. Typically, they'd play quarters to see who the designated driver would be. Whoever lost would abstain, and the other two would take down a couple buckets of beer. The three of them normally ate at least a pound each of boiled crawfish, and they always ordered the fried shrimp basket.

Tonight, however, the normally upbeat gathering was all business. Instead of the three of them, there were five. Jason Rich's presence wouldn't have changed anything. In fact, they enjoyed when Jason tagged along, because then they had an all-time designated driver.

But no one was drinking at the moment, and that had everything to do with the fifth member of their party.

Tyson Cade sat at the end of the rectangular table. This was a power play by the drug dealer, as he'd moved the chair the second he'd sat down. "I want to be able to see your faces," he'd said. "And don't get any crazy ideas. No one is with me, but the cavalry isn't far."

"Good to know," Satch had said in his gravel-laced tone. "Thank you for coming."

"Fuck you, Colonel," Cade said. "I didn't come because you asked."

"Then why did you?" Jason snapped, looking directly into Cade's hazel-colored eyes.

"I guess I was curious. Do you know how many times I get summoned for a meeting?" He made a zero with his thumb and forefinger.

"It's an emergency," Jason said.

"Then get on with it."

Jason let out a breath and looked behind him. They were sitting at the "Tootsie Table," which was a private spot to the right of the bar. There were no other tables in sight, and at 4:45 p.m., the barstools were empty. That would all change when the dinner crowd swept in, but for now, it was as quiet as a country church during communion. "Trey won't tell me his whole story. Says he can't. Says you own him and that I'll have to get the full story from you."

Cade drank a sip of Coca-Cola and wiped his mouth. "Well, sucks to be you, then."

"I can't represent him if he won't tell me what happened."

"What has he told you?"

Jason chose his words carefully. His communications with Trey Cowan were protected by the attorney-client privilege. He was duty bound not to disclose them to anyone. But with Trey not talking and pointing him to Cade, he didn't have much choice. "Not much. Says he and Flowers were old friends that had gotten cross with each other. Flowers was giving him a hard time about a failed baseball tryout with the Barons, and that's what led to their scuffle at the Brick. He went home, got his shotgun, and went to his mom's. Remembers nothing else until morning. Was depressed and off his meds. Went to the football field because he didn't know where else to go." Jason paused. "That's pretty much it."

Cade put a toothpick in his mouth and began to chew. He wore a T-shirt, jeans, and a baseball cap. For all the world, he could have passed as a friend or even a young relative of the Tonidandels. At five feet, ten inches and only around 165 pounds, he wasn't physically imposing. But, as he glared at Jason, the young man's presence was unmistakable. "What do you want to know?"

"The full story," Jason said. "Or I'm gonna withdraw as Trey's counsel."

Cade laughed. "You realize that I could have your daughter and girlfriend arrested at any time for drug possession."

"I know you've threatened that, which means you must have an in with the sheriff's department."

"Man, you're good," Cade teased. "Nice thinking, Sherlock." He chewed some more on his toothpick. "All it would take is one phone call, and Nola is looking at a drug conviction that will make getting into a good school next to impossible. And, as I'm sure you know, Chase has had her share of trouble with the law. A possession . . . and a distribution charge would send her to prison."

"Distribution?"

"Who do you think got your little niece started on meth?"

"What? You're a liar. Nola's been getting her drugs from Kevin Martin." Jason felt a boot cover his foot and press down. He almost yelped but stopped himself. He looked at Satch, who was giving him a death stare.

Cade chuckled. "I've got a printed photograph in my pocket that I think you will find interesting. Colonel, may I?" He looked at Satch.

"Get on with it," Satch said.

Cade reached into his front pocket and pulled out a folded piece of paper. He slid it across the table to Jason, who unfolded it and brought it up to his face so he could see better.

In the grainy color picture, Chase was handing Nola a tiny container that was about the size of a pill bottle. It was a closeup, so Jason couldn't tell their location.

"This could be anything," Jason said, his voice dry. He took a sip of water from the glass in front of him.

"Oh really. I have a video, boys. OK if I show it to Mr. Rich?"

Satch nodded, and Jason felt a sinking in his stomach. He remembered the last time Tyson Cade had showed him a video.

Cade reached into his other pocket and pulled out an iPhone. He brought up the video and then slid the device across the table. Jason took it with both hands and peered down at the screen.

The footage wasn't zoomed in and was taken through a window. Chase and Nola were sitting at the kitchen island in Jason's home. They were talking. There was some white powder on a charcuterie board. Nola leaned over and snorted some of it through a straw. Then Chase took a turn. Then Nola. They laughed. Then did some more.

"Look at the container next to the board," Cade said.

Jason did and then compared it to the zoomed-in photograph.

"Could have been a gift," Jason said, his tone weak.

"Contributing to the delinquency of a minor," Cade said. "Worst case, she'd be charged with that and possession. But I think a tracking of Ms. Nola's bank account will show that she paid for the drugs."

Jason wanted to puke but tried to stay focused. What he'd just seen was unbelievable. Nola had gone to Perdido with him. She'd seen Chase's condition, and yet she said nothing to him about using with Chase. Or that she'd bought from Chase. *She's a teenager,* Jason reminded himself. *Who lost both parents last year . . .*

"Why is Nola buying from K-Mart if Chase was her source?"

"Chase only distributed once to Nola," Cade said, his voice matter of fact. "Just enough for us to get pictures and video."

"What?" Jason didn't believe it.

"Hurts, doesn't it? If it makes you feel any better, we insisted that she do it if she was going to continue getting her own stash."

"We?"

"Me . . . through my colleagues."

"Which were who?"

Cade flicked his toothpick on the ground and drank another sip of Coke. "That's not for you to know." He paused. "But you see what's at stake here, Jason. If you don't continue to represent Trey Cowan, the people you care about most are going to be hurt."

"It's not enough," Jason said. "I can't defend Trey without knowing his story. Besides, these are your drugs. How can you bring Nola and Chase down without implicating yourself and your whole operation?"

"Oh, I'm insulated, Counselor. There are so many layers before you ever get to me. Plus, remember what you said earlier about having a source inside the department." His mouth curved into half a grin. "Perhaps making sure your niece and lover go to jail isn't a big enough threat. Remember what I did last year to your older niece. What's her name? Niecy? Isn't that cute?"

"She's being watched twenty-four hours a day," Satch grunted.

"Just like she was last year. When one of my guys put her in the hospital and could have killed her if that was my desire."

"We have a different crew this year," Satch said.

But Cade ignored him, looking at Jason. "You really think you can protect yourself and the people you love from me?"

"Yes," Jason said.

"OK," Cade said, standing from the table. "If there's nothing further."

"There is," Jason said. "Can you tell me anything else? Or at least give Trey the green light to tell me everything he knows. Whatever me and Trey talk about is protected by the attorney-client privilege."

"Which you just broke by talking to me about what he said."

Jason gritted his teeth. "True, but you didn't leave me much choice."

"I don't trust you, Jason. And Trey's right. I do own him."

"Tyson, I can't represent him effectively on what I know now. I don't have an alternate suspect, and the physical evidence against him is substantial. Is there anything you can give me? You said you have a source in the department. Have they told you anything about Flowers?"

"Not a word," Cade said.

"Well, do you know anything about him? He's from Alder Springs, and that's Sand Mountain. Can you tell me anything about his family? He has a sister, right?"

"Bella," Cade said, grinning. "She was so fine back in the day."

"Did you know her?"

"Not really. Only in my wet dreams." He chuckled, and Mickey Tonidandel let out a guffaw. Satch and Chuck both glared at their brother, and Mickey looked down at the table.

"What about Kelly? Were you friends? Enemies? Did he ever investigate you?"

"I knew him, but we were never friends. When he joined the dark side, we became enemies. I think the sheriff's department had him investigating me, because Kelly's from Sand Mountain."

"And did Kelly get too close? Is that why you had him killed?" Jason asked the question deadpan.

Cade snickered. "You trying to play a Jedi mind trick? I didn't kill Kelly. I was safe in my bed, having made sweet love to Dooby Darnell."

"Who is she?"

"My fuck buddy. She's a clerk at the Alder Springs Grocery."

Jason didn't bother to ask any more questions about Darnell or his alibi. A man like Cade wouldn't do his own dirty work. "Did you hire someone else to kill Flowers and set Trey up? Maybe now you're feeling guilty about it and want to see if I can get him off."

Cade leaned his elbows on the table. "Let me explain something to you, Counselor. Guilt is not an emotion that I'm capable of feeling. If

I did hire someone to take out Kelly Flowers, then you best be sure I wouldn't be feeling guilty about it."

"Then why are you involved?" Jason asked, his tone saturated with exasperation. "Is it because Trey works for you? Because of the deliveries he made."

Cade gave a subtle nod. "That's one of the reasons. I'm also very fond of his mother. She was good to me and my mom when I was young." He grabbed another toothpick from the pack on the table and began to chew.

"Tyson—"

"I've told you all I'm going to tell you. Trey's a Sand Mountain boy. He did some work for me, and I feel responsible for him, and I'm loyal to folks like Trudy Cowan who've been loyal to me. That's that."

"Then why me?" Jason asked. "You could've hired anyone with your drug money. Why involve me?"

"Because I had the goods on you, Jason. I don't trust anyone, but I thought we worked well together in Jana's trial. She was guilty, and you got her off. I'm hoping you can do the same for my friend."

"Your friend?"

Cade smiled and started to turn away. Then, stopping, he returned to the table and leaned close to Jason's ear. "There's one other reason I hired you."

Jason waited.

"Trey is innocent," Cade whispered.

"How in the hell do you know that?"

"Because I know who Kelly Flowers was meeting at Branner's Place the night he was killed." Cade rotated the toothpick in his mouth. "And you do too."

Jason's throat clenched, and he tried to swallow. He coughed and drank a sip of water.

"He'd been meeting her quite a bit in the weeks before he was killed."

Jason's eyes watered as he glared at the drug dealer. "How do you know that?"

"I make it a point to check out the people who are investigating me."

"What are you saying?" Jason glanced at Satch, who gazed back with a poker face. If he had heard what Cade had whispered, he wasn't letting on.

"I'm saying that it's déjà vu all over again, Jason." Cade's whisper sent gooseflesh running up on Jason's arm like wind over a field of hay. "A woman that you love is right in the middle of this case." He paused. "Another . . . *guilty* woman."

44

Hatty got to Hitt's Place at 6:15 p.m. and ordered a gin and tonic to calm her nerves. By the time her friend arrived fifteen minutes later, she was well into her second one.

"Hey," Hatty said, as the woman sat down at the table. She was still in her khaki uniform, and there were sweat beads on her forehead. "Long day?"

"The job is the job."

"And so it is," Hatty said, reaching across and taking the woman's hands in her own and giving them a squeeze. "It is so good to see you, Frannie."

Frannie Storm had light-brown skin and was in her midthirties. At a tad over six feet tall, she had a statuesque, lean frame. She'd been an All-State basketball player at Giles County High School and Little All-American at David Lipscomb College and had spent several years in the WNBA before deciding to pursue a career in law enforcement. Hatty had met Frannie when the latter was an inexperienced deputy almost a decade earlier. During Frannie's first couple of years, Hatty had served as a mentor of sorts for the young and eager law woman. Whenever Frannie had a question or encountered a problem, she came to Hatty for advice and counsel. Even after Hatty left Pulaski to become an investigator in the Marshall County Sheriff's Office eight years ago, the two had remained close. As she looked over her former protégé and the words "Chief Deputy Sheriff" on her lapel, Hatty beamed with pride.

"It's good to see you too," Frannie said. She waited as the bartender took her drink order. She asked for a Yuengling in a bottle, and Hatty ordered another gin and tonic. Once the drinks were on the table, Frannie held out her bottle. "To old friends."

"And good times," Hatty chimed in, looking around the bar, which advertised on its front window in big blue letters that it had the COLDEST BEER IN TOWN.

"Remember when we used to come here after work?"

Hatty snorted. "I remember you peppering me with every question in the book. Procedural? Strategy for stakeouts? How to handle informants? You never stopped."

"And you were like a living and breathing encyclopedia for a young kid who didn't know shit from Shinola."

"I'm proud of your success," Hatty said. The gin had made her face warm, and seeing her old friend had made her forget, at least for a few minutes, her predicament. Catching herself, she glanced down at her glass and gripped it with both hands.

"What's wrong, Hatty?" Frannie's voice had lost its softness. She knew this wasn't a social call, and it was time to cut to it.

"I'm in trouble."

"What do you mean?"

"Did you hear about the officer killed in Marshall County?"

"Yeah, of course. Can't remember his name, but he got shot by a high school friend of his, right? The perp was then arrested on the football field where they'd both played ball together."

Hatty nodded. Guntersville was less than two hours from Pulaski, and an officer death of any kind was news. She wasn't surprised that Frannie had heard about it. "The officer's name was Kelly Flowers."

"I'm sorry. Did you know him well?" Frannie asked.

"Not exactly. But I . . . was investigating him."

"What for?"

"Being an inside source to Sand Mountain's biggest meth dealer."

211

"Oh, Jesus," Frannie said, leaning back and crossing her arms. "Hatty, I've skimmed over most of the articles online about the murder. I don't remember hearing anything about Flowers being a dirty cop." Frannie squinted. "I'm assuming that's because your investigation cleared him."

Hatty took a long sip from her glass. "I wish."

Frannie drank the rest of her beer in one gulp. Then she waved the bartender over. "One more," she said. Then she leaned forward and whispered, "What do you mean, you wish?"

"I mean what I said. My investigation revealed some things. The preliminary hearing was yesterday, and I was feeling pressure to . . ."

"Pressure to what?"

". . . not mention it."

"Are you kidding?"

"No. It's an election year. The Flowers murder is big news in Guntersville. If word gets out that he was an—"

"Stop," Frannie said, her voice loud but not quite yelling. "Don't say anymore. This is information you need to be telling an attorney. Anything you say to me isn't privileged."

"I'm sorry. I wanted you to know the nuts and bolts of it so you would understand."

"You're worried you are going to lose your job if you don't cover up your investigation. And you're worried that if you do the right thing and blow the whistle, that you'll never be hired to work in law enforcement again."

Hatty gave a swift nod. "Yes, but that's not everything."

"Isn't that enough?"

Hatty bit her lip. "I'm also worried for my safety. I've noticed a car following me the past couple of days. I think the meth dealer may be tailing me, and I'm worried that if I don't cooperate, he might take matters into his own hands. I don't think he . . . or our department . . . wants it getting out that Flowers was an inside source."

Frannie raised her eyebrows.

"Don't worry," Hatty said. "I drove out of Guntersville at three in the morning, and I didn't see the tail. Then I went all the way past Montgomery before I turned around and headed here."

"But here is home, Hatty. Don't you think if someone were looking for you, they might look here?"

Hatty finally couldn't stop the tears as they trickled down her cheeks. "Yes, that's a risk. But here I have a friend." She paused to collect herself. "And I don't have many of those in the world."

This time, Frannie grabbed hold of Hatty's hands. "You came to the right place." Then, forcing a laugh, Frannie added, "Goodness gracious, girl, you in some high-level shit."

Hatty couldn't help but laugh too. "That's one name for it."

Frannie's grin faded. When she spoke, her voice was firm. "How can I help?"

"I need a place to stay. To hide out, I guess, until I figure out what to do."

"You can stay with me. I've got an extra bedroom, and I would enjoy the company."

"Thank you, Frannie." Hatty's lips trembled as she privately thanked God as well.

"What else?"

"You've already mentioned it. I need a lawyer. Someone I can tell this whole crazy story to in confidence and who can help me out of this mess."

Frannie raised her eyebrows. "That's why you really came here."

Hatty returned the gesture. "You did say you were kind of dating him in one of your recent texts."

Frannie rolled her eyes. "We're just . . . very good friends."

Hatty took a sip of her gin and tonic and winced. "I don't think he ever cared much for me. He'll probably say no."

"Only one way to find out," Frannie said, pulling out her phone.

"What are you doing?"

"Sending a text."

Hatty took another sip from her drink and closed her eyes. She opened them when she heard a ding coming from Frannie's phone. "That was fast."

"He'll meet with you next week. No promises, but he'll hear your story."

"Next week? Frannie—"

"He's in depositions this week, and then he's visiting his son in Tuscaloosa. He'll be back in town on Monday, and he'll see you that morning."

"I may not have a week."

"You'll be safe here. I've got your back."

Hatty drank down the rest of her gin and tonic. *This is why I came,* she told herself. Then, looking at Hatty, she asked, "He's still the best attorney in Pulaski, isn't he?"

Frannie snorted. "Hatty . . . he's one of the best in the world."

45

Jason didn't say a word on the way home from Crawmama's. As he was getting out of Satch Tonidandel's truck, he asked the colonel if they could talk in private.

Once they were both inside the home, Jason spoke while gazing out at the cove. "Does Chase have a twelve-gauge shotgun?"

"Yes."

"Are you sure?"

"As shit. I've seen them."

"Them?"

"She had an older model that was her daddy's, and she had a new one she bought a few years ago."

"Ever seen her shoot it?" Jason turned and looked at Satch, who was rubbing his chin.

"Can't say that I have. At the range, she normally shoots handguns and rifles. Most folks don't shoot a scattergun like a twelve gauge at the range." He snapped his fingers. "Now I did see her giving Nola a lesson with the older shotgun on one of the weeks where you were gone. They were out on the dock, and she was showing Nola how to hold the gun. How to load it, that sorta thing."

Great, Jason thought.

"Satch, can you check her home and see if you can find either of the shotguns?"

The colonel grunted. "You don't really believe that sorry sumbitch, do you?"

"I'm just doing my due diligence. If Cade is right and Chase was meeting Kelly Flowers at Branner's Place the night he was shot and killed with a twelve gauge . . ." He trailed off.

"All right," Satch said. He walked toward the door and then turned back to Jason. "You OK?"

"Yeah, Satch. Thanks for setting the meeting up."

Once the colonel was gone, Jason went downstairs to his garage gym. He didn't even bother to change into shorts. He took off his button-down and worked out in his T-shirt, slacks, and dress shoes. He didn't want to think. He didn't want to do anything but punish his body. He told Alexa to play songs by Metallica and then lifted weights at a deliberate pace, trying not to think.

He knew he was on the verge of another breakdown. Forty-eight hours after his last near relapse. But if he pushed his muscles to the brink and let the loud music infiltrate his veins, he knew the urge would go away.

I will not let that sonofabitch break me. I will own this situation, and I will claw myself out of it.

About an hour in, the desire to have a shot of whiskey went away. Two hours in, even the impulse for a cold beer was gone. He was drenched in sweat, and his feet hurt from doing dead lifts in Allen Edmonds lace-ups.

He could deal with the pain. Anything was better than a hangover. And the disappointment that falling off the wagon . . . again . . . would bring.

After warming down by jumping rope and doing a ten-minute stretch, Jason trotted upstairs and made himself a protein shake. Looking around, he noticed that—big surprise—Nola wasn't there. It was 10:30 p.m. on a school night.

He picked up his phone and checked his Life360 app. It showed she was on Buck Island. Then he called the number for the guard assigned to her. "Where is she?" he asked, forgoing any pleasantries.

"At the Martin kid's house," a gruff voice answered. "She's been here for a while."

"*Damnit*," Jason hissed through his teeth.

"Do you want me to engage, sir? I can tell her that she needs to come home."

Jason wiped sweat from his forehead. "No, that won't be necessary."

"Ten-four." And then the line went dead.

Jason drank down the shake and then hopped in the shower, turning the dial as cold as the water would get. As the icy water cascaded over him, his mind began to clear.

And he knew what he had to do. It was time to step up. As an uncle and guardian. As an attorney. As a human being.

Jason dressed in jeans and a golf shirt and headed to the front door, making sure his Glock was concealed in his pocket.

His phone buzzed as he climbed into the Porsche. It was Satch, who was watching the house tonight. Jason clicked on the phone.

"Where are you going?"

"To bring Nola home."

"Good," he said. Then, grunting, he asked, "Want Mickey or Chuck to follow you?"

"No. I've got this myself."

"All right then. Watch your back."

"Will do." Jason ended the call and pulled out onto Mill Creek Road, and then hung a right on Highway 79. For early May, the night was cool, and Jason wished he'd thought to bring a windbreaker.

It'll do me good, he told himself. Like a cold shower, cool air was another defuser. Something that opened his pores and made him return to the present and away from his torturous thoughts.

Jason turned left on Highway 431. Five minutes later, he hung another left on Buck Island Drive. As he returned to the scene of last year's case—the murder of his brother-in-law, Dr. Braxton

Waters—Jason felt a pit in the bottom of his stomach but pushed past his feelings of guilt and anguish.

When he reached the address, he parked in the grass front lawn because the driveway was full of cars. He didn't see his security detail, but he knew the guard was out here somewhere. He got out of the car and walked toward the front door, hearing the sounds of loud music beyond it. Because the mansions were spaced a good ways apart, this type of high school party could get off without causing too much of a commotion. Jason knocked and, when there was no answer, turned the knob, which wasn't locked, and walked inside.

The house opened to a large open area where teenagers were talking, dancing, and drinking. He scanned the crowd but didn't see Kevin Martin or Nola. He went up to the first kid he saw. "Have you seen Nola Waters?"

The kid smiled, eyes bleary. "No, dude. I mean, Dad." He laughed, and Jason pushed past him.

"Has anyone seen Nola Waters?" he asked the crowd of people. No response. He grinned and took out his phone. He began to snap pictures of the people in the room.

"Hey, man. What are you doing?" It was a young woman's voice. Jason turned toward it and noticed her. He'd seen her at his house a few times. "Harley?"

Her eyes went wide. She was holding a Truly seltzer in her hand. "Where's Nola?"

She combed back her hair. "I . . . I'm not sure."

Jason clicked a photo of her. "I think your parents will like that one."

"Mr. Rich, please—"

Jason clicked a few more pics, and a boy approached him. "Hey, Mister. You need to get on outa here."

"I'm not leaving until I see Nola. Now, where is she?"

No one answered.

"All right, I'm calling the police." Jason made a show of punching the digits with his phone.

"She went with K-Mart, I mean Kevin," Harley said.

"That doesn't tell me much. Where'd they go?"

"For a Jet Ski ride," Harley said, taking a few steps toward him. Though she was holding an alcoholic beverage, her eyes were clear. "To her old house. The new owners are hardly ever there."

"OK," Jason said, pressing end on his phone and putting it in his pocket. "Does she do that a lot? Visit, I mean."

Harley nodded. "Pretty much every time she comes over here."

Jason turned to leave.

"Mr. Rich, are you going to tell my parents about . . . ?"

But Jason was out the front door before he heard the rest of it. He unlocked his car and looked down the road. The old Waters homestead was a quarter mile away. Hesitating for only a second and patting his pocket to make sure his Glock was still there, he locked the door and began to walk. As he did, he called his security guard. "She took a Jet Ski ride with K-Mart down to her old house. It's a little ways down the road, and I'm going to walk it. I don't want to startle them."

"I'm sorry, Mr. Rich. I can't see the Martin boathouse from out here."

"It's OK. Look, I've got things from here. Why don't you take the night off?"

"Are you sure?"

Jason wasn't sure of anything anymore, but he thought he needed to do this by himself. "Yes."

Jason hung up as Buck Island Drive hooked around to the left and the old Waters homestead came into view. He felt a nervous tickle in his stomach. When had he last been here? *Nola comes every time she sees K-Mart . . .*

Jason took a deep breath, feeling his heartbeat racing. He tried to think about what he might say to her.

Jason arrived at the house and saw that all the inside lights were off, and the circle driveway was devoid of cars. There was a light above the garage, but that was the only illumination.

Jason didn't bother to try the front door. He knew it was locked, and he doubted that any key that Nola might still have to the home would work. Besides, even if the door was open, he doubted that's where she would go.

He walked around the house and saw two silhouettes down by the boathouse. They were close to each other and appeared to be in an embrace. A song was playing, and, as he got closer, Jason recognized it as Darius Rucker's version of "Wagon Wheel." He thought back to the investigative report on Braxton Waters's death. An Alexa device had been playing songs by Rucker.

Jason's feet hit the dock and he realized that he hadn't actually been in the boathouse since before Braxton's death. He'd visited the home, but last year the boathouse and dock had been a crime scene. At some point, after Braxton's murder and the close of the trial, the yellow crime scene tape had been removed. Jason wondered if the fact that a murder had occurred on this spot bothered the new owners or if they were the kind of people who might think that was a cool side plot to the home. A conversation piece at dinner parties.

Perhaps . . . but that's not what it was to Nola.

As Jason got closer to the covering where Braxton Waters had been hitting golf balls into the lake the night he died, he felt a solemness come over him. He also noticed that the two people on the dock weren't hugging each other any longer. Nola was sitting on the dock with her legs dangling over the edge, while Kevin Martin was lying back in a lounge chair and checking his phone. Jason watched Nola and saw that she was swaying back and forth and humming to the music.

When K-Mart saw Jason, he rose to his feet and stuck his phone in his pocket. "Who are y—"

Jason put his index finger over his mouth to shush him, but, as he got closer, he could tell the boy now recognized him. "I'm Nola's uncle."

"Yes, sir." K-Mart extended his hand, and Jason took it. K-Mart was about five feet, ten inches tall and looked to be around two hundred pounds. His arms and shoulders were thick from weightlifting, and his grip was strong. He had dark hair and olive skin.

Jason glanced at Nola, and she was still swaying to the music and humming. "How much has she had to drink?"

"A couple Trulys," K-Mart said, his voice matter of fact. If he was shocked or startled by Jason's presence, he was doing a good job of keeping calm.

"And how much meth?"

The boy blinked twice. "None that I'm aware—"

"Cut the crap, K-Mart," Jason said. "What drugs has she done tonight?"

He rubbed his neck. "Two lines of meth. A Xanax. That's all I've seen her do."

"And where did she get the meth?"

"Beats me."

"Right. You're a liar, K-Mart."

"And you've had someone following me, Mr. Rich. Haven't you?"

Jason didn't answer.

"I should report you to the police."

At this, Jason laughed. "And tell them what? That me allegedly having an investigator follow you has cut into your meth trade?"

"Listen, man—"

"No, you listen," Jason said. "I want you to hop on that Jet Ski . . ." Jason pointed to the watercraft tied to the back of the dock. ". . . and get your punk ass out of here."

K-Mart took a step forward, moving his pecs back and forth. "You really think you can tell me what to do? I'll have you put in jail." K-Mart pushed Jason in the chest, knocking him back a few steps.

"This is her parents' boathouse," Jason said. "Her dad was murdered pretty much exactly where she is sitting. Do you hear me?"

K-Mart didn't look at Nola. He took another step toward Jason. "I know. She's told me all about it. Now, I think it's time you leave."

Jason didn't move. "I know all about you, K-Mart. I know what you sell and who you sell for. You really think it's a good idea working for Tyson Cade?"

"Who?" K-Mart asked. "I don't have the foggiest clue who you are talking about."

"Right."

Instead of his gun, Jason took out his phone. "I'm going to call the police if you don't leave right now."

K-Mart turned and grabbed his own device from the chair behind him. "Me first."

"I'm going to call them to your house, where a bunch of kids are underage drinking and doing the meth you sell them. How'd that be?"

"And when they get there, I'm going to tell them how you threatened me."

Jason smirked. "And in the next breath, I'll mention how you drugged my niece and took her down to her old boathouse to do God knows what with her."

K-Mart seemed to force a smile. "I'd watch my back if I were you."

"I always do." Jason reached into his pocket and lifted the handle of his Glock just a few inches up so that K-Mart could see it. "Now, you've already assaulted me, and I'm feeling a bit twitchy, and I really don't like it that you are out here with Nola, so . . ." Jason glared at him. ". . . like I said, get the hell out of here."

K-Mart stuck his phone in his pocket. He walked over to Nola and kissed her cheek, whispering something into her ear. Nola said something back that Jason didn't hear. Then he strode to the end of the dock and climbed on the red-and-black Kawasaki. He undid the rope and kicked off the edge. Once the craft was a few feet away from the dock, he pushed the ignition, and the Jet Ski roared to life. K-Mart extended his middle finger toward Jason. "I'll be seeing you, Mr. Rich," he shouted.

Then he sped away without looking back.

Jason almost called after him but thought better of it. His heart was pounding, and his adrenaline gauge had almost reached the top. Taking a deep breath, he approached his niece.

"Nola?" He walked toward her and squatted. "Honey, are you all right?"

She glanced at him as the song changed to "Beers and Sunshine."

"H-h-hey," she said. Her eyes were glassy and she slurred her words.

Jason took a seat beside her. "It's time to go home, honey."

She shook her head. "No."

Jason started to say yes but caught himself. He gazed out at the water and saw the Veterans Memorial Bridge in the background.

"This was D-D-Daddy's favorite. He loved Darius."

"I know, honey. I remember."

"I was here when they pulled his body out of the water," Nola said, her words coming out as a low whine. "Mom and me. We saw it. They pulled him out." She wiped her eyes, which were now brimming with tears. "I already knew he was dead. I'd seen his golf hat floating on the water, and I knew. But s-s-seeing his body was still . . ."

"Nola, I'm so sorry. I know it's hard."

"No, you don't. Nana and Papa lived long lives before they died. My parents were both murdered. Do you hear me? Someone killed them. I didn't even have a chance to say goodbye. Not to either one of them."

"I know."

"We had a good life, Uncle Jason. I mean, Mom was a little crazy, and they didn't have the best marriage, but we had a life." She sobbed. "And now it's all gone. And Niecy is in college. And . . . ." She hiccuped and rolled her eyes. ". . . all I've got is you."

"The drugs don't help."

"*They do for me!*" she screamed and pulled herself to her feet. She stumbled, and Jason grabbed her arm to steady her. She snatched it away and punched his shoulder.

"Don't touch me!" she wailed.

"Nola, let's go home."

"You aren't my dad. You aren't my parent. You're *nothing*." She spat on the boathouse floor. "And when I turn eighteen, you can best believe I'll be outa here. You'll be alone, Uncle Jason." She stumbled again, getting very close to the edge of the dock.

"Sweetheart, please let me take you home. I know I'm not your father. But I am an addict, and I know one when I see one."

"Oh, fuck off. An addict? Like you? Like Chase? No, I am not. This is by choice. I don't have to do any of this stuff. I want to do it. I want to die, you hear me?"

Jason felt warmth on his cheeks. He reached out with his hand. "Please don't say that, sweetie."

"Why? It's the truth."

Jason stepped toward her.

"Don't get any closer to me, or I'll jump in. It's eight feet deep over the edge of this dock. Sometimes twelve. I'll swim out to the middle, where it's even deeper, and you'll never find me."

"Nola—"

"Shut up."

Jason's mind scrambled to find something to redirect her. Whatever drugs she'd done had taken over. "Nola, what happened to Chase? I know you started using with her. Why did she relapse?"

Nola howled with anguished laughter. "You are so clueless, Uncle Jason. I didn't start using with her. Chase started using with me. I got her back in the game. Me!"

"But I've seen pictures of you being given meth by her."

She hiccuped again. "That was K-Mart's idea. Once Chase started using with me, he said it would be good if we had a picture of her selling to me." She hiccuped again and then burped. "As protection for him."

"You set her up?"

Nola opened her mouth wide. "Surprise!"

"Nola, please let me help you. You and Niecy are the only family I have left. I love you." Jason felt tears misting in his eyes. Had he ever told her that before?

Nola opened her mouth for a moment as if she were stunned by what her uncle had just said. "I . . ." She bit her lip and looked out at Lake Guntersville.

"Please come with me, honey," Jason said.

Nola's lip began to tremble. "I'm sorry, Uncle Jason."

And then she fell backward into Lake Guntersville.

46

Kevin Martin waited until he had parked his Jet Ski in his boathouse to make the call. He described what happened on the dock with Jason Rich in as much detail as he could, keeping his voice and tone measured. K-Mart was in his third high school in four years, and he'd been popular in each one. Part of his attraction was the drugs, which he had always had a knack for finding and selling. But the other part was confidence. He knew who he was and didn't care what others thought of him. That made him golden.

In business and with the ladies.

"All right, kid, thanks for calling. Mr. Rich won't be bothering you anymore." A pause. "Are you still dating his niece?"

K-Mart grinned as he approached his house. "We're friends with benefits."

A chuckle on the other end of the line. "Well, try to keep that going."

"Will do, Mr. Dean."

K-Mart strode up the lawn to his home, feeling in total control again. His parents were out of town, and Matthew Dean—or, more likely, Mr. Dean's boss—would make sure Jason Rich didn't bug him anymore. He looked over his shoulder at the lake, regretting that his interlude with Nola had been broken. As he entered his home, he figured his chances of getting lucky tonight were over.

As he shut the door, Harley Rogers came toward him and touched his arm. "Did Nola's uncle find y'all?"

"Yep. Did you tell him where we were?"

"I didn't have a choice. He was threatening to call the police."

"Yeah," K-Mart said, giving his head a jerk. "He made the same threat to me."

"Did Nola go with him?"

"Yep, she's gone."

"So . . ." She leaned in close, and he could smell her perfume. ". . . do you have any meth upstairs?"

K-Mart grinned. Perhaps his chances were improving. "Let's go find out."

———

Matty Dean ended the call with the kid and let out a deep breath. *Tyson ain't gonna like that,* he thought, shuddering and taking a long sip of beer. He was sitting at the bar at Fire by the Lake, a waterfront restaurant off Highway 69. He'd spent most of the day fishing after making a delivery for Tyson by boat to Ditto Landing in Huntsville.

He'd had a good day, catching twelve bass. His further reward was a couple of brews at the bar and some flirting with the redheaded barmaid, Teresa. Now, though, the good times were gone. Jason Rich was making more trouble.

As he left the bar and walked toward his truck, he glanced up and saw one of the lawyer's massive billboards.

You have no idea the hell you are bringing on yourself, he thought, gazing up at the stubble-faced attorney. Then, climbing into his pickup, he noticed a maroon SUV out of the corner of his eye. Had it been here when he arrived?

He thought it had. He didn't turn but instead climbed into the cab of his vehicle. He glanced into the rearview mirror and noticed a man behind the wheel. Thinking fast, Matty hopped out of the truck and snapped his fingers, as if he'd forgotten something. He walked fast down to the dock where he'd moored his boat in one of the slips. *Just a man who's forgotten his cap,* he thought as he strode toward the boat. He hopped in and opened the storage closet by the front console. He pulled out a hat, which he hadn't forgotten but which he typically left in the boat. Then, putting it back on his head, he walked away from the boat in similar fashion, head down and snapping his fingers. He pulled his phone out of his pocket and held it to his side as he approached the maroon SUV, which was a Ford Explorer, and snapped two photographs of the back, making sure he captured the license tag, and two more of the side.

Then he hopped inside the truck. Once he was out on Highway 69, he dialed the number.

"This better be good," Tyson said, his voice high and his breathing labored.

"The kid was accosted tonight by Jason Rich at a party he was throwing at his home. Rich accused him of working with you."

"Really?" Tyson asked, his breath more under control.

"Yep. And that's not the worst part."

"What is?"

Matty glanced in his rearview mirror, and the Explorer was about six car lengths behind him. "I'm pretty sure I'm being followed."

Silence on the other end of the line. When Tyson spoke again, his voice was as cold as the lake in December. "Maroon SUV?"

"Yep."

"You get a photo and the plates?"

"I did."

"Have our guy run them. Jason Rich better hope this is some kind of massive coincidence."

Matty said nothing for a second, glancing again in the mirror. "Will do, boss." He let out a breath. "But we both know it's not."

47

Jason wasn't a good swimmer. He dove in after Nola, and the cold water sent shock waves through his body. Early May was still a few weeks before the lake's temperature warmed up, and at this time of night, it was freezing cold.

Jason swam downward and opened his eyes, knowing she couldn't have gone far. He thrashed in front of him and felt her foot. He tried to latch on, but she wiggled away.

He dove down farther, hoping like hell they hadn't drifted under the boathouse. For a second, he saw nothing. He knew if he went up for air, it was over. He'd never find her again, and if he did, she'd probably be too far gone.

If she is swimming out to the middle, I'll never catch her, he thought, as he felt the silty, sandy bottom of the lake. He opened his eyes as wide as he could, thinking he saw an outline of a leg moving a few feet away. He lunged for it and felt skin in his grasp. Then he had his arms around her. He tried to pull her up, and she resisted.

He screamed in her ear, "Nola, please help me!"

But they were underwater, and he couldn't understand his own words.

He again tried to bring her up, but she wasn't budging. Nola only weighed about 115 pounds, but the water weight, the depth of at least twelve feet, and Jason's weakness as a swimmer were too much to overcome. He relaxed for a second and closed his eyes. He was dizzy and weak. And then . . .

Don't quit, baby brother. You promised.

Jana's voice. His eyes shot open, and his heart pounded. For his whole life, Jana had gaslighted him. She'd made him feel like he was crazy. She'd had some kind of psychotic hold on him and pretty much everyone in her inner circle. They'd all wanted to please her despite the crazy things she'd done in her life. Jason had finally cut himself off from her, but then Braxton's murder and Jana's arrest for the crime had brought him home.

And now he was drowning in Lake Guntersville.

Don't be a pussy. Jana's voice again, just as he'd heard it a million times in his thoughts every time he'd ever failed at something. Constantly tormenting him. He hadn't heard it, or perhaps he'd blocked it out, since her death.

You were always weak, Jason. Now you're gonna take my daughter down with you.

Jason screamed into the water and directly into Nola's ear. He turned her around and brought her face to his, screaming again. She didn't open her eyes. *No* . . .

Then he hugged her close and pushed off the bottom. His thighs and hamstrings burned as he pushed his legs against the water as hard as he could. He could see the light of the moon above them. Just a couple more feet. *Don't be a pussy* . . .

Jason's head came out of the water, and he lifted Nola's face out. He saw the ladder a few yards away and swam toward it, hooking Nola under his left arm and keeping her head above the surface of the lake. He grabbed the wooden rail and turned to Nola. She was foaming at the mouth but still alive.

"Nola, grab hold of my neck, honey," Jason said, pulling her arms around him and clutching both her hands with his left. He took a deep breath and leaned into the ladder, taking two steps up and then falling forward. He managed to get his right elbow on the dock and then pressed off of it as hard as he could. He and Nola both fell onto the deck, and Nola rolled over on her back.

He crawled toward his niece and wiped the foam from her mouth. He pulled her up to a seated position and patted her back.

Nola began to cough, and then her eyes rolled back into their sockets. She coughed again and spat water out of her mouth. Then she vomited. Jason reached into his pocket for his phone, and it was drenched. He tapped it with his hand, but the screen was blank. It was no use. He looked around the boathouse for a purse, a bag, anything that might have Nola's phone in it, and didn't see anything. "Damnit!" he screamed.

He needed to get Nola to a hospital, but how? He had no phone, and his car was a half mile up the road. And he'd sent his security detail home. *You are such an idiot.* This time, the voice in his thoughts was his own, but he knew his deceased sister would agree.

Jason rose to his feet, and his legs were wobbly. He looked in either direction. Buck Island was so spread out that he'd have a hike regardless of which way he went. It would be impossible to carry her that distance.

Nola's stomach heaved again, and she threw up on the dock. Bile was flowing from her mouth. Had K-Mart lied about how much she'd had? Or was he telling the truth, and this was her reaction to the combination of Xanax, meth, and alcohol?

Jason tried to think. He reached into his pocket and pulled out the Glock. It was obviously wet, but would it still work? Perhaps the gun would be more durable than the phone. He pointed it at the lake and pulled the trigger.

Boom.

Jason felt a shiver of adrenaline run through his whole body. The gun had fired. Satch had instructed him to always keep it loaded, because he'd be dead in a gunfight if he had to take the time to load it.

Jason scrambled up the hill toward the house. When he reached the patio, he tried the door first, knowing it would be locked. Then he pointed his gun at the window portion of the door and fired. One, two, three shots. He reached through the jagged glass and turned the knob as alarms sounded in every direction.

Jason breathed a sigh of relief. He went inside, looking for a landline and not finding one. He cursed, wondering if anyone used anything but a cell phone anymore.

But that was OK. The alarms would bring the police as fast or faster than a 911 call. He ran back down to the dock, and Nola was lying on her back. He knelt to the ground and rolled her over, patting her back again until she coughed.

"Thank God," Jason whispered. Then, gathering all his strength, he picked her up and began to walk.

When they reached the front of the house, Jason fell to his knees and laid Nola on the ground. He checked her pulse, and she was still breathing. He stumbled toward the road, praying that a car would come along. But there was nothing. *Why did I send my security detail home?* Jason again cursed his stupidity, wondering if he should run to K-Mart's house or wait for the police.

"Help me!" he screamed. "Someone help me!"

But the only response was the wind rustling through the trees. Jason walked over to Nola and checked her again. Still breathing but not conscious. "Damnit!" he yelled. He paced back and forth to and from the road a couple of times and then decided he'd run back to K-Mart's. But he didn't make it thirty yards before he heard a siren coming from behind him. He turned, feeling an immediate sensation of relief as he saw red and blue flashing lights approaching on Buck Island Drive.

A patrol car came to an abrupt stop, and an officer jumped out of it, wielding a gun. Jason held up his hands, which were shaking. "Please help her," he said, nodding toward Nola. "Please help my niece."

48

Two hours later, Jason was sitting in a plastic chair in the emergency room lobby of Marshall Medical Center North, his clothes still damp. Next to him, Satch Tonidandel sat with his arms crossed tight across his chest. Jason had ridden with the police car to the hospital and borrowed a phone to call the colonel as soon as they arrived. Now, Mickey was watching the house, and Chuck was patrolling the hospital parking lot.

When Jason and Nola had arrived at the hospital, the emergency room staff had insisted on checking Jason out. He'd had his vitals taken and been given an IV. When everything came back normal, he was discharged.

Now he waited on news about Nola. She'd been unconscious for the whole ride from Buck Island, which had been about ten minutes. He hadn't been allowed back to see her.

Finally, a nurse emerged from the double doors and walked toward him. "We've got her in a room now. You can come back."

Jason nodded at Satch, who remained in the lobby. Then he followed the nurse through the maze of hallways to a small room with a full-length glass window. When he saw Nola hooked to a monitor with a long tube poked down her throat, his knees gave, and he leaned into the glass.

"Are you OK?" the nurse asked.

"Yes . . . what's that tube?"

"We had to intubate her," a strong voice said from behind him.

Jason turned to see a woman with blondish-gray hair wearing a white coat. "I'm Dr. Squire. Your daughter swallowed a lot of lake water and was suffering from alcohol and drug poisoning. We had to pump her stomach, and we were forced to intubate her when she began to aspirate."

Jason wrinkled his eyebrows.

"She was choking, so we intubated her to clear the airway."

"OK," he managed. "She's my niece."

"I assumed daughter. I'm sorry."

"It's fine. Dr. Squire . . ." Jason gritted his teeth to keep his emotions under control. ". . . is she gonna—"

"She was on the verge of an overdose when you brought her in, and she's still unconscious. The next few hours are critical, but I think she's going to pull through." She paused. "Her blood test revealed almost three times the normal limit of alcohol along with a good deal of methamphetamine and alprazolam. Once she regains consciousness, we'll need to move her to the detoxification unit."

"I understand," Jason said, breathing a deep sigh of relief. "Thank you."

———

Jason sat at the bedside for thirty minutes, watching his niece breathe, hoping for any further sign of life. Finally, needing to stretch his legs and also inform Satch of the status, he returned to the lobby.

And found an entourage of police officers waiting for him. One of the officers approached and started to open his mouth, and Jason put up his index finger. "Give me one second," he said, pushing past the officer and walking over to Satch, who was standing and bouncing on his toes. The bearded man's eyes were bloodshot red, which was typical of the colonel. "She's gonna be OK," Jason said to Satch.

The older man stuck his hands in his pockets and looked at the floor. "Good," he grunted.

"Still unconscious," Jason continued. "But the doctor says she should make it." He let out a breath. "Gonna be a long haul," he said.

"She's been through a lot," Satch said.

Jason nodded.

"And so have you."

"My problems are just heating up," Jason said, glancing at the group of uniforms. "Let me get this over with."

Jason ambled over, and the lead officer, Sergeant George Mitchell, asked him to sit down. "Long time, no see," Jason said, hoping to strike up some humor with the lawman he'd cross-examined for several hours a couple of days prior.

Mitchell's face was blank. "Mr. Rich, I'm sorry about your niece. I do have some questions about the incident."

"I'm sure you do."

Jason then answered every one of them, basically telling the truth, choosing his words carefully when it came to his conversation with Kevin Martin. All he said about that was that he had asked Martin to leave the dock so that he could take Nola home and that Martin had agreed. He didn't mention K-Mart's drug dealing or anything about Tyson Cade. He also agreed to pay all charges related to shooting up the house and make full restitution. "I'm sorry," he said. "I just didn't know what else to do."

"We still have to charge you with destruction of property and breaking and entering."

Jason couldn't believe his ears. "No, you don't."

"We'll also check and see if you have a gun permit. If you don't, then that'll be another charge."

"I do have a gun permit, and I was trying to save my niece's life when I broke into the Waters's old home. My *family's* old home."

"Sir, I'm just doing my job." He paused. "The Martin kid says you threatened him with a gun."

Jason gripped the side of his chair and squeezed. He couldn't believe how stupid he'd been to talk. The shock of the last few hours must have drained him of his senses. "I did no such thing. He's lying."

"Your word against his."

"He pushed me. If you charge me with anything, then I'm going to file a report against him."

"Funny. You didn't mention him pushing you just now when you were describing what happened."

"It wasn't relevant. I thought you were investigating the near drowning of my niece and my shooting of the back door of the house."

"We decide what's relevant. Now . . ." His expression was cold and unwavering. ". . . you have the right to remain silent."

49

Jason didn't waste his one phone call.

Izzy answered on the first ring. "We are going to own the Marshall County Sheriff's Office, you hear me? I'm going to have the deed to that place in seven days." Her voice shook with fury.

"Glad you're on it. You can start by getting me out of here. But first, check on Nola."

"The colonel is staying at the hospital. Last word from him—he doesn't say much, you know—was that she still hadn't woken up, but he won't leave until you come back."

"Good," Jason said, feeling a rush of relief.

"I can't get anyone on the phone because it's so late, and the clerk I spoke with said that the earliest that a judge would be available to set bail would be nine in the morning. I'm sorry, Jason."

"I understand." Jason leaned his head against the old pay phone on the wall that the inmates had to use. He was exhausted. "Before you talk about bail, go see Shay. The last conversation I had with her was pleasant. Given the facts, my arrest seems clearly retaliatory."

"You think? She is the first person I plan to see."

"Good. Thanks, Iz."

"I told that clerk if a hair on your beautiful head is out of place when I see you, I'm going to sue them for everything under the sun. That they better make sure all their surveillance cameras are working and that I would not stand for any retribution against you for representing the man accused of killing one of their peers."

"I hope that works."

"I think I was very persuasive."

"I bet you were. Bye, Iz."

Jason was led back to a tiny holding cell. Inside was a cot with a thin white sheet as covers. He sat down, and the mattress was as hard as the concrete floor. He thought back to the speech he'd given himself a few hours earlier.

"I'm really stepping up," he whispered, lying down on the cot. *Nola almost died tonight, and I'm in jail.*

Jason closed his eyes, trying to wish away the last thought that came into his mind, but it was no use.

I need a drink.

50

He was back under the water. How deep was impossible to tell. He had his arms wrapped around Nola, and he was struggling for breath. He turned her around and tried to push off the floor of the lake, but his feet dug into the sand. Instead of going up, he began to sink deeper. He looked at Nola, and her eyes were open. She mouthed *"Help,"* but her look was vacant. Jason squatted and tried to dig himself out of the sand, but he only fell farther down. Now, half his body was submerged in the sand. He looked up, and Nola was gone. Now, Jana was staring at him. She was shaking her head.

You are so weak.

Jason heard the words as if they were breathed into his ear. He ground his teeth. He was now covered to the chest in the lake's sandy bottom. He saw a snake slither past him. He reached toward Jana, and she was gone. In her stead was the silhouette of Tyson Cade. "I liked your sister," Cade said. "I really liked her."

Jason was now covered to his neck. He looked at Cade.

"She was strong, but you're weak."

Weak. Cade's voice.

Weak. Jana again.

Then, as his mouth filled with sand, he saw his father, Lucas Rich. Even ten feet under water, he was wearing a suit and tie.

You're weak, son.

Jason's head submerged under the sand. He heard a clanging sound. He tried to move, but he couldn't. Nor could he breathe. But he could still see. Next to him were Nola and Niecy. Chase. Izzy. Harry. Satch. Mickey and Chuck. Their eyes were closed. They were dead.

You've always been weak. Jana again. *And now they're all dead.*

More clanging.

"Rich?" A strange voice.

Dead. Jana. Now louder.

"Jason?" He felt hands on him, and he screamed, turning away from all the noise.

———

Jason's eyes flew open when his shoulder hit the concrete floor, and he yelped in pain. He gazed upward, and his vision was blurry. A woman wearing a dark suit was standing above him. He scrambled to his feet, breathing hard.

"It's OK," Shay said. "You were having a nightmare."

Jason continued to pant and placed his hands on his knees.

"Why don't you sit on the cot," Shay said.

Jason eased himself down on the hard surface and folded his arms tight across his chest. He was shaking.

"I talked with your partner this morning," Shay said. "I was able to get Judge Barber to set bail."

Jason raised his eyebrows.

"It was $15,000. Ms. Montaigne is in the process of wiring the funds. You should be out in an hour. Tops."

Jason swept a hand through his hair and looked himself over. He was still wearing the clothes he'd worn when he'd jumped into Lake Guntersville last night. He smelled like dirt and sweat. He peered at Shay and felt heat on his cheeks. "I was trying to save my niece's life."

"I can't talk with you about the facts."

"I didn't do anything wrong."

Shay bit her lip. It appeared as if she wanted to say something but stopped herself. "I just wanted you to know that you will be out soon."

"Are you going to dismiss the charges?"

"I need to talk with Sergeant Mitchell first and circle the wagons with my officers."

"Shay, please. I was trying—"

"I have to do my job, Jason." She was gazing down at the floor, her shoulders slumped. She had her left hand on her hip, and her right hand was massaging her neck as if she might have a crick in it.

"Shay . . ." He trailed off. He could think of nothing else to say. He was exhausted and still reeling from the nightmare he'd just had.

The prosecutor sighed and turned away. As the cell door clanged shut, she finally met his eyes. "I'm sorry."

"I bet," Jason said, scowling at her.

As Shay walked away, Jason rubbed his face with his hands.

Despite the district attorney's seeming reluctance, Jason knew the score. His arrest was a gift to the sheriff's department. They could slander him now all in the name of doing their job. *Destruction of property. Shooting up a Buck Island mansion. Threatening a minor.*

And on and on. Regardless of her demeanor in the cell, Shay Lankford had to be loving this development. The jury would already be slanted against Trey Cowan. Marshall County was a conservative venue, where the police were revered. Add to that Cowan's attorney being a criminal, and things went from bad to impossible.

Jason stood and rested his face against the cold iron bars. But that wasn't the worst of it. He'd have to report the charges to the Alabama State Bar. He was operating under a zero-tolerance policy, and he might be put on probation again. *Or worse . . .*

He'd jeopardized his career. Again.

Jason squeezed the bars, trying to maintain his composure.

And then there was Nola. And Chase. What was he going to do?

It's my fault, Jason thought, gazing around the tiny confines of the holding cell and trying not to let depression consume him.

Focus, he thought. *Focus only on what we can control.*

It was a lesson of AA. As Jason gazed through the opening in the iron bars of the holding cell, he knew he would need to lean on everything he'd learned to get himself out of this mess.

He thought back to the nightmare he was having when the district attorney entered the cell. He was no psychiatrist, but he thought he knew what it meant.

"I'm in over my head," he whispered.

And I'm going to take everyone I love down with me.

51

At 10:00 a.m., Jason walked out of the Marshall County Jail to a cascade of flashbulbs and microphones. He still wore the golf shirt and jeans from the night before, and he knew he must look terrible. Izzy, who gripped his forearm and wore a charcoal-gray suit, said that he needed to look the part. Today, he was the victim.

"Mr. Rich, are you going to contest the charges?"

"What were you doing at the old Waters home on Buck Island?"

"Mr. Rich, isn't it true that you are on probation with the Alabama State Bar? Will these charges affect that?" The voice sounded familiar, and Jason glanced and saw his friend Kisha Roe. Her face was all business. She was a reporter, and this was her job. As Jason climbed into the back seat of the waiting SUV, he saw Harry in the driver's seat.

"Amigo," Harry said.

Jason nodded. His mouth was dry, his brain frazzled.

Jason listened as Izzy addressed the mob of reporters. "My partner dove into Lake Guntersville last night and pulled his niece out of the water. He's a hero who should be treated as such. Instead, the Marshall County Sheriff's Office has filed a bunch of frivolous charges in a clear effort to defame his name and to retaliate against him for taking the Trey Cowan case. Their behavior will not stand."

"Are you going to sue the sheriff's department?" Kisha's voice again.

"We're going to sue the sheriff, his office, the district attorney, and anyone else who had anything to do whatsoever with these ridiculous charges."

"Is Mr. Rich all right?" Kisha asked again, concern in her voice.

"He almost drowned last night. He was treated in the emergency room. His niece almost died. What do you think? No more questions." Izzy opened the door, and Jason scooted to the left to make room for her. "Drive," she said to Harry.

As the Explorer pulled onto Blount Avenue, Jason looked at her. "Thank you."

"No need for that, Jason Rich. Charging you with those crimes was a declaration of war." She stared at him, her eyes ablaze. "They don't have any clue who they're dealing with."

52

"Mind telling me how all these reporters found out that Jason Rich was being held at the jail?" Shay glared at Sheriff Richard Griffith.

"Small town, Shay. Jason Rich is a celebrity around here. There's literally no telling. Someone at the hospital could have tipped them off."

"Or a deputy in your office . . . at your direction."

"I would never do that."

"Right."

"Forget the press coverage, Shay. Rich's arrest is good news for us. This is Marshall County. Folks around here don't like showboaters, and they do like cops. Rich being charged with a crime is completely in line with who everyone probably already thinks he is."

"What if he sues us? You ready for that?"

"We have qualified immunity, and he shot up a house and threatened a teenager with a pistol. I'd say we're in good shape. If his partner wants to file a lawsuit over that, then I've got two words for that crazy bitch. Bring it."

"Tough talk, Griff. That *crazy bitch* is smart as hell. If she can show an intentional act of retaliation, she could get around qualified immunity, couldn't she?"

He put his hands on his hips.

"Couldn't she?"

"I don't know. You'd have to ask our civil rights lawyers."

"And isn't that just what we need? A lawsuit on the heels of Hatty Daniels's disappearance."

Griff's face reddened. "What's wrong with you? I thought you'd be happy about this. Jason Rich has been a thorn in our side since he returned to Guntersville."

"I don't want a tainted victory."

"He did this to himself, Shay." Griff walked toward the door.

"Any leads on finding Hatty?"

He stopped and glared at her. "No."

53

Before going home, Jason stopped at Marshall Medical Center North. He went to her room, where Nola was lying in the bed. The tube that had been down her throat was out, but an IV was still latched to her arm. Jason walked toward her and planted a kiss on her cheek. He saw her chest move up and down. Then, her eyelashes batted, and she squinted up at him. "Uncle Jason?"

He felt a rush of emotion that came out in an anguished sob. He pressed his face into her neck. *Thank you, God.*

"Uncle Jason . . . I'm s-s-so tired."

He patted her forehead and turned to the man sitting at her bedside.

Satch had his legs crossed and his arms folded across his chest. His eyes were alert, albeit a bit redder than normal. If he was tired from staying up all night, he didn't show it. "She regained consciousness about three hours ago."

"Man, that's good news," Jason said.

"It is," Satch said. "Afraid I've got some bad."

"What?"

"We found Chase's shotguns."

Jason frowned. "Go on."

"The newer one was still in its gun case. Dust on the barrel and handle. Looked like it hadn't been used in a while."

"And the old one?"

"In the trunk of her car. Next to a five pack of Remington buckshot shells." He paused. "The pack was open."

"How many were left?"

"Three."

Jason felt dizzy. Kelly Flowers had been shot twice from close range. *Two shots. Two missing shells . . .*

"Uncle Jason?" Nola whimpered.

"Yeah, honey?"

"I'm sorry."

It was the same thing she'd said before diving into the lake.

"It's not your fault, honey," Jason said. "None of this is." Then, turning to Satch, he added, "It's mine."

PART FOUR

54

Hatty Daniels waited in the reception area of the law office. One week had turned into two and a half, but he'd finally agreed to meet with her. A woman with strawberry-blonde hair who'd introduced herself as Lona sat at a desk a few feet away, typing furiously on her computer. Her phone buzzed, and she picked it up, glancing at Hatty. Then she put the receiver down. "He'll see you now."

She was escorted down a narrow hallway and into a conference room. Lona asked if she wanted coffee, water, or a soft drink, but Hatty declined. Her stomach had twisted into a knot, and she doubted she could eat or drink anything until after this conference was over. She took a seat and waited, feeling her heartbeat thudding in her chest. For the past eighteen days, she'd stayed as a houseguest of Frannie Storm. She hadn't checked in with Griff or Shay or anyone else with the Marshall County Sheriff's Office. According to Frannie, there'd been a bulletin asking for any information regarding Hatty's whereabouts, but Frannie had ignored it. *Not until you see him,* she'd said. In the interim, Hatty had taken long walks in the morning and reviewed the materials in her investigative file of Kelly Flowers at least once a day. She did Google searches related to her predicament, which only confused her more. She was a law enforcement officer, a damn good detective, but she wasn't a lawyer.

When he entered the room, he took up almost the entire door. "Hatty Daniels," he said, his voice deep and firm. "It's been a long time."

"Bo," she managed, biting her lip. "Thank you for agreeing to a meeting."

Bocephus Aurulius Haynes had practiced law in Pulaski for almost thirty years. Before going to law school, he'd been an All-American linebacker for Coach Paul "Bear" Bryant at Alabama and would have likely enjoyed a long professional career if he hadn't blown his knee out. At six feet, four inches tall and at least 240 pounds, Bo still looked every bit the former football player he had been. He wore blue jeans, a black button-down shirt, and boots. His bald head made him look a bit like Michael Jordan. He was the only Black trial attorney in Pulaski, and even now, some twelve years since she'd last seen him, he was still a good-looking man.

"I followed that Odell Champagne case a couple years ago," she said. "You did a phenomenal job. As always."

"Thank you," Bo said, taking a seat at the head of the table and placing a notebook and a pen in front of him.

"Is the General still kicking everyone's ass?"

Bo laughed, and Hatty joined in. "The General" was Helen Evangeline Lewis, the district attorney general of Giles County, Tennessee.

"Yep," he said. "Would you expect any different?"

She shook her head. "I heard you helped her out of a jam a few years back too. Her husband's case."

Bo nodded. "She's a fine lady. Very good at her job." He paused. "Just like you. Hatty, I'm sorry we couldn't meet sooner. My schedule's a bit crazy. But I'm here now. What's going on?"

For the next hour, she told him everything she knew. Bo took a few notes, asked several questions, and eventually stood and began to pace around the conference-room table.

"Can you help me?" Hatty asked.

Bo sat on the table and folded his arms. "I'm a trial lawyer, Hatty. I've handled contract cases, but it's been a while. You might be better with someone else."

She snorted. "Better than Bocephus Haynes? Surely you jest."

"I don't," Bo said. "I'm not a magician, and I have a wheelhouse. Personal injury plaintiff's work and the occasional criminal defense is my toolbox."

"You're the only one I trust. I remember going against you, Bo. In our cases, you were tough but fair." She sucked in a breath. "And you're smart. You always seemed to have an angle."

For a long moment, Bo gazed at her.

"I'll pay you whatever your rate is for this kind of work. I have money." She swallowed, and her mouth tasted dry. "At least I do now."

"I'll have to check the whistleblower laws in Alabama, but I don't think you really have that here. No one has threatened you with retaliation for coming forward with the results of the Flowers investigation, correct?"

"Correct. But someone in that office deleted files on my computer, and I know I was being followed when I left. Either by my own employer or—"

"This meth dealer," Bo interrupted, beginning to pace again. "Hatty, sometimes these types of cases involve stuff that goes on outside the courtroom. Believe me, I've had a few . . . especially here recently . . . where just staying alive to get to the verdict was as much a consideration as the case itself." He looked at her. "Do you know what I mean?"

"I think so."

"I'll do some research, and let's regroup in a few days."

"That sounds great, Bo." She stood and approached him. "I appreciate this so much."

"I haven't done anything yet."

She walked to the door.

"Hatty?"

"Yes." She turned to face him.

"What's your endgame?"

"What?"

253

"Your goal. What do you want here?"

Hatty had thought about little else over the course of the past eighteen days. "I want to return to my job. I've worked hard to be the head of investigations. I have at least ten active cases that need to be worked."

"You realize your actions could be seen as abandonment."

"Yes, but I didn't have any other choice." Her voice began to shake. "I was scared, Bo. I've been scared before. This job isn't for the faint of heart." She bit down on her bottom lip. "But nothing like this. Please . . ." She took a deep breath and looked at the hardwood floor. "Please help me."

For several seconds, there was silence. Then she felt his large hands cover her own, and she looked up into his dark eyes.

"If I can, I will."

55

The arraignment of a capital murder defendant was a big moment in a criminal trial. As Jason glanced over his shoulder, he saw that all rows of courtroom 1 of the Marshall County Courthouse were filled. He noticed media people he recognized, including Kisha. There were also several town and county dignitaries. Mayor Annie Caudle. A couple members of the Guntersville Chamber of Commerce. County Commissioner Rex Patterson. He figured the politicos were here to show their public support for a fallen officer. Any chance to stand behind the police was an opportunity to stoke the flames of support leading into November elections.

Sitting directly behind the prosecution table was a young woman with dark-brown hair. She wore an elegant black dress. *Bella Flowers,* Jason thought. There'd been a picture of her in the *Advertiser-Gleam*'s article on the funeral of Kelly Flowers, and Jason recognized her right off. In fact, it appeared that she might be wearing the same dress. As Tyson Cade and Bull Branner had both mentioned, she was attractive, though, in her conservative outfit, it was hard to imagine her "dancing the pole," as Bull had said. Seeing her was a reminder that he needed to meet with Bella if she was agreeable. That was a box he needed to check. Kelly Flowers seemed to be kind of an enigma. Perhaps a family member could shed some light on the man behind the uniform.

The bailiff announced the judge's presence, and Terry Barber walked to the bench with what seemed to be a spring in his step. Barber also was facing reelection, and was there anything better for a judge than to be seen wearing the robe and making rulings in a high-profile case? Jason doubted it.

Especially when there were two cases that would put him in the public eye.

Jason kept his expression neutral as His Honor ascended the bench, but inside, he was seething. He knew that Barber had intentionally set his arraignment in the state's bullshit attempted assault of a minor and destruction of property charges on the same day as Trey Cowan's capital murder case to turn the dial on the publicity all the way to the right.

Jason took in a deep breath, knowing that today was going to be a kangaroo court but resolving that there wasn't a damn thing he could do about it.

"State of Alabama versus Trey Jerome Cowan." Judge Barber spoke with his nasal southern twang. "Are the parties here?"

"Yes, Your Honor," Shay said, standing and pressing down on her burgundy suit.

"And the defendant?"

"Yes, sir," Jason said.

"OK, then. The defendant shall remain standing. Mr. Cowan, you have been charged with the intentional murder of Sergeant Kelly Flowers, and the state is seeking the death penalty." He paused. "Do you understand the charges levied against you?"

"Yes, sir." Trey's voice was calm and firm.

"How do you plead?"

"Not guilty."

"All right, Counsel, please approach."

Once Shay and Jason were both below him at the bench, Judge Barber put on a pair of spectacles and looked down at what appeared to be a calendar. "Today is June 3. When do you think this one will be ready for trial?"

"The defendant would like this case set as quickly as possible," Jason said.

Barber smirked. "The defendant or his lawyer?"

Jason didn't take the bait. He kept his mouth shut and gazed at the judge.

"Well . . . we can do that. But, regardless of how quick a setting Mr. Cowan receives, the charges brought against you, Mr. Rich, will be set first. A capital murder case will take longer to get ready for trial than an attempted assault and destruction of property case. Isn't that right, Madame Prosecutor?"

"Yes, Your Honor."

"Mr. Rich, don't you have a hearing in front of the state bar's disciplinary commission pretty soon?"

"More of a meeting than a hearing, sir. But yes, in a few weeks."

"And you are currently operating under a consent order, correct?"

Jason worked his jaw, knowing that he must maintain his composure. "Yes, Your Honor."

"Perhaps Mr. Cowan would be better off retaining a different lawyer. You don't want to add ineffective assistance of counsel to your list of problems, do you, Mr. Rich?"

"I've explained my situation to my client, and he wishes to proceed with me as his attorney. The defense can be ready for trial in sixty days."

Barber turned to Shay. "And the state?"

"We would recommend six months, Your Honor. At a minimum."

The judge took off his glasses and chewed on the stem. "Let's go with four months. That's one hundred and twenty days and splits the baby." He licked his fingers and turned a page in his calendar. He returned his spectacles to the bridge of his nose and cleared his throat. "Trial is set for October 14."

Jason returned to his table and put his arm around his client. "Now the real work begins."

"Thank you for sticking with me," Trey said. "I know you're dealing with a lot."

"You're welcome," Jason said. He could have said "I have no choice," but what was the point? At least Trey was beginning to appreciate the sacrifices being made.

As two uniformed guards led Trey Cowan away, Jason slid over into Trey's chair, and Isabel Montaigne took his former seat.

"State of Alabama versus Jason James Rich." Barber's voice boomed out into the courtroom louder than it had for Cowan's arraignment. Jason glanced over his shoulder. None of the crowd had left. Every spare seat was taken, and there were folks standing in the back.

"Well, since everyone is still here, let's get to it," Barber continued. "Will the defendant please stand?"

Jason and Izzy stood together. "Mr. Rich, you have been charged with attempted assault of a minor, harassing communications, destruction of property, and trespassing. How do you plead?"

"Not guilty to all charges," Jason said.

"Counsel, please approach." Jason and Izzy both walked to the bench, meeting Shay below the pulpit.

"Do we anticipate a trial in this one?" Barber looked at the prosecutor, but Izzy was first to speak, her tone confident and full of energy.

"Your Honor, Mr. Rich has already paid full and complete restitution to the owners of the home, who have informed the state of their desire that the destruction of property and trespassing claims be dropped. The other claims are also based on the word of a seventeen-year-old kid without any further support." Izzy paused. "Unless all the charges are dismissed, we do expect a trial."

"Ms. Lankford?" Barber asked, a trace of irritation in his tone.

"The state has offered several plea deals, and the defendant has refused. Obviously, paying restitution to the Cornelius family for the damage to their home is a key consideration, as are their wishes."

Jerry and Susan Cornelius had bought the old Waters home and had been happy to accept a $50,000 check to repair the door and windows in return for a full and complete release of all civil claims they could have brought against Jason.

"What are your thoughts regarding a trial date?" Barber looked at Shay.

"Ninety days," Shay said, her voice tired.

"And what does the defendant say regarding trial, Ms. Montag . . . ?"

"Montaigne," Izzy said. "The *g* is silent. We would like a trial date as soon as possible."

"Really?" Judge Barber asked. "I would have thought Mr. Rich would have wanted to wait as long as he could, given that the outcome of these charges could affect his ability to practice law."

"On the contrary, Your Honor," Izzy said. "My client wants a speedy trial. As soon as the jury's not-guilty verdict is rendered, we have a civil suit that we will be filing."

"That so?"

"Yes, sir."

"I'm going to set trial in this matter for October 7."

"Your Honor, that's—" Izzy started, but was cut off by the judge.

"My final ruling." Barber stood from the bench. "We're adjourned."

56

Fifteen minutes later, they holed up at a table at JaMoka's Coffee Company a block from the courthouse. The mood was somber.

"I'm sorry," Izzy said.

"You did the best you could," Jason said, sipping from a steaming cup of black coffee, which was the best in town. "The charges are frivolous, and Shay knows it."

"Can't we get some help from our resident drug dealer?" Izzy said. "I mean, the Martin kid works for him, and it is this *K-Mart* that is the state's star witness."

"I've had Satch reach out to him, but Cade is probably enjoying having leverage over me."

"But couldn't we implicate Cade if your case ever goes to trial?"

"The kid will never give Cade up. Besides, he could probably truthfully testify that he's never seen Tyson Cade." Jason snorted. "I'm sure we could finagle some testimony from someone—hell, Nola if we had to have it—that K-Mart sold them drugs, but he would just deny it."

"You could threaten to pull out of the Cowan case."

"I've already done that."

"And?"

"Cade said that if I withdrew as counsel for Trey, I was a dead man. And that he'd kill you. And Harry. And Nola, Niecy, and Chase. And the Tonidandels."

"Damnit," Izzy said. "Remind me again how we all got mixed up with this rattlesnake? Oh, yeah. Your sister, Jana. The gift that keeps on giving."

"Izzy, please, she's—"

"I'm sorry," she said. "I know you loved her and that she's dead, but damnit, Jason Rich. Was she worth the shitstorm you've been in ever since you got here?"

Jason gazed into his cup. "I was in a shitstorm of my own making when I came here. At least this one's Jana's fault." He forced a smile.

"We aren't getting anywhere with this talk." Harry's firm voice finally broke through. "Are we going to sit here and whine, or are we going to play the hand we've been dealt?"

"Harry's right," Jason said, putting his hands on the table. "We have a lot of work to do. Izzy, I still need a meeting with Colleen Maples. Any luck?"

"She's a broken record. Nothing to say and refuses to meet."

"Then threaten her with a deposition. That we'll subpoena her and make her answer my questions."

"That would be risky and foolish."

"I didn't say we'd actually do it," Jason fired back. "Just throw it out there and see if that helps persuade her. All I need is fifteen minutes."

"OK."

Jason turned to Harry. "Anything new in the surveillance on Matty Dean?"

"Nothing. Still haven't seen him and K-Mart together. I think it's a waste of time."

"Satch says Dean has been with Cade from the beginning. If we're liable to catch a break, it's from watching him. Have you learned anything else about the relationship between Flowers and Cowan?"

"Nothing," Harry said. "Every avenue has been a dead end. Sand Mountain folks are tight lipped and stick together. I'm sorry, J. R. You may want to ask the Tonidandels to help with that line of investigation. Being local, they may have better luck."

"Good idea," Jason said, knowing he was stretching the brothers pretty thin with the security they were doing for him. Also knowing that he'd already asked Satch to look into Cowan and Flowers, and he'd turned up nothing either.

"Or maybe Trey will finally break his silence."

"You know he won't," Jason said.

Harry grunted in begrudging agreement, and Jason turned to his partner. "Iz, Flowers's sister was in court today. Did you see her?"

"Yes."

"Have you been able to speak with her yet?"

"No. I'm not sure the number Harry found is still good. And, even if it is, she may be screening us."

Jason looked at his investigator. "Have you determined which strip club she dances at?"

"Her current spot is Jimmy's Lounge. Do you want me to approach her?"

"Oh, I'm sure you'll love that," Izzy teased, elbowing him.

"Business is business," Harry fired back, and she pointed her index finger at him.

"Why don't we go together?" Jason volunteered. "We can keep each other out of trouble."

"Good idea," Izzy said.

"All right, what about Detective Daniels?" Jason asked.

"Still AWOL," Harry said. "All I've been able to discern from the sheriff's department is that she's taken an indefinite leave of absence."

"Something is up there," Jason said, running his thumb down his mug before taking another sip. "Iz, in our discovery, let's be sure to ask for her personnel file and all information regarding her current whereabouts. And Harry, do some digging on your own. Find out all you can on Daniels. Background, prior jobs, et cetera."

Harry nodded while Izzy took out her phone and began moving her thumbs. "On it," she said.

"Harry, one more thing. Remember how you tracked Walt Cowan to the Highway 30A area of the panhandle last year."

"Need him again?"

"I do. One thing Trey has told me is that he's not a good shot and has only fired a weapon a few times in his life."

"Amigo, it's not all that hard to shoot a twelve gauge and hit something from only a few feet."

"From the cab of a truck? Isn't that kind of tight space for a shotgun?"

Harry scratched his face. "Awkward for sure."

"Based on Mitchell's limited testimony at the prelim and Daniels's investigative report, the state's theory will probably be that the first shot was fired from inside the truck while the second blast came from outside."

Harry was nodding along. "Based on the fact that one spent shell casing was found in the cab of Trey's truck while the other was discovered near Flowers's body."

"Exactly." Jason licked his lips. "Trey was intoxicated and not experienced with firearms. The state's theory hinges on the killer successfully pulling off an awkward shot from inside the cab of a truck and through the opening in a window."

Harry continued to nod. "No glass, so, if the shot was fired inside the vehicle, it must have been through either the passenger-side or driver's-side window. Which, with a bulky twelve-gauge shotgun, would be a bit tedious." Harry mimicked the move a person would have to make, turning his shoulders to the left and pulling his right arm back to attempt a driver's-side blast and then twisting his whole body to the right for the passenger window shot. "Easier out the driver's side, in my opinion, especially if he gets the whole gun out the opening. Much easier. The passenger-side shot would require a bit more twisting." He sipped his coffee. "Not impossible."

"But for a drunk not familiar or very good at shooting?" Jason pressed.

"It's something," Harry said. "But how are we going to get around the fact that the shotgun that killed Kelly Flowers was likely our client's, found in his truck with only his prints?"

Jason grinned. "Still working on that one."

Harry scoffed. "All right, I'll find Walt Cowan."

Jason gave him a fist bump. "Good man." Then he turned to Izzy. "How does our calendar look the rest of the week?"

She gazed back at her phone. "Status conferences in Birmingham and Tuscaloosa tomorrow, both at nine in the morning. I thought I'd handle Birmingham, and you can take Tuscaloosa."

Jason nodded his agreement.

"Motion docket in Mobile Wednesday with depositions in Biloxi, Mississippi, on Thursday and Friday in that Loggins trucking case. I can take the depos if you—"

"I've got them."

"Jason, what if the state bar suspends you again?"

"Innocent until proven guilty, Iz. They won't do that on a charge."

Izzy grabbed his hand. "The commission has discretion to do whatever it wants and . . ." She stuck her tongue out at him. ". . . they don't like you."

"My earlier suspension was related to alcohol abuse, and the current charges aren't related in any way. I think the bar's attorney will have my back, and so will Ashley."

"Ashley? Your *mentor*?"

"Iz, I don't trust anyone either, including Ashley, but she's been supportive so far, and she said she'd go to bat for me in front of the commission."

"I hope you're right."

Jason stood. The discussion about the week ahead had charged him up. He had work to do, and action of any kind was better than sitting around feeling sorry for himself. "The plane ready?"

"Yep."

"All right. Anything else?"

"Yes." Harry's voice was grave.

"What?" Jason asked.

"Sit down."

Jason almost protested but thought better of it. He took his seat. "What?" he repeated.

"J. R., I know you don't want to hear this, but there seems to be a rather obvious person that you need to interview in the Cowan matter."

For a moment, the table was silent. Jason looked from Izzy to Harry and then into his mug.

"It's been almost sixty days," Izzy finally said.

"I know," Jason said.

"We know what you're afraid of, J. R.," Harry continued. "But you owe it to your client . . . and yourself . . . to go hear it from the horse's mouth."

"You're right," Jason finally said, standing again and looking at his partner and then his investigator. "Iz, tell the pilot that we're staying in Mobile on Wednesday. I can rent a car and drive to Perdido from there."

"Will do," Izzy said as Jason walked around them to the door. "Hey," she called out.

Jason turned to her.

"This is all going to work out."

He forced a smile and walked out the door.

57

Six hours after the arraignments of Trey Cowan and Jason Rich, Shay Lankford strode into Sheriff Griffith's office and shut the door. She dropped several stapled stacks of paper on his desk.

"Discovery from Rich in the Cowan case," Shay said. "He wants the personnel file of Hatty Daniels and all documents related to her current leave of absence."

Griff crossed his arms. "What does any of that have to do with Kelly Flowers's murder?"

"Nothing," Shay said. "I'll serve objections, but I may have to turn over some of it. What's the status?"

"She has an attorney in Pulaski, and we've negotiated a paid leave of absence."

"Is she going to come back?"

"I don't know."

"Griff, what's the deal?"

"The less I tell you, the better. The county attorney instructed us to keep quiet."

Now Shay folded her arms. "Well, that's good advice, but it doesn't help me any. I'd like Hatty back for the Cowan trial. I think I can keep out any evidence of her leave of absence if it truly has nothing to do with Trey Cowan or Kelly Flowers." She took a step toward the sheriff. "Can you confirm that her leaving isn't related to either?"

"Like I said . . . I can't talk about it."

Shay bit her lip and leaned over the desk. "Griff, if there is some correlation, I need to know as soon as possible. We have four months to trial, but you can't spring something on me at the last minute. That could cost us the case." She paused. "And us both the election."

"I won't," he said.

"Good."

58

Tyson Cade sat on a bale of hay inside the barn. He took a piece of grass and stuck it in his mouth. Like every teenager who grew up in Alder Springs, he'd enjoyed drinking and partying at Branner's Place. He'd lost his virginity not far from here in the cab of his first truck. *Good times,* Tyson thought, pushing off the stack and pacing the huge area. Now, he used the space for his business.

Since the murder of Kelly Flowers, he'd avoided this location, but given who he was meeting tonight, he figured this was an appropriate meetup spot.

The barn door creaked open, and a figure walked in wearing the khaki uniform of the Marshall County Sheriff's Office. Tyson sucked on the stem of grass and waved the man over to him. "So?" Tyson said, squinted up at him.

"Detective Daniels is in Pulaski. She has a lawyer. We are trying to negotiate her return."

"Is she going to testify in the Flowers murder trial?"

"Still up in the air, but if the district attorney has any say in the matter, then yes."

"And if she testifies, that puts Flowers's former position as my inside source in jeopardy."

"It does. In fact, the defendant has requested the personnel files of Flowers and Daniels and all documents related to investigations of either." He sighed. "Hatty's disappearance is fishy, and Jason Rich isn't stupid. If he obtains Hatty's file . . ."

"I thought you deleted that."

"I did, but Hatty Daniels isn't stupid. I'm sure she made a copy of everything. In fact, her attorney all but confirmed it."

"And who is her attorney?"

"Bocephus Haynes. A local Pulaski lawyer."

"Any good?"

"Very good. He has a reputation as a strong trial attorney and an overall badass."

"Well . . . that's not a good development. Would have been nice if you had just let me handle her before she left town." He sucked on the grass. "Instead of saying you could do it yourself."

The lawman stuffed his hands in his pockets. "I had hoped . . . there'd be another way. I like Hatty."

Tyson guffawed and threw the string of grass on the barn floor. He approached the other man and patted his shoulders. Then he kneed him in the groin, and the officer grunted and knelt to the ground.

Tyson circled him and then kicked him in the ribs. Another groan, and the man fell onto his back.

Finally, as the other man gasped for breath, Tyson knelt beside him. "You can't do business with me if you are going to let your emotions and selfish interests get in the way of our needs. That was Kelly Flowers's downfall. Now, you are an upgrade over Kelly, but there will be times when you have to follow through with my wishes if you want to continue receiving that nice chunk of cash I'm giving you each month." He thumped him over the ear, a trick his mother used to do on Tyson to get his attention. "You need that money, don't you?" He lowered his voice down to a whisper. "Your girlfriend in Huntsville . . . still needs her stipend, doesn't she?"

The new mole in the Marshall County Sheriff's Office pulled himself to his knees. Then to his feet, clutching his ribs.

"You came to me, remember?" Tyson continued. "After Detective Daniels had figured out that Kelly Flowers was my inside guy. It was you that offered to take Kelly's place, provided of course that I pay your number. Remember?" When there was no answer, Tyson backhanded him. "Do you?"

"Yes."

"But you got impatient, didn't you?" Tyson teased. "Is that why you killed Kelly?" He paused. "Or maybe it has something to do with that girlfriend of yours . . ."

"Trey Cowan killed Kelly."

"Ah, yes. Trey Cowan. The wunderkind quarterback." Tyson walked over to another bale of hay and snatched a piece of grass, smelling it. "The ultimate patsy."

"All the evidence points to Trey as the killer."

"You were supposed to let me handle Flowers," Tyson said, sticking the string of grass in his mouth and beginning to chew. "I could have made him disappear."

"How was I supposed to know that Trey Cowan would go off the deep end?"

"You screwed up. With Flowers. And now again with Detective Daniels. I'm beginning to wonder if you are an upgrade after all."

The other man swallowed. "I don't see a way that Hatty can take the stand and not reveal the results of her investigation of Flowers."

Tyson approached him and threw the wet blade of grass at him. "Then there seems to be only one solution. Are you going to stay out of my way?"

The lawman frowned. "She's my friend."

Tyson squinted at him. "I don't think you understand the magnitude of the deal you've made."

"I just wish there was another—"

Tyson kicked him as hard as he could in the knee. The lawman fell in a heap, and Tyson stuck his foot on his neck.

As the officer struggled for breath, Tyson spoke in a low voice. "Your first loyalty is to me. Not Marshall County. Not your friends.

Me." He removed his foot, and the mole gasped for breath. Tyson walked over to the bale of hay he'd been sitting on when the other man arrived and snatched the briefcase. He brought it over and dropped it on the lawman's chest. "Your monthly draw."

Tyson started to walk away.

"Tyson?"

Tyson made his way to the barn doors.

"Cade?" the officer's voice was desperate.

As he opened the door and strode into the hot summer night, Tyson Cade shook his head and looked over his shoulder. "Evening."

Then he slammed the door.

59

Jason stood with Harry on the tarmac as the pilot made his final preparations.

"How long do you think you'll be gone?"

Jason stuffed his hands in his pockets. "A week. Maybe two." He sighed. "Maybe longer. Between the hearings, status conferences, and depositions, I just don't know how long it's going to take with Chase. And I need to make sure Nola is OK too."

Harry spat on the pavement. "You know, J. R., a person can only do so much. I'm worried."

"About what?"

"That we might not make it out of this one."

"Why do you say that?" Jason had never seen Harry Davenport exhibit one ounce of fear. Concern, yes. Worry? Maybe a little. But he'd never seen or heard Harry be scared.

"Because we are way out of our lane, J. R. I hate to always be the voice of reason, but you are a personal injury lawyer. You have billboards and commercials that ask people to call you if they have been injured so they can get rich. You run a racket, for God's sake, and you know it. That's what we do. We run cases. You, Izzy, and me. We run cases and settle them. It's a nice living."

"Harry—"

"Let me finish." He spat again. "There's a fine line between investigating a person's driving history in a wheels case and scoping out a methamphetamine dealer. You understand that, don't you?"

"Yes. Look, Harry, I know I've asked a lot of you and Izzy. This case is more about my life than it is my career, and I don't have many choices."

"I know that, amigo. And I know you have me watching K-Mart and Matthew Dean in the hopes that we might gain some leverage on all the things he has on you, but my gut tells me that we're playing checkers and Cade is playing chess." He grabbed Jason's shoulders. "Someone's going to get hurt."

Jason squelched a chuckle. There was nothing funny about what Harry was saying, and yet a sad smile still came. "Harry, my sister is dead. My brother-in-law is dead. Niecy almost got killed last year. Jackson Burns did get killed. Chase and Nola are both in rehab. People have already been hurt."

"Things can always get worse, J. R."

Jason sighed as the pilot gave him the thumbs-up sign. "Maybe so . . . but we have to try."

60

Matty Dean cast his line from the rocks above Mill Creek. As he reeled it in, Tyson sat down beside him.

"The counselor gone?" Tyson asked, as they both gazed across the water at the home of Jason Rich.

"Left this morning."

Tyson stretched his legs out over the rocks and cracked open a Sun Drop. He hadn't brought his pole tonight. This meeting would be short and to the point. "We've got a lot of balls in the air," he said.

"No one has ever juggled this business better than you."

Tyson sighed, wondering if that was true. His desire to control every aspect of the aftermath of Kelly Flowers's murder—his image in the Sand Mountain community, his new inside source in the sheriff's office, and, of course, Trey Cowan's lawyer—was beginning to catch up to him. Perhaps he should back off. Cut his losses and move on. Tyson took another long sip of Sun Drop and gave his head a jerk. *No. My instincts have never failed me. Focus on the problem at hand.*

"I need your help with a couple of . . . *projects.*"

"Say the word."

"Detective Hatty Daniels. I told our new mole that we would handle her before the Flowers trial."

"And by *handle*, can I assume you mean—"

"Yes . . . with a caveat."

"Damn, T. C., stop using words I don't understand." He snickered.

"An exception."

"Which is?"

"Daniels is a detective. A lifer in law enforcement."

"Which means she'll be packing."

"It means more than that, Matty. She has training, and she's smart. We can't just go in with guns blazing. We'll need to be subtle."

"Subtle is my middle name."

"I can't have us taking a shot and missing. I've got enough problems."

"If we don't kill her, I doubt we'll be able to persuade her to have a selective memory. We both know the Wittschen woman was ratting Flowers out."

"But we don't know what Wittschen learned and whether it leads back to me."

"Didn't our mole—"

"We have different agendas. Daniels's investigation of Flowers may include enough smoke to conclude that Flowers was dirty. But that doesn't mean there's enough there to charge me with a crime." Tyson paused and took a sip of Sun Drop. "Those two things are apples and oranges."

"I agree, but wouldn't the safest play be to kill her?"

"Yes. But I'm not sure it can be done without collateral damage."

"Why is that?"

"The name Bocephus Haynes mean anything to you?"

"No."

Tyson took a pebble and threw it sidearm into the lake, watching it skip one, two, three times. "He's Daniels's attorney. A bad dude. I had a client in Pulaski for a while. A big shot named Zannick whose right-hand man was Finn Pusser. Remember Finn?"

"Yeah, but I haven't heard much from him in a while."

"That's because Bo Haynes basically put him away. I think he's out of jail now, but he's not in the business anymore."

"So if we try to take out Daniels, we'll have to deal with Haynes." Matty snickered. "I mean, he's just a lawyer, right?"

"No," Tyson said. He'd always trusted his instincts, and they were sending distress signals now. "He's more than that."

"So what are you saying?"

"That we have to be careful. I want you to get the lay of the land in Pulaski and report back. If we think we have a good shot, then take it. If not or, God forbid, we do and we miss . . . then we move to plan B."

"Which is?"

"You let me figure that out. For now, I want you to get a couple of guys you trust and go to Pulaski. Find Daniels and size up the prospects of taking her out. Then call me."

"What about Rich's investigator?" Matty asked, casting his line again. "He's still tailing my ass, though I haven't seen him today." Matty had run the plates on the maroon SUV from Fire by the Lake, and sure enough, the vehicle was registered to Jason Rich. A couple of days later, they had photographs depicting Harry Davenport behind the wheel. Since then, the investigator had been following Matty on a regular basis. As of yet, they hadn't made a move on him.

Tyson Cade took a long sip of Sun Drop and then hurled the empty bottle into the lake. "I know," he said.

"Shouldn't we take him out before I head to Pulaski?"

Tyson walked up the rocks to the overpass, and Matty reeled in his line. "Tyson?"

The meth king opened the door to the car that had stopped to pick him up and squinted back at Matty. "Or . . . we could kill two birds with one stone."

61

The Perdido Addiction Center had a campus that included a few hundred yards of sand fronting the Gulf of Mexico. When he was in rehab, Jason had avoided the ocean because it made him think of all the times he'd been drunk with friends in college, law school, and even during seaside conferences. Then, he'd felt the beach might be a trigger for him. He'd even left the PAC and headed straight for the Flora-Bama lounge and ordered a Corona just minutes after his discharge. He'd been saved by a phone call from Jana, or he might have taken a sip.

That was the rub for him. He knew Harry and Izzy both hoped he would sell his house at Mill Creek and move back to Birmingham. They'd never wanted him to go home in the first place. But, for him, coming home to represent Jana had saved him. Sure, his journey had led to a lot of heartache and problems. But what would have happened if he hadn't come?

Jason didn't like to ponder that question very long.

Now, as he watched the waves roll into the sand from behind the full-length glass window, the memories flooded back to him. Some good. Many bad. He didn't see the beach as a trigger so much anymore, but he couldn't say he enjoyed it either. Almost two months ago, when he'd dropped Chase off at rehab, he'd spent almost all night walking on the sand. Would he have given in to the temptation to drink if Nola hadn't been with him?

"Jason?"

He turned as a woman in a navy blouse and white shorts walked toward him. She wasn't Chase, but Jason was still glad to see her. "Michal, it's been a long time."

"You look good," she said, extending her hand, which Jason shook. Despite the swirl of emotions he was struggling with, he managed a smile. Michal had been his counselor when he was a patient at the PAC. He couldn't remember her last name, but he could recall much of their work together. She had pushed him to explore his feelings toward Jana and, in particular, his father. Though he was still walking a tightrope with sobriety, he knew he'd be a full-fledged drunk if he hadn't come here, if Michal hadn't spent so much time with him.

"Thank you. I'm surprised to see you. Where's Chase?"

She grimaced and glanced at the window. "Can we take a walk?"

———

A few minutes later, Jason's shoes were off, his pants were rolled up, and he was walking on the beach. He had hoped to meet Chase as soon as he got here. Had spent the whole ride in the rental car from Mobile rehearsing his questions. He needed answers and didn't have a lot of time. He had depositions in Biloxi all day tomorrow and Friday and had yet to crack open the file to prepare. He'd spend tonight holed up in a hotel trying to get in good enough shape to wing it. As he walked, he felt his heartbeat racing as fast as his mind.

"Jason, Chase doesn't want to see you," Michal finally said after they'd walked about fifty feet.

Jason stopped and crossed his arms. "Why couldn't you have told me that back there?" He pointed to the building. He tried to control his breathing, but it was no use. "Michal, this is ridiculous. I'm paying for her to be here. I need to talk with her."

"You're a trigger for Chase. She says that you know this. Do you want her to relapse?"

Jason glared down at the sand.

"Jason, she's been here fifty days. She really needs another two months at a minimum." Michal hesitated. "Her counselor states that they're only just now beginning to make progress."

"You aren't her counselor?"

"No."

"Then why are you talking to me?"

"Because her therapist won't be able to disclose any of the things they have been working on. Chase hasn't consented to disclosure. So there's nothing her counselor can tell you . . . other than a meeting with Chase, especially now, is not advisable. Because I have a preexisting professional relationship with you, it was decided that I should tell you."

Jason began to walk again, looking out at the gulf. The waters were rough today, and the waves were crashing onto the shore and over Jason's feet and calves. "Can we talk confidentially?"

"Of course. That's another reason why I'm here."

"Chase could be a . . ." Jason fought the urge to say *suspect*. ". . . *key witness* in a case I'm handling."

"You're talking about the Kelly Flowers murder case?"

Jason glanced at her. "How did you—"

"I can't say."

"Chase has mentioned things about it?"

Michal smiled. "I can't tell you any specifics. Only that I'm aware of it."

"Do you know why I need to meet with Chase?"

"I'm sorry, Jason. We take the psychotherapist-patient privilege very seriously around here."

Jason thought it through. "I have a trial date of October 14. We're now in late June. I don't have forever."

"I know. But we're talking about more than just a case here, Jason. This is Chase's life. If you speak with her now, her counselor is very worried that she'll go backward."

"She can't hide in here forever."

"Do you think that's what she's doing?" Michal snapped the question back at him. "Hiding? Is that what you were doing?"

"My situation was different."

"Was it?"

"Michal, I wasn't an important witness in a murder trial." He stopped again. "Look, she may be more than a witness. There is someone who puts her with Flowers on the night of the murder. I think Flowers was either blackmailing her or supplying her with meth. I'm not sure which, and it might even be both. But my theory is that he was a dirty cop, and, if Chase was with him the night of the murder . . ." He trailed off.

"You think she might have killed him?"

"No, I don't think that. But until I talk to Chase and get some answers, I can't be sure."

"Jason, I'm not a lawyer, but don't you have a conflict of interest? You're representing a client who has been charged with a murder that you think your ex-girlfriend may have committed?"

"I don't think that, but the facts suggest that she could be a potential alternative suspect."

"Isn't that a conflict?"

"Not if she's innocent," Jason said.

Michal stuffed her hands in the pockets of her shorts and peered up at Jason. "And what if she's not?"

Jason again looked at the ocean. "She is," he finally said.

62

It was a two-hour drive from Perdido Key to Biloxi. Jason rolled the windows down and tuned the radio to a rock station. He tried to drown out the noise in his mind, particularly the last thing Michal had said to him.

"Jason, you really need to take care of yourself now. I can tell that you're struggling. There is an AA meeting tonight in Gulf Shores. It is a good group. Why don't you go to that?"

The meeting was at a restaurant, and Jason pulled into the parking lot. For several minutes, he sat there watching people enter. He knew Michal was right, but he was so frustrated. Then his cell phone rang.

"Hey, J. R."

"Harry."

"How'd it go?"

Jason closed his eyes and leaned back in his seat. "I'd rather not talk about it."

"OK then. Listen, we've got a situation."

Jason cracked open his lids, surprised by the intensity in Harry's tone. "What?"

"I'm in Pulaski."

"What? Tennessee?"

"Yeah, amigo. Matthew Dean drove here this afternoon. He's got one guy with him, and there's another car with three others."

"What's in Pulaski?"

"I don't know. Could be a drug deal. But it also could be something related to our case."

"How so?"

"Detective Daniels. I've done some digging, and Pulaski is her hometown. She also worked in the Giles County Sheriff's Office before coming to Guntersville. It very well could be where she is."

"Have we heard anything about what's going on with her?"

"Negative. The sheriff's department has been stone silent, and my source has dried up. Has your reporter friend mentioned anything?"

"No." He'd asked Kisha Roe to let him know if she heard any scoop about Hatty Daniels, but so far, even Kisha had not been able to unearth any information.

"Don't you think it's weird how hush-hush everything is with Daniels?" Jason asked. "I mean, what's the big secret? Seems like your source could give you something?"

"All we've got is the company line."

"An indefinite leave of absence related to personal matters," Jason muttered.

"That's it," Harry said. For a minute, there was a pause, and Jason heard an exhale. He smiled, envisioning his investigator lighting a cigarette. Harry did his best thinking with a slight nicotine buzz.

"What's your gut telling you?" Jason asked.

"Honestly?"

"Always."

"To get the hell out of Dodge." He exhaled again.

Jason gazed out the window as more people began to enter the restaurant. Had they come for the meeting, which was in a private room in the back? Or just to eat? Jason closed his eyes, trying to think. "Pulaski is, what, a couple hours from Guntersville?"

"Yeah, a little more but not much."

"So it is plausible that Dean is making a delivery or picking up product."

"Yes, it is." Another exhale.

"But you don't think so."

"No."

"Why?"

"Because there are too many people for that. Dean would come alone, or he'd have a wingman. That's all that would be necessary. Five people and two cars doesn't fit for a drug deal." He coughed.

"But it does fit an ambush," Jason said. "But why?"

"Cade hired you to represent Trey Cowan. Presumably, he wants Cowan to win. Hatty is lead detective for the case. If he takes her out . . ." Harry trailed off.

"Not enough gain for such a bold move," Jason said. "I mean, putting out a hit on a cop? The state can win without Daniels. Sergeant Mitchell was Daniels's partner. He was there for everything, and the physical evidence pointing to Trey as the killer is formidable. As is the videotaped motive." Jason shook his head. "If this is really and truly shaping up to be a hit on Daniels, there's gotta be some other reason."

Silence and then Harry grunted. "I agree."

Jason tapped the steering wheel with his fingers. "Could just be trying to scare her. Maybe he feels if he puts a little heat on her, then she'll stay away. The number of folks would fit that theory."

"Could be," Harry said. Another exhale. Then a cough. "I don't know, J. R. Something is off here."

Silence filled the line, and Jason felt his heart thumping again. He had so many decisions to make. He remembered Harry's advice before he got on the plane Tuesday morning. *Maybe we should stay in our own lane . . .*

"Harry, do you think they're on to you?"

A long, slow exhale of smoke. "I don't think so, but . . ." He trailed off.

"But what?"

"But these guys are professionals, Jason. They are used to watching their back."

Jason squeezed the wheel again, feeling helpless. *I'm a lawyer. Not a CIA agent . . .*

"I don't know what to tell you, Harry. If they are there for Daniels, either to scare her or kill her, then that is obviously important."

"It's also criminal, J. R."

"They haven't done anything yet."

"When they do, it'll be too late."

Jason sucked in a deep breath. "Harry, I trust you, man. If you think you've been made or if you feel threatened in any way, then get out of there, OK?"

"Ten-four, amigo. I'll see you when you get back."

"Harry."

"Yeah."

"Be careful."

Jason heard the phone click dead in his hand. He looked at the entrance to the restaurant and then the clock on the dash. The meeting started five minutes ago. Jason grabbed the door handle and then let his hand fall to his side.

He put the car in reverse.

Seconds later, he was back on Highway 98 headed to Biloxi.

63

Harry Davenport had fought in Afghanistan. He was an army Ranger. He'd been in scrapes before, and he had killed at least five people during his military service.

He'd also seen men and women officers in his regiment killed.

It had been years since he was in active combat, but the memories were still fresh. At the time, he had only reacted. You couldn't think in the trenches, or you'd wind up dead. But he did a lot of thinking when he got home. Of the lives he'd taken. Whether any of those men had been married. Did they have children? A mother and father who would receive the news of their son's death in the middle of dinner or on a Saturday morning. Those ruminations had led Harry to see a psychologist when he'd returned from overseas. They'd also contributed to his departure from the army. He'd told himself that he'd never again get involved in life-and-death situations. That was one of the reasons he'd enjoyed working for Jason Rich.

Investigating personal injury cases or even criminal charges against a client on behalf of a law firm should not ever necessitate a risk to his safety or anyone else's. But as he watched Cade's henchmen pull into a strip club off Highway 64 on the outskirts of Pulaski, Harry sensed a clear and present danger.

Matthew Dean and the man with him went inside the establishment, which had a neon sign that advertised its name: THE SUNDOWNERS CLUB.

The other three walked into a field behind the building and disappeared into the trees. *What the hell?* Harry thought, watching from his parking place in the gravel lot.

He got out of the Explorer and lit a cigarette, then blew a plume of smoke above him. Then, after taking three quick puffs, he threw the unfiltered cancer stick on the ground and stepped on it.

In combat and in his civilian life as a bouncer at a place similar to this club and now as an investigator, sometimes the only answer he'd ever been able to reach were two words that might very well sum up his philosophy on life.

Fuck it, he thought, heading for the front door.

64

Matty Dean paid no attention to the topless woman dancing above him. He peered down at his cell phone, waiting for a reconnaissance report. He'd been in the club nearly two hours, and he'd already spent fifty dollars. It was 8:45 p.m., and he was willing to stay all night until he got what he wanted. Which had nothing to do with the skin being flashed in front of him.

He sucked on his teeth as his phone finally vibrated, announcing a new text. He peered down at his phone.

We found the cabin.

Then, seconds later, another message from the same number.

She's alone.

Matty gazed up and took out a one-dollar bill as if on autopilot. He put it in the stripper's G-string and then returned to his phone. He typed his response: Do we have a shot?

Nothing and then three dots appeared on the screen. Seconds later, the response.

If we act now . . . Yes.

Matty took a sip from his glass of Diet Coke and then let out a long, slow breath. He hadn't thought things would happen so fast. He'd dispatched a man to Pulaski hours after his talk with Tyson at Mill Creek, and Hatty had been located by him following her attorney, Bocephus Haynes. She was camped out on a piece of land Haynes owned where he ran an orphanage for teenage boys and girls. While secluded and protected with security, the location was promising if they could get inside the fence. It had taken the man another twelve hours, but he'd been able to bust the code. Then he'd sent for reinforcements, and Matty had rounded them up.

He spoke to his partner without looking at him. "Is our friend still here?"

"Yep. Three tables away."

Matty grinned up at the dancer and stood. He flung two more ones on the stage and began to walk to the door. It had been a while since he'd done a hit.

He pushed through the opening and saw Harry Davenport's Ford Explorer in the parking lot. *And tonight could be a two-for-one special.*

Matty spat on the gravel and walked to his car. He grabbed two handguns and a twelve-gauge shotgun while his partner pulled out an AR15 assault rifle.

Then they both strode toward the woods behind the Sundowners Club.

65

Harry left the club about thirty seconds after Matty Dean. He walked to his car and noticed that Dean's vehicle was still parked in its original spot. He glanced toward the woods and saw a couple of shadows enter the same area where the three other men had gone almost two hours earlier.

Harry lit a cigarette and took a long pull on it. He had no idea what the men were doing, but it didn't make sense to him that a drug deal would be made on the Roosevelt Haynes Farm for Boys and Girls.

Perhaps the odd location is what made it an ideal site? he asked himself. Then he shook his head. *No.* That didn't feel right. Not with five of them going in.

What in the hell are they doing?

Harry took another drag on the cigarette and stomped it out. *Only one way to find out,* he thought. He pulled out his cell phone and typed a text message to Jason and Izzy.

I've tracked them to the Sundowners Club off 64. All five of them just went into the woods behind the place. I'm going to take a look.

He retrieved his concealed carry handgun from his pocket and checked the magazine. Then, without further hesitation, he walked around the building until the gravel turned to grass.

66

Hatty Daniels had enjoyed living on the farm. The seclusion allowed her to take long runs, and there was also a fitness center where she could lift weights. Since moving here from Frannie Storm's house at the invitation of Bo Haynes, she'd gotten in excellent physical condition.

She'd also found a couple of trees on which to practice her shooting.

In terms of ranking a place to serve out purgatory, it wasn't bad.

But it was also temporary. She knew she couldn't live out her days waiting for the other shoe to drop. Eventually, she'd have to return to Guntersville. To Marshall County. She might've run, but she couldn't quit. Bo was in the process of negotiating her return, and she was growing impatient.

She sat in a rocker on the porch in front of her cabin and peered out at the moon. Lights out for the teenage residents was thirty minutes ago, and she'd seen several girls scrambling back to their cabins from the many various after-school activities on site.

Now, though, the only light was from the moon and sky above.

In her prior life as a hard-driving deputy in the Giles County Sheriff's Office, she'd seen Bocephus Haynes as an aggressive, ruthless, and intimidating defense lawyer. Separating the lawyer from the man had been difficult, but seeing his vision for a place for boys and girls without parents to grow up was a revelation. She was proud of him.

And honored to have him as her attorney.

Hatty heard a rustling sound to the north, and she stood and leaned over the railing, peering in that direction. The farm had many sounds on summer nights. Crickets and frogs chirping, the whistling of the wind through the trees, and the occasional cry of a bobcat.

She figured the sound she'd heard was of some kind of animal, but as she squinted into the darkness, she saw a shadow of a human figure. Hatty felt her pulse quicken.

Then she heard two loud booms, and her right shoulder exploded in pain. Hatty hit the floor as the window above her shattered into a million pieces. She crawled toward the front door on her side, reaching into the back of her waistband for her Glock. When the explosions paused, she rose to her knees and fired three shots to the north, where she'd heard the rustling.

Then the unmistakable patter of machine gun fire started again. Hatty rolled into her house like a barrel and kicked the door closed, but then it exploded on top of her as more shots rang out. She took out her phone and dialed 911.

Hatty heard a loud alarm ring out over the farm. She touched her shoulder and looked at her hand.

Blood.

The shots had died down, and she assessed herself on the floor. She was hit on the right shoulder and in the stomach.

The room began to spin as a large Black man entered the opening. "Hatty?! Are you all right? Hatty?"

She felt huge arms embrace her and lift her to her feet.

Then her eyes rolled into her head, and the world went dark.

67

Harry Davenport flinched and dropped to the ground when he heard the first gunshot.

What the hell? He crawled forward, trying to get a better look, but Cade's men were about a hundred yards away. They were at the edge of a clearing, and there appeared to be a cabin in the distance.

The target was in that cabin. Harry could see three of the shooters, but he didn't have a line on any of them, and even if he did, he wasn't sure what was going on. Slowly, he stood and looked around a tree.

Now he could see four of the men. Matthew Dean was missing.

He barely heard the shot before it penetrated his back. It was the muffled pop of a Glock with a silencer.

Despite the searing pain in his lower back, Harry dropped to his knees and rolled to his left, coming up in a firing position. He pulled the trigger as his chest and neck exploded in pain.

The gun fell from his hands, and Harry plunged backward onto the grass.

He blinked his eyes as a man came into focus. "Dean?" Harry gasped, as the other man walked toward him. Harry's legs began to feel numb, and the world was spinning.

When he saw the stubby barrel of the pistol above him, he tried to move but couldn't.

"I'm sorry, Iz," he whispered.

68

Ten miles south of Pulaski, off of Highway 31 and just past the Buford Gardner Bridge, Matty Dean pulled off the road. Tyson had a meth maker who had a trailer and a barn on a half acre fronting the Elk River.

Matty and two others took the supplier's boat and motored about three miles out into the main channel. Then they tied a cinder block to the body of Rich's investigator.

And dumped him in the water.

Once back on shore, Matty made the call. "We got one bird for sure. Just buried him in the middle of the Elk River."

"And the other?"

"Not sure if she's dead, but we hit her."

"Good. Did you make sure there were no outside surveillance cameras?"

"Ten-four. There were none at the Sundowners, and we disabled the ones at the farm."

"Hell, yeah," Tyson said. "That's my Matty boy." Then there was a whistling-through-teeth sound and a quick snort. "Get your ass home."

———

Tyson Cade did a happy dance around the king-size bed in the Hampton Inn. He took a long sip of Sun Drop and allowed himself a rare treat. He drew out a line of his best product on Dooby Darnell's stomach and did it all.

"Hell, yeah," he said. "How do you like me now?"

"Are you talking to me?" Dooby asked.

"No, sweetie." He pulled open the curtains and pointed out toward the highway. "I'm talking to that sonofabitch." Cade smirked at the huge billboard on Highway 431.

"You're my bitch now, Counselor."

69

Jason was in the middle of his last deposition when he got a text from Izzy that sent a dagger of fear through his chest.

Detective Daniels was almost killed last night in Pulaski. She's in the hospital barely hanging on. Shot at the Roosevelt Haynes Farm for Boys and Girls. It's off Highway 64 less than a mile from the strip club that Harry texted us from. Jason, I still haven't heard from him. I'm scared.

Jason told the other lawyers he had a family emergency and ended the deposition.

Then he drove straight to the Mobile Regional Airport. He'd planned to fly to Gainesville next and see Nola. She was currently a patient at the Florida Recovery Center, which was the recommendation of the folks in Perdido when Jason said he didn't want Chase and Nola at the same place.

But his plans would have to change. "Where to?" the pilot asked, as Jason ran from his rental car to the tarmac.

"Pulaski, Tennessee," he said.

"Closest we can get will be Huntsville, Alabama."

"Good enough," Jason said, climbing into the plane and trying to calm his nerves.

Don't be dead, Harry, he thought, but as the wheels lifted and the jet ascended from the runway into the skies above Mobile Bay, Jason had the awful realization that his investigator . . . his friend . . . was probably gone.

70

Izzy picked Jason up at the Huntsville International Airport. As he got off the plane, she hugged him. Then he looked at her. She wore a white T-shirt, jeans, and tennis shoes. Her eyes were red from crying.

"He's got to be all right."

"Come on, let's go. I'll drive."

They took Izzy's BMW and made it to Pulaski in thirty minutes. When they pulled into the Sundowners Club on Highway 64, it was 9:00 p.m.

Harry's SUV was still in the parking lot. "When was the last time you tried calling him?"

"Right before I picked you up at the airport. No ring. Straight to voice mail."

Jason pulled out his cell phone and pushed in the number for Harry. He got the same thing. Jason let out a deep breath. "Did you call the police?"

"Yes. But they're a lot more worried about the shooting than they are about a missing private investigator from Alabama."

Jason sighed. "That makes sense. Well, let's go inside and see if anyone remembers anything."

If his partner seemed squeamish about going into a strip club, she didn't act like it. "After you," Izzy said, gesturing toward the neon sign.

———

An hour later, Izzy and Jason returned to Harry's car. "We need to check it out."

"I agree," Izzy said. She found some Kleenex in her vehicle and wrapped it around her hand. Then she took the extra set of keys that she'd brought with her and unlocked the SUV. She opened the door and peered inside. Outside of some jumper cables in the back and a few notepads, the car was empty.

No clues.

"Look, Iz, did you read Harry's last text to the police?"

"I did more than that. I copied and pasted it to them. The Giles County Sheriff's Office has done a complete search of the farm, looking for Detective Daniels's attackers. They have found nothing."

Jason closed his eyes and leaned his frame against Izzy's car. *Harry's gone . . .* He forced his eyes open. "Come on," he said, walking around to the driver's side.

"Where are we going?"

"The sheriff's office."

"At this time of night?"

"What else are we going to do?"

Izzy slammed her door shut. "Good point."

———

Fifteen minutes later, they walked into the lobby of the Giles County Sheriff's Office. Jason was wired, running on adrenaline. He checked in at the front desk and asked to speak with the officer leading the investigation into the disappearance of Harry Davenport.

The clerk wrinkled her face up and then made a phone call. "If you two will have a seat, Chief Storm will be right with you."

Thirty minutes later, a tall, lanky Black woman in a blue uniform came out of the double doors. She looked agitated and tired. "I'm

Frannie Storm. I'm sorry you had to wait, but I'm investigating an attempted murder. It takes precedence over a disappearance."

"We understand," Jason said. "But I can give you the name of at least one of the people who tried to kill Detective Daniels."

She cocked her head at him and said, "Follow me."

———

Frannie tapped her pen on a pad that she had been making notes on. "So your investigator, Mr. Davenport, was following Matthew Dean. He went into the Sundowners after Mr. Dean, and then, according to this last text you received, he followed them into the woods behind the club."

"Correct."

"Mr. Rich, I agree this is a promising development for our investigation. We'll run this Dean fellow's picture by the employees of the Sundowners, and hopefully we can confirm his attendance last night. But you realize that this text message and anything Mr. Davenport told you is—"

"Hearsay," Jason said. "I do realize that, but it doesn't change the fact that Harry followed Dean to Pulaski and into those woods. And Dean works for Tyson Cade."

"The Guntersville meth dealer," Frannie said.

"Right."

"So, in your opinion, this was a hit on Hatty Daniels from this Cade fellow."

"Nothing else makes sense," Jason said.

"I agree," Frannie said. "I just don't know that we can prove any of it."

"Can we speak with Detective Daniels?" Izzy asked. "Maybe she could have seen our friend."

"I've already done that," Frannie said. "She's still very groggy, but she doesn't remember seeing anything but shadows. I'm sorry." Frannie stood and walked a circle around the long conference-room table. "Assuming your theory is correct, why would Tyson Cade want Detective Daniels dead?"

"We think she must have been working on something that would have exposed him to criminal prosecution."

Frannie crossed her arms. "Makes sense, but what would that be?"

"That's another reason why we need to talk with the detective," Izzy said.

Frannie buried her chin in her chest. "It's probably going to be a few days before Hatty is up to anything like that. She's out of ICU but still very weak."

"Please, Chief Storm . . ." Izzy's voice cracked.

"And when she is healthy enough to talk, she may not want to talk with you. I mean, you're on opposite sides of a murder case in Marshall County."

Jason pushed his chair back from the table and crossed his legs. "Detective Daniels's leave of absence has always seemed fishy to me. Now she's almost murdered by Marshall County's meth king. There has to be some relationship between the attempt on her life, her leave of absence, and our case." He stood and placed his hands on the table. "Chief Storm, please help us. Our friend may be dead, and your friend is still in danger."

"I never said Hatty Daniels is my friend. Is that some kind of racist conclusion because we're both Black?"

"No, ma'am," Jason said, flabbergasted. "I can tell you're concerned for her. And I know Hatty is from Pulaski and worked in this department before coming to Guntersville."

Frannie's face softened. "Look, I'm sorry. It's been a long day, and you're right. Hatty was my mentor, and she is my friend. And I'm worried as hell for her, and now I'm concerned that a Sand Mountain drug lord is trying to kill people in my county."

"Is there anything you can do to help us?"

Frannie walked to the door and peered down at the ground. Then, nodding, she turned back to them. "I believe there is."

71

By the time they reached the house, Jason was running on fumes. It was 11:00 p.m., and he'd been going all day. Three depositions. A two-hour flight. The trip to Pulaski and then the investigation at the Sundowners Club and the sheriff's office. If he was exhausted, Izzy looked like death warmed over. Her skin was pale, her eyes were bloodshot, and her voice was dry and hoarse.

As Jason started to knock, the front door swung open, and a huge man stood in the opening. He waved them inside and extended his hand. "Bo Haynes." His voice was a deep baritone. He wore a black T-shirt and gray athletic shorts. Even in only his bare feet, Jason figured he must be at least six feet four.

"Jason Rich," Jason managed. "This is my partner, Izzy Montaigne. Thank you for meeting us on such short notice and at such a late hour."

"Frannie said you had information on the people that tried to kill my client on my farm. As you might imagine, I'm pretty upset about that."

"Yes, sir," Jason said.

"And we're very upset that our friend is missing," Izzy croaked.

Bo rubbed his chin. "Yeah. I'm sorry. Listen, let's go out on the porch," he said. "Can I offer either of you a drink? Water? Beer? Whiskey?"

"Water would be great," Jason said.

"Jack Daniel's over ice," Izzy said, coughing. She sounded terrible. "I'm sorry, Jason," she said, looking down at the ground.

"You don't have to apologize, Iz," Jason whispered.

"Coming right up," Bo said. A minute later, he returned with a bottled water for Jason and a glass of whiskey over ice for Izzy, and he cracked open a bottle of Yuengling for himself. "All right, tell me what you can."

Jason went through the key facts, leaving out only the part where Tyson Cade had blackmailed him to take the Cowan case. Bo Haynes sat in a rocking chair, sipping his beer, occasionally asking a question but mostly just listening.

Finally he cleared his throat and asked them if they needed anything else to drink.

Izzy held up her glass. "Can you make it a double?"

"Sure," Bo said. He returned a minute later with a brown-and-white English bulldog following behind him. "Lee Roy won't bother you," he said. "I put him in the utility room, but he was scratching to get out."

Izzy petted the dog behind his ears, and Jason smiled. "He's a cute, big boy," Izzy said, taking her glass from Bo.

"He's got a face only a mother could love, but he's a hell of a good dog." Bo opened a bottled water for himself and sat down, leaning forward on his elbows. "I'm sorry, but I can't tell you much about Hatty's situation. Everything she's discussed with me is protected by the attorney-client privilege. I'm duty bound to keep it confidential. I'm sure you understand that, Mr. Rich."

"Call me Jason."

"OK . . . Jason."

"Can you at least confirm that you're representing her in connection with her leave of absence?"

"I can do that," Bo said.

"And that her leave has something to do with the Kelly Flowers murder case."

Bo stood and walked to the screen door, and Lee Roy scampered out. He took a long sip of water. "Jason, I'll make two promises to you. One is that I will do all I can to help the Giles County Sheriff's Office bring in the people who broke into my farm and tried to kill Hatty. If it's this meth king, as you say it is, then I will do everything in my power to help bring that sonofabitch down."

"Thank you," Izzy said.

"And the second promise?" Jason asked.

Bo peered at him. "That I will advise my client to meet with you before the Flowers trial and answer the questions you've asked me. The conference will be in my presence at a place I select."

"That would be great," Jason said.

"I wish I could do something else," Bo said. "You've given me more than I've given you. And . . . based on what you've told me and the man you've said we are dealing with . . . I'm worried about your investigator."

Izzy choked out a sob and covered her mouth. Then she drank the rest of her whiskey.

"We understand," Jason said. "And we appreciate your time."

Bo extended his hand, and Jason took it. As he tried to let go, Bo grabbed hold, looking at Izzy. "I'll make you one last promise. By the time your trial is over, we'll be even."

Jason nodded as Bo let go. He escorted them out the front door and grabbed Jason's shoulder as Izzy continued to walk to the car.

"She all right?" Bo asked.

"She and Harry were dating."

Bo took in a deep breath. "Damn . . . I'm sorry."

"Thank you." Jason turned to walk to his car, and Bo's baritone voice stopped him.

"Hey, Jason."

He turned.

"Watch your back, dog."

72

Jason booked two rooms at the Hampton Inn in Pulaski and had to help Izzy to hers.

"He's going to be OK, isn't he?" Izzy asked, shaking his shoulders. "Tell me that I'll get Harry back."

"We've got the chief deputy sheriff working the case as well as one of the best lawyers in this county trying to help us. We're doing all we can do, Iz."

"You think he's dead, don't you?"

Jason didn't know what to say. He was still looking at her when she slammed the door in his face.

———

Once in his own room, Jason lay on the bed and gazed at the ceiling. He was exhausted, but he couldn't sleep. He called Satch, who answered on the first ring.

"Any word on Harry?"

"No," Jason said. "The sheriff's office here is looking for him."

"He's dead."

Jason closed his eyes, not wanting to believe it. "Have you heard from Cade?"

"No, but I suspect we will soon."

"OK, let me know if he calls."

"Jason, we've made some progress on the Sand Mountain angle you had us looking into. I've got a few pieces to the puzzle."

"And?"

"And I think we need another meeting with Bull Branner."

"Set it up."

"This time, we need to catch him off guard. He lied to us before, Jason. He lied to *me*, and that won't fly."

"I trust you, Satch. Whatever you think is best. What else?"

"That's the main thing. The other is just a working theory. I'll run it by you when you get back."

"OK. Thanks, Satch."

"Hey, Jason. I'm sorry about Harry."

Jason clicked End and slammed the phone down on the bed. He thought about his last few conversations with Harry. His investigator, a former army Ranger, had been afraid they were going too far. Jason should have listened to him.

He closed his eyes, and the dream came to him again. The one he'd had in the holding cell. Of being underwater and sinking in the silty, muddy bottom of the lake. Of seeing the people he cared about under there with him. Dying.

If Harry was dead, then his nightmare was coming true.

73

Jason awoke to loud banging on his door. He stumbled out of bed, wondering how long he'd slept. It couldn't have been more than a few hours. When he opened the door, Izzy was standing in the hallway. Tears streaked both of her cheeks. She held her phone out to him.

Jason took it and Izzy entered his room, crumpling on the floor by his bed.

"Hello," Jason said.

"Good morning, Counselor." The voice of Tyson Cade.

"What's going on? How'd you get my partner's number?"

"I have my ways. Anyway, like I was telling your feisty young colleague, your investigator, Mr. Davenport, isn't coming home."

"What do you mean?" Jason asked.

"I mean what I said."

"You killed him."

Silence for several seconds. Jason looked down at the floor, where Izzy was beginning to convulse.

"I would have expected more from an army Ranger," Cade finally said. "I'll say this for your team. They're loyal."

"Why?" Jason asked, squatting and touching Izzy's shoulder.

"Meet me today. Same place as last time. Same time. Alone."

"Wait, what—"

But Cade hung up.

Jason cradled Izzy in his arms. She was still shaking. "I'm sorry, Iz," he said, feeling tears welling in his own eyes. "I'm so sorry."

———

Jason drove Izzy's car back to Guntersville. She said nothing, sitting in the passenger seat with her knees pulled up to her chin. Jason tried a couple of times to engage her, but it was no use. Izzy was in shock, and he would have to give her time. If she didn't come out of it soon, he might have to take her to the hospital.

Jason pulled onto Mill Creek Road around eleven in the morning. He helped Izzy into the guest bedroom, and she lay down on the bed, curling herself up into a fetal position. Then he called Satch.

The colonel came over, and the two of them talked while standing in the kitchen.

"Bad idea," Satch said, after Jason had broken down Cade's request for another meeting. "You can't meet that SOB without at least one of us there."

"He killed Harry, Satch. I can't take any more risks."

"He may kill you."

"No," Jason said. "He won't. He needs me to represent Trey."

Satch rubbed his chin, gazing out at the water. "He was teaching you a lesson. That's all Harry was."

Jason knew it was true, but coming from Satch, it still felt like a gut punch. He winced and looked at the floor. "It's my fault."

"Don't be too hard on yourself, Jason. Harry was a grown man. A Ranger. No one was more equipped to deal with Cade."

"He wanted out," Jason said. "He said we needed to stay in our lane, and I didn't listen."

"He was worried about you. And your partner in there. That may have been how they got him. In combat, you can't be thinking about stuff like that. It blinds you. All you can think about is your prey." He walked toward the door. "That's why so many of us can't ever go back to a normal life." He grunted. "I mean, look at me, Chuck, and Mickey. We were decorated soldiers. I'm a full fucking colonel. And here I am living in my parent's run-down shack on the wrong side of the road in Mill Creek. Unmarried. No kids. Making a living teaching folks how to shoot assault rifles." He rubbed the back of his neck. "I admire Harry. At least he tried to have a normal life."

"And I took that from him," Jason said.

"No, you didn't. Cade did. If Harry were here, he wouldn't blame you."

Jason walked over to Satch. "I'm not going to have any more casualties, Satch. I can't deal with it. I want you and your brothers to stand down. I don't want you getting killed."

Satch grinned, his eyes creasing into slits. "Jason, my brothers and I care about you. We care about Nola and Chase too. We aren't soulless." He paused. "But we ain't like Harry. I never came back from the war, you understand? Neither did Mickey or Chuck. We've been looking for prey for a long time, and you've given us that." He grabbed Jason rough around the arms. "We ain't doing this for you. We're doing it for us. And don't ever—and I mean *ever*—tell me to stand down again. Don't forget who I am."

Jason felt an odd sense of relief wash over him. "Yes, sir, Colonel."

74

Jason sat down at the Tootsie Table at Crawmama's at 4:45 p.m. Tyson Cade was already there and was sucking on the head of a crawfish. When he finished, he flicked the shell into a basket. Then he took his phone out, entered a code, and slid it across the table.

Jason peered down at the screen and into the blank, dead eyes of Harry Davenport. He had a gunshot hole in his forehead, and his mouth was open.

Jason felt vomit in his throat and coughed. He forced his eyes off the screen and onto a sign on the far wall that said **MEN. URINAL ONLY.** He blinked his eyes and took a deep breath. Then he got up and walked toward the restrooms. He entered one of them that had a toilet and dropped to his knees. He threw up and wrapped his arms around the porcelain bowl. Then he vomited again. He felt dizzy, the world spinning. He'd known Harry was dead. Had known it in his gut, and Tyson Cade had all but confirmed it this morning. But seeing Harry's corpse . . .

Jason beat his fists against the toilet. He stood and looked for a faucet, but there was none. He stumbled out of the bathroom and saw a community sink. He ran water over his hands and washed them. Then he splashed his face. He grabbed a paper towel and dried his hands but left the dampness on his cheeks. He swallowed and tasted bile. He moved his eyes around the room. There was hardly anyone in Crawmama's this time of day. Jason took another deep breath. Then another. Finally, he walked back to the table and sat down. He looked across the table at Cade, who was eating another crawfish. "Why?" Jason asked.

"Because you crossed the line."

"What line?"

"You don't follow me or my men, Counselor. I do the following. Mr. Davenport had been tailing one of my best hands for a couple of months, and he finally got caught in the cross fire."

Cade had taken his phone back, but Jason didn't need it to envision Harry's dead face. It would be stamped in his memory forever. He thought of his investigator's last text. Going into the woods and following the man Jason had asked him to follow. Then he thought of Izzy, lying on the guest bed in the fetal position. Nola in rehab in Gainesville. Chase in Perdido, so far gone she couldn't bring herself to talk to him. Niecy, in Birmingham, hadn't come back in months. Why would she? Jana had asked him to come to Guntersville last year, and she was dead.

Had he helped anyone since he'd arrived?

I'm a curse.

"Jason, you have one job, and I hope you understand what it is."

"Represent Trey Cowan," Jason mumbled.

"More than that. I expect the same result you obtained for your sister."

Jason looked at him as he rose from the table. "What if I can't deliver that?"

Cade leaned over the table. "Then more people that you love are going to end up like Mr. Davenport." He threw two twenties on the table. "Feel free to order something, Counselor. I'm kinda busy, so I need to be leaving."

As he started to walk away, Jason called after him. "It'll be a lot harder with Harry gone."

Cade returned to the table. "You should've thought of that before you sicced him on one of my guys." He leaned in closer. "And before you threatened my high school distributor."

"You ask the impossible," Jason said, feeling sick to his stomach again.

"No, I don't. I've already told you who Trey was meeting at Branner's Place. And I suspect, after you talk to your girlfriend . . . or is it ex-girlfriend . . . that you will see that she makes quite a promising alternative suspect."

"What is your play here?" Jason asked, beginning to sense a numbness coming over him. "I don't get it. You hire me, but then you seem to do everything you can do to keep me from succeeding and then still expect me to somehow win."

Cade grinned. "Don't you worry about that, Jason. Stay in your lane."

Hearing the drug dealer throw Harry's advice to him was almost too much, and Jason's gag reflex kicked in. He coughed and grabbed for a water that wasn't there.

Cade slapped him twice on the back, and the fit subsided. Then the drug dealer leaned down and whispered in his ear. "Just win, baby."

75

Jason walked out of Crawmama's on shaky legs. He'd drunk two glasses of water before leaving, but he still felt dehydrated and weak from all the vomiting. His heart was also beating hard, and no amount of deep breaths seemed to calm him. All he could see in his thoughts was Harry. Blank eyes. Gunshot wound to the forehead. Open mouth.

He got in the Porsche and gazed at his reflection in the rearview mirror. Feeling hate building inside him. He put the car in gear and squealed his tires as he pulled onto Highway 431.

He drove to the jail on autopilot, slammed the door, and walked into the reception area. "I need to see my client, Mr. Cowan."

"It's a bit late for an attorney consultation, Mr. Rich. We are way past normal hours."

"This is an emergency, and it won't take long." He took out his cell. "If you don't set it up, I'm going to call Shay."

The reception clerk gave him a tight smile and snatched a phone. "Just a moment."

———

Five minutes later, he was seated in the small room looking across the metal table at Trey Cowan.

"What's up?" Trey asked.

"Tyson Cade murdered my lead investigator. His name was Harry Davenport. He worked for me and . . . he was one of my best friends in the world." Jason spoke in a deliberate manner, forcing his voice not to break. "One of my only friends."

"I'm sorry," Trey said. His tone sounded sincere but also stupid.

"You're *sorry*."

"What else do you want me to say?"

Jason stood and placed his hands on the desk, glaring at Trey. "I want you to tell me the whole deal, Trey. Perhaps if you come clean with me, no one else that either one of us cares about will die."

"Mr. Rich, you need to calm down."

Jason grabbed him by the collar. "Don't tell me what to do. I'm in this mess because of you, and I need you to help me dig us out. Tyson Cade expects me to win this thing. That's the only way I protect my family and friends. Do you understand?"

"Take your hands off of me."

Jason relinquished the man's shirt and pushed himself back off the table. "Now I'm going to ask you a series of questions, and I want you to answer them with a nod or a shake of the head."

Trey scowled back at him.

"Did Kelly Flowers work for Tyson Cade?"

No response from Trey.

"Trey, it doesn't make sense to me that you would threaten to kill Flowers just because he shamed you for not doing well at a baseball tryout. I mean, come on. You and he are talking in low voices, and all of a sudden you go off the deep end. You're both from Sand Mountain. You were teammates on the football team. You have already admitted to doing deliveries for Cade. It is a very easy stretch to assume that Flowers was also working for Cade."

Again, Trey sat there with no expression.

"Damnit, man," Jason said. "What is the deal? Don't you want to live?"

"There are some things worse than dying."

"Like what?"

"Like watching the people you love die. Like what you are feeling right now, Mr. Rich. I don't want to feel that."

"Who are you talking about? Your mom? Your dad? Colleen Maples?"

Trey looked down at the table. "Yes. Mostly Mom and Colleen. I know if I talk, Tyson will hurt them."

"Do you really think Tyson Cade is going to hurt your mother? Didn't she practically raise him? Isn't she the reason that I'm here? She begged Tyson to hire you a lawyer, and he got me as a favor to her."

Trey put his face in his hands, and Jason returned to his seat.

"Please, man. I'm at the end of my rope, here. I can't tell if Tyson hired me to help you or to guarantee that you lose."

At this revelation, Trey looked up. "What do you mean?"

Jason thought of Chase, who Tyson Cade said was meeting Kelly Flowers the night he was murdered at the very place he was killed. Teresa Roe had seen them together at the Brick. Why? What was the deal? Was Flowers leaning on her as a cop? As one of Cade's men? Or was he just dating her?

"I mean he has hamstrung me by killing my investigator. By scaring you into not talking." Jason sighed and pulled out his phone. He found a photograph of Chase and pushed the device over the table to Trey. "Have you ever seen Flowers with this woman?"

Trey shook his head, and Jason breathed a sigh of relief.

"Who is she?" Trey asked.

"A woman named Chase Wittschen."

"Don't know her. Why's she important?"

Jason stood and scratched his neck. "I'm not sure that she is." He closed his eyes and hung his head. "Trey, please, can you give me something? Someone who might know something."

"Have you talked with Colleen yet?"

"She's refused our requests for an interview."

Trey crossed his arms. "Try her again."

"Why? What could she possibly—"

"A lot," Trey said, walking around the table to the door and banging three times. "I haven't seen Kelly with the woman you're talking about . . . but I have seen him with Colleen."

"What?"

"Try her again," he repeated as the door swung open.

76

Colleen Maples lived in a lake cottage off Highway 69. To get there, Jason had to drive right past Fire by the Lake restaurant, a key site in his sister's case. Then he turned right onto Browns Creek Road.

Maples's house was about a half mile down the road.

Jason parked in the driveway and saw that a BMW 3 Series sedan was nestled under the carport. He remembered the vehicle from the last time he'd stalked Maples for an interview. Then, in the parking lot of Marshall Medical Center North, she had almost run over him. He didn't think this visit could be any worse than that, but he wasn't willing to make any guarantees given how the day had gone thus far.

He knocked on the door and waited. Nothing. He knocked again. And again. After ten minutes, he tried the knob. It was unlocked. He leaned his head inside. "Hello? Ms. Maples? Colleen?"

Nothing.

He took a full step into the room. "Is anyone here? Colleen? Ms. Maples?" For a split second, he worried he was about to see another dead body.

"Wh-wh-who is it?" a groggy voice called out from the darkness.

Jason blinked his eyes and saw a woman emerge from the dark. Her brown hair was tousled, and her eyes were creased with sleep. She wore a long T-shirt that fell to her knees. Still, even in complete disarray, Colleen Maples was an attractive woman. She flipped on a light and put up her hands against the glare. Then she looked at him. "What are you doing here?"

"I'm Trey's lawyer. He said that you knew some things that might help me."

She crossed her arms. "I should call the police. What? Did you jimmy the lock?"

"It was unlocked." Jason glanced to his right and saw a kitchen table with an open bottle of vodka. It was a fifth of Grey Goose that might have a couple shots left in it.

She put a hand over her face. "Look, it's five forty-five. My shift starts at seven p.m."

Jason frowned. "Why would a CRNA work the night shift?"

She glared at him. "When the CRNA has her license suspended and has to work as a registered nurse for a hospital who's about had enough of her."

"Ah," Jason said. "I'm sorry."

"It's my own fault. I'm sure you know my story very well."

"I thought you got a relatively light punishment. A fine and probation."

"I did for the stuff with Braxton. But then, a few months ago, I failed a drug test. That led to a suspension, and now I'm lucky to be working as an RN. One more screwup and my career is toast."

Jason stared at her with an open mouth. "I'm sorry. I have a similar situation with the Alabama State Bar."

"I know."

For a moment, Jason wasn't sure what to say. "I'm sorry I woke you," he finally managed.

She breathed through her mouth and poked her lip out, causing her bangs to fly up out of her eyes. "It's OK. I was about to have to get up anyway." Then she sighed. "Want some coffee?"

"That'd be great."

———

A couple of minutes later, they were sitting at the kitchen table with two mugs of coffee in front of them. Colleen hadn't removed the still-open vodka bottle, and Jason glanced at it. "Grey Goose was always my favorite vodka."

Colleen took a sip of coffee. "Well, it's about the only thing getting me through the hours I'm not working."

Jason almost said "I'm sorry" again but stopped himself. "How long had Trey been working for Tyson Cade?"

She grimaced. "I'm not exactly sure. Trey and I broke up right after your sister's trial. But I know he hated it. Every second of it. But Trey was stubborn. He wanted to make another run at the Majors, and Cade paid very well."

"Forgive me if this sounds insensitive or direct, but what were you doing with him? You're a beautiful, successful, professional woman. He's only a few years removed from high school."

She leaned back from the table. "When word got out about me and Braxton, I felt like I was walking around with a scarlet letter on my chest. All my friends and colleagues shunned me. I'm midthirties, never married, and had spent five years of my life hoping that Braxton Waters would leave his wife for me. Then we have a spat during Trey's surgery, Trey ends up with a broken leg that never heals, and I'm investigated for the first time by the Board of Nursing. Then Braxton was killed. I guess I was spiraling out of control. I felt guilty. I went to see Trey to say I'm sorry, and we ended up having a drink and . . ."

"One thing led to another," Jason finished, remembering how Trey had described their relationship on the stand during Jana's trial.

"Yep. I'm still not sure what I was doing. At the end of the day, I guess I was lonely. Then, after Jana's trial . . . after you outed us . . ." She pointed a finger at Jason. ". . . I was embarrassed, and I guess I became very depressed. And then I got involved with someone else . . ."

"Kelly Flowers?"

Her eyes widened for a second, and then she gazed at her mug. "Trey told you."

"What can you tell me about Flowers?"

She looked up with a smirk. "I'm sure Trey has filled you in on all the sordid details."

"Trey hasn't said a word. He advised me to ask you about it."

Colleen peered down at the table. "I guess that's not surprising." Then she chuckled, and the bitterness in the sound was palpable. "Look around you, Mr. Rich. My life is a shambles. I work the graveyard shift as a staff nurse. I used to be a CRNA. I'm two months late on the mortgage to this place, and I'll probably be evicted soon. I drink a quart of vodka a day."

"How did you get mixed up with Flowers?"

"I went out with some friends to Wintzell's. I drank too much, and on my way home, Flowers pulled me over. I failed the field sobriety test, and he was going to take me in. I begged him not to—said that I'd lose my license—and he offered me a deal."

"What kind of a deal?"

"If I went with him to the Hampton Inn, he'd tear up the ticket."

"Did you?"

Her lip began to tremble. "Yes."

"Then what?"

"He made me do that a few more times."

"Always at the Hampton Inn?"

"No, after the first encounter, we usually came here since I live alone. Finally, I said no." She scoffed. "The next day, I was randomly drug tested."

"Do you think Flowers was behind that?"

She cocked her head at him and opened her mouth. A nonverbal *duh* if there ever was one.

Jason felt a buzz of adrenaline combined with anger pulse through him. What Colleen Maples had just described was an absolute abuse of power. An officer using his badge to coerce sex in exchange for leniency. Could Flowers have pulled the same sting with Chase? Despite his fatigue, Jason's heart was pounding now. Kelly Flowers was a dirty cop. He gritted his teeth. *Very dirty . . . just awful . . .*

What also made sense was that Colleen Maples would have every reason to want misfortune to befall Sergeant Kelly Flowers. *As would Chase, if he was blackmailing her . . .*

. . . but, if Flowers stole Trey's girlfriend under these circumstances, it also enhances my client's motive . . .

"Trey has told me that you texted him the morning of Kelly Flowers's murder." Jason forged ahead. "You let him know that the cops were staking out his apartment. Why'd you do that?"

She shrugged. "I drive by Trey's apartment from time to time. When I saw all the police vehicles, I got worried."

"Ms. Maples, is there anything else you can tell me about Kelly Flowers?"

She bit her lip and crossed her arms. "Yes. There was only one person that Trey interacted with in Tyson Cade's organization. That's why Trey hated Kelly so much. It was Kelly that convinced him to work for Cade. And since Kelly was a police officer, he could lean on Trey and threaten to arrest him. It was a dangerous game Kelly was playing. I mean, Trey could have turned him in." She took a sip from her mug. "Or he could have killed him."

"You could have reported him too," Jason said. "Or . . ." He let his voice fade out. Then he decided to press. "Ms. Maples, where were you the night of April 8? Were you working?"

"I was here. At home."

"Alone?"

"Just me and a bottle of Grey Goose. Look, I know where you're going," she said, her voice reeking of sarcasm. "It's kind of obvious. But I didn't kill the bastard. I don't own a shotgun."

"Did you know that Trey owned one?"

She blinked, and Jason thought it might be a tell. Perhaps she hadn't considered that possibility. "No."

He couldn't discern whether she was lying, so he decided to change direction. "What do you think happened to Flowers?"

She drank a last sip of coffee and walked to the sink, then poured the rest down the drain. "I don't have a clue, but I really don't think Trey could have killed Flowers. So the only thing that makes sense is that Tyson Cade had him killed. Maybe Cade got word that Flowers was using his badge to solicit sexual favors from women, and he thought that behavior was too risky for his inside man? Or perhaps Cade found someone else in the sheriff's office to siphon him information. Cade kills Flowers and sets Trey up for it. Then, because Trudy practically raised him, he hires you as Trey's lawyer, knowing full damn well there's no way you can win."

"Why would he do that?" Jason asked, knowing that he had been bothered by the same thoughts.

"To make it look like he's protecting his people. According to Trey, Tyson has a godfather-like reputation in Sand Mountain. He takes care of his own, and Trey and Trudy are his own."

"So this is all a sham orchestrated by Cade."

She shrugged and walked toward a hallway. "That's my two cents, and I'm sure that's what it's worth. But if Trey is innocent, and I believe he is, what else makes sense?"

Jason pondered the question as he stared into his coffee cup. Then he felt a hand touch his shoulder. He looked up at Colleen.

"Good luck to you."

"Thank you, Ms. Maples."

"You can call me Colleen," she said as she walked away. "I get off at seven a.m. Monday through Friday and sleep from ten to six. If you need to see me again, come in the morning." She cocked her head toward the almost-empty bottle of vodka on the table. "I might even let you buy me a drink."

"OK."

77

At 7:00 p.m., Top O' the River was hopping. Jason got a booth and asked for Trudy Cowan. His head was spinning, but he knew he couldn't stop. He had to keep moving. Otherwise, he'd think about Harry. And Izzy. And Chase. And Nola.

He wasn't hungry, but he ordered the catfish plate to be agreeable. He drank a few sips of sweet tea and waited. While he did, he received a text from Satch.

> Bull Branner reserved a bay at the range tomorrow morning at eight. Let's plan on meeting him then.

Jason sent back the thumbs-up emoji.

A few minutes later, a woman sat down across from him. She wore a navy-blue golf shirt with the words TOP O' THE RIVER over the heart along with a miniature picture of the restaurant. She was a stocky woman with thin silver hair. She had blue eyes that pierced him with a "this better be good" stare.

"Ms. Cowan, thank you for making time for me."

"I don't have but a couple minutes. What can I do for you? Is Trey OK?"

"He's fine. Except he's not giving me all the information he knows."

"Now why would he not talk to his lawyer?"

"Because he's afraid Tyson Cade is going to hurt you."

She waved a hand at him. "Tyson ain't going to lay a finger on me. I practically raised the boy."

"Tell me about that," Jason said, scooting up in his seat.

"Well, Tyson's daddy run off before he was even born. His momma was a nice lady. A real pretty woman. Worked at Wayne Farms on the line before she started hooking. Because of her *profession*, she was out late a lot. Tyson spent many evenings over at our house. I probably fed that boy supper almost every night. Trey was little then, and my husband, Walter, was a drunk. You might say me and Tyson kept each other company for a lot of years." She paused. "I loved that boy. Once Trey got to be a little older, we were so busy with his games that we didn't see Tyson as much. Of course, part of that was that he was a grown man and had gotten his own place." She looked down at the table. "But he still came around. And when he became well off, he always looked after us. He's been really great since Walt left."

"What happened to Tyson's mom?"

"She ended up getting sick with fever and never got over it. Didn't have health insurance and was too stubborn to go to the hospital. That was when Tyson was in college."

"What about Trey? How has Tyson been with him since Trey has been an adult?"

She shrugged and stared off into the distance. "Trey didn't approve of Tyson's line of work."

"You mean drug dealing?"

She crossed her arms. "Folks have to make a living, and Tyson grew up hard."

"Are you saying you approve?"

"No. I'm saying I understand."

"But Trey didn't."

"No. Trey was naive. He was a gifted athlete since he was in kindergarten. People always treated him special because of his arm, or because of how big and strong he was. Kissing his ass. Wanting him to play on a travel team or an AAU basketball team or whatever. Sports came easy. So did the girls. Everything. And grades? Hell, they didn't matter to Trey no matter how hard I tried to convince him different. He was going to play football in the NFL."

"Then he broke his leg."

"And everything went to shit in a minute. No thanks to your brother-in-law. God bless his soul. But Trey wasn't tough. He'd been the golden boy for so long that he didn't know how to scrap."

"He never went to college."

"Couldn't afford it. He probably could have worked his way through a community college, but Trey wasn't interested in anything. The injury got him depressed, and then the medications kept him that way." She flung up her hands. "That's just an old woman's opinion."

"How did he feel about working for Tyson?"

She gritted her teeth. "He never told me, and I never asked."

"But you knew."

She nodded.

"How?"

"One of his good friends kept me abreast of everything."

Jason felt a tickle. "Kelly Flowers."

"Remember that old show *Leave It to Beaver*?"

"Vaguely."

"Remember Eddie Haskell? Always being nice to Mrs. Cleaver, while he was bullying the Beaver and trying to get Wally in trouble. That was Kelly."

"What did he tell you?"

"That I needed to watch Trey. That he was in with Tyson."

"What did you do?"

"I asked Trey about it, and he denied any such thing. But I knew he was lying. Trey could never get away with nothing as a kid, because he was a terrible liar."

"How'd you know?"

"When Trey lies, he can't make eye contact with you. Easiest tell in the world."

Jason made a mental note of that, though such a general statement could be made about pretty much anyone.

"Did you ever suspect Kelly of working for Tyson?"

"What?" She snickered. "No way. Kelly loved being a police officer. Hell, he wore that damn uniform everywhere. Was proud of it."

"You knew him well too."

"I knew all the boys Trey's age in Alder Springs."

"Kelly have any enemies?"

"Not that I'm aware of. But being a cop is a risky job. I'm sure he put away some folks that got out that may have wanted revenge."

Jason nodded his agreement. One of the things he had requested in discovery was the names of all people that Kelly Flowers had arrested since joining the force, along with copies of their files. It was too broad, and Shay would likely object, but he should be able to at least get the names of anyone convicted that was out of jail or prison on the day Kelly was murdered. It was a long shot, but so was everything in this case.

Jason pulled up a photograph of Chase on his phone and slid it across the table. "Ever see Kelly with this woman?"

"Pretty girl." She shook her head. "No. Who is she?"

"Her name is Chase Wittschen. A few folks have placed her with Flowers in the weeks before his murder." Jason paused and decided it was better not to mislead his client's mother. "She's my ex-girlfriend." The words pained Jason to say, but they were true. Chase had left him. And she might never come back.

"Oh." Trudy squinted at him. "That must be awkward for you."

"It won't affect my representation of your son. If she's implicated, I'll bring it out. I just . . . don't quite understand what she and he were doing."

"Look, I've got to get back to work, but I want to pass along something I believe. Tyson Cade is a drug dealer, but he makes no bones about who he is. He's also always done right by me, and despite Trey poor-mouthing him, Tyson gave Trey a job and paid him money. That's a sight more than Kelly Flowers ever did. Kelly was a chameleon. A hypocrite. Nice and friendly on the outside but rotten where it counts. I never trusted the boy, and I'm not all that sad he's gone. I heard rumors that he would arrest women and give them a warning in exchange for . . . well . . . you know."

Jason felt his stomach tighten as Trudy Cowan described exactly the situation that Colleen Maples had told him.

"Did your ex get into any trouble?" Trudy asked. "Was she ever arrested by Kelly?"

"I don't know," Jason said.

"Well, I'd check that out if I were you." Trudy stood and extended her hand. "Thank you for helping my boy."

"You're welcome."

He watched her walk away, thinking Trey was fortunate to have such a strong mother. And Tyson Cade was lucky to have her as well.

She didn't know about Flowers and Cade . . .

That was strange, but her explanation made sense. It was Flowers who told her about Trey working for Cade. But if she didn't trust Flowers, wouldn't she have confronted Trey about it?

A waitress set a plate of catfish and fries in front of him. Jason wasn't hungry but forced himself to eat a few bites. Nothing about this case was adding up.

And now Harry is dead.

Jason squeezed his eyes shut. He'd kept himself busy for four hours, but the image on Tyson Cade's phone was back. Harry's dead eyes. The bullet hole. The open mouth.

He asked for the check and paid. Then he hustled out into the night. He got behind the wheel of his Porsche and squealed his tires as he left the lot.

Tears had begun to fall, but Jason made no move to wipe them. He needed an AA meeting. A talk with his counselor. Lunch with Ashley. Something. But he didn't want any of that.

What he wanted was to get drunk.

Keep moving, he thought. *Harry wouldn't want that. He wouldn't want me to quit.*

As Jason motored up the Veterans Memorial Bridge, he glanced to his right at the lights of Buck Island. Then he took out his phone and called Nola.

"Hey," she answered.

"Hey."

"It's pretty late, Uncle Jason."

"I'm sorry, honey. I keep forgetting it's eastern time there."

Silence.

"So . . . how have things been going?"

An impatient sigh. "It's rehab. It sucks."

"I know. I . . . I know it does."

More silence.

"What can I do for you, Uncle Jason?" Her voice was cold. Distant. Just as it had been every time he'd called since her admission.

"Nothing." He knew he couldn't tell her about Harry. "I guess I just wanted to hear your voice."

"Does it sound the same?" The sarcasm was palpable. "Want me to sing you a song? Maybe one of your cheesy favorites. How about that 'I Wanna Be Rich' song? Or maybe, given where I am, 'Cocaine,' by Eric Clapton?" She mimicked the opening guitar chords to the famous song.

"That won't be necessary."

"Good. Look, I've got a group meeting I have to attend in the morning. Hi, my name is Nola, and I'm an addict." She whined the words out. "Going to bed. Later."

The phone clicked dead.

Jason sighed as Highway 79 came into view. "Later," he whispered to himself.

———

When Jason got home, he noticed that Izzy's car was gone.

He ambled up the steps and saw a note on the pillow in the guest room. He grabbed it and unfolded the paper.

> Jason,
> I've had a lot of time to think today, and I can no longer be a part of what you're doing here in Guntersville. Ever since you opened a satellite office in this town, your life has gone haywire, and I've done everything I can do to keep the firm on solid footing. Harry did everything he could do, too, and he all but begged you not to have him follow Tyson Cade's dealers. Now he's dead, and if you keep up what you're doing, you'll probably be joining him. I can't relive this day ever again. I loved Harry, and I love you. But I just can't do this anymore. Please accept this letter as my resignation from the firm. I will also be withdrawing as your lawyer in the case the state has against you. I'm sure you'll have no trouble finding someone else.
> Good luck, Jason Rich. I love you, and I'm sorry.
> Izzy

78

At 8:00 a.m. sharp the following day, Bull Branner walked into the gun range. He checked in at the front desk and was given a target. Then he walked to the back with his case draped over his shoulder. As Bull knelt to pick out which weapon he was going to shoot first, Satch grabbed the man by the collar and jerked him up against the wall. "Need a few words, Bull."

"What the . . ."

Satch stuck his forearm up under Bull's neck, and the other man gasped. "Now, no one else is here, and the video cameras, for some reason, aren't working this morning. Unless you want me to call 911 here in a few minutes and report a shooting accident, I'd suggest you answer a few questions. You understand?"

Bull nodded.

Jason stood next to Mickey and Chuck in the shooting bay. No one else was in the range, and Mickey had hung the **CLOSED** sign as soon as Bull had checked in.

"Now, I have spoken to at least fifty residents of Alder Springs in the last month, and about half of them have told me that you are allowing drug deals to be made and consummated at your old barn. You know, the place where Kelly Flowers was murdered back in April. The place you told us you never go to anymore and hardly ever use."

Bull moved his eyes around the small space. They had narrowed to two little black dots. "You can't prove anything, Satch. This is bullshit."

Chuck kicked Bull in the knee, and the stubby man fell to the floor. Then Mickey kicked him in the chest. Chuck picked the other man up by his hair and slung him against the wall. "When you talk to my brother, you address him as Colonel."

Bull sank to the ground and held his stomach. "I think you broke my ribs."

"We're gonna break more than that, son," Satch said, his voice as menacing as Jason had ever heard it. "Now my friend here has some questions."

Jason stepped forward and squatted next to Bull. "Did Tyson Cade pay you an incentive to use your barn for his business?"

"I can't answer that," Bull said. "I'd rather you kill me."

"We might take you up on that," Satch said.

"Let me ask you this," Jason said. "Did you ever see Kelly Flowers at the barn prior to his murder?"

"Yes."

Jason felt a surge of adrenaline. He hadn't slept a wink last night after reading Izzy's resignation letter. He had sat out on the sunporch staring at the water until the sun began to rise. Numb all over until Satch had knocked on the door to take him to the range.

"When?"

"Several times."

"Did Flowers work for Cade?"

Bull touched his ribs and winced. "I don't know."

Satch pulled his arm back to strike, and Bull held up his hands.

"I really don't. There were a lot of rumors that he did. I'm sure you heard those when you did your talking to folks."

"I did," Satch said.

"Well, the truth is I don't know. All I know is that Kelly told me he'd be at the barn at certain times, and I made sure it was open for him."

"Did he pay you?"

"No, but Kelly is a police officer, and he said he knew what I was doing with Tyson. I couldn't take the risk."

Savvy, Jason thought. Flowers was playing the double-dealer to perfection.

"Did Tyson know Flowers was using the barn?"

"Yes. I told him." Bull licked his lips. "He said he'd take care of it."

"Those were his words?" Jason asked.

"Yes."

Jason straightened his legs. That was good information, but he wasn't going to get anywhere pinning Flowers's murder on Cade.

"Did you ever see who Flowers was meeting?"

Bull grinned, showing a gold front tooth. "A woman. I know that."

"Do you know what he was doing with her?"

Bull's grin widened. "Yeah, hoss. He was fucking her. I think it was some bitch he'd arrested, and he'd cut a deal with her."

"Sex in exchange for no charges," Jason said, his voice losing steam as he remembered Trudy Cowan's insinuation last night at Top O' the River and Colleen Maples's haunting story of Flowers blackmailing her with the same setup.

"Yep."

"When'd they meet?"

"All different times. Sometimes morning. Other times night."

"When was the last time Flowers used the barn to meet with her?"

Bull's eyes narrowed. "I can't remember," he said, with a twinkle in his eyes. "But I do recall him reserving it for twelve thirty a.m. the morning he was killed."

Jason ground his teeth together. "Are you sure?"

"As shit."

"Then why didn't you tell the police that?"

"What do you think I am? Stupid or something? I can't tell the sheriff's office that I've been letting a cop use my building to blackmail a woman into giving him sex. And if I did, then I'd open the door to them investigating my other uses of the barn." He whistled. "And then I'd be as dead as Kelly Flowers."

"Did you ever see the woman?" Jason asked.

He nodded, and Jason winced. "What did she look like?"

"Pretty. Had short brownish-blonde hair. Nice ass."

Jason pulled up the same picture he'd showed Trey and Trudy Cowan. They hadn't recognized Chase, but he knew this time would be different. "Is this her?"

Bull started laughing immediately. "Yeah, man." Then he looked from the screen into Jason's eyes. "Well, I'll be dipped in horseshit. Was he fucking your girl?"

Jason's left hand formed a fist and flung out at the man's face without conscious thought. He heard Bull's nose crack, and then he threw his right fist into his cheek, seeing blood fly out his mouth. He punched once, twice, three more times, before he felt his feet being lifted off the floor, as he continued to flail his fists in front of him.

Jason was taken into a small office and pushed up against the wall. "Easy now," Satch said. "Easy. Don't make me hurt you."

Jason tried to calm his breathing. He doubled over and grabbed his knees. When he finally caught his breath, he straightened.

Satch was staring at him with his slit-like eyes. "You're going to have to talk with Chase."

"I tried. They wouldn't let me."

"Jason, where there's smoke, there's fire. And it is a fucking chimney right now. Cade said that Flowers was meeting Chase the night of the murder, and Bull just confirmed it. And, if Flowers was using his position as a police officer to force her into sex, then that's a powerful reason to kill him." He grabbed Jason's shoulders. "But it might also offer a defense. I'm not a lawyer, but seems like this could be self-defense or insanity or something."

Jason stared at him, not quite believing what he was saying. "Satch, what—?"

"I told you I had a working theory, remember?"

Jason nodded, feeling numb.

"Chuck found a witness," Satch said. "I didn't want to say anything to you until we talked with Bull, but everything Bull just said is consistent with our conclusion."

"A witness?"

"Ms. Eva Claire Cobb. Lives on Hustleville Road. She's been in and out of the hospital with congestive heart failure, but she was home the night of April 8, and at just past midnight the morning of April 9, she was sitting on her front porch when she saw a uniformed officer walking by."

Jason's heart fluttered. "How close was she to Branner's Place?"

"She lives almost exactly between the Alder Springs Grocery and Bull's place. Didn't you say Flowers's vehicle was found at the convenience store?"

"Yes," Jason said. "Which means he could have walked to Branner's Place."

"Could have? He definitely walked. Ms. Cobb saw him."

"Did she recognize him as Flowers?"

"No, but she saw his uniform. That's good enough, isn't it?"

"Probably. Satch, did she see the shooting?"

"No. From her porch, you can't quite make out the barn, and she's worn earplugs for years. She didn't hear the blast and probably wouldn't have heard the shot if it had happened in her front yard."

"So . . . what's the deal, then? She saw him. If she didn't see the killing, then what—?"

"She saw something else."

"What?"

"The officer was carrying a bag under his arm. She couldn't make out the color, but it had a strap."

Jason blinked his eyes, his mind racing. Had there been anything about a bag or a satchel being recovered at the scene of the crime? *No . . .*

"The police didn't find a bag," Jason said.

"I didn't think so." Satch had a glint in his reptilian gaze. "And I bet they didn't discover one on your client, either, did they?"

Jason shook his head, as Satch's theory dawned on him.

"Stands to reason that the true killer may have taken the bag," the colonel said, pausing. "Especially if she was an addict, and there was meth inside it."

Jason swallowed, and his mouth was as dry as sandpaper. "Satch . . . are you saying you think Chase killed Flowers?"

"No. What I'm saying is that if Cowan didn't kill him, what else makes sense?"

79

Jason called the Perdido Addiction Center from the parking lot of the gun range. As he waited while the receptionist paged Michal, he caught sight of Bull Branner limping back to his truck. He had a paper towel pressed against his face. He looked at Jason and shot him the bird.

Jason gave him a thumbs-up.

"This is Michal."

"Hey, it's Jason Rich. I'm sorry to bother you, but it is an emergency."

"What's going on?"

"I know I said I'd wait until Chase finished the program, but I just can't do that anymore. I have to see her."

"And risk any progress we've made with her."

"Yes." Jason chose his words carefully. "It's possible that she may be the only witness to a murder."

Jason heard breathing on the other end of the line. "Michal, please. I have no choice. I checked Chase into rehab. I'm her sponsor. And I have to talk with her."

"OK," she finally said.

"I'll be there this afternoon."

———

Jason drove himself to the airport. Satch had offered to take him, but Jason declined. "There may be pushback with what we did to Branner,"

Jason had said. "He's connected to Cade. He didn't admit it, but he wouldn't answer the question. That's enough for me."

"Me too," Satch had agreed. Before leaving the house, Satch had leaned his huge frame against the Porsche and offered Jason some much-needed advice. "I know you got a lot swirling around your head right now. In the army, I always told the soldiers under me to stay in the present. Solve the problem right in front of them. You can't fight a war with a distracted mind."

Jason had thanked him and shook his hand.

Now, as he trudged up the steps and into the plane, Jason tried to follow the colonel's instructions. *Nothing is going to make sense until I talk with Chase. That is the current problem.*

As the plane lifted off, Jason gazed out the window at Lake Guntersville. It was so beautiful. So natural. How could evil live in such a place?

Jason pressed his head against the glass. He wasn't that naive. If he had learned anything as a lawyer, it was this . . .

. . . *evil lives everywhere.*

———

Jason knew something was wrong the moment he checked in at the Perdido Addiction Center. "They'll be right with you, Mr. Rich," the receptionist said, her face tense.

Jason waited less than a minute before three people came toward him. Michal was one of them, but an older woman was out front flanked by a bald-headed man with glasses. Jason recognized the older woman as Dr. Sylvia Otto, the owner, who he had spoken with when he'd checked Chase in.

"Jason," Dr. Otto said. Behind her, Michal nodded but didn't smile.

"What's all this?" Jason asked. "Where's Chase?"

"She checked out three hours ago."

"She did *what*?" Jason asked.

"She asked for a discharge, Mr. Rich," the man said. "My name is Bill Kettlebaum. I'm the physician following her, and I would not approve her leaving." He sighed. "So she checked out AMA."

"Good lord," he said, shooting an accusatory glance toward his old counselor. "Michal, what did you—"

"It wasn't her fault, Jason," Dr. Otto said. "After consulting with Dr. Kettlebaum and Chase's counselor, Michelle, we all thought it would be best if we told Chase you were coming. We didn't think it would be productive if she felt we had ambushed her."

"And now she's gone. How productive is that?"

"How could we have known she would check herself out against medical advice?"

"Why didn't you call me?"

"We tried, but the calls went straight to voice mail."

Jason ground his teeth together, knowing he wouldn't have had service on the airplane. "I can't believe this."

"I'm sorry, Jason," Michal said. "We all are."

"Mr. Rich, this isn't a prison," the doctor said. "Patients can leave when they want."

Jason found a nearby bench and collapsed onto it. He placed his face in his hands. Then he looked up at Dr. Otto. "Did she say where she might be going?"

"No. But she did leave you something."

———

An hour later, as the wheels of the jet curled up under the fuselage and the plane took flight, Jason cursed under his breath as he held the piece of notebook paper to his face. He'd already read it at least ten times, but he was a glutton for punishment. Chase's letter was shorter than Izzy's but no less painful.

J. R.,
I know you know what I did. I hope one day you'll
forgive me.
Chase

Jason finally wadded up the page and threw it across the plane, hitting the window on the other side. "Good riddance." He felt his eyes beginning to moisten, and he wiped his face hard with both hands.

He was three and a half months out from a trial he wasn't sure he could win unless he pointed the finger at the woman he loved most in the world. Jason glared at the wadded-up note on the floor. *Who left me for drugs and a tryst with an officer who she may very well have murdered.* Jason felt anger and bitterness building within him.

He reclined his chair and gazed out at the dark sky. He hadn't slept in almost thirty-six hours, and he felt exhaustion finally taking over. Before he passed out, visions of each of the people he had lost popped into his mind, finishing with his sister.

Poor baby. Jana's voice in his mind. *Always so weak, J. J.*

She had called him J. J. despite the fact that he'd hated it and much preferred J. R. It was her pet name for him, and he cringed when he heard it again in his thoughts.

Big sister can't bail you out of this one.

Jason squeezed his eyes shut, trying to block out the voice that terrorized his thoughts, but it was no use.

You're weak.

Weak.

Weak.

80

Bull Branner's nose was broken. He hadn't had it x-rayed, but he knew by the crooked way it set and the perpetual ache he felt every time he touched it.

"Rich really do this to you?" Matthew Dean asked, as he steered the runabout boat out into the main channel.

"Yeah, but only after the Tonidandels cracked my ribs and took my knee out."

"What did you tell them?" This voice came from behind him and sent a shiver of fear up both his arms. He'd spoken with Tyson Cade before—enough to recognize his voice—but it had been a long time. Matty Dean and Kelly Flowers were Bull's main contacts. Now that Kelly was dead, all communication had been with Matty.

Until tonight.

"That Kelly had met a woman at the barn a few times before he was killed. And that he had set up a meeting the night he was shot." Bull sucked in a breath. "Just what you told me to say if the Tonidandels or Rich ever got after me."

"Did Rich believe you?" Matty asked.

"I mean . . . he seemed pretty messed up by it. He didn't start punching me until I told him about the woman."

"Did you tell them about Flowers's association with me?" Tyson asked.

"No."

"Did you tell them anything about any of my meetings at your barn?"

"No. I promise."

"What about the night of Flowers's murder? Did you say anything about me being at your barn then?"

"Tyson, I'm not a fool. I'd never do that. I'd never say anything about you being there." He swallowed. "Or the other officer."

Silence for several seconds as the boat continued to head toward Scottsboro. Then a muted laugh. "What?" Tyson asked. "I never said anything about another officer."

Bull bit his lip and gazed at Matty Dean, who was pointing a small handgun at him. "I didn't get a good look at him. Just saw the uniform."

"Ah, Bull. Damnit, man," Tyson said. Then he snapped his fingers, and three gunshots rang out.

Bull slumped forward and grabbed his chest. He looked up at Matty, who now had the barrel of the gun pressed against Bull's temple.

"Please," Bull whimpered.

"I'm sorry, Bull," Tyson said from behind him. "But there are some things you can't unsee."

"Or unhear," Matty added.

Then he pulled the trigger.

———

Matty drove the boat until he was well into Tennessee. Then, using two cinder blocks this time, he and Tyson threw the body of Bull Branner overboard.

For a few moments, the two men rested and gazed up at the stars.

"We'll need to stop for gas," Matty said.

"Let's anchor and sleep for a few hours."

"Ten-four," Matty said.

Tyson stretched out on the back console, while Matty did the same in the middle. "You really think that was necessary?" Matty asked.

"We can't take any chances," Tyson said. "Bull knew too much. If those crazy Tonidandels came after him again, he might have spilled all the beans."

"What are we going to do about those bastards?"

Tyson closed his eyes and chuckled. "Matty, have you ever heard the story of the old bull and the young bull?"

"What? No."

Tyson gazed up at the stars, remembering the story that King Hanson had told him in prison just before Tyson became the leader of the Sand Mountain meth business. "Young bull and old bull are sitting high up on a hill looking down on a valley full of cows. Young bull says, 'Hey, Dad, let's run down this hill and fuck one of them cows.'" Tyson snorted. "Old bull says, 'No, son. Let's walk down this hill . . . and fuck 'em all.'"

Matty Dean howled with laughter.

"When you're in my position, you always have to be the old bull, Matty. Colonel Tonidandel and his brothers have to be handled with care. And I'm still using Jason Rich." Tyson paused and closed his eyes. "So I'm going to walk down the hill. When the opportunity presents itself, we'll take out the brothers."

"What about Rich?"

Tyson grinned, keeping his eyes closed. "My bet is that he takes himself out."

81

Jason woke up in the front seat of the Porsche. He was still at the air-field. When the plane had landed, he'd decided to close his eyes and take a quick nap.

And he had slept for seven hours. He stepped out of the car on shaky legs. Then he took out his phone. It was 7:45 a.m. There were a few planes getting ready on the runway, but otherwise the place was barren.

He had several texts and emails, but none of them were from Izzy. He still held out hope that his partner would reconsider, but he knew he couldn't press her. If Izzy wanted to come back, he would welcome her with open arms. She had every reason to leave him.

Chase, on the other hand . . .

Good riddance, Jason thought again. If she wanted to come back, then that was up to her. Whether she came back or not, he'd have to decide what to do with the information that Tyson Cade had given him and Bull Branner had confirmed. Could he really set up his defense around Chase being the alternate killer? Satch Tonidandel seemed to think he could, especially with Hustleville Road eyewitness Eva Claire Cobb testifying that Flowers had been carrying a bag, presumably full of meth, that wasn't found at the murder scene or in Trey's car, apartment, or mother's home.

Jason wasn't sure, but he was closer to saying yes today than he'd been yesterday.

He cranked up the Porsche and pulled onto Highway 431. *You have an obvious conflict of interest,* he thought. *You should withdraw as Trey's lawyer.*

Jason shook his head, thinking of Harry. He couldn't quit. Not now. He'd lost too much.

He saw a liquor store up ahead and turned on his blinker. He wasn't going to quit. But it was time to stop being something he wasn't.

———

Fifteen minutes later, he pulled into the driveway on Browns Creek Road. This time, the door was locked. He rapped his knuckles three times on the door and waited.

Colleen Maples answered the door in green scrubs. Her eyes looked tired. "Hey."

"Hey," Jason said. He felt an odd rush of adrenaline mixed with guilt that he was trying his hardest to repress.

"You look awful," she said.

"Thanks," he said.

"What's in the bag?"

Jason pulled a fifth of Grey Goose vodka out of a brown paper sack. "Thought it was time I bought you that drink," he said.

Colleen took a step backward and then walked back into the house. She left the door open.

Jason took a deep breath and exhaled. Then he moved forward and shut the door behind him.

PART FIVE

82

October.

If there was a sweet spot in terms of weather on Lake Guntersville, or, in Jason's opinion, Alabama in general, this was it. Still warm enough to play in the water, but cool in the evening for cookouts, back porch gatherings, and, of course, Friday night lights on the high school gridiron.

And pretty much perfect for college football Saturdays in Tuscaloosa and Auburn.

Jason Rich's favorite time to be on the water was in the fall. He enjoyed the way the leaves turned orange, yellow, and brown and framed the water with their beauty. And his favorite activity, riding the Sea-Doo, was even more enjoyable because the wind that filled his lungs was cool and fresh.

On Saturday evening, October 5, 2019, nine days before the capital murder trial of Trey Cowan, Jason leaned forward on the Sea-Doo and pressed the throttle all the way down. There were few boats or watercraft on the lake at this time of day, as it was getting late, and Auburn was battling Florida in the SEC Game of the Week.

Jason enjoyed the smooth feel of the ride, and at least for a few precious minutes, his mind rested. When he reached his destination, he cut the ignition.

And gazed up at the cliffs at Goat Island.

He moved his eyes around Honeycomb Cove, taking it all in. The last time he'd been here was on Christmas Day last year. He undid the latch on the front console and looked inside, seeing the small box that contained the engagement ring. He still hadn't touched it since Chase's rejection.

Jason slammed the compartment shut. He wouldn't be touching it today. Now, his mind began to race, and he took in a deep breath, forcing himself to stare at the top cliff. He had never had the guts to jump, but that was going to change today. He gritted his teeth as his phone buzzed in his pocket. He took out the device, saw the name on the screen, and groaned. Then he answered. "I know what you're going to say."

"Jason, where in the hell have you been?" Ashley Sullivan's voice sounded frantic. "I've been trying to talk with you for weeks. Normally, I can't get you, and when you do answer, you blow me off."

"Ashley, I'm sorry, but I'm busy. Now's not a good time."

"Well, tough shit."

Jason held the phone out from him. He wasn't sure if he'd ever heard the director of the Alabama Lawyer Assistance Program cuss before. "What do you want?"

"For starters, a meeting. On Monday. My office in Cullman. I want you to be prepared to tell me why you haven't seen me in almost three months. Jason, there are rumors swirling at the state bar office that you are drinking again. Please tell me that's not true."

"It's not true," Jason said.

"But not cooperating with the Lawyer Assistance Program is, and guess what? You're currently not cooperating."

"Look, Ashley. I have a murder trial in little over a week, and I'm running my law firm right now without a partner and with several brand-new associates. Can you give me a break?"

"No, I can't. I'm worried about you, Jason. You don't sound like yourself. You're all hyped up every time we get on the phone."

"This is who I am, Ashley. I'm just being myself. Now I have to be in court Monday morning in Guntersville. It is actually in the bullshit case the state has brought against me, so I don't have any choice but to be there. How about dinner at the All Steak? I'll buy."

"No. No dinners. No schmoozing. My office at six p.m. If you don't show, I'm reporting you to the Alabama State Bar. I'd be there if I were you."

"Yes, ma'am," Jason said, but she had already hung up.

Jason closed his eyes for a second and then opened them. He undid the console again and took out a pill bottle of NoDoz. He popped two in his mouth and swallowed.

"Yeah, baby!" he screamed, as he gazed up at the cliffs.

He turned the Bluetooth on his Sea-Doo to his "kick-ass" playlist. As the beginning of "A Country Boy Can Survive" cranked through the speakers, Jason jumped into the cool water.

———

Five minutes later he was standing on the top cliff, at least sixty feet above the surface. He could hear the music, and the song had changed to "The Needle and the Spoon," by Lynyrd Skynyrd. Jason took a deep breath and slowly exhaled. He gazed down at the water and slapped his hands together.

"Jump, you pansy," he said out loud, but the climb had made him a bit light headed.

"Ohhhhh, yeahhh," Jason mimicked the "Macho Man" Randy Savage but found his energy was waning. He blinked his eyes and then sat down on the rocks, trying to steady his nerves.

He hadn't lied to Ashley. Despite buying vodka for Colleen Maples a few months ago, he hadn't suffered a relapse. He'd watched Colleen drink herself into a slight buzz, but though he'd poured himself a drink, he hadn't taken a sip. When Colleen had invited him back to her bedroom, he'd politely declined and thanked her for the company.

She'd been confused, and he knew he'd probably hurt her feelings, but Jason hadn't cared. He'd walked out of her house and run to his car. Then he'd spent the rest of the night driving before finally returning home. Jason had been too tired to lift weights, so he'd searched YouTube, finding some of his favorite old pro wrestling moments.

The best of seven series between the Russian Nightmare, Nikita Koloff, and Magnum T. A.

The Saturday Night's Main Event when Hulk Hogan saved the Macho Man from the Hart Foundation and the Honky Tonk Man, referred to as the meeting of the Madness and the Mania.

When Sting dropped from the top of the United Center in his Crow outfit holding a baseball bat. Taking on the New World Order by himself.

When the urge to drink had finally passed, Jason had pulled up Dusty Rhodes's famous "Hard Times" speech after the Four Horsemen had broken his leg and practiced his own version of it in the mirror.

"Tyson Cade put hard times on Jason Rich," he mimicked Dusty's high-pitched southern accent and pointed at the mirror. "Hard times!" he screamed.

Finally, he'd managed a laugh. He had sat down on the floor and cackled. Then, thinking of Harry, and Izzy, and Chase, his laughter had turned to sobs.

He'd finally passed out from exhaustion on the floor of the sunporch.

———

Now, some three and a half months later, Jason was still hanging on, but he knew it was by a slim thread. The urge to imbibe was constant, and he had to keep coming up with more drastic defusers. Today, less than thirty-six hours from a court appearance that could mean him losing his license, he had thought the only way to keep from drinking was to jump from the cliffs.

But maybe he didn't have to jump. The climb had seemed to quell his desire for a drink. Jason breathed in the cool autumn air and thanked God that he had beaten the urge again.

Then, with great care to keep from slipping, he descended the cliffs.

When Jason arrived home, Satch Tonidandel was sitting in a rocking chair on the pier. The colonel was smoking a cigar and gazing at the water.

Jason docked the Jet Ski in the boathouse and placed a chair next to him. "Thought you'd be watching the Auburn game."

"They lost." Satch's mouth formed a tiny grin.

"And this makes you happy? I know you're a Bama fan, Colonel, but don't you cheer for Auburn when they aren't playing Alabama?"

"Hell no," Satch said. "I cheer for Alabama and anyone who's playing Auburn. And any self-respecting Auburn fan roots for the Barn and any team playing us. It ain't the best rivalry in sports for nothing."

Jason, who'd never been a college football crazy, just shook his head, knowing Izzy would be saying amen to Satch. Thinking of his former partner gave him a sinking sadness.

"Has Nola called?" Jason asked, bracing for what was coming.

"No," Satch said.

Jason sighed. Nola had been back from rehab a couple of months. If he had thought their relationship was bad prior to her time at the Florida Recovery Center, it was even worse now. Before, she'd argued and fought with him. Rolled her eyes. Been agitated. Now, and especially since turning eighteen, Nola ignored Jason as if he didn't exist. Though she hadn't officially graduated from Guntersville High, she'd obtained her GED and was now spending most of her weekends, including this one, with her sister in Birmingham. She was taking a gap semester and planned to go to college in January. He suspected that part of the counseling she'd been given in Gainesville was to create boundaries with those people that caused her stress or triggered her impulses.

Namely . . . me, Jason thought.

Though she was still technically living at home, Jason knew that was only temporary.

She'll be gone for good soon.

"What are the boys doing tonight?" Jason asked, not wanting to think about Nola.

"Mickey's out with a woman."

Jason raised his eyebrows. "What?" He had never known any of the Tonidandels to date.

"Yeah, cute girl named Tiffany. Cuts hair during the week but likes to fish in her free time. She and Mickey were fishing the same hole a few weeks ago, and I guess they hit it off."

"Sounds . . . so romantic," Jason said, snorting.

Satch grunted but smiled. "Yeah, Mick hasn't spent the night at home the last couple of Saturdays. I think things are going pretty well."

"And Chuck?"

"He's at Camp Sumatanga. Chuck is big in the Emmaus Community, and there's a walk this weekend. Chuck is one of the spiritual leaders."

"Awesome," Jason said. "So you're all by your lonesome."

"Yep, just me and Alexa."

Jason grinned. He'd gotten Satch the device for his birthday in August and was glad to hear him using it.

"Who woulda thunk it? I can have Lady freakin' Gaga right in my living room."

Jason guffawed. "You like Lady Gaga?"

"Sexiest damn woman alive," Satch said. He was so serious about it that Jason forced back his smile.

"I figured you for old country."

"I like some of that, too, but I get tired of it. There's something about Gaga, Jason. The way she tells a story with her words and her costumes and the way she's so damn unapologetic about being herself . . . I don't know, man, it's like Viagra for the soul."

Jason laughed out loud. Over the past few months, especially with Harry dead and Izzy gone, he'd come to cherish these moments with Satch.

"Well, what's the latest?" Jason finally asked.

"Still no word from Bull," he finally said. "I'm afraid that he must be sleeping with the fishes."

"Do we have any other leads or angles from Sand Mountain that you can think of?"

"Nothing besides Ms. Eva Claire Cobb, who's prepared to testify about seeing Flowers carrying a bag down Hustleville Road just before he was killed. Chuck served her with a subpoena yesterday before leaving for Sumatanga."

"Good deal," Jason said. He'd met with Ms. Cobb a few weeks ago and thought she made a credible witness. But she was eighty-six years old and battling a number of health conditions, including congestive heart failure, which would make her ripe for a soft but effective cross-examination from Shay Lankford.

Jason got up and spat into the lake. "I've got a meeting with Detective Daniels tomorrow. I'm hoping that leads to something."

"I hope so too," Satch said, crossing his legs. "Otherwise . . ."

"We're probably screwed," Jason said.

Satch grunted his agreement.

83

Jason was wired when he entered the law office of Bocephus Haynes. "Thank you for setting this up," he said to Bo, as the big man escorted him down a hallway and into a conference room.

Detective Hatty Daniels was sitting in a chair in the middle of a long rectangular table. She stood when Jason entered the room, and they shook hands. "Detective Daniels, thank you for agreeing to meet."

She nodded. Her face was tight and tense.

Jason took a seat at one end of the table and Bo the other.

"I'm sorry about your investigator," Hatty said.

"Thank you. How are you doing since the shooting?"

She shrugged. "My left shoulder still hurts a little from the surgery. All in all, though, I was lucky."

"And my investigator, Harry Davenport, wasn't so fortunate," Jason said. "And there're apparently no leads on the killers even though I told Chief Storm who did it."

"Frannie's doing all she can do, Jason," Bo said. "Since the shooting, our primary focus has been to keep Hatty safe, and she's now living at an undisclosed location and being watched at all times by two armed security guards hired by me as well as a Giles County sheriff's deputy. But no one's forgotten about Mr. Davenport or how close Hatty came to being killed. I have my own investigator, and he's damn good. We're going to get that Dean fellow. You just have to give it time. Guys like that eventually screw up."

For a moment, there was silence. Jason took a deep breath as his mind raced with questions. Finally, he started with the obvious. "Detective, are you still employed by the Marshall County Sheriff's Office?"

"Yes."

"When are you going to return to the office?"

"Monday will be my first day."

"Why did you leave?"

"She can't answer something that broad, Jason."

Jason glared at Bo. "Why not?"

"Because the settlement we've reached with Marshall County is confidential."

"I didn't ask about the settlement. I asked why she left in the first place."

"Ask it a different way," Bo snapped.

"All right. Did the Cowan case have anything to do with your leave of absence?"

"Yes," Hatty said.

"In what way?"

Hatty leaned forward and began rubbing her hands together. "I was doing an internal investigation of Kelly Flowers at the time of his murder."

Jason felt a flutter in his heart. "What were you investigating him for?"

"We had a person come forward. An informant. Who said that Flowers was selling her meth in exchange for sexual favors and for not prosecuting her for drug possession."

"An informant?"

Hatty nodded. "I believe you know her."

Jason's stomach jumped.

"Chase Wittschen," Hatty continued. "We were planning a sting with Ms. Wittschen, but then Flowers was murdered."

A surge of relief flooded through Jason. "So Chase was working with the department in an effort to have Flowers arrested?"

"Yes."

"When did she first present with information on Flowers?"

"I'd have to look at my file to be exact, but I think it was March 14."

Jason's stomach clutched. "Your file? You mean, the department has a file on this investigation? I have asked for that in discovery and received nothing but objections."

"The sheriff's office *had* a file. The day before the preliminary hearing in the Cowan case, I checked my hard drive to review the file, and it was gone. All materials in my internal investigation of Kelly Flowers had been deleted."

"Holy shit," Jason said. "Is that why you left?"

"That and the fact that I started noticing that I was being followed."

Jason leaned back in his chair and looked at Bo. "Did you threaten a whistleblower action?"

"I did. Since she was never technically retaliated against, the claim wasn't ripe. But we've negotiated her return in a way that is very favorable to Detective Daniels."

"Who deleted the files?"

"We don't know," Bo said.

"To my knowledge, there were only two people in the department who knew about my investigation of Flowers." Hatty looked at Bo, who nodded. Then back to Jason. "Sergeant George Mitchell, who participated in the investigation, and Sheriff Richard Griffith."

"This is unbelievable," Jason said. "Does Shay know all of this?"

"I would think she would have to know by now," Hatty said.

"And what about at the time of the prelim?" Jason's mind was racing. Had George Mitchell perjured himself? Had he asked a question direct enough to bring out the investigation? He'd have to look back at the transcript.

"I doubt it. But I can't say for sure."

356

"But Detective Mitchell would have known."

"Absolutely. He was in on the investigation of Flowers from the start. In fact, he was who first brought allegations of Flowers's misconduct to me. Quite reluctantly I might add. George had stopped Ms. Wittschen walking along the Sunset Drive Trail along Lurleen B. Wallace Drive. She was unsteady on her feet, and he was about to write her up for public intoxication when she started rambling about Flowers. George brought her in, and that's when our investigation cranked up."

Jason was scowling. "Detective Mitchell called Flowers 'a good cop' at the prelim."

Hatty pursed her lips. "George was very hesitant about confronting Kelly. George isn't a trusting soul and . . . he didn't think Ms. Wittschen was credible."

"Whatever," Jason said. "He sounds as dirty as Flowers to me." Jason turned to Bo. "Thank you for this."

"You're welcome," he said. "Jason, I suspect this information is evidence you may seek to use during your defense case."

"You think?" Jason scrunched his face up.

Bo chuckled. "I'd use it too if I were you. I've done a little criminal defense in my time. But you know as well as I do that putting the victim on trial is risky."

"Nobody likes a dirty cop, Bo. Not even the staunch conservatives in Marshall County, Alabama. And Kelly Flowers was filthy, and George Mitchell isn't far behind."

Bo nodded. "I tend to agree."

"So would I," Hatty said. "And I'll tell the truth about my investigation of Flowers when I'm put on the stand in this case. The truth is that we had an informant and that Flowers was being investigated. While it certainly appeared that he might be 'dirty,' as you say, we had not made any conclusions."

"But you had Chase."

"A drug user." She paused. "Who has now completely disappeared after checking out of rehab AMA." She raised her eyebrows.

Jason looked at his hands. "I see what you mean." He paused. "But it doesn't change the fact that Mitchell either lied or gave misleading testimony at the prelim."

"Agreed," Hatty said. She popped her knuckles and pierced him with a steely gaze. "But I still believe that Trey Cowan murdered Kelly Flowers. My leave of absence and return doesn't change any of that."

"What about the attempt on your life?"

She didn't blink. If it was possible, her expression became harder. "I haven't forgotten, nor will I ever forget. You said Mr. Davenport indicated that Matthew Dean was one of the men at the Sundowners who went into the woods, right?"

"Yes."

Hatty cleared her throat. "To my knowledge, Dean has no connection with the sheriff's office."

"He's connected to Tyson Cade."

"So you say."

"Ma'am, don't you want to find the people that tried to kill you and bring them to justice?"

She bit her lip. "Very much."

"Have you thought about why Tyson Cade would want you dead? Or perhaps . . ." Jason was thinking out loud. ". . . that your own colleagues might have wanted to silence you because of this embarrassing investigation of Flowers."

"I have thought . . . about *both* of those possibilities." Hatty spoke through clenched teeth.

"And have you come to any conclusions?"

She leaned back in her chair and folded her arms. "I can't tell you. Not until I'm sure."

Bo walked Jason to his car. "Thanks for setting that up," Jason said.

"I told you I would," Bo said. "You OK? You seemed really jittery in there."

Jason rubbed his neck. "Too much to do and too little time." He looked at Bo. "But that's the gig, isn't it?"

"Can I offer you some unsolicited advice?"

Jason straightened and looked up at the huge man. "I'd appreciate that."

"I'm Hatty's lawyer in her dispute with the county, and I've done my job. I don't have a dog in the hunt in your murder case, and Hatty will tell the truth. What she just told you is what she'll tell the jury . . . if the judge allows it, which I suspect he will." Bo hesitated. "But here's the rub. Most times in these cases . . . the answer is right under your nose." He sighed. "And, unfortunately, in our line of work, a lot of times the answer is that our client did it." He slapped Jason on the shoulder. "Good luck, man."

84

Jason stopped at the Tonidandels' shooting range on the way home. He waved at Mickey and then went to his customary bay. He hadn't gone back to drinking, in part because he had upped his time with, as Ashley Sullivan called them, his defusers.

In addition to watching old wrestling videos, one of his top activities to release stress was target practice with his Glock.

For an hour, Jason practiced. Five yards. Ten. Twenty. He shot until his shoulders began to ache.

When he got home, he lifted weights for an hour and took a dip in the lake. Then he stood in front of his mirror, asked Alexa to play "Real American," and did the entire Hulk Hogan after-match flex routine that the Hulkster had made famous, complete with holding his hand to his ear for crowd noise even though there was, of course, no crowd. He enjoyed the way his muscles were popping and thought, for the first time, that his arms were "guns," as the kids liked to say. If he got any stronger, he'd have to update his billboards. He looked kind of scrawny on them now.

Embrace your inner narcissism, Jason thought, shrugging and then thinking, *Fuck it. Whatever works . . .*

After showering, he went back to work. Returning emails. Saying yea or nay on new cases. And prepping for the next round of depositions and hearings. It was a lawyer's life, and he dived into his work now like a lifeline. He hadn't let Tyson Cade break him. If anything, he'd gone the other way. He could see it in Satch's, Mickey's, and Chuck's eyes. In their demeanor around him.

He was one of them now. He hadn't served in the army, but he felt like a soldier. He was in a war, and he hadn't run. He was fighting.

He grilled a steak and gazed out at the half moon, which danced its light across the cove. He didn't know what time it was and didn't care. He ate when he was hungry now.

While he had quelled his urge to drink with shooting, lifting, and work, he was dealing with another struggle now.

Sleep.

Regardless of what he tried, he couldn't seem to ever get a good night's rest. The nightmare of him sinking at the bottom of the lake came to him every night. As did Harry's cold, dead eyes. And Jana's voice, always tormenting him no matter how strong he felt. Calling him weak. Motivating him from the grave as she had when she was living.

He'd tried everything. Every bed in every room in the house. On the couch upstairs and down and even in a sleeping bag on the floor.

The only time he ever really dozed off was when he slept on the old raggedy couch on the open-air patio on the bottom floor.

Now, after finishing his steak, he sat out on the couch and cracked open a novel by Greg Iles. He was reading fiction more now, too, as both a defuser and an attempt to help him sleep. He couldn't say it helped much in the way of rest, but he enjoyed the adventures of Penn Cage. Somehow, they made him feel a little better about his crazy life.

Jason finally set the book down, fixed the alarm on his phone, and lay back on the old couch that had been in his family since before he was born. He glanced out at the water and thought of Tyson Cade.

I'm still here, you sonofabitch.

85

Matty Dean sat on the rocks below the Mill Creek overpass. Tonight, he was the only fisherman. His phone buzzed, and he picked up. "Yeah?"

"What's the status?" Tyson asked.

"Same old. Nothing new. Our folks said he went to Pulaski for a meeting at Bo Haynes's office."

Silence. And then a sucking sound. "Damnit."

"What's the end game here, T. C.?"

Silence for a few more seconds. Then Tyson cleared his throat. "Same as always. To stay on top."

"You tell me what to do, and I'll do it."

"For now, we sit tight. I underestimated the counselor. And Detective Daniels too. But neither of them have figured it out. If . . . or when . . . they ever do . . ." A pause. ". . . it'll be too late."

Matty fought to keep irritation out of his tone. "What does that mean, T. C.?"

"It means what it means," Tyson snapped.

"What about me, boss? The Giles County Sheriff's Department has been all over my ass since the shooting. They haven't charged me with anything because they've got nothing. But I can feel eyes on me. The local authorities in Guntersville have been poking around about Bull Branner too." Matty found that he couldn't stop the words from tumbling out. "Bull was a regular down at the auto shop. Kelly Flowers and I were Bull's main contacts, and a lot of people saw me with Bull. Not you, me, because that's the way you've always wanted it. I'm being the good soldier, T. C., and I know we covered our tracks with Bull and Davenport, but all the questions are making me nervous. Bull was who discovered Kelly's body, so the district attorney isn't going to stop looking for him. You can bet your ass they are going to keep watching me."

More silence and then Tyson's firm, unwavering voice. "All we can do right now is hang tight, brother."

The phone clicked dead, and Matty gazed at the device before putting it back into his pocket. He had never doubted the wisdom of Tyson Cade, but he was beginning to feel the pressure.

And he still didn't quite understand his boss's motives.

What's the endgame, he again wondered as he cast his line out into the dark water.

86

"State of Alabama versus Jason . . . James . . . Rich."

Judge Barber seemed to relish drawing out Jason's name in his nasal southern twang. "Is the defendant ready?"

Jason stood and buttoned his coat. "Yes, Your Honor."

"And I see that you haven't hired another lawyer since Ms. Montaigne's withdrawal?"

Jason grinned. "I'm a lawyer, Judge. And I don't need any help defending against these frivolous charges."

Barber scowled at him and then turned to the prosecution table. "Is the state ready . . . where is Ms. Lankford?"

Sergeant George Mitchell stood and looked to the back of the courtroom. "She stepped out a second ago. Let me go check." As Mitchell walked toward the double doors in the rear, Jason watched him, thinking about the officer's testimony at the preliminary hearing. Though he hadn't outright lied—Jason had never asked whether Flowers had been investigated—Mitchell had volunteered that Flowers was a "good cop." Jason's gut feeling was that Mitchell was dirty, but he wondered how much so. Could Hatty Daniels's partner have been involved in the hit on her in Pulaski? And what about Flowers? Could it be that Mitchell used his inside information to take out Flowers so that he could replace him as Tyson Cade's inside man? As these thoughts swirled in his mind, Shay Lankford busted through the double doors.

"I'm here, Your Honor," Shay said, her tone agitated as she strode in. Jason turned, looking past Shay and scanning the crowd. Outside of Kisha Roe and a couple of other reporters, the courtroom was barren. Apparently, his own personal travails weren't as big a news item anymore. He was dismayed. When part of your brand was the circus you created, it was depressing when there was no audience.

"Is the state ready, Madame Prosecutor?"

Once she had made it to her table, she glanced at Jason and then back up at Barber. "Your Honor, may we approach?"

He motioned them up, pulling his spectacles down around his nose. "What's going on, Ms. Lankford?"

"Judge, I am having difficulty with our witnesses."

"What do you mean . . . difficulty?"

Shay bit her lip. "Mr. Martin isn't here."

"Didn't you subpoena him?"

"A subpoena was issued, but Mr. Martin moved out of state before it could be served."

"Well, where is he?"

"Mr. Martin is in college now. He's at Georgetown in Washington, DC. I spoke with him yesterday, and he said he would be here."

"Did you try serving an out-of-state subpoena?"

"Your Honor, that process is difficult and expensive. We didn't think it a good use of the state's resources. Especially when Mr. Martin said, on numerous occasions, that he would be here."

"Well . . . why isn't he?"

She held out her palms. "I don't know, Your Honor. Mr. Martin hasn't returned any of our calls. I assume an emergency has arisen."

"I see," Barber said, his tone seesawing between disappointment and disapproval.

"The state would respectfully request a continuance."

"And I would respectfully oppose," Jason said. "Your Honor, the state has had more than three months to get ready for this trial, and they literally only have one witness. If the state isn't ready, then the charges should be and are due to be dismissed."

Barber took off his glasses and frowned. His disappointment was now palpable. Finally, he glared at Jason. "And if one of your witnesses, Mr. Rich, had an emergency and couldn't appear for the Trey Cowan murder trial, would you expect me to proceed with that trial?"

Jason felt light headed. He'd taken a couple of NoDoz pills this morning, and his hands shook as the caffeine combined with adrenaline and anger. *You prick,* Jason thought, glaring at His Honor. "There has been no showing of any emergency, Judge Barber. And if I requested such a continuance without any justifiable grounds, I'm sure you would deny it. I expect the same treatment of the prosecution."

"I'm going to grant the state's motion," Barber said, his tone authoritative and flicking out his wrist at Jason as if he were a small child whose foolish pleas needed batting down. "This case is reset for trial on October 21. Court adjourned." He banged on his gavel, and Shay turned to walk back to her table. Jason stood stock still, continuing to stare at His Honor, who gazed back at Jason like he had just put a sour pickle in his mouth.

"Is there something else, Mr. Rich?"

Jason said nothing, and Barber put his hands on his hips. "Answer me, Counselor, or I'm going to hold you in contempt."

"No, Your Honor," Jason said. "There's nothing else."

Jason trotted down the courthouse steps and forced a smile for the smattering of TV cameras. While the courtroom had been relatively quiet, the media presence outside was a tad more substantial.

"Mr. Rich, do you have any comment on Judge Barber's ruling to continue the trial on the charges the state has brought against you?" Kisha Roe asked.

"I'll be ready to defend myself in two weeks," Jason said.

"And, if you succeed at trial, will you be filing any type of lawsuit against the county as Ms. Montaigne threatened months ago?"

Jason looked around at the various cameras, letting them all get a money shot of his determined mug. "Let's just say I'll be evaluating all options."

87

Jason walked back to the office and went straight to the library. While he had restaffed his Birmingham office, he hadn't added anyone new here in Guntersville. He still had two assistants answering calls, but that was it.

Truth be known, he wasn't sure how long he was going to keep this office open.

Jason fired up his laptop. As he waited, he heard a voice from the front that he recognized.

"Is Mr. Rich in?"

"Do you have an appointment?" his assistant, Kimberly, asked.

"Send her back!" Jason yelled, standing and waiting.

When Shay Lankford entered the room, she didn't wait to be offered a seat. She plopped down in one of the leather chairs and put her hands on the table. "Look, I know this doesn't matter to you, but I want you to know anyway. I didn't want to prosecute you. I told the sheriff as much, but he and Sergeant Mitchell insisted. We had Kevin Martin on board when we filed the charges, and we also had the cooperation of the Cornelius family, whose house you broke into. When you made restitution, I again recommended dismissal, but sometimes I have to go along with my officers."

"Even when they're wrong?" Jason snapped. He'd heard enough. "Even when they are doing unethical things?" He hesitated. "Like deleting files related to an internal investigation of a murder victim who, in actuality, was a dirty cop."

Shay opened her mouth to speak, but no words came. Her face turned crimson. "How do you know about that?"

"Because I got it directly from the horse's mouth. Hatty Daniels was one of those officers you do so much to protect. She'd had enough of the tactics of the sheriff's department, and she left." He paused. "I can only imagine how sweet her deal must have been to return."

"She didn't tell you that too."

"Oh, no. She didn't reveal any of the terms of her settlement. Only that her investigative file had been deleted, and that only Sergeant George Mitchell and Sheriff Richard Griffith knew about it." He raised his eyebrows. "Those are your wingmen, Shay. I'd watch my back and lock my office door if I were you."

Shay said nothing. Finally, she stood. "Are you going to sue us?"

"I don't know."

Shay walked to the door and stopped. "I'm sorry, Jason. I guess that's why I came over." She looked at him. "To say I'm sorry."

88

Shay Lankford had a visitor sitting in her office when she returned from the Rich Law Firm. Shay looked at the woman sitting in the chair across from her desk and took her time walking to her seat. A dozen thoughts went through her mind. When she got around the desk, she decided not to sit. She crossed her arms and stared at her old friend. "It's been a minute, Hatty."

"I wanted you to know that I was back. And I'm ready to work."

"For the sheriff's department . . . or Jason Rich?" Shay regretted the attack the minute it came out of her mouth, but she couldn't help it. The sting of her conversation with Trey Cowan's attorney was still fresh.

"I'm not going to justify that question with an answer." Hatty's tone was as tense as her face.

"It would have been great if you hadn't filled in Rich about the deletion of your investigative file on Kelly Flowers."

Hatty didn't even flinch. "It would've been great if I had gotten some backup from the prosecutor I've worked cases with for a decade when an officer in the sheriff's office decided to delete those documents."

"I didn't know anything about that, and you never returned a single one of my calls."

"Forgive me if I was in an untrusting frame of mind after my file was destroyed and I started noticing a car following me around at all hours of the night." She paused. "My faith went out the window when someone tried to kill me."

"Hatty, I obviously heard about that, and I'm very sorry. Are you OK?"

"What do you think?"

Shay finally sat down, collapsing into her chair and sighing. "I can't even imagine. Physically, have your wounds healed?"

Hatty shrugged. "Pretty much. My shoulder still hurts from time to time."

For several seconds, the two women were silent. Shay was exhausted from the stressful hearing and her clash with Jason Rich. She hadn't expected to have a confrontation with Hatty, and she didn't have the energy for it. "I'm sorry, Hatty. I really am. I've always thought of you as a friend, and I've enjoyed working with you." She hesitated. "You can't think that someone in Griff's office . . . or mine . . . was behind the attack on you."

"I don't know what to think anymore."

Shay took in a deep breath. "I guess I can understand that."

Hatty pushed herself up out of the chair. "Well . . . I just wanted you to know that I was back." She turned for the door.

"Hatty, we need to brainstorm the Cowan case," Shay said. "I presume that you're willing to support your own investigation and, in particular, your conclusions."

Hatty leaned her elbow against the doorframe. "I am. But I'm not going to forget what happened to me." Shay could feel the intensity resonating from the detective's eyes. "And I won't rest until I have some answers."

89

Jason walked into Ashley Sullivan's office at 5:59 p.m. with a dozen roses. "Honey, I'm home." He set the flowers down on a reception desk and looked around the dark office. "Ashley? Anyone here?"

"Coming." Ashley trudged toward him wearing a T-shirt, jeans, and no shoes. Glasses covered her face, and her hair was up in a ponytail. "Sorry for the casual dress. I'm prepping for a trial myself tomorrow."

"No worries. Understood. Brought you a present since I've been so derelict in seeing you."

She rolled her eyes but grabbed the flowers anyway. "My hero." Then she frowned. "Heard about the continuance. I saw it on Twitter. I follow the *Advertiser-Gleam*."

"I've notified the state bar," Jason said. "Ted sounded . . . disappointed." Ted Raleigh was the executive director of the Alabama State Bar, and he'd been a thorn in Jason's side since his first billboard went up. Jason had already undergone an informal meeting with the commission in late July, where he had told his side of the story with respect to his confrontation with Kevin Martin and his shooting up the Waters's former home on Buck Island in the aftermath of Nola nearly drowning in Lake Guntersville. The commission had said then that they would withhold any ruling on whether discipline would be imposed until after the criminal charges against him were disposed. Now Jason would have to wait two more weeks. But first, he'd have to get through the Cowan trial.

Ashley managed a tired smile. She gestured toward a couch in the lobby. "Sit."

Jason did as he was told.

"So tell me how you're doing?"

Jason looked at her and felt an odd charge come over him. Ashley Sullivan probably thought she looked terrible, but to Jason, seeing her like this felt intimate.

"I'm fine, Ashley." He opened his mouth to say more but thought better of it.

"Why haven't you checked in with me?"

"Because I've been so busy."

"Jason, I know about what happened to your investigator. There was a news story about the attack on Detective Daniels's life, and his disappearance was referenced as something that might be related. And I know your partner left you. How are things with your niece?"

"Nola is out of rehab and doing well. But . . . she wants nothing to do with her dear old uncle."

"What about Izzy? You talked so glowingly about her. Do y'all still talk?"

Jason gazed down at his shoes. "No. She . . . blames me for Harry's death."

"His death?"

"Disappearance," Jason corrected.

"You think he's dead?"

Jason continued to peer at his feet, seeing the photo that Tyson Cade had showed him of Harry's dead body in his mind. He knew he couldn't burden Ashley with this information. The last thing he wanted to do was jeopardize the health of anyone else he cared about, and, if he were honest with himself, he knew he was beginning to have feelings for the red-haired attorney from Cullman. "Harry wouldn't have just vanished. I believe he was killed by the same people that tried to kill Detective Daniels."

"Goodness," Ashley managed. "You know you fell off the wagon last year when things got out of control."

"I know, but I haven't this time."

"How?"

"I've been leaning hard on my defusers. Shooting. Weightlifting. Reading fiction." He crossed his legs and averted his eyes. "Watching eighties and nineties pro wrestling videos."

"Get out," she said, but the tease in her voice wasn't mean. "I used to love . . . who was that guy . . . the Heartbreak Kid?"

"Shawn Michaels. The Showstopper. Came to the ring to the song 'Sexy Boy,' which he sang himself. Leader of the faction D-Generation X." Jason stopped when he saw Ashley staring at him.

"Damn, you know your stuff. That's him all right."

"It's getting harder to quell the desire."

"What about AA meetings? And your counselor?"

"No. Talking things out doesn't do any good."

"Why not?"

"Because that makes me explore my feelings, and I don't want to do that."

"Repressing them is only going to make the inevitable fall worse."

"Maybe," Jason said, standing and beginning to pace around the small lobby. "But I can't afford to let my guard down right now. I'm in the biggest crisis in my life, and I just can't do it."

"That's why you haven't come to see me."

Jason nodded. "I let you inside, Ashley." He looked at her. "And it makes me feel vulnerable. I can't feel that way and deal with . . ." He almost said Tyson Cade but stopped himself. ". . . this case."

"Is it just the Cowan murder trial? I mean, I know that's a big deal, but—"

"No. It's not just that. I want justice for Harry. And for Izzy. They were a couple. I want justice for my nieces too. And for Jana." He squeezed his hands into fists. "For me."

"All of that ties into the Cowan trial?"

"Yes," Jason said.

For a moment, she didn't say anything. Then she approached him. "Promise me something."

"What?"

"If you get the urge to drink, call me. Don't fall off the wagon until you've seen me, OK?"

He looked into her green eyes and felt the same charge of warmth. "OK," he said.

He extended his hands at the same time she stretched her arms outward for a hug.

They both laughed, and Ashley took his hands in both of hers and squeezed. "Don't go so long without calling again. I was worried about you."

Jason didn't want to leave, but he knew he must. "Good luck with your trial," he said. Then he walked to the door.

"Hey, Jason."

He looked over his shoulder at her.

"Ditto."

90

Jason drove home with the windows and top down on the Porsche. He relaxed to the mellow sounds of Christopher Cross's "Sailing" and several other numbers from the eighties crooner before he switched to "Africa," by Toto, and "Listen to the Music," by the Doobie Brothers. When he took the Veterans Memorial Bridge, he played "Crazy Love," the Aaron Neville version, and sang along.

He couldn't remember the last time he'd felt this good.

When he hung a left on Mill Creek Road, he had dialed it up slightly with "Live and Let Die," by Guns N' Roses. He was still pumped and thought he might take a dip in the lake.

He pulled into the driveway with the music still reverberating out of his speakers. He continued to sing, but then he saw the visitor sitting on his steps.

Jason's heartbeat almost skidded to a stop as fast as the Porsche did. Gasping, he hopped out of the car and walked cautiously toward the steps.

"I think you woke up the whole neighborhood. Even the folks across the cove." She shook her head. "Guns N' Roses? That's so high school."

Jason swallowed. Her hair was longer, and she wore a pair of faded blue overalls over a white T-shirt.

"Jason James Rich," she said. "Cat got your tongue?"

"Savannah Chase Wittschen." Jason's voice cracked on her last name. He reached out with his right arm but didn't take a step closer. His feet felt like they were in wet concrete.

She rose and stuck her hands in the pockets of the overalls. Then she walked toward him, stopping when she was a couple of feet away.

"It's . . . been a long time," Jason finally said.

Chase nodded. Then she reached for his still-outstretched hand.

———

"I just couldn't handle it," Chase said. They were sitting side by side on the steps now. Jason was in shock. He was having a hard time thinking straight. It was good to see her. But also so painful, as flashes of what he knew hit him like lasers.

"What?" Jason asked.

"You asking to marry me," she said. "I didn't feel worthy. I'd already started, even before Christmas, drinking again. At first, it was just a few beers on my boat. Then, after the proposal and after I left the cove, I got the whiskey out. I came back one weekend when you were gone, and I saw Nola and that kid doing meth together. At that point, the alcohol wasn't doing the trick. Once I did my first line again, I was hooked."

"Tell me about Kelly Flowers, Chase. I know you got mixed up with him. How'd it happen?"

Tears filled her eyes.

"Chase, I have to know."

Her lip quivered. "He caught me doing meth. I'd gotten drunk at Wintzell's and was doing a line in my car. He knocked on the door and put cuffs on me. Put me in his police cruiser and drove off. I should have known something was up when he turned off the video camera."

"What happened?" Jason felt a deep sense of foreboding.

"He told me that he didn't really want to arrest me." Her hands and arms were shaking, and she crossed them.

"Then what happened?" Jason asked, thinking that her story was very similar to that of Colleen Maples.

"He took me back to my car and told me that if I wanted to avoid arrest, I needed to check in to the Hampton Inn."

Jason felt an invisible sword slice his chest. *Just like Maples . . . a pattern of abuse by Sergeant Flowers,* he thought, envisioning the argument he would make before the jury. There was no doubt about it anymore. He'd be putting the victim on trial.

"Did you go to the hotel?"

She nodded.

"Then what?"

Despite clutching her knees, she began to shake again. "He met me there, and . . ." She glared up at him. "Are you really going to make me say it?"

The blade in Jason's sternum sank deeper, and he almost groaned. He felt a myriad of emotions churning inside him, but white-hot rage was winning the battle for supremacy. He looked away from her and peered out at the road. Smoke was fluming behind the Tonidandel house, and Jason knew the boys were taking out the trash.

Jason finally just said it. "In exchange for him not arresting you . . . you had sex with him."

"Yes."

"Did you see him again?"

"Yes."

Jason stood and paced a few steps away. He took several deep breaths, reminding himself that Chase was a material witness in his capital murder trial. "Was that the deal?" he asked. "Did you have to have multiple encounters with him before he'd drop the charge? Or were the subsequent times by choice?"

When she didn't answer, he looked back at her. "Well?"

"That wasn't the deal . . . and I barely remember it."

"Why then?"

More tears and she shook her head. "He said he could get me meth. And not what I had been doing, but the best in Marshall County. All

I had to do was keep . . ." She trailed off, and Jason glared down at the concrete and tried to keep his composure.

"Where was Flowers getting the meth?"

She sighed and let out a quiet sob. "He never said . . . but we both know it had to be Cade."

Jason looked up at the sky. The night was cloudy, and he saw no stars. "When did you go see Hatty Daniels?"

Chase stood up and looked at him. He'd finally shocked her.

"I'm a lawyer, Chase, and I'm investigating Flowers's murder. Hatty Daniels has incurred her own bit of drama these past few months."

Chase sat back on the steps. "I heard."

"Detective Daniels told me that you were her informant and that she was investigating Flowers. She said you came forward after being threatened with a public intoxication arrest by Sergeant George Mitchell out at the Sunset Drive Trail. Daniels, Mitchell's partner, was brought in, and the two of them were trying to organize a sting . . . and then Flowers was killed."

Chase looked down at her feet.

"Is all of that true?" Jason asked.

"Yes."

"All right . . . when you would meet with Kelly Flowers, did he have a spot that he preferred?"

"You already know the answer to that."

"Branner's Place." It wasn't a question.

"Pretty much every time after the arrest."

"How many occasions?"

"I don't know."

"Ballpark it." Jason spat the words, trying hard to keep his cool. *Keep your attorney hat on,* he thought. *You have to check this box.*

"Maybe six," she said.

"Did you meet with him on the night of April 8 . . . or after midnight on April 9 . . . at Branner's Place?"

"I was supposed to," Chase finally said.

"What time?"

"We normally met at nine, but he had to do something that night, so he moved it back."

Jason licked his lips and swallowed. His throat was dry. "How far back?"

"Twelve thirty," she said.

"And did you meet him then? At thirty minutes past midnight?" Jason paused and closed his eyes. "Chase, did you kill him?"

She looked past him to the road. "I can't believe that you would actually think that of me."

"Go back over what you've already admitted to doing," Jason said. His voice was cold. "Did you kill Kelly Flowers?"

Chase began to cry again. Softer this time.

"Chase?"

"No," she finally said. "I didn't show. I stood him up."

Jason let out a long breath that he had been holding. He took a seat next to her. "Why'd you stand him up?"

She snorted. "I wish I could give you a heroic reason, but the answer is far simpler."

"What?"

"I needed a meth fix, and I couldn't wait."

"Where'd you get it?"

Chase's tears were falling harder now. "Oh, Jason, I was such a mess. I'm so . . . *sorry*."

"Where'd you get it?"

She sucked in a breath and looked at him. "Nola."

Jason howled like he had never howled in his life. He jumped off the steps and ran his hands through his hair.

Chase was off the steps too. "Jason, I'm sorry. I'm so—"

"I'm not mad. I'm just . . ." He grabbed her arms. "When were you with Nola?"

"It wasn't really Nola I was with."

He blinked his eyes in confusion. "What?" He removed his hands. "All right, tell me what happened?"

"After I had done meth with Nola and her boyfriend at the house, the boy left me his number in case I ever needed any more. Before Flowers, my source was him. So . . ."

"You called Kevin Martin?" Jason asked. "K-Mart?"

"Yes," Chase said. "I ended up meeting him at the gas station there at the intersection of 431 with Buck Island Drive."

"What time did you meet him?"

"I don't know the exact time. Flowers called right at nine. I was already at Branner's Place then. I waited for about fifteen minutes, and then I called K-Mart. I went straight to the gas station, and he met me there."

"Then what?"

"I bought a gram from him, and he asked me if I wanted to get high with him." She shrugged.

"Oh, Chase."

"My brain was cooked by then, J. R. I just wanted to float away."

"What happened?"

"He drove me back to his house. His dad was still at work, and his mom had gone out with friends. We went to his boathouse. Did a couple of lines. Then he asked me if I wanted to go out on the boat."

"When was this?"

"I have no idea. After ten."

"Then what?"

"I remember he drove toward Goose Pond a ways. We did another line, and he had some hard seltzer drinks."

Jason gazed at the ground. He knew he shouldn't be surprised, but he was anyway.

"Then I got sick," Chase continued. "I started throwing up over the side of the boat. I lay down on the console and . . ."

"And what?"

"I don't remember anything else. The next thing I remember was waking up on the floor of a warehouse with the door locked." She rubbed her arms. "I was there for a while. A guy they called Matty kept me fed and full of meth. I'm not sure how long I was there, but they eventually brought me home." She paused. "And then you took me to Perdido on the plane."

Matthew Dean, Jason thought, feeling anger boiling over. "Did you tell anyone that you were supposed to meet Flowers at twelve thirty a.m. at Branner's Place?"

Chase sucked in a breath. "Officer Mitchell was my primary contact with the sheriff's office. I told him about the nine p.m. meeting, and I called him when the time was moved to twelve thirty."

"So, just to be clear, you told Detective Mitchell that you were meeting Flowers at Branner's Place at twelve thirty in the morning."

"Yes."

"Are you sure?"

She scowled at him. "As shit."

Jason looked up at the sky, thinking through the possibilities. Why wasn't any of this in Mitchell's or Daniels's investigative report? *Good grief . . . Maybe Mitchell is Cade's new inside source. He offed Flowers and framed Trey. The attack on Flowers by Trey at the Brick was reported to dispatch. Mitchell . . . as well as any other officer on the force . . . could have had knowledge of it . . . especially if they were looking for an opportunity.*

Jason's mind switched gears. "Other than Officer Mitchell, did you tell anyone else about the twelve thirty rendezvous with Flowers?"

"I think I may have told K-Mart."

And the kid could have told Matty Dean, who told Cade, who showed up at thirty minutes past midnight and killed Flowers . . . or hired one of his goons to do it . . . or maybe Cade already knew about Flowers's arrangements with Chase. Flowers could have told him directly, never expecting the drug lord to turn on him. Or maybe Bull Branner told Cade. Flowers reserved the barn at twelve thirty for the meeting with Chase, and Bull could've squealed.

Especially if Cade leaned on him. Or hell . . . maybe Mitchell, Cade's new inside source, told Cade, and they worked together to kill Flowers.

There were a lot of possibilities, none of which were simpler or better than the obvious one. *Flowers got into an argument with his old teammate, Trey Cowan, at the Brick over a drug deal, and Cowan, fed up with his life and blaming Flowers for getting him in with Cade and for stealing his girlfriend, killed him.*

Jason continued to gaze up at the stars. "What happened to your car?"

"I left it at the gas station." She looked across the yard to her home, where her truck was parked under the carport. "I don't know how it got home."

"So, if K-Mart were to tell the truth, then you'd have a complete alibi."

"You don't think I'll be charged, do you?"

Jason's mouth formed a faint smile. "No. But, up until a few minutes ago, you were my most plausible alternative for someone other than Trey Cowan being the killer." Jason breathed a sigh of relief. "I was sweating whether I was going to have to present that theory to the jury."

"Do you believe me?"

"Yes," Jason said. "I do. But even if I didn't, there's no witness that can place you at Branner's Place at the time of the murder. For that matter, there's no one that can put you there at any time unless you were to testify. And to do that, you'd have to incriminate yourself. To testify truthfully, you'd have to go through buying meth from Flowers and then K-Mart. You can take the Fifth Amendment to all that." Jason rubbed his hands together. "None of it comes in."

Chase cocked her head at him. "Are you happy or sad about this?"

"Neither," Jason said, walking a few steps away from her. "I'm shocked by almost everything you've said. But I'm also relieved."

For a long moment, the two stared at each other. Though the distance was only a few feet, it seemed much further. "Why'd you come home, Chase?"

A lone tear fell down her cheek. "I didn't have anywhere else to go."

91

The next day, Jason met Trudy Cowan at Top O' the River. They'd started meeting every week for coffee around 4:00 p.m., just before her shift started.

"What's the good word?" Trudy asked.

"Well, we've confirmed that Kelly Flowers was working for Tyson Cade. Detective Daniels was investigating him at the time of his murder and had an informant ready to roll on him."

Trudy crossed her arms. "Well . . ."

"You didn't know."

"I didn't. Oh, I thought he abused the power of the uniform. But I didn't figure him for a double-dealer."

"Trey never said anything."

"Nope. I'm assuming this helps Trey, though. The fact that Kelly was dealing for Cade."

"It doesn't hurt. I'm just not sure how much it helps."

"What about that girl you said might be an alternative theory."

"She has an alibi. And even if she didn't, we don't have a witness that puts her there at twelve thirty a.m. on April 9." Jason paused. "She was Daniels's informant, so there's that, but I don't see us making much hay with her as an alternative. The better play would be to point the finger where it really belongs."

She scrunched up her face.

"Tyson Cade," Jason said. "Daniels will have to testify that she was investigating Flowers in connection with Cade, and we may be able to get in that Flowers was using Branner's Place to do drug deals."

"May be able to get in?"

"It's hearsay. I think we have a strong argument that it falls within an exception, but we may lose."

"Shit, boy. Even if we do get it in, you really gonna try to pin this on Tyson?"

"I didn't say that. I'm just saying it would be the better play."

"No, it wouldn't. Why the hell would Tyson want to kill his inside source?"

"I'm thinking that Tyson had tired of Flowers and was getting ready to replace him."

"What makes you say that?"

"The investigation file was deleted by someone in the sheriff's office. Obviously, one reason for that is to cover up any wrongdoing on Kelly's part. But the other reason—"

"Is whoever deleted the file is Cade's new source."

"Right," Jason said, pointing at her. "Nothing else makes sense. Listen, Trudy, there is something I want to ask you. Trey mentioned that he was not a good shot and had only fired a gun a couple times in his life. That ring true to you?"

"Yeah. I can't say for sure about the last few years, but I don't remember him shooting much as a kid."

"Well, I've done a little shooting myself. Even at five yards, at least with a handgun, a person can miss if they haven't been trained."

"You ever shot a twelve-gauge shotgun?"

"No," Jason admitted.

"You ain't goin' miss with it."

"He was still a few feet away and likely shooting from the inside of a vehicle. At least on the first shot. Not the easiest thing to do with a twelve gauge."

"I see your point," Trudy said, rubbing her chin, which had some peach fuzz on it. "If I'm being honest with you, I don't have a clue. You might ask his old girlfriend, the nurse anesthesia lady, whether he did any shooting."

"What about Walt?"

"What about that lowlife sonofabitch?"

"Did he and Trey ever go hunting together? Dove hunting? Quail? Target shooting? Anything?"

"I don't know of them ever shooting together, but I've worked two jobs my whole life trying to feed everyone. You should ask him."

"I've tried, but I can't find him. My investigator was working on that when he was killed. Do you know where he is?"

"He's on the Gulf Coast somewhere. Working construction by day and drinking beer and chasing tail by night, if I had to guess."

Jason remembered that Harry had tracked Walt to Watersound on 30A last year, but so far, Jason had not been able to pin the elder Cowan down. "OK, if you hear anything about Walt, let me know."

"Will do." She stood and shook his hand. Her grip was firm, her hand heavily calloused. "Thank you, Mr. Rich."

92

Once Jason was back in his car, he sent Colleen Maples a text.

> In the time you dated Trey, did he ever go shooting? Ever hunt or spend any time with a gun?

He wasn't sure if she was working tonight or not, but her quick response made him think she was off.

> No. Never. Like I told you before, I didn't even know he had a gun.

Jason thought about it. Then he fired her another text. You think he could have been an avid hunter or gone shooting and maybe he kept that from you?

Her response came back in seconds. Anything's possible, but I don't think so.

Jason cranked the ignition and began to pull out of the parking lot. By the time he was back on Highway 431, Colleen had sent him another text.

> Busy tonight? I'm off. Haven't seen you in a while . . .

Jason sighed and put the top down on the Porsche. He put his phone on the passenger seat and tapped his fingers on the wheel. He was tempted. But with Chase back . . .

. . . so what if she's back? he thought. *She cheated on me multiple times. Abandoned me. I don't owe her anything.*

He thought back to how he'd felt with Ashley Sullivan the night before. The warmth he'd sensed. The intimacy.

At the stoplight by the Hampton Inn, he picked up his phone and thumbed a quick response to Colleen. Can't tonight. Working.

As he drove back to his office, Jason put the top down on the Porsche and breathed in the cool night air. He was starting to finally see his defense case taking shape. He'd bring out Kelly Flowers's inappropriate and abusive behavior with Chase and Colleen Maples. He'd have Detective Daniels admit that Flowers was being investigated by internal affairs and that she had an informant, Chase, who was ready to roll on him. Daniels would testify that her file was deleted and that an attempt was made on her life. When the state called Detective Mitchell, he would tear into him with questions about his knowledge of the investigation into Flowers and the victim's whereabouts the night of the murder.

Someone in the sheriff's office, either Mitchell or perhaps the sheriff himself, wanted to sweep the Flowers investigation under the rug. And perhaps that same someone was Tyson Cade's new source in the sheriff's department.

The murder was an inside job, Jason thought, squeezing the wheel and knowing he had to be right.

But by whom? Tyson Cade or the sheriff's department?

Jason sucked in a deep breath. *Or both . . .*

As he pulled into his lot, Jason felt his heart and mind racing. He was six days out from trial, and he had a theory.

But he needed more. There were additional boxes to check, and he was running out of time.

Damnit, Harry. I need you, man, he thought. Then he had an idea. He took out his phone and clicked the number for Bo Haynes.

Seconds later, a deep baritone voice answered, "What's up, Jason?"

Jason closed his eyes. *Six days . . .* "I need your help."

93

Jason worked until just past nine o'clock. By the time he arrived home, he was worn out and thought he might actually be able to sleep tonight. But, as he was getting out of his car, Satch's voice stopped him.

"Hey, Jason."

He turned and saw the big man crossing the street holding something in his hand.

"What's up?"

"Chase asked me to do something with this. I guess she had kept a stash hidden in her house and didn't want it in there anymore." Jason glanced over at Chase's house. The light above the carport was on. He hadn't spoken with her since their conversation on the steps the night before.

"Why are you showing it to me? Get rid of it."

"I've got a better idea. I was thinking we keep it. You never know when we might want to put it somewhere, you know what I mean?" He squinted and grinned.

"I like it," Jason said.

94

On Wednesday, October 9, Jason decided he'd procrastinated long enough. There was one box he knew he had to check that he'd been purposely avoiding.

I was supposed to do it with Harry, Jason thought. But Harry was gone, and Jason was five days from trial. There were valid reasons for his delay.

For one, he doubted this trip would lead to anything.

And two, perhaps more importantly, he knew he'd be triggered to drink.

At 4:30 p.m., after a good lift session, Jason got in the Porsche and headed toward Huntsville. *I can do this,* he thought, remembering Ashley Sullivan's words from several months earlier.

———

Jimmy's Lounge was one of the oldest surviving strip clubs in north Alabama. The exterior was bland and almost blank except for the red sign in block capital letters.

JIMMY'S

Jason was no stranger to exotic dance clubs. In college and law school, he and his friends hit Sammy's in Birmingham and the Cheetah in Atlanta. But since beginning the practice of law, he hadn't been a frequent flier, though he reminded himself that he'd interviewed several dancers at the Sundowners Club in Pulaski after Harry's disappearance.

Jason walked inside the doors and was greeted with the sounds of "I Touch Myself," by Divinyls, blasting from the ceiling speakers. He looked around, taking the place in. The lighting was dim, and there was a long bar in front with several tables in front of it. There appeared to be a layer of stalls to the left where dancers were leading men for private lap dances. The huge room smelled of cigarettes, cheap perfume, sweat, and beer.

Jason felt his stomach tighten as he brushed past several women wearing nothing but G-strings and bikini tops. As he sat down and saw a woman with blonde hair and huge breasts dancing on the stage to the right of the bar, he had an odd thought.

When was the last time I had sex?

Jason was still pondering the question when a female waitress came by, wearing a lacy black bra and Daisy Duke cutoff jeans. She asked for his drink order, and he swallowed. Every fiber in him wanted to order a beer or a whiskey drink. Instead, he said, "Club soda and lime."

She looked at him funny and walked away. When she returned, he'd regained his composure. "Is there a dancer here named Bella Flowers?"

She blinked. "Who wants to know?"

He took out his business card and slid it across the table.

She giggled. "I've seen your commercials."

Jason nodded.

"This about her brother?"

"Yes," Jason said.

"She in trouble?"

"No. I just have a couple questions."

"OK. She's on the center stage next. Then she'll be available for lap dances." She grinned. "Or a VIP dance if you have the green." She winked and walked away.

Jason took a sip of his soda and took out his phone. He had a text from Bocephus Haynes. My investigator is on it. He said he should have some information for you by midmorning tomorrow. Watch for an email.

What's his name? Jason replied.

Albert Hooper, but he only answers to Hooper.

Jason smiled and replied with the thumbs-up emoji.

Then, as he was about to surf his social media sites, he got a text from Nola. I heard Chase came back. Is she alright?

Better, Jason responded.

What are you doing?

Jason looked up as the blonde woman was exiting the stage and another song began to play. It took him a few seconds to recognize it, but he eventually tabbed the number as "Crazy in Love," by Beyoncé. It took him no time to recognize the woman on stage.

Gone was the elegant black dress she'd worn at her brother's funeral and Trey Cowan's arraignment. In its place was a see-through lace gown and nothing else but a black G-string.

She ran her hands through her dark-brown hair and jumped onto the pole in the middle of the stage, sliding seductively down it. Jason watched as several men began to place dollar bills on the stage. Based upon her presentation, he figured Bella was one of the more popular dancers.

Jason returned his eyes to his phone, where Nola's question remained.

Working, he typed back.

———

Forty-five minutes later, Bella Flowers, now wearing a black halter top and pink shorts, walked over to his table. "You wanted to talk with me?"

"Yes," Jason said. "It won't take more than five minutes." Jason took a hundred-dollar bill out of his wallet and slid it across the table.

"That's enough for a VIP dance. Did you—"

"I don't want that," Jason said. "I just don't want you to lose any money by talking to me. I can see that you're very popular."

She put the money in her G-string and peered back at him without saying thank you. "What do you want?"

"How often did you talk with your brother in the months before he died?"

"We texted about once or twice a week. Kelly liked to come to Huntsville to eat, so we'd meet a couple times a month for dinner." She paused. "We were the only family either of us had. Our parents died young."

"I'm sorry," Jason said.

"Did he ever say anything about Trey Cowan?"

"Not to me."

"Do you remember Trey?"

"I was several years older than Kelly, so I didn't know many of his friends that well."

"Did you know any of Kelly's friends in the department?"

She looked down at the table. "I mean . . . sometimes he'd bring one or two of them with him when he came to visit."

Jason sensed an opportunity. "Did he ever take any of his colleagues here?"

She chuckled. "Oh, no. Kelly was embarrassed by all of this." She waved her arm around the room. Her eyes were blank, and she occasionally pursed her lips and moved her mouth in a circle. *A tic,* Jason thought. *Is she on something?*

"Did Kelly ever mention any involvement with a man named Tyson Cade?" Jason asked.

"Only that he wanted to bust that motherfucker's ass."

Jason smiled. "Anything else?"

"No." She punched his shoulder. "You're cuter in person than on your billboards."

Definitely on something, Jason thought. "Are you aware of Kelly having any enemies?"

"No," she said.

"When was the last time you talked to him?"

"He called me the day before he died. Said he would be coming up later in the week and wanted to go to lunch at Rosie's Cantina."

Jason jotted a few notes down on his phone. "I'm assuming you've told all of this to the sheriff's department."

She nodded. "George interviewed me."

Jason felt a flutter in his chest and raised his eyebrows.

"George Mitchell," Bella continued. "He was one of Kelly's friends in the department. I'd met him before." She reached out and ran a finger up his arm. "How about that VIP dance?"

Jason ignored the question, thinking about Officer Mitchell. *Everything and everyone in this case seems to be one step away from George Mitchell . . .* "Did any officers from the Marshall County Sheriff's Office ever come here to watch you dance?" he asked.

She removed her hand and crossed her arms. "No."

"Not a single one?"

She made a zero symbol with both hands and laughed. "Bye, Mr. Rich." Then she stood and walked away.

Jason watched her go, knowing that he didn't have any more questions but also feeling as if she hadn't been completely truthful.

He thought it through. Kelly Flowers was a young officer whose incredibly attractive older sister was a stripper at a club forty-five minutes from Guntersville.

Would any of Kelly's colleagues have come to see her dance?

Hells to the yes, Jason thought, throwing a five-dollar bill down for the soda and heading for the door.

———

As he exited the club, his nostrils still saturated with the scent of sin, Jason felt an overpowering urge that had nothing to do with alcohol. He was both relieved that he didn't want a drink and agitated that he wanted something else that he couldn't have.

He saw an image of Chase in his mind. The last time they'd been together was Christmas Eve at her house. He imagined her fruity perfume and earthy scent. Then another, somewhat surprising, vision came to him. Ashley Sullivan in her T-shirt and jeans. Freckles on her nose. The intimacy of their last meeting.

Jason fired up the Porsche, thinking a cold shower was in his future. Before pulling out of the lot, he checked his email.

There was a message waiting from Albert Hooper.

Mr. Rich,

Attached is the information your requested on Walt Cowan. I haven't completed my work on the officers in the department, but I'll have you that tomorrow afternoon.

Jason clicked on the attachment, skimmed through it, and then dialed the Guntersville Municipal Airport.

After the dispatcher answered, Jason spoke in a firm voice. "Please get my plane ready and find me a pilot."

"When are you leaving, Mr. Rich?"

"Tomorrow," he said, putting the Porsche in gear and spinning his tires as he peeled out of Jimmy's Lounge.

95

Three hours later, after quickly changing in the dressing room, Bella Flowers slid into her truck and clicked on a contact in her phone that she hadn't called or texted in several months. When he answered, she didn't bother with pleasantries.

"Trey's lawyer came to visit me tonight."

"And I presume you told him nothing about . . . us."

"You presume right."

A sigh of relief. "Good."

"When are you going to come see me again?"

"You know I can't. Not until after the trial."

"OK," she said. Then she clicked End.

96

The Pearl was the nicest hotel on the Emerald Coast. Located in Rosemary Beach, on the northern tip of Highway 30A, its exterior was painted white with a black canopy, giving it a regal presentation.

But Jason hadn't picked the accommodations for their plushness.

No, he'd chosen the Pearl for one reason and one reason alone.

Every weekday night at 5:00 p.m., Walter Cowan had a smoky old-fashioned at the first-floor bar. The bar was known for the drink, and from five to six, it was happy hour. Walter had two drinks each night before heading home to Panama City. He was working on a couple of new houses being built in nearby Seacrest. Jason had obtained the intel from Albert Hooper's detailed report and was impressed with the quickness with which Bo Haynes's investigator had tracked Cowan down.

Now, on Thursday afternoon, October 10, four days from the start of trial, Jason was sitting at the bar, waiting for Walt.

At almost 5:00 on the dot, the man appeared. Jason had been texted a few pictures of him by Trudy, and he recognized him right off. Gray, thinning hair, same height as Trey but much skinnier, with a reddish face made all the redder, Jason assumed, by years of abusive drinking. Walt sat down, and the bartender flashed him a wink.

"Usual, Walt?"

"Yes, sir. And I'll be finishing it fast, so you might want to go ahead and make two."

The bartender, whose lapel read **JOE**, laughed. "Coming right up."

Jason walked over and waved at Joe. "This one's on me."

Walt smiled, but in an instant, as recognition set in, his face went blank.

"Mr. Cowan, I'm—"

"Jason Rich. My son's attorney. You didn't have to buy me a drink."

Joe brought the cocktail over, and Walt took a long, slow sip. "Damn, that's good." He turned and looked at Jason with red-rimmed eyes. "What do you want?"

"Kelly Flowers was killed with a twelve-gauge shotgun. Have you ever seen Trey fire that type of weapon?"

Walt took another long sip and shook the ice in his glass. "I haven't seen much of Trey in the last few years, so I'm speaking only from my experience raising him. But Trey never liked guns. He loved team sports, and he liked to go fishing with me. But I'm not sure I've ever seen him fire a gun of any kind. I took him to a couple dove hunts when he was a kid, but I'll be damned if I remember him firing a shot."

"Do you know if anyone ever taught him how to shoot?"

Walt finished off the glass and made a circle in the air with his index finger. "You mind getting this one, too, Jason?"

"Not at all," Jason said. "I came four hundred miles for this meeting."

"I didn't teach him," Walt continued. "Hunting and shooting just wasn't something we did together. Hell, I barely shoot any myself. I have a concealed carry handgun, but I haven't gone to the range in years, and I never took Trey there." He smiled, and his face turned redder. "I threw a lot of football with him. Pitch-and-catch baseball. We had a basketball goal, and I'd shoot baskets with him. I loved doing that stuff and could keep up pretty good till my knees got ruined laying brick." He looked into his empty drink and took a sip of ice, crunching the cubes in his mouth. "Playing ball with Trey was the most fun I ever had in my life. He was a natural."

Joe brought over the next smoky old-fashioned, and Walt took it out of his hand.

"Do you think Trey could kill someone?" Jason asked.

"No, I don't. I believe my boy is innocent. But my opinion and a quarter will buy you a gumball, and that's it." He took another sip. "I'll tell you this. I spoke with Trey more than his momma knows. I'd call him at least once a week. I even sent him some money when he was going for that tryout with the Barons, even though I knew he wasn't going to make it. Don't have the wheels anymore. No team is going to take a chance on a one-legged player." He swirled the ice cubes in his glass. "Anyhow, I've never seen Trey as down as he was the last few months before he was arrested. Honestly, if you'd told me he had fired a shotgun and that's all you told me, I'd have assumed he'd used it on himself."

Jason peered down at the bar, remembering what Trey had said in the consultation room a few months ago. He'd grabbed the shotgun because he'd thought he wanted to kill himself. "Trey said he went off his depression meds a couple weeks before the murder to help with the tryout," Jason said.

"That was dumb. All that did was make him more depressed. Unless he could reconstruct the leg that your brother-in-law butchered, he was never going to be given a chance by a Major League club."

Jason watched as Walt killed the rest of his drink. "You mind buying me one more?" Walt asked. "All this talk about Trey's situation is depressing me."

Jason ordered the drink. "Is there anything you can tell me about Tyson Cade? Or Kelly Flowers? Any nugget of information you think might be useful?"

"Trey was drunk that night, wasn't he?"

"Yes," Jason said. "He'd had five beers at the Brick and then drank a half a fifth of whiskey."

"That'll hurt your aim," Walt said, taking a long drink from the glass. "I've never tried to shoot while drunk, but I've done a lot of other things hammered, and I can't say it's improved anything."

"Why do you do it then?" Jason asked. Just one alcoholic asking another the seminal question.

Walt gazed at the mirror behind the bar. "I've got nothing else. If I stopped drinking, I'd have to accept the fact that I've got nothing. No family no more. I used to work all day so I could come home and play ball with Trey. I lost that after his injury and buried my head in the bottle." He took another sip. "Been there ever since."

"I'm an alcoholic," Jason said. "I went to the Perdido Addiction Center for ninety days and got clean. You might want to try it." Jason pushed himself off the stool. "Are you going to come to the trial, Mr. Cowan?"

"Trudy would probably kill me if I do."

Jason looked at him. "I think you should come. I may have to call you as a witness."

He laughed out loud. "To say what?"

"That you never saw Trey fire a shotgun or a firearm of any kind."

"I've barely seen him the last three years. Doesn't that matter?"

Jason sighed. "I'm grasping at straws, Walt. We need everything we can get."

Walt drained the rest of his third drink. "All right then. For Trey, I'll be there."

Jason took down his cell phone number and gave Walt all of his contact info. "Call me when you get into town, and I'll get you a hotel room."

"Thanks."

Jason turned to leave, but Walt grabbed his arm. "I hope to hell you have another theory. A shotgun is literally the easiest gun to shoot in the world."

"From inside a truck. Through a window."

Walt squinted.

"Police report says there was one shell casing found in the cab of Trey's truck. Another was discovered near the victim's body. Since Flowers was killed with two blasts to the chest, that means the shooting, at least in part, must have been done from inside the vehicle. That seems pretty awkward with a twelve gauge."

Walt grinned, and his eyes were bleary. "Not bad. Not good, either, but . . . better than nothing."

"Thanks," Jason said, walking out of the bar and toward the elevator.

Better than nothing, he thought, as he pushed the up button for the elevator and exhaled with relief.

He'd take that.

97

On Friday morning, October 11, Sheriff Richard Griffith sat down at the head of the table in the sheriff's office war room. On the other end of the table sat Detective Hatty Daniels.

Between them was district attorney Shay Lankford.

"Are we all going to make nice and play in the same sandbox?" Shay finally asked, looking first at Griff and then Hatty.

"Depends," Griff said. "Are you both going to throw me under the bus next week?"

"I'm going to tell the truth," Hatty said.

"And what's that?" Griff asked. "That you were too weak to hack it around here, so you abandoned your job for three months only to hire a hotshot lawyer that made it so we had to take you back."

"You'd be wise to watch your words, Griff," Shay said.

"You're not my boss," Griff snapped. "I answer to the people of Marshall County that elected me. Same as you. Now Hatty . . ." Griff nodded toward the detective. ". . . she does answer to me. Or at least she should. Maybe now that's she's gotten away with her little stunt, she doesn't feel that way."

"You . . . or George . . . deleted my file on Kelly Flowers."

"I can't speak for George, but I did no such thing. And do you really think George Mitchell, mild-mannered, straight arrow George, would destroy evidence? Come on, Hatty."

"Who then?"

"Are you sure you didn't do it yourself by accident?"

Both women gave Griff the stink eye, and he looked away.

"Look . . . ," Shay finally said. "There's a hearing this afternoon where we're asking the court to exclude all of this as irrelevant and highly prejudicial, so it may not even be a consideration. But, if we do have to address it, Hatty is going to tell the truth next week," Shay said, looking at Griff before turning to Hatty. "Which is that the file was deleted, but she doesn't know who did it."

"And the only person that I told about it was you and George," Hatty snarled.

Griff stood. "I've heard enough. I hope you win your hearing, Shay." He glared at Hatty. "For her sake."

The sheriff stormed out of the conference room. Shay peered at Hatty. "It's not easy playing referee," she said.

"I'm sorry, but I'm not backing down. Someone tried to kill me, do you understand?" Hatty pressed herself up. "Think about something, Shay. Who benefits the most if I'm dead? If I can't come back and tell the county what happened? How an entire investigative file was deleted? How a cop working under Sheriff Griffith's watch had turned dirty and was working for Tyson Cade?"

Shay looked down at the table.

"By my count, two folks win in that situation," Hatty continued. "George Mitchell ascends to my position in the department . . . and perhaps becomes Tyson Cade's new inside source." She shrugged. "And the sheriff avoids a very embarrassing situation . . . and also perhaps becomes Cade's man."

"Hatty, you're talking out of your mind," Shay said. "I'm not going to feel comfortable calling you as a witness if you keep this up."

"Rich will call me if you don't, and he'll make you and the state look even worse for destroying evidence." She stormed toward the door.

"Hatty?"

"Think about it, Madame Prosecutor," Hatty said, turning and glaring at Shay for a full second. Then she walked out of the room and slammed the door behind her.

98

At 1:30 p.m. on Friday, Jason sat at the defense table looking over his notes. Other than the trial itself, the single most important part of the case was about to transpire. Looking behind him, he saw there was no fanfare. No patrons. No reporters. Not a single soul seated at any of the benches.

But regardless of the lack of an audience, this motion hearing would determine whether he could plant the seed of Kelly Flowers as a dirty cop.

Judge Barber strode to the bench with no announcement. He wore a golf shirt and slacks and, if Jason knew His Honor, was probably headed for a round of golf at Gunter's Landing immediately after this hearing.

Jason glanced at Shay Lankford, who was dressed in her customary dark suit. The prosecutor had said hello upon his entrance but nothing else.

"OK, on the Cowan case, we are here for the party's respective motions in limine. Let's get started." He looked down at his court reporter. "You ready, Jill?"

"Yes, Your Honor."

"All right, let's get on the record."

———

As expected, Barber saved the most important motion for last. "Now, turning to the state's motion to exclude any evidence of the sheriff's office's internal investigation of Kelly Flowers, the leave of absence taken by Detective Daniels, and the deletion of Flowers's investigative file . . ."

Barber took off his glasses. "I have read each party's respective briefs, and I want to compliment both the prosecution and the defense for arguing their positions so eloquently and persuasively. But here is the thing I keep coming back to, Mr. Rich. What does the investigation into Kelly Flowers have to do with his murder? Do you have any evidence linking the investigation to some alternative defense theory? There is a lot of highly inflammatory stuff in here. Leniency offered for sex. Drugs offered . . ." He gave his head a jerk. ". . . also for sex. I mean, if the jury hears this type of content, it could be incredibly prejudicial and to what end? Can you link any of it to the murder?"

"Your Honor," Jason said, feeling a desperate sense of exasperation. "With all due respect, Mr. Cowan has been charged with capital murder. Any evidence that might exculpate him in any way ought to be and is due to be allowed. The investigation of Flowers is straight-up Brady material and should come in. Not only that, but the state's attempt to destroy evidence violates my client's due process rights."

"How is any of this mess exculpatory, Mr. Rich?" Barber challenged again.

"That Mr. Flowers's double-dealing and monstrous abuses of power led to him being killed by either of his two masters. The sheriff's office . . . or the Sand Mountain drug trade. The defense is allowed to present an alternative theory for the murder, and that is ours."

"Ms. Lankford?"

"Your Honor, Mr. Rich's argument is preposterous. There is no evidence whatsoever linking anyone in the sheriff's office or any alleged drug dealer with this murder. Mr. Rich is reaching, and he knows it. He wants to put the victim on trial, and any probative value of this investigation by the sheriff's office into Sergeant Flowers's conduct would be greatly outweighed by prejudice to the state. Not to mention, it would be completely irrelevant."

"Your Honor—" Jason started but stopped when Barber beat on the bench with his gavel.

"I've heard enough." He looked at Jason and then Shay. "The state's motion is . . . denied." The disappointment in Barber's voice was obvious. "I agree with Mr. Rich that the evidence fits under the Brady rule and should be allowed."

"Your Honor, please reconsider," Shay pleaded. "Kelly Flowers's legacy as an officer shouldn't be tarnished in this way."

"I've made my ruling, Madame Prosecutor."

———

Jason sat at the defense table for a long time. He could hardly believe it. It had sounded as if Barber was going to grant the state's motion, but he hadn't.

I won.

When Shay finally spoke, he hadn't realized that she was still in the room.

"You're going to do it again, aren't you?" the prosecutor asked.

"Do what?"

"Turn this court into the Barnum & Bailey circus."

Jason looked at her, wondering what she was still doing in here. "If he had granted your motion, that would have been reversible error. Do you really want to have to try this case twice?"

"No. But I was hoping that the jury wouldn't be put through a shitshow of you cross-examining Hatty Daniels and George Mitchell on things that may stink to high heaven but don't have a damn thing to do with how or why Kelly Flowers was murdered."

Jason looked at her and then smiled. "See you on Monday, Madame Prosecutor."

Shay managed a weary return smile. "You're a fighter, Jason. I admire that about you. But we both know you aren't going to be able to pull a rabbit out of your hat this time."

Jason narrowed his eyes. "We'll see."

99

Jason waited until he was inside his Porsche before he let himself react to the ruling.

"Wooooo!" he screamed, giving his best Ric Flair imitation. "Woooo! Woooo! Woooo!"

He beat his fist on the steering wheel and took a deep breath. Then he put the car in gear and looked at the clock. It was 2:00 p.m. on a Friday. He might not be able to win this trial, but at least he had a puncher's chance.

He wanted to celebrate. To howl at the moon. To get loose.

I want a drink.

He gripped the wheel and tried to calm his breathing. Normally, the triggers for alcohol were bad things. He snatched his phone out of his pocket. Ashley Sullivan had said he could call her if he ever was about to fall. This would be an odd time, but he could feel a strong craving coming on.

A swig of champagne right from the bottle.

An icy-cold beer followed by another.

A shot of Jack Daniel's.

Jason felt sweat on his forehead. He tried to find Ashley's contact information, but he realized his phone was off. He'd powered down when he'd gone into the courthouse. When the device came on, he had a text message and a voice mail from the same contact.

Bocephus Haynes.

All the text said was to call him, and Jason didn't wait to listen to the message. He clicked call.

Bo answered on the first ring. "I got something on our boy Matthew Dean."

"What?"

"He hasn't renewed his boat registration."

"What?"

"When you own a boat, you have to renew your tag every year, just like a car."

"Right, I know. I do that for my Sea-Doo."

"Yep. Well our boy Matthew hasn't renewed his, and it was due in August."

"Well . . . that's something," Jason said.

"I've had my investigator looking for an angle, any kind of leverage. He mentioned this to me in September and said most officers would give a boater a grace period. But we're into October now."

"Past any grace period."

"It's not much, but you may be able to use this to mess with him. Especially since you have an in with the police department."

"I do?"

"Hatty Daniels. Dean tried to kill her, remember?"

Jason felt a tickle inside his brain, and he didn't want a drink anymore. "Bo, thank you. I think . . ."

. . . Jason's eyes widened, and his pulse quickened as an idea hatched in his brain.

"Jason?"

". . . *this is exactly what we need.*"

———

Jason called Satch on his way home.

"I like it," Satch said. "And I'm on it. That sonofabitch takes his boat out every Saturday. Looks like Chuck and Mickey and I will be doing a little fishing tonight."

Jason next called Hatty Daniels.

She listened to his pitch. Then, without hesitation, she answered: "Hell yes."

100

Matthew Dean got an early start on Saturday morning. He fished the waters around Honeycomb and then thought he'd try Browns Creek before heading in for an early dinner at Fire by the Lake. He'd drunk a few beers and was feeling good.

That is, he was until he saw blue and red lights close in behind him. *What the hell?*

Matty waited as two uniformed officers hopped aboard his boat. "Mr. Dean, do you realize that you are operating an unregistered boat?"

"What?" He snapped his fingers. "Oh, shit. I haven't gotten my renewal in. I'm sorry, Officer. I'll get that done on Monday. Can we go with a warning this time? My record is clean."

"No, Mr. Dean, we can't. Have you been drinking?"

"We got a report from another boat operator that you were driving your boat at a high rate of speed and in an unsafe manner. Are those empty beer cans in the floorboard?"

Matty blinked his eyes as another man entered the boat. "Mr. Dean, I'm a sergeant with the Marshall County Sheriff's Office. Do you mind if we search your boat?"

"Why do you want to do that?"

"Because we've received multiple reports of erratic movement from your boat. It'll just take a second."

Matty put his hands on his hips but said nothing.

The sergeant and the two other officers searched for several minutes. Then one of the deputies brought his hand out of the storage bin. "Well, well, well. Lookee here."

Matty felt a chill run up his legs to the middle of his spine. "You planted that."

"I found it, Mr. Dean. What are you doing with three grams of methamphetamine?"

"Planning to sell it or snort it?" the other officer asked.

Then the sergeant stepped forward. "Matthew Dean, you're under arrest for possession of an illegal substance, operation of an unregistered watercraft, and operating a boat while under the influence of alcohol or controlled substances." He paused and took a card out of his pocket. "You have the right to remain silent."

101

Tyson Cade rarely lost his cool. Even when he attacked someone, he did it with deliberate malice. But when he saw his mole with the Marshall County Sheriff's Office enter the tiny cabin in Mentone, Alabama, he couldn't contain himself.

He kicked the man as hard as he could in the shin and then brought his knee into the other man's chin.

The officer fell onto the plywood floor and grunted.

"What in *the fuck* is going on?"

"Your guy fucked up," the lawman managed.

Tyson kicked the officer in the stomach, and the mole fell backward. Tyson started to kick him again but stopped himself. The lawman was breathing heavy, and he was sweating profusely despite the temperature being fifty-five degrees outside and there being no heat in the cabin.

"My operation depends on Matty Dean. He's my lead distributor. I can't lose him."

The officer pushed his back against the wall. "He says the drugs were planted, but by who? Who would or could set you up like that?"

"Detective Daniels?" Tyson said.

"You said you were going to kill her," the officer said. "Remember?"

Tyson ground his teeth together. "I need you to make this go away."

"It's not that simple. He had an unregistered boat. There was a complaint of erratic operation. He was drinking on the boat. And they found the meth. We can't let it go."

"What good are you if you cost me my best man?"

"I didn't cost you him. He messed up. Plain and simple."

Tyson crossed his arms. "You're welcome to stay here tonight. You may want some time to think about your situation. But you have forty-eight hours to figure this shit out. Come Monday evening, Matty Dean better be out of jail."

"Or what?"

"Or I'm gonna kill your children. And their mother. *And your girl-friend.*" He squatted in front of the lawman. "I'll bury them all in the lake. The kids I'll just shoot, but . . . I'll take my time with the women."

"Leave my family out of this."

"When you signed up to work for me, you signed up your family and everyone you care about. That's the deal." He grabbed the doorknob and glared down at the lawman. "Forty-eight hours."

102

At 8:45 a.m. on Monday, Jason stared at himself in the mirror of the men's room on the second floor of the Marshall County Courthouse. "Fifteen minutes till go time," he said out loud, taking a deep breath and then splashing water on his face.

He'd spent the entire weekend preparing for trial. Much of that work involved reviewing the materials uncovered by Bo Haynes's investigator, Albert Hooper.

Jason had asked Hooper to do background checks on every single officer in the Marshall County Sheriff's Office. Most of that information had turned out to be irrelevant.

But one nugget Jason found interesting. George Mitchell had gone through a divorce in the last year. Jason knew from his experience with Jana's trial that divorce files could contain all sorts of potentially helpful information.

Mitchell's divorce was final and a decree entered. Infidelity had been raised on his wife's part, but much of the file was under seal. Jason had subpoenaed the attorneys on both sides of the Mitchell divorce late Thursday afternoon, asking for all documents produced during the divorce proceeding. He knew objections would likely be filed, but he ought to be entitled to any documents or information not protected by the attorney-client privilege. He'd filed an emergency motion seeking either a response within a week or a continuance of trial, and Judge Barber had granted the motion for an expedited response. He should know by this Thursday what, if anything, relevant was in the files.

Would that be soon enough?

Jason splashed more water on his face. Then he walked inside one of the stalls and locked it. Once inside, he flexed like he might be the Incredible Hulk and let out a silent scream. *Now or never,* he thought, walking out the door into the hallway.

My third jury trial, he thought. As he reached the defense table and sat down next to Trey Cowan, he felt his phone vibrate in his pocket. He had placed it on silent instead of turning it off. He looked at the screen and felt a pang in his heart.

The message was from Izzy Montaigne.

He clicked it open and stared at the text for a long time.

Kick their ass.

Jason smiled and set the phone on the table. He was still looking at the screen as another message from his former partner came through.

You're Jason Motherfucking Rich.

103

By 4:00 p.m. on Monday afternoon, the seven men and five women who would decide the fate of Trey Cowan were seated in the jury box.

"We are going to adjourn for the day, and we will start with opening statements in the morning at nine a.m.," Judge Barber said.

Back in the attorney consultation room thirty minutes later, Trey gazed across the metal desk at Jason. "What do you think of the jury?"

"I've seen worse," Jason said, which was a bit of a ridiculous statement since he'd only seen two other juries in his life. "There are three under thirty, and younger jurors tend to be more defense friendly." He'd experienced this firsthand and also heard it from Knox Rogers and Bo Haynes, who both stressed that Jason should seek out younger jurors for their more liberal leanings.

"Trey, it's do-or-die time. I've told you everything I've learned in my investigation. Flowers was dirty. He was working for Cade. We know this now. The trial has officially started. Can you tell me the deal? What was Kelly Flowers giving you such a hard time about at the Brick?"

Trey gazed past Jason to the wall. "What does it matter? We can't win."

"Maybe not, but you'll never know unless you come clean with me. I'm an attorney. Whatever you tell me is protected by the attorney-client privilege. Please, Trey."

After several seconds of silence, Jason sighed and walked to the door. Before he could knock, Trey spoke behind him.

"Kelly wanted me to make a delivery for Tyson. I refused."

Jason turned and sat down. "What kind of delivery?"

"Pick up a truck and take it somewhere. I'd find out at the pickup time where I was going."

"Why didn't you agree?"

"Eventually . . . I did. Out on the sidewalk. After the dustup in the bar."

"After you told him you were going to kill him in front of about twenty camera phones?"

"Yep."

"Why did you threaten to kill him? What made you so mad that you attacked him?"

Trey ground his teeth. "He said he'd found out about my failed tryout with the Barons from Colleen. He said I was stupid all day long and that it was no wonder Colleen left me." Trey sighed. "I snapped."

Jason made a tent with his hands, thinking it through. "When was your tryout?"

"First week of April. I had gotten the rejection text a few hours before going to the Brick on the eighth."

"Did you tell Colleen about the tryout?"

He peered at the table. "Yeah. Sent her a text and asked her to wish me luck a couple days before."

"Why? Y'all had broken up by then, hadn't you?"

"We had, but I hadn't told anyone but her and my folks about my comeback attempt. I guess I was hoping I might be able to see her again. Hell, I don't know what I was doing."

"Did she respond?"

"She sent a text saying 'good luck.' That was it."

Jason rubbed his chin. All of these mentions of Colleen Maples had made him think back to his own initial meeting with the CRNA. There was something he had asked her that he thought she might be lying about. What was it? "OK . . . ," Jason continued, still thinking about Colleen but forcing himself back to the present. ". . . so that explains the fight and why you were so mad. After the brawl, you tell Kelly you'll do the delivery out on the sidewalk. Then what?"

"I'd been off my meds for a while. I wanted . . ." Trey's eyes filled with tears. ". . . like I told you earlier, what I really wanted was to kill myself. I got drunk and grabbed my shotgun and some shells, because that was my plan. I was going to drive somewhere and do it." He wiped his eyes. "But instead I drove to my momma's house." He shook his head. "Like a big sissy."

Jason took a few notes. "Did you talk to anyone else before you went to your mom's?"

"No."

"Did you fire your shotgun before you got there?"

Trey shook his head.

"And, like you and your dad have both said, you didn't have much experience shooting a gun of any kind, correct?"

"That's right."

"When you got to your mom's, did you leave the gun inside the truck?"

Trey blinked his eyes. "Yes."

"Did you lock the doors?"

"Nah, never. Nothing in there to steal."

"Just the shotgun," Jason said, looking Trey in the eye.

"But it wasn't stolen. It was there when I left Mom's the next morning."

"Maybe someone borrowed it," Jason volunteered. "Someone trying to frame you for this murder."

Trey raised his eyebrows but said nothing.

"How drunk were you by the time you went to your mom's?" Jason asked, shifting gears.

"I was hammered. I could barely walk. I went to her house, drank some more bourbon, and then passed out."

Jason pushed his chair out from the table and laced his hands behind his head. "Trey, we need to make a decision about whether you're going to testify. There is some good stuff here, but it could also be a land mine of trouble. Your anger over the breakup with Colleen and Flowers's involvement is definitely a negative that gives you more motive to kill him."

"And I can't say I delivered drugs for Tyson Cade. Wouldn't that be admitting a crime?"

"Yes, but a much lesser one than murder. It would give you credibility in front of the jury."

"Tyson paid you to represent me. Won't he kill us both . . . and everyone we care about . . . if I say I delivered drugs for him on the stand?"

Jason peered down at the floor, growing frustrated. *He's right.*

"That's one of the reasons I've never told you what happened until now," Trey continued. "What's the use? I'll never be able to say what really went down without bringing a painful death to everyone I . . . and everyone you . . . care about."

Jason sighed and banged on the door three times. "I'm doing all I can do, Trey."

"I'm not going to risk my mom or dad getting hurt. Or Colleen. Or any more of the people you care about."

Jason felt a pang of guilt but shook it off. Then, at the mention of the nurse anesthetist's name again, his memory came back to him. "Trey, did Colleen know you had a shotgun?"

At this, the prisoner managed a grin. "Actually, yeah. She was with me when I bought it."

Jason felt a cold tickle run up his arms. "See you tomorrow."

———

After stopping by his office and printing something off his computer, Jason drove the streets of Marshall County for an hour and a half. He blared music from Waylon, Hank Jr., and Johnny Cash and tried to process the story Trey Cowan had just told him. Finally, he had his client's version of what happened the night of the murder. And while Trey's reasons for the barroom fight with Kelly Flowers were now crystal clear, it was the last thing Trey had said that had Jason buzzing with adrenaline.

"She was with me when I bought it."

At 6:15 p.m., Jason pulled to the curb outside of Colleen Maples's home. He walked to the front door and rang the doorbell.

She answered in green scrubs. "Hey, there."

Jason took the document he'd printed at his office and handed it to her. "This is a subpoena to testify in Trey's case," he said. "I know you said you'd be there, but I have to protect my client."

"I understand," she said, taking the subpoena and glancing at it. "Is there anything else? I have to go to work."

"Trey says that you were with him when he bought his shotgun. That true?"

She crossed her arms, hesitating only for a second. "Yes."

"He also claims that Kelly Flowers mentioned hearing about Trey's tryout with the Barons from you." Jason paused. "You told me that Flowers had moved on from you and that you hadn't seen him since your demotion at work."

Colleen gazed past Jason to the street. "I never said that. I only said that he was the one who prompted my drug test that led to my CRNA license being suspended."

"You kept seeing him after that?"

She nodded.

"When was the last time you saw him?"

She gazed down at the ground.

"The week of Trey's tryout?" Jason pressed. "First week of April?"

"That sounds right."

"Which was a week before Flowers was murdered."

She narrowed her gaze. "Yes, it was."

"Where did you see Flowers? At your house?"

She shook her head, and her lip began to tremble. "No."

Jason's eyes widened. "Where then? At the Hampton Inn?"

"No. I . . . lied about that too."

"What?"

"After our first encounter at the hotel, we always met at the same location . . . and it wasn't my house."

Jason's stomach twisted into a knot. He knew what she was going to say, but he asked anyway. "Where?"

"A barn on Hustleville Road," she whimpered. "He called it... Branner's Place."

104

Later that night, Jason lay on his back on his dock and gazed up at the stars. He was reeling from his encounter with Maples. Jason had asked her why she had lied to him about the shotgun, and she had said, *"I was scared. I didn't trust you, and I knew how all that might look to you. I don't have an alibi, and I had every reason to want Flowers dead. But I didn't kill him. And, if I had done it, I would not have set Trey up for it. And that's what you think happened, right? A setup?"* Jason had pondered the question and then asked one of his own. *"But it was Trey who cost you a future with Dr. Braxton Waters, wasn't it? The argument you had with Braxton during Trey's surgery and the botched follow-up leading to you being investigated by the Board of Nursing and Braxton cutting things off. You could have blamed Trey for everything and decided you'd kill two birds with one stone."* Colleen had stormed off her porch steps then, telling him that if he believed that, then he was crazy. *"I was in a relationship with Trey, and I cared about him,"* she had pleaded at her car.

"And it ended, and you got mixed up with Flowers, an old friend of Trey's. My deductions still add up. Plus, why were you hanging around Trey's apartment the day after the murder? That's never made sense to me."

"Because I care about him, and I saw police officers in the parking lot. I was trying to help." Her voice had cracked on the last word, and she'd glared at him. *"Don't come visit me again."* She'd waved the subpoena at him. *"I'll see you in court."*

Then she had driven away, leaving Jason to ponder what in the hell it all meant. Hours later, after working out in his garage gym and showering, he was still pondering. He'd hoped the dock and the lake breeze would provide some inspiration, but thus far, they hadn't.

"A penny for your thoughts?" Chase asked, walking up to him and lying down beside him.

"I asked you to stay away from me until after you testify. I don't want you to be cross-examined about our conversations. Shay may try to insinuate that I've coached you up."

"Well, you haven't. And when was the last time I did something you asked me?"

"Uhhhh . . . never."

She laughed, but Jason didn't. "How you doing?" she asked.

"I'm losing," Jason said.

"You can't win them all."

"I'm missing something. I think I have a fighting chance, but . . . I'm still missing something. I can feel it."

"You said the same thing about Jana's case. And you figured it out at the end."

He let out a deep breath. "How are you doing?" He had kept his distance from Chase since her return, not calling her and not dropping by her house. He wouldn't be a trigger for her anymore. He wasn't sure what, if anything, they would be to each other.

"I'm . . . OK," Chase said. "I miss you."

Jason closed his eyes and breathed in her earthy scent. He felt an ache in his loins and his heart. "Miss you too."

For a long moment, there was only silence. Jason could hear his heart thudding in his chest. He wanted to say more, but he was afraid. He wanted to know how Chase felt, but he didn't want to trigger her. Finally, he decided to change the subject.

"Chase, you've shot guns your whole life, haven't you? If you were trying to shoot someone from the driver's side of a truck, would you use a shotgun?"

"No. Would be awkward to shoot a twelve gauge from the cab. Unless you had a sawed-off shotgun."

Jason had thought of that, but Trey's gun had been a regular-size twelve gauge.

"But if that was all I had, I suspect I could pull it off." She peered at him. "And a shotgun is a scattergun, so you don't have to be as precise."

"Damnit," Jason said, feeling a growing sense of desperation. Eventually, he trudged up the hill to his house and lay on the raggedy couch on the covered patio.

I'm missing something, he thought again.

105

At 8:45 p.m. on Monday, Matty Dean was released from the Marshall County Jail. Bond had been set at $50,000, and it had been paid thirty minutes earlier. Matty walked out the visitor's entrance and into the parking lot, where an SUV was waiting on him. He climbed into the front passenger's side, and the vehicle surged forward.

"You all right, Matty?" Tyson asked from the back seat.

Matty didn't turn to face him. "Be better after I get a shower. Is your new inside man going to get the charges dismissed?"

"First things first," Tyson said. "We had to get you out, and he made that happen."

"I was set up, T. C., and I have a good mind who done it."

"Rich," Tyson said.

"Yeah, but he would have needed help in the sheriff's office."

A pause. "Daniels?" Tyson asked.

"Who else? She thinks I tried to kill her, and Rich knows damn well that I killed his investigator."

Tyson took a swig from a drink, and Matty knew it had to be a Sun Drop. The boss was a creature of habit, and one of these days, his patterns were going to get him killed. He had strung them all out over the past few months. He was juggling too many balls in the air, and he'd finally and inevitably dropped one of them. His obsession with control had cost the operation.

And I paid the price, Matty thought. *And may pay more . . .*

"All scores will be settled," Tyson finally said, putting something in his mouth, which Matty knew had to be either a Twinkie or an oatmeal creme pie. He began to chew, adding, "We just have to lie low and get through this trial without any collateral damage."

"Too late for that," Matty said. "I'm collateral damage."

"The charges will be dismissed," Tyson said, but he didn't sound as confident as he normally did, and Matty didn't respond.

"What about our new inside guy?" Matty asked, turning to face Tyson, staring into the younger man's hazel eyes. "Is he going to hold up? Or crack like an egg?"

Tyson put the rest of his snack—a Twinkie—into his mouth and grinned at Matty. Like his tone, the expression felt forced. "We'll see."

———

At the cabin in Mentone an hour later, Tyson Cade was keyed up and antsy. "After this trial is over, I want the charges against Matthew Dean to disappear, do you understand?"

"Yes." The lawman's voice was tired. Weak.

"You don't look good—are you going to stay strong? Or do I need to replace you already?"

"You can't replace me. You're in too deep with me."

Tyson grinned. "Keep thinking that and see where it gets you. Remember the threats I've made on your family. I'll carry out every one of them if you even think about rolling on me."

The mole looked away, unable to maintain eye contact. "Tyson, this trial is going to be a shitshow. The judge has allowed Rich to go into all of the investigation of Flowers. That implicates you."

"No, it doesn't. While there may be proof that Flowers was a crook, there're no direct links to me. Come on, man, you're better than this."

The lawman put his face in his hands and began to cry. "I wish I had never gotten involved with you."

Tyson Cade cackled. "Everyone always blames me. The truth is that your problems started when you began cheating on your wife with Bella Flowers. Then Kelly started leaning on you, and that's when you seized on an opportunity that would solve all your problems."

"You're wrong."

"I'm right. And Bull Branner saw you do it. He couldn't make out who it was, but *Bull saw*."

"But Bull has disappeared. There's a missing person's report out on him."

"And someday, years from now, his remains may wash up on a shore."

The lawman looked at Tyson with wild eyes. "You killed Bull."

"I did you a solid. Now it's time for you to hold up your end of the bargain." Tyson walked to the door. "Don't worry," he said, as he gripped the knob. "This will all be over shortly, and you'll be rolling in money and in the hay with Bella Flowers. Just get through this week."

"Are you setting me up?" the lawman asked, his voice a low whine. "All this time I thought you'd hired Rich to represent Cowan as some kind of show but that you were sabotaging him the whole way. Trying to hold down your reputation as some kind of Sand Mountain savior while throwing your boy under the bus." The mole licked his lips. "But maybe that's not it. Maybe you're loyal to your kind, and you're messing with me." He paused to catch his breath and took a tentative step toward Tyson. "If you bring me down, I'm gonna take you with me."

Tyson turned his head and glared at the lawman. "Did you just threaten me?"

The mole said nothing, but he didn't back away. "It's time for you to pick a team, Cade."

Tyson grinned. "Roll Tide." Then he slammed the door shut.

106

At 8:30 a.m. Tuesday morning, Jason met Hatty Daniels at a wooden bench on the Sunset Drive Trail. For a few seconds, they sat side by side, staring out at Lake Guntersville. Jason was holding a Styrofoam cup of coffee that he'd picked up from JaMoka's a few minutes earlier. Daniels had her hands clasped in her lap. Finally, she spoke without looking at him.

"Matty Dean was released on bond last night. $50,000. Given the charges, the bond was actually pretty high, but he was able to pay it."

"You mean Cade was able to pay it."

"Whatever. The money came in from a bonding company." She sighed. "I'm going to have him watched. Maybe he'll screw up again. I'm sure he figures it was us that set him up." She finally turned to Jason. "Watch your backside. You know how Cade operates. If he thinks we're behind Dean's arrest, then he may make a play."

Jason snorted. "Hatty, if I watched my ass any closer, my head would be screwed on backward. But thanks for the warning. Let me give you one. I had Matty Dean watched, and my investigator's now dead. I don't want that to happen to your guy, especially if it's Bo's private eye, Hooper."

"I'm not asking anyone else to handle this," Hatty said, standing and peering at the water. She looked back at Jason. "I'm watching Dean myself."

"Do you think that's wise?"

"I don't care. He tried to kill me and almost succeeded. I'm going to bring him down. And if he worked with George Mitchell, I'm going to bring George down too."

"Have you spoken with Sergeant Mitchell since your return?"

She shook her head. "I had one come-to-Jesus meeting with Shay and the sheriff. Since then, they've excluded me from all trial preparation. I'm not even sure she's going to call me as a witness."

Jason grinned. "I hope not. That will make my theory even more plausible."

Hatty bristled. "I don't like this little dance we are doing, Mr. Rich. It makes me uncomfortable. You know how I feel about the murder."

"You think Trey did it."

"The evidence begs only that conclusion."

"Well . . ." Jason stood and walked a few paces toward the lake. ". . . I beg to differ."

"Good luck today, Jason."

He turned. It was the first time she'd called him by his first name. "Thank you."

107

For jury selection, the courtroom had been barren except for the potential jurors. That was at the express order of Judge Barber, who hadn't wanted a circus during voir dire. But on the Tuesday of trial, with the jury that would decide the case in the box and the trial about to officially start, His Honor had lifted his ban.

And the place was a madhouse. Every available seat was taken, most by members of the media, but there were also quite a few town luminaries, including the entire Guntersville Chamber of Commerce, the mayor, and both county commissioners. Jason wondered if the political brass would be around after he dragged George Mitchell and Hatty Daniels through the mud of their internal affairs investigation of Kelly Flowers. The thought made him giddy. Outside the courthouse, he heard chants of "Blue lives matter," and today he had taken Shay up on her offer to enter through the back way of the courthouse. The town had not forgotten that one of their youngest and most beloved boys in blue had been shot down, and they had come out of the woodwork today.

Jason moved his eyes down the rows, nodding at Kisha Roe and winking at Colonel Satch Tonidandel, who was sitting in the back, wearing a sports coat and slacks. Satch was here to provide security and to be Jason's eyes and ears away from what was happening in front of the jury, and he was grateful for it. Nola was at home, being watched by Chuck, while Chase's home was being guarded by Mickey. If anything, all three Tonidandel brothers seemed wired and hyperalert.

Ready for war.

Am I ready? Jason wondered as he watched Judge Terry Barber stroll into the courtroom after the bailiff announced his presence.

After calling the case to order, Judge Barber looked at Shay and then Jason. "Counsel, are we ready for opening statements?"

"Yes, Your Honor," Shay said. The prosecutor had on a royal-blue suit today. Her voice was firm.

"Yes, Your Honor," Jason fired back.

"Very well then," Barber said, ratcheting up his southern accent and seeming to relish every second he had in the spotlight. "The state may proceed."

———

"May it please the court," the district attorney began, standing and bowing to Judge Barber. "Your Honor." She turned to Jason and gave a nod. "Counsel." And then she walked to the edge of the jury railing. "Members of the jury." Shay paused, and when she resumed speaking, her tone was fierce and aggressive. "On the morning of April 9, 2019, just off of Hustleville Road in the community of Alder Springs in Marshall County, Alabama, Sergeant Kelly Flowers was brutally murdered. Shot twice from close range with a twelve-gauge shotgun. The evidence in this case will show that the defendant, Trey Jerome Cowan, had threatened to kill Officer Flowers just a few short hours before doing just that. We will show you video evidence of the defendant's threats. We will also present to you the defendant's own shotgun, with only his prints on the handle, which a ballistics expert will testify is the weapon that murdered Kelly Flowers. Finally, we will prove beyond any reasonable doubt that the defendant, Trey Jerome Cowan, had ample motive, sufficient means, and, since he lived less than a mile from the murder site, all the opportunity in the world to commit this crime. The defendant murdered Sergeant Flowers, and the evidence is conclusive . . . and overwhelming."

It was a strong start, and Jason saw that every juror was leaning forward in their seat. Shay spent the next few minutes going over the operative facts in detail. The coroner's report showing that Flowers died from two shotgun wounds to the chest. The Remington shell casing found in the cab of Cowan's truck and the second one located on the ground by the victim's body. The fingerprint testing showing only Cowan's prints on the handle of the gun and the ballistics report confirming that the shell casings as well as the shell fragments found in the victim's body were all consistent with a twelve-gauge shotgun.

She then went through Trey's motive, mentioning the threat to kill Flowers made by Cowan at the Brick and reiterating that they would see video proof of Cowan swearing to God he would kill Flowers.

Finally, Shay frowned at Jason and spoke to the jury while moving her eyes between Jason and Trey. "It's our belief that the defense will try to put Sergeant Flowers on trial in this case and try to demean his good name. They will do that by introducing evidence of an internal affairs investigation into Flowers's behavior that reached no conclusions and the possible testimony of two drug addicts." She paused. "No matter how hard the defense tries to shine the spotlight elsewhere, the facts will remain. Kelly Flowers was shot and killed with Trey Cowan's shotgun. Cowan was caught with the murder weapon. He was also caught on camera threatening to do exactly what he did." She licked her lips. "After you've seen the mountain of evidence the state has against the defendant, I am confident that you will render the only verdict that justice allows." She paused. "Guilty."

———

"Do you smell that?" Jason hurled the question from his seat without standing. Judge Barber had just told him to proceed with the defense's opening statement, and he decided on the fly that he'd take the gloves off from the get-go.

There would be no bowing to His Honor or opposing counsel. No "May it please the court" or any other flowery statement. No bullshit. If he had any chance of winning, he had to make the jury smell and breathe the stench of the state's cover-up.

"Do you?" Jason stood and looked out at the capacity crowd, catching the eye of Bella Flowers in the row behind the prosecution. Her eyes were blank, and she seemed to look right through him. He moved his gaze to Kisha Roe, who was leaning forward in her chair, her eyes alert and on edge. Then he walked toward the jury, stopping just short of the railing. "You don't smell it now, because the prosecutor decided to tiptoe around the utter and complete mess that the Marshall County Sheriff's Office has made of this case." Jason glared at Sergeant George Mitchell, who sat next to Shay.

"Your Honor, we object. This is opening statement, and counsel is arguing."

"Sustained," Judge Barber said, but Jason didn't bother to look at him. He focused his eyes on the jury. He was grateful for the interruption, which gave him a dramatic lead-in to his theme.

"You're going to learn in this case that the sheriff's office didn't want you to know the whole story. You see . . . you're going to hear evidence in this trial from not one but two women that Sergeant Kelly Flowers abused in his role as a police officer in exchange for sexual favors." Jason's voice carried to the back of the courtroom, and he saw that Bella Flowers was now looking down at the floor. "That's right," he said, looking at the jurors, several of whom had pale faces. He then moved his gaze to Shay, who was glaring at him with pure contempt in her eyes.

"Sergeant Flowers arrested a woman named Colleen Maples for a DUI. Driving under the influence of alcohol. But then he decided to turn his camera off and offered her a deal. No arrest in exchange for sex. After a while, he added that he could get her the best methamphetamine on Sand Mountain in exchange for more sex." He lowered his voice. "Members of the jury, you are going to learn in this trial that Kelly Flowers was a monster." He pointed his finger at George Mitchell. "And the sheriff's office knew about it. That's right, Detective Hatty Daniels, the lead detective on the case, will testify in this case that she . . ." He continued to point at Mitchell. ". . . and Officer Mitchell were investigating Flowers for being involved in the Sand Mountain drug trade. You're also going to hear from Sergeant Daniels that, just prior to the preliminary hearing in this case, her entire file was erased and that only people in the department knew about the file. Sergeant Mitchell . . . and the high sheriff himself, Richard Griffith." Jason paused and took a big, exaggerated sniff.

"Do you smell it yet?"

After waiting five full seconds, he nodded at them. "You will." Jason walked back to the defense table. "Mr. Cowan, will you please stand?"

Trey did as he was told, and Jason put his arm around him. "This is Trey Jerome Cowan. Pride of the Guntersville Wildcats. There was a time in this town when little kids asked for this man's autograph. After a broken leg ended his football career, Trey went to work for the city doing sanitary work and umpiring baseball games. He isn't perfect. His mother, Trudy, who has lived in Marshall County all her life, will testify regarding her son's depression since the injury and his drunkenness the night of April 8, 2019. You'll also hear testimony from multiple witnesses in this case who saw Trey in an intoxicated state the night of the murder. Finally, you'll hear from Trey's father, Walt, and his mother, Trudy, that Trey Cowan was not a marksman. In fact, his father had never seen Trey shoot a gun in his life. The shot from the vehicle in this case was an awkward maneuver that would require someone with more shooting experience than Trey Cowan." Jason paused and moved into the well of the courtroom. "The defendant doesn't have to prove anything in this trial. Mr. Cowan doesn't have to put on a defense case at all. On the contrary, the burden of proof rests entirely on the prosecution to prove each of the elements of murder beyond a reasonable doubt."

For the next fifteen minutes, Jason highlighted the questions that the prosecution would not be able to answer, including what happened to the bag that Eva Claire Cobb saw Flowers holding minutes before the murder but which wasn't found at the scene of the crime or in Trey Cowan's possession, as well as where the evidence was that showed that Trey knew Flowers was going to be at Branner's Place at 12:30 a.m. Jason also explained how Flowers had engaged in the same monstrous abuse of power with Chase Wittschen as he had done with Colleen Maples, and that the real reason the officer was at Branner's Place at 12:30 a.m. on April 9 was to deliver methamphetamine to Wittschen. He described how Wittschen would testify that she had become an informant for the sheriff's office and was cooperating with Sergeant Mitchell and Detective Daniels as they investigated Officer Flowers. Wittschen would describe for the jury how she had told Sergeant Mitchell exactly when the rendezvous at Branner's Place would occur. Finally, Jason asked the jury to consider why the sheriff's department would delete its investigative file on Kelly Flowers. "What were they trying to hide?" Jason asked, looking right at Sergeant Mitchell.

Jason again faced the jury and took in a deep breath, slowly exhaling as he looked into each of their eyes. "Members of the jury, where there are this many questions . . . there has to be reasonable doubt. I am confident that, when you reach your decision at the end of this trial, you will reach the result that justice demands. That Trey Cowan is not guilty." He nodded at them. "Thank you."

―――

As Jason took his seat, the courtroom erupted in a smattering of murmurs. Judge Barber banged his gavel and asked the counsel to approach.

Jason's heart was thudding as he walked to the judge's bench. He was completely buzzed on adrenaline.

Barber scowled at Jason, his eyes glowing with indignation. "Mr. Rich, I knew your opening was going to be inflammatory, but you have me considering ordering a mistrial right now. I am beginning to doubt the wisdom of my ruling in limine."

Jason gave a reassuring smile. "Judge, you made the correct ruling. Any evidence that has any exculpatory value, under the Brady test, has to be allowed. If you'd ruled differently, I would have appealed, and your order would have been reversed."

"That sure of yourself?"

"Yes, sir."

He leaned back in his chair and sighed. "All right, let's get on with it." He flicked his wrists at them. Jason walked back to his table, and Trey whispered in his ear, "Great job, man."

"Madame Prosecutor," Barber bellowed. "Is the state ready to call its first witness?"

"Yes, Your Honor," Shay said. "The state calls Dr. Clem Carton."

Jason leaned toward his client, whispering, "Buckle up."

108

Dr. Clem Carton had been the county coroner for Marshall County for over twenty years. His testimony was methodical and almost impossible to counter. He testified that the cause of Kelly Flowers's death was two gunshot wounds to the chest from a twelve-gauge shotgun, that the time of death was between midnight and 2:00 a.m. on April 9, and, based on the presence of a twelve-gauge shell casing in the cab of Trey Cowan's truck and another one on the ground near the victim's body, that the victim had likely been shot once from inside a vehicle and a second time from outside the car.

On cross-examination, Jason decided to try to plant one of his big seeds.

"You would agree, wouldn't you, Dr. Carton, that shooting someone from inside a vehicle with a twelve-gauge shotgun would be a difficult mark?"

"Not necessarily. A shotgun is a scattergun, so it is easier to hit a target."

"But harder from inside a vehicle than outside one?"

"Maybe . . . but I couldn't say one way or the other."

Jason decided not to belabor the point. He'd planted the seed. "No further questions."

The state's next witness was Dr. Arthur VanderMeer from the state crime lab, who provided lengthy and tedious testimony regarding his ballistics analysis of the shell casings, the fragment retrieved from Flowers's chest cavity, and the twelve-gauge shotgun found in Trey

Cowan's truck. His ultimate conclusion, as expected, was that the victim was probably shot and killed by the shotgun found in Cowan's truck.

On cross-examination, Jason was able to get VanderMeer to admit that the ballistics examination of a shotgun was not as precise as other guns.

"The analysis is certainly not as definitive as linking a handgun to a bullet," VanderMeer testified. "With a shotgun, there are just too many variables. What we can say, based on my experience and training, is that the shell casings found inside Mr. Cowan's truck and on the ground next to the victim's body were the same type of shells contained in a package in Mr. Cowan's car and, based on my analysis of the firing pin markings on the casings, probably were fired from Mr. Cowan's shotgun."

Jason figured that was the only concession he was going to get, so he decided to quit while he was ahead. "No further questions."

By the time VanderMeer left the witness stand, it was 4:45 p.m., and the faces of the jury looked exhausted.

"OK, we are going to adjourn for the day," Judge Barber said, also sounding tired and stifling a yawn. "We will resume at nine o'clock in the morning."

———

Jason met with his client in the attorney consultation room immediately after court was let out. "Tomorrow will probably be the most important day of trial. My bet is they call Mitchell and Daniels both tomorrow, and I'll be ready to light into them on cross. Then they'll end their case with all of those videos where you threaten to kill Kelly."

Trey winced.

"That's what I'd do if I were them. The last piece of evidence they want the jury to hear is your voice swearing to God that you were going to kill him."

"And then it'll be our turn," Trey said.

"Yep."

"Do you think I need to testify?"

Jason let out a deep breath. He was exhausted and wasn't ready to answer this question. "Let's table for now. We may have to make a game-time decision."

"OK," Trey said, as Jason got up to leave. "Hey, Mr. Rich."

"Yeah."

"Your opening was awesome, man. For a minute there, I think we jumped into the lead." Then he sighed. "For a minute."

"Thanks, Trey." He winked. "Hopefully, we'll have some of those moments tomorrow."

109

At 9:30 p.m., Sergeant George Mitchell was sitting in his favorite rocking chair, trying to unwind. He was streaming the second season of *Stranger Things* and was on episode 5. The popular sci-fi show was one of his favorites and made him wish for a return to his own childhood. George had been in the Scouts as a kid and been devoted to his father, who was a police officer in Huntsville. His favorite times in life had been on scouting retreats where he and his dad would camp out under the stars, roast marshmallows over a real fire, and tell ghost stories. The family homestead had been in Arab, which was one of the four flagship towns of Marshall County. Guntersville, Albertville, Boaz, and Arab. George had graduated from Arab High School in 1997 and Jacksonville State University in 2001, where he, like his father, had majored in criminal justice. He was in his first year as a deputy with the Marshall County Sheriff's Office when his parents were killed by a drunk driver on Highway 231. George had been devastated by their deaths and went on to dedicate his life to making sure that drunks and drug addicts stayed off the road. He loved his job. Loved wearing the uniform, just as he'd been proud to wear the Scouts uniform as a kid.

And now I've disgraced and dishonored my parents . . . and everything I believe in . . .

George squeezed his eyes shut, unable to watch the television show any longer. He turned it off and paced his empty house, which was only a couple of miles from his childhood home. His wife, Jan, had left him four months earlier. He'd seen where Jason Rich had subpoenaed the divorce file, and he wasn't entirely sure what would be produced.

The truth could come out . . .

George looked at the photographs of his two children. George Jr. and Grace. His son, a high school freshman, and Gracie, a seventh grader. When was the last time he'd seen them?

Labor Day, he thought. Since then, he had been working on the weekends when the court order allowed him to see them, and Jan hadn't compromised on working out other dates for him to see them.

George stopped at the wet bar in the den and poured himself a glass of George Dickel over ice. His hand shook as he brought the glass to his lips. *I'm cracking,* he thought. *I have to testify tomorrow . . . and I'm cracking.*

Three loud knocks on his front door caused him to almost drop his glass of whiskey. He was able to gain control of the tumbler and set it gently on the counter before walking with caution toward the door. He looked through the peephole, felt his stomach tighten as he recognized his visitor, and cleared his throat. "What do you want?"

"To talk, George," Hatty said. "Please let me in."

"I got nothing to say to you."

"Fine, I'll talk. I'm just wondering if you're going to perjure yourself tomorrow?"

"Fuck you, Hatty. Now, if you don't leave, I'm going to call 911. Or I might arrest you myself."

"Bring it," Hatty said. Then, she raised her voice. "You know what I think, George. I think you're hiding something. Something big. Something that involves Tyson Cade . . . and the attempt on my life."

"You're crazy," George said, but his voice shook with fear.

"I don't think so."

There was a long pause, and George thought she had left. Then her voice boomed out a final time. "Hey, George."

"What?"

"Good luck tomorrow." She paused. "You're gonna need it."

110

"The state calls Detective Hatty Daniels to the stand," Shay said, her voice slightly hoarse after two full days of trial. Jason watched as Detective Daniels strode through the double doors in the back of the courtroom and walked briskly to the stand. He hadn't heard from her since she'd wished him luck at the Sunset Drive Trail yesterday morning, but he had heard from Bo Haynes last night. Bo had said, based on his conversations with his client, that he thought Hatty would be the first or second witness this morning and that he was planning to attend to protect his client's interests, just in case he were needed if either side tried to dive into the merits of the deal he'd negotiated for Hatty.

Sure enough, Bo was seated six rows behind the state's table. The attorney wore a charcoal suit, white shirt, and red tie, and his presence had caused a bit of a stir, as Jason had seen many of the media types, including Kisha Roe, glancing his way since his arrival ten minutes earlier. Haynes had a reputation in southern Tennessee and north Alabama as a fierce trial lawyer who had successfully handled several high-profile criminal cases.

Jason nodded at Bo, who returned the gesture. Then he shifted his focus to the witness, who was now seated and taking her oath to tell the truth. Jason could feel the tension emanating from the state's table. Hatty Daniels hadn't been sitting with Shay during the first two days of trial, which begged a question.

Where was George Mitchell this morning? Mitchell had been present and seated right next to Shay the first two days, but there was no sign of him today. Instead, Sheriff Richard Griffith had taken Mitchell's place.

Perhaps the switch was meant to be a subtle message to the jury, driving home the seriousness of the spectacle. The sheriff was now here.

But Jason didn't buy that. Shay Lankford seemed like a no-nonsense and no-frills prosecutor. She wouldn't want the jury asking where Mitchell was.

So the question remained. *Where the hell is he?*

"Detective Daniels," Shay began, gesturing toward the twelve human beings who would decide this case. "Would you please introduce yourself to the jury."

————

Once Hatty took the stand, she fell back into her role like slipping on a comfortable glove. Despite the looks of distrust she saw from Sheriff Griffith and several of her other colleagues this morning and the unease she saw in the district attorney's eyes, the Trey Cowan investigation was her baby. She'd been the lead, and she was prepared to defend her actions and tell the truth when it came to her investigation of the victim.

She gazed over the top of the prosecutor's head and saw Bo Haynes seated several rows behind the state's table. His presence calmed her, and she was relieved that he was here. She then glanced to her left and saw Jason Rich. She'd felt a growing kinship toward the billboard lawyer since their meeting in Pulaski at Bo's office last week, but she knew whatever truce they had come to in bringing Matty Dean to justice would be thrown out the window this morning. Jason Rich would be coming after her on cross like his life depended on it.

And his client's probably does.

Hatty finally stole a glance at Trey Cowan. Despite everything, she still felt he was guilty of murdering Kelly Flowers and that the evidence that she'd unearthed before being forced to leave the county was staggering. Hatty took a controlled breath as Shay asked her to introduce herself to the jury. She turned to them and spoke with clarity and confidence.

"My name is Detective Hatty Daniels."

———

Shay took Hatty through her experience as a detective first, establishing her two decades of collective work in the Giles County and Marshall County Sheriff's Departments. After establishing Hatty as a long-tenured and very experienced law enforcement officer, she went through the department's investigation into Kelly Flowers's murder in step-by-step fashion, covering the initial call from Bull Branner and the inspection of the crime scene. The district attorney then made a show of introducing three separate photographs and had her describe each of them for the jury.

At the motion hearing last Friday, it had been decided that the state would be allowed to show the jury a limited number of photographs of the victim's body. Shay had wanted to introduce twenty, and Jason had objected to any of them being shown, arguing that the prejudice to his client greatly outweighed any probative value. Barber had compromised by telling Shay she could introduce three photographs but that the state wouldn't be allowed to use any blowups or show the officer's corpse on the wide-screen television in the courtroom.

"These are pictures taken by one of my deputies of the deceased's body," Hatty said, her voice matter of fact as she went through them one by one.

"Thank you, Detective," Shay said. "At this time, Your Honor, we'd ask that these photographs be admitted as state's exhibit four, and we'd like to publish them to the jury."

"Please proceed," Barber said.

Shay gave the jury ample time to review the gruesome photographs of the victim. Then she went through the strongest part of the state's case, which was the physical evidence. Hatty described the discovery of the shotgun in Trey's truck and finding shell casings at both the scene of the crime and on the floorboard of the defendant's vehicle. The district attorney made a show of introducing the twelve gauge as well as the fingerprint testing confirming that only Trey's prints were on the weapon. After a solid start, Shay eased into the uncomfortable aspects of Hatty's testimony.

"Detective Daniels, were you the head of internal affairs for the Marshall County Sheriff's Office?"

"Yes. Still am."

"And did you investigate Kelly Flowers in connection with that role?"

"Yes. Officer George Mitchell and I handled that investigation."

Jason could have kissed Hatty for mentioning Mitchell, who was still absent from the courtroom.

"And can you describe for the jury the nature of the investigation?"

"Yes. We had an informant come forward who claimed to have had drug-possession charges dropped by Sergeant Flowers in exchange for sexual favors."

"And who was this informant?"

"Typically, I wouldn't disclose the name of an informant, but, given the circumstances of this case and Flowers's death, I will do so here." Hatty paused. "Our informant was Chase Wittschen."

"Who brought forward this story when she was about to be charged with public intoxication." Shay looked at the jury as she talked.

"Yes."

"And who's had multiple trips to rehab for methamphetamine addiction."

"Correct."

"Which I'm sure affected her credibility in your eyes."

"It did, but the allegations were very serious. We had to investigate."

"Of course," Shay said, again looking at the jury. "And did you draw any conclusions?"

Hatty shifted in her chair. "Nothing concrete before Flowers's death."

"Did you have a written file of your investigation?"

"I did. I noticed my file was deleted a few weeks after Sergeant Flowers's murder."

"But you made a copy, didn't you?"

"I did."

"So none of the materials in your investigative file were lost, were they?"

"No. Thankfully."

"Officer Daniels, to your knowledge, who was aware of your investigation into Flowers?"

"Like I said, Sergeant George Mitchell assisted me with the investigation." She paused. "And I told Sheriff Griffith about it after Flowers's murder."

"Do you know who deleted your file from the hard drive of your computer?"

"No."

"Sergeant Daniels, did you look into the altercation that Trey Cowan had with the victim just hours before Officer Flowers's murder?"

"Yes, I did."

It was an artful examination, Jason thought, as Shay smoothly covered the internal investigation of Flowers and moved right into the second strongest part of the state's case. Trey's threat to kill the victim.

"What did your probe reveal from your interviews of the patrons of the Brick?"

"That there were multiple witnesses . . . over fifteen people . . . who saw Trey Cowan assault Sergeant Flowers."

"What else?"

"That these same patrons heard Cowan threaten to kill Flowers."

"There were actually videos of this threat, weren't there?"

"Yes."

Shay faced the jury, nodded several times, and then looked at Hatty. "Thank you, Detective Daniels. No further questions."

———

As with his opening, Jason launched his first question from the chair. "You were investigating Kelly Flowers for being a dirty cop, weren't you, Detective?"

"For engaging in potentially abusive behavior."

"Oh, it was a bit more than that, wasn't it?" Jason hopped out of his chair, feeling light on his feet and pulsing with adrenaline. He approached Daniels and put himself at a forty-five-degree angle so he could look at the witness and the jury without moving. "Sex in exchange for not charging her with a crime, correct?"

"Yes. That was one of the allegations made by Ms. Wittschen."

"Drugs, namely methamphetamine . . . in exchange for sex, correct?"

"Yes."

"Your informant told you that Officer Flowers had done these things to her?"

"Yes, she did."

"And, in fact, your informant, Ms. Wittschen, was supposed to meet with Sergeant Flowers the night of April 8? Isn't that true?"

"Yes, it is."

Jason took out a three-page narrative that had been given to him by the state after Hatty had turned over her copy of the internal affairs file. He handed it to Daniels and then looked at the jury. "Detective, what is that?"

"It's my timeline of the investigation."

447

"And is that the original of that document?"

"Yes, it is."

"Your Honor, we'd ask that this timeline be marked as defendant's exhibit one."

"No objection," Shay said, her tone nonchalant.

"Prior to April 8," Jason continued, "how long had you and Officer Mitchell been in contact with Chase Wittschen?"

"Three weeks."

"And what was the objective, here?"

"Excuse me?"

"What did you and Officer Mitchell hope to accomplish?"

"Well . . ." Hatty paused, looking down at the timeline and then back up at Jason. "We wanted to see if Ms. Wittschen was telling the truth. To do that, we hoped to set up a sting on Officer Flowers and catch him in the act of either soliciting sex from Ms. Wittschen or distributing drugs to her."

"And had you achieved that goal prior to April 8, 2019?"

"No. Each time we thought we had a sting arranged, Flowers would back out of the meeting."

"And was there a sting on for April 8?"

"Yes, but it was called off."

"Please read the last line of your narrative."

Hatty looked down at the document and flipped to the last page. "April 8, four p.m. Informant called to say that she was meeting KF at nine p.m. Location TBD."

"And 'TBD' is 'to be determined,' correct?"

"Yes."

"Was a location ever chosen?"

"Not to my knowledge."

"And is it your testimony that this meeting was called off?"

"Yes. Officer Mitchell told me that Ms. Wittschen had informed him that Flowers postponed it."

Jason looked at Shay, a bit surprised that there was no hearsay objection. Of course, the calling off of the meetup between Wittschen was good news for the state. *Hence . . . no objection.*

"Do you know whether the time was simply moved back?"

"I don't know that."

"If Chase Wittschen were to testify that Kelly Flowers didn't postpone the meetup, but rather moved it back a few hours . . ." He looked at the jury. ". . . to twelve thirty a.m. the morning of April 9 and selected Branner's Place as the rendezvous point, would you have any reason to dispute her?"

"Well, she didn't tell me that."

"But, wouldn't you agree, that her primary point of contact with the sheriff's office was Sergeant Mitchell?"

"Yes."

"Detective Daniels, based on your experience as an investigator, did you find Ms. Wittschen sincere in her remarks about Sergeant Flowers?"

"Yes, I did."

"Did you believe her?"

"Objection, Your Honor. The detective's personal belief is irrelevant."

"Overruled," Barber fired back. "The witness shall answer the question."

Hatty looked at the jury and paused a beat. "Yes. I believed her."

Jason turned his gaze to the jury box and then back to Judge Barber. "No further questions, Your Honor."

"Redirect?" Barber asked Shay.

"Yes, Your Honor." Then, mimicking Jason, the prosecutor asked her first question while seated. "Regardless of your belief, did your and Officer Mitchell's internal investigation ever determine that Kelly Flowers was guilty of any wrongdoing whatsoever?"

"No," Hatty said.

"And, as the lead investigator on this case, were you able to find any evidence linking any other suspect to the murder of Kelly Flowers?"

"No, I wasn't."

"Nothing further," Shay said. She'd never gotten to her feet.

"Recross, Mr. Rich?"

"No, Your Honor," Jason said, figuring he'd notched all the points he was going to score.

"All right then. Let's take a short break, and then the state may call its next witness." As Barber banged on his gavel and adjourned the jury, Hatty Daniels exited the witness stand, not looking at Jason as she strode to the back.

"Good job," Trey whispered next to him.

Jason nodded. He'd done the best he could. *Would it be enough?*

111

"*Where in the fuck is George, Sheriff?*"

Though her tone was just above a whisper, Shay's demeanor and delivery were so intense that they caused Griff to take a couple of steps backward as they gazed at each other in the sheriff's department war room.

"I don't know."

"Not good enough. He needs to be sick. Or undercover. Or doing some extremely important shit for your office. There needs to be some explanation for why in the literal fuck he's not here. I had wanted to call Hatty after George and limit my questions to her, but instead I had to give all my questions to Hatty."

"And you did a damn fine job," Griff said. "Maybe the best examination I've ever seen you do. Under the circumstances, top notch."

"Don't flatter me. I need you to find George or figure out where the fuck he is."

"I will, but you keep doing what you're doing."

Shay walked to the door. "I expect you to sit with me the rest of the way. Maybe I can play it off as you replacing George as the representative for the state given the seriousness of the crimes."

"Sounds good, and I'm right behind you."

She turned, but his voice stopped her.

"Shay?"

"*What?*"

He smiled. "We're winning."

"We're supposed to be. It's our case in chief. We'll see what kind of case we have when Rich starts calling witnesses."

"Surely you don't think the jury is buying his bullshit?"

"They did last year," Shay said.

And then she slammed the door shut.

112

Shay's next witness was Ronnie Kirk, the longtime head football coach of the Guntersville Wildcats. Kirk described his interaction with Trey just before the defendant was taken into police custody at the football field and, in particular, Trey's despondent demeanor and his admission that the police were not there to arrest him for trespassing.

The state spent the rest of the day calling several patrons who'd witnessed Trey's assault on Flowers at the Brick.

During the testimony of the last of these, Shay played the best video of the interaction for the jury on the big-screen television adjacent to the jury box. After she pushed play, the scene came into view, with Trey lunging for Flowers and missing.

As the two men faced each other on the television, Trey glared at Flowers and yelled, "I'll kill you. I swear to God, I will."

Shay pressed pause, and the screen showed a closeup of Trey Cowan's angry face seconds after making his threat.

"No further questions," the prosecutor said.

For his part, Jason didn't ask any of the Brick patrons any questions on cross-examination.

"Call your next witness," Judge Barber instructed.

"Your Honor," Shay said, speaking with a deliberate, forceful calm. "The state rests."

113

When Jason arrived at his office at 5:30 p.m., he had a surprise waiting on him. A plump man wearing a crimson golf shirt with a white script *A* over the heart, khaki pants, and tennis shoes was waiting for him in the firm library. A mess of papers was scattered in front of him.

"Albert Hooper," the man said, not extending his hand. "I hope you don't mind, but I went by both of the lawyers' offices in George Mitchell's divorce, and I was able to obtain the nonprivileged divorce documents from both."

Jason plopped down in a chair across from Bo Haynes's investigator. "I don't mind at all. Is there anything good in them?"

Hooper grinned and slid a piece of paper across the table to Jason along with two photographs. "Does it help you that Officer Mitchell was seen by his wife's lawyer's private eye in Alder Springs on the night of April 8, 2019?"

"Holy shit," Jason said, gazing at the color pictures before looking up at Hooper. "That's—"

"Trudy Cowan's home," Hooper interrupted, unwrapping a cherry Blow Pop and sticking it into his mouth. "Interesting, huh?"

Jason couldn't believe his eyes. Another divorce file was about to save his case.

"It does beg the question," Hooper continued, "what exactly was Officer Mitchell doing sitting in an unmarked car, which wasn't the vehicle registered to him by the sheriff's office, at eleven oh two p.m.?"

"It does indeed," Jason said, extending his fist, which Hooper rapped with his own.

"RMFT," Hooper said, walking around Jason to the door.

"What?"

"Roll motherfucking Tide. And is there a good place to get a burger around here?"

———

They ate at the Rock House, and Hooper filled Jason in on the rest of the respective divorce files. None of it was nearly as interesting as what he'd shown Jason at the office and, in fact, told a sad story. While Jan Mitchell's attorney's files turned up the surveillance of the detective in Alder Springs the night of the murder, there was no proof of any infidelity on his part. George's attorney's materials, however, did reveal that Jan had been engaged in an illicit affair with a banker in Huntsville.

"There's not much, really, other than what I showed you at the office."

"Which puts Mitchell at the same spot as Cowan an hour and a half before the murder. With the same opportunity to kill Flowers."

"Doesn't give him motive, but it does fill in opportunity, and that picture shows him just a few feet from Cowan's truck, where the shotgun was found."

"He could have had the means too. Trey says he never locked his truck at his mom's house. Mitchell could have put gloves on, grabbed the twelve gauge, driven the mile to Branner's Place, and killed Cowan. Then returned the gun to the truck."

"He could have indeed."

"But what's his motive?"

"I think he was Tyson Cade's new inside man. His wife divorced him. He'd lost everything, and he'd decided to go rogue."

"Breaking bad, just like the TV show."

"Exactly."

"I understand from Bo that Mitchell wasn't in court today."

"That's right," Jason said. "Which begs another rather obvious question," he continued, using the investigator's own lingo.

"Where the hell is he?"

114

Tyson Cade entered the cabin in Mentone and couldn't believe his eyes.

Empty, he thought, taking a long sip of Sun Drop. His instructions had been clear. He'd told the lawman to be here at 9:30 p.m.

But his mole wasn't here.

Tyson sat down at the small kitchen table and placed a phone call. "Matty, we got a problem."

"What's that?"

"I think our mole may be on the verge of turning his back on me."

"What do you want me to do?"

"Nothing, for now. But we may have to circle the wagons soon."

"Just say when, boss." A sigh. "I'm ready to kill them all. Rich. Daniels. Our mole. Every damn one of 'em."

Tyson Cade took a long sip from his favorite soft drink. "Patience, Matty," he said, feeling anything but as he walked out of the empty cabin and into the cool night. "All in due time."

115

Jason arrived home to a strange but welcome sight. Nola was sitting out in the sunroom, her attention seemingly rapt on two men engaged in a lively discussion. As Jason entered the room, Colonel Satch Tonidandel gave him a wave. Then Satch turned to the other man in the room. "Anyway, go on. Finish the story."

Bocephus Haynes peered up at Jason with a tired but hearty smile and continued in his baritone voice. "Well, we all came out of the irrigation tunnels in Hazel Green at around the same time. We saw Wheeler about to open fire on the Professor's grandson, and we all fired. General Lewis got the kill shot."

"The woman prosecutor?" Satch asked.

"Yes."

"She sounds like one badass lady."

"You have no idea," Bo said, standing and stretching his legs. He extended his hand to Satch. "Enjoyed your stories about the Screaming Eagles, sir."

"Not as much as I enjoyed yours about playing for Coach Bryant and bringing JimBone Wheeler to justice. I remember when he was a fugitive."

"Yes, sir." Bo nodded and looked at Jason. "You talk to Hooper?"

"Yes, I did," Jason said. "And I think we may really have an angle with Sergeant Mitchell. Is there any word on what happened to him today?"

"Not that I'm aware of. Listen, you got a second?"

———

They talked in the driveway next to Bo's silver Chevy Tahoe. "You did a good job today. I appreciate you staying away from Hatty's disappearance and her negotiated return to the sheriff's office."

"I tried to focus on what was most helpful to Trey's case."

Bo nodded. "You accomplished that . . . and I thought Hatty held her own as well. It was awkward to watch, because I feel like, even though you and Hatty are on opposite sides of this case, we're all trying to be on the side of justice."

"And what's justice here, Bo?"

"Finding the truth."

"I think your man Hooper uncovered it tonight. I just have to confront Mitchell with it."

For a moment, there was silence, and then Bo continued, his voice grave. "I'm worried about Hatty. She seems obsessed with bringing this Dean fellow down."

"I know. She told me she was staking him out." Jason hesitated. "That's what my investigator was doing when Dean killed him."

"I know, and I'm worried. She also seems determined to find a link between Dean and the sheriff's office."

"I think Hooper may have found that for us."

"Perhaps, but keep your eyes, ears, and most especially your mind . . . open. The truth sometimes does its damnedest to remain hidden."

The two men shook hands, and Bo climbed into the Tahoe. After cranking the ignition, he rolled down the window after Jason rapped his knuckles on it.

"Can I ask you a question?"

"Shoot."

"I feel like this case is moving ninety to nothing, and my pants are on fire. There are so many moving parts that my brain is scrambled, and I'm so tired that I can barely think."

Bo grinned at him. "But you're loving it, aren't you?"

Jason grinned back, feeling tired and goofy. "Yeah. Does that make me weird?"

"Nope. It makes you a trial lawyer." He winked. "And you've reached my ideal pace."

Jason wrinkled up his face, and Bo guffawed as he put his vehicle in gear and spoke over the sound of the engine.

"Wide ass open."

———

When Jason entered the house, Nola was still sitting in the sunroom. He approached and sat down in the chair next to her. "What's up, honey?"

"Just thinking."

"About what?"

Nola sighed and looked away from him. "About how I need to tell you something."

For a moment, Jason didn't know what to say. Finally, he sighed. "Just spit it out."

"I got into Alabama. I found out earlier today."

"Nola, that's wonderful." He leaned forward and kissed her on top of the head. "I'm proud of you."

"Thanks."

"Is that it?"

"No." Her voice had begun to quiver. "I'm leaving, Uncle Jason. I'd already accepted a job in Birmingham at the campus bookstore at Birmingham-Southern. Niecy got it for me. I'm going to live with her the rest of this year and then start in Tuscaloosa for the second semester."

Jason looked down at the floor. He'd known she'd be leaving soon, but the finality of it still hurt.

"I hope you understand," she said.

"I do," Jason said.

"When are you going?"

"Now."

"But Nola, it's past nine o'clock. Why not wait until—"

"I can't. I don't want to be here any longer . . . than I have to be."

Jason managed a nod. He knew it was no use stopping her.

"Are you already packed?"

"Everything's in my Jeep."

"Ah," Jason said, feeling a deep and palpable sadness enveloping him. He bit his lip, trying to keep his emotions in check. He remembered being greeted by Nola when he'd returned to Guntersville last year. She'd been happy to see him then. It had been Nola's desperate text that had sealed the deal on Jason's decision to come home. He remembered how he'd felt in the hospital a few months earlier, after she'd nearly drowned. The sheer relief that had flooded his veins when she had opened her eyes again.

"Nola Frances Waters," Jason managed, his voice cracking. "I'm gonna miss you."

Nola wiped a tear from her eye but said nothing. She didn't go in for a hug, and Jason didn't either. He knew she was guarding against him. Keeping her boundary clear. And now she was making that chasm permanent.

As they stood there in the sunroom, the silence becoming unbearable, Jason could barely control his emotions. Nola, who had her mother's eyes. Jana's crystal blues. He squeezed his lids shut to force back the tears.

"Uncle Jason, there's one more thing I need to tell you." Jason didn't want to look, but he forced himself to open his eyes and locked them on his niece, who was peering at the ground.

"Thank you for saving my life." Nola stole a glance at him that sent a dagger right into his heart. She tried to say more but could only nod. "Gotta go now."

———

Jason sat in the rocker in the sunroom for a long time. Tears streaked his face, but he didn't wipe them away. He felt numb. He knew he'd lost Chase. Regardless of what happened tomorrow at trial or how relatively friendly things had been since her return, he'd never be able to forget what had happened.

And neither would she.

Whatever they'd had—whether it was some wistful love that Jason had imagined but that didn't really exist or whether there actually had been something there—was gone forever. Lost in the dark waters below the cliffs at Goat Island.

Or, perhaps more accurately, in a line of Sand Mountain SlimFast.

Now Nola was gone. Jason was alone. He had worked so hard for the ones he loved, and he had managed to lose them all.

Jana was dead.

Harry was dead.

Izzy had left him.

Chase.

Niecy.

Nola.

All of them . . .

At some point, through fresh tears, he gazed across the room and saw Satch Tonidandel sitting with him. Looking at him.

"I know it hurts, but Nola will be safer and happier in Birmingham." He paused. "We're in the endgame now."

What did that even mean? Eventually, the colonel left to retake his post, and Jason was again left alone in the home he was raised in. As he peered out at the lake, he had a sad, unwavering thought.

I could win this case . . .

Jason lay down on the twin bed in the sunroom and prayed for sleep that wouldn't come.

. . . and still lose everything I care about. He sighed, seeing a last vision of the look Nola had given him before walking out the door.

Maybe I already have.

116

George Mitchell had rented a car on Wednesday morning at 9:15 a.m. When he should have been taking the stand to testify in the Trey Cowan murder trial, he was pulling out of Hertz Rental Company in Huntsville in a gray Chevy Cavalier.

George drove to the Space & Rocket Center and toured the museum, riding the Millennium Falcon ride several times and eating two cups of Dippin' Dots. Wired on sugar, he'd spent the rest of the afternoon and early evening walking Big Spring Park in downtown Huntsville before getting a room at the Embassy Suites hotel. After tossing and turning most of the night, he managed to get a few hours of merciful sleep once the clock struck midnight. He'd woken at 6:30 a.m., eaten breakfast in the hotel restaurant, and then checked out. He'd then driven back to Arab, but he hadn't gone home. He knew they'd be looking for him there. Shay Lankford was probably about to lose her mind.

Instead, he parked in a strip mall on Highway 231 and watched the front of a gift shop called Fine Things.

At 9:00 a.m., as day four of the murder trial of Trey Cowan was about to start, George was twenty miles from the courthouse, out of uniform, and hoping for a glimpse of his ex-wife.

His heart began to pick up speed as he saw her park near the front of the store and exit the vehicle. George got out of his own car, trying to work up the courage to yell her way. But he didn't.

Jan Mitchell entered Fine Things and shut the door behind her. In a couple of minutes, she was sitting behind the checkout desk.

George sighed and hung his head.

"We need to talk, George."

He wheeled toward the voice and saw Detective Hatty Daniels approaching him and stepping between him and the Cavalier.

"What the hell? Are you stalking me?"

"I'm not the one hanging outside my ex-wife's place of employment."

"How did you know—"

"Your divorce files were produced yesterday. I know everything." She handed him the two photographs depicting his vehicle in front of Trudy Cowan's home.

"The date and time when those images were taken were April 8 at eleven oh two p.m. Cowan's lawyer has copies of these, and you can bet your ass he's going to use them. How could you not tell me this?" Hatty stuck a finger in his chest. "How could you compromise our investigation like this?"

"Hatty . . . I . . ." George started to cry.

"You're Tyson Cade's inside man, aren't you?" She grabbed him by the collar. "You tried to kill me, didn't you? You were working with Dean. It was you, George."

He shook his head. "No."

"What do you mean, no?"

"It wasn't me. I didn't kill Trey Cowan, and I didn't have anything to do with the attack on you."

"Bullshit."

"No. It wasn't me."

"Whatever." She turned and started walking away from him. "It's time I had a heart-to-heart with the sheriff. I think he'd like to hear about your jaunt to Trudy Cowan's house the night of Kelly Flowers's murder."

"He already knows," George said. His tone was flat. Defeated.

Hatty stopped in her tracks. "What?"

George spoke while looking down at the asphalt. "The sheriff knows everything."

117

"Mr. Rich, is the defense ready to call its first witness?" Judge Barber asked.

Jason stood as if on autopilot. He hadn't slept at all the previous night and felt nauseous and a bit dizzy. "Yes, Your Honor. The defense calls Ms. Savannah Chase Wittschen."

As she took the stand and was sworn in, Jason felt like he was having an out-of-body experience. He glanced to his left, trying to focus. He noticed that George Mitchell was missing his second day in a row of court. Perhaps Shay had permanently replaced him with the sheriff. *Who the hell knows?*

"Would you please introduce yourself to the jury?"

"Chase Wittschen," she said.

Jason remembered the first time he'd met the girl that grew up to be the woman on the stand. She'd been eight years old. Tomboy haircut. She'd invited Jason to go on a canoe ride, after Jana had taken off in a boat with some of her friends.

Jason had accepted. He blinked his eyes, trying to control the flurry of emotions raging in his soul. He hadn't realized how hard this was going to be. *Torture, more like it.*

"Mr. Rich, is there something wrong?" Judge Barber asked, after Jason had not asked a question for over ten seconds. "The jury is waiting. Are you going to examine the witness?"

"Yes, Your Honor. Ms. Wittschen . . ." He sucked in a deep breath. *Do your job, J. J. Don't be such a drama queen.* The voice of his perpetually helpful dead sister. Always there when torturing her baby brother was on the agenda. "Can you please describe to the jury how you first met Sergeant Kelly Flowers?"

It was indeed like Jason was a spectator. He heard himself asking the questions, but he had checked out emotionally. Perhaps it was a survival instinct, as the woman he'd loved since she'd first taken him canoeing almost thirty years ago began to describe the abuse she'd endured from Kelly Flowers, which was brought on and hastened by her own weakness and addictions.

She described in detail her first arrest outside of Wintzell's and the clandestine meeting later that night at the Hampton Inn, where she had engaged in sexual relations with Sergeant Flowers in exchange for him not charging her with drug possession. And then she testified to each subsequent session leading up to April 8, 2019.

"At some point, did you report Sergeant Flowers's behavior?"

"Yes. I told Sergeant George Mitchell after he brought me in for public intoxication. Then, I told Detective Hatty Daniels."

"And did you agree to become an informant for the sheriff's office?"

"Yes. In exchange for them dropping the public intox charge, I agreed to inform on Sergeant Flowers."

"And what was their plan?"

"They wanted me to wear a wire and catch Flowers in the act."

"And did you ever do that?"

"No."

"Why not?"

"He was killed before we could go through with it."

"Were you supposed to meet Sergeant Flowers the night he was murdered?"

"Yes, I was. At nine, but he changed it to twelve thirty a.m."

"And did you meet him then?"

"No. I got antsy for my meth fix, and I went and found it some-where else."

Jason paused and looked at the jury. Every eye was on Chase. "Did you tell Sergeant Mitchell that the meeting with Flowers had been moved to twelve thirty a.m. on April 9 at Branner's Place?"

"Objection, Your Honor," Shay said, rising to her feet. "Hearsay."

"Mr. Rich?" His Honor turned to Jason.

"Any statements attributable to Sergeant George Mitchell would be an admission against interest by a representative of the state. By definition, that would not be hearsay."

"Agreed," Barber said. "Objection overruled."

"But, Your Honor, these aren't statements by Mitchell but by the witness herself to Mitchell. That's hearsay."

"Overruled," Barber said. "It's the witness's own statements."

"Yes," Chase said, deciding she could continue. "I told Sergeant George Mitchell."

"Did Officer Mitchell ask you to wear a wire?"

"No, he didn't. He said he wanted me to report back after the meeting, and we'd set up a sting the next time. He said he wanted to lull Flowers into a false sense of security."

"Did you tell Officer Daniels that the meeting had been moved?"

"No. I assumed Sergeant Mitchell told her."

Jason again looked at the jury and then to Judge Barber. It was finally over. "No further questions."

———

On cross, Shay led with the obvious. "You're a meth addict, aren't you, Ms. Wittschen?"

"I'm in recovery," Chase said.

"From being a meth addict, correct?"

"Correct."

"You're also Mr. Rich's ex-girlfriend, aren't you?" Shay made a show of walking over to Jason and pointing at him.

"Yes."

"And isn't it true that you still care very deeply for Mr. Rich?"

Chase looked at Jason. "Yes. That's true."

"And you'd do just about anything to get him back, wouldn't you?"

Chase shook her head. "No, I wouldn't lie."

"Oh, come on, Ms. Wittschen. Isn't it true that Mr. Rich broke up with you because of your addictions, and you're now trying to win him back with this ridiculous story on the stand?"

Chase scowled at Shay. "No, that's entirely false. I *am* a meth addict, and I'm in recovery. But Jason didn't end the relationship." She paused, and Jason saw fire in her eyes. "I did."

Shay walked with nonchalant grace back to the state's table and snatched up a yellow notebook. She looked completely in control, but Jason knew that Chase had just stunned her. But the district attorney was quick to pick up her fumble. "Ms. Wittschen, isn't it true that you didn't report any wrongdoing on behalf of Sergeant Flowers until you were facing an arrest for public intoxication?"

"Yes," Chase said. "That's true."

"No further questions."

"Recross, Mr. Rich?"

Jason made eye contact with Chase and shook his head. "No, Your Honor."

As Chase walked past him, she was crying. He wanted to reach out and touch her arm. Give some sign of support. But he knew he couldn't do that in front of the jury.

Please, God, don't let today be a trigger for her. Please . . .

"Mr. Rich, call your next witness."

Jason rose from his seat. "The defense calls Ms. Colleen Maples."

———

Colleen Maples entered the courtroom, wearing a conservative black dress. She took the stand, was sworn in, and looked at Jason with a distrusting gaze. Jason had not spoken to her since their conversation Monday night at her house, and he had half expected her to ignore the subpoena. But here she was, on the stand.

Do your job, Jason told himself, still thinking about Chase and reeling from fatigue and lack of sleep.

The beginning of the direct of Maples was almost identical to Jason's examination of Chase, except there was no informant agreement between Maples and the sheriff's department. Jason established the key pattern of abuse.

An arrest outside of Wintzell's followed by sex at the Hampton Inn in exchange for no charges being brought. A continuation of these trysts with the threat of arrest being held over her head. Finally, the addition of meth being provided by Flowers in exchange for sex. After establishing these facts, Jason decided to dive into the new stuff that Colleen had revealed on Monday night.

"Did you ever meet Officer Flowers at Branner's Place off of Hustleville Road?" Jason asked.

"Yes. That was typically where we met."

"And when was the last time you met Officer Flowers there?"

"The first week of April," she said, without hesitation.

Jason then went into Colleen's relationship with Trey Cowan and their subsequent breakup, as he knew that Shay would go into this questioning in her cross.

"Did your relationship with Sergeant Flowers begin after the breakup with Trey?"

"Yes."

"Did you ever tell Trey about your relationship with Flowers?"

"No."

"Did Trey ever say anything to you about your relationship with Flowers?"

"Yes. He said I was making a big mistake getting mixed up with Kelly." Colleen looked at Trey. "And he was right."

Jason walked all the way back to the defense table before asking his last question. "Did you know Trey owned a twelve-gauge shotgun?"

"Yes, I did."

"No further questions," Jason said, peering at Trey, whose face had gone pale.

"*What are you doing?*" Trey whispered as Jason sat down.

"My job," Jason whispered back.

———

On cross, Shay fired the questions as if they were coming out of a machine gun. "You were Trey Cowan's girlfriend, and then you began having sex with Sergeant Flowers?"

"Because he threatened to arrest me if I didn't."

"And also because he supplied you with methamphetamine, right?"

"That was after."

"Your license to practice as a CRNA was suspended by the Alabama Board of Nursing, wasn't it?"

"Yes . . . because Kelly Flowers notified the hospital that I was using, and they ordered a random drug test."

"Ah . . . so your testimony today is an effort to get back at the man who ruined your career."

"No, it's not. I'm here to tell the truth. Nothing more. Nothing less."

"You were the defendant's girlfriend."

"I've already said I was."

"And then you started your sex-for-leniency, sex-for-drugs tryst with Sergeant Flowers, right?"

"Yes."

"And, Ms. Maples, wouldn't you agree that your ex-boyfriend, Trey Cowan, was pretty upset when he told you he knew about what you were doing with Flowers."

Maples sighed. "Yes. I agree."

"No further questions."

———

The defense's next witness was Ms. Eva Claire Cobb. Ms. Cobb shuffled to the stand with the use of a rolling walker. She wore a faded yellow blouse and had silver hair, bright-red lipstick, and an infectious laugh that was somewhat inappropriate for the occasion.

"Would you please introduce yourself to the jury."

"Eva Claire Cobb. Two words. Eva. Claire." She let out her high-pitched giggle, and a couple of the jurors joined in while a few others opened their mouths. It seemed to Jason like they might be wondering if this woman was for real.

She was, and her testimony provided an effective piece to the defense case and several much-needed moments of levity. After establishing that she had seen an officer carrying a bag over his shoulder down Hustleville Road at a little past midnight on April 9, Jason said he had no further questions.

The real drama happened on cross.

"Ms. Cobb, you're eighty-six years old," Shay said.

"Young," the witness declared. "I'm eighty-six years young. Age is a state of mind."

"Uh, yes, ma'am. And isn't it true that you have difficulty with your distance vision?"

472

"No, that is not true. Not when I wear my glasses. I wear *corrective lenses*. That means I can see like a hawk."

"OK, ma'am. Didn't you just get out of the hospital right before April 8, 2019?"

"True enough. Dang congestive heart failure."

"And, at the risk of offending you, wouldn't you agree that one of your diagnoses is mild dementia?"

"Everybody over seventy years old has mild dementia, ma'am. You just wait."

Laughter from the jury box rang out in the courtroom. Jason turned and breathed in a sigh of relief. *A laughing jury doesn't convict,* he'd heard Professor Adams at Cumberland say on more than one occasion.

"Please answer the question, Ms. Cobb," Barber said, but even the crusty old judge was smiling.

"Yes, I suppose I have been diagnosed with a *mild* case of dementia."

"Which means, if we're being fair," Shay said, "that you could be wrong about what you saw in the early-morning hours of April 9."

Eva Claire Cobb was shaking her head before the question was even finished. "Naw. Naw. What it means is that, every once in a while, I might wake up in the middle of the night and not know if I'm at my house or in the hospital. Or sometimes I forget the names of presidents." She shook her head again. "But I remember what I see, especially when there's a murder reported the next day." She leaned forward in her chair. "I remember that *real* good."

Shay smiled at the jury and raised her eyebrows, as if to say "O . . . K . . ." Then she looked at Judge Barber. "No further questions."

As Eva Claire Cobb shuffled out of the courtroom, Judge Barber leaned forward on the bench. "Mr. Rich, it's four fifteen p.m. Do you have a witness whose examination you can finish within forty-five minutes?"

"Yes, Your Honor."

"Then please proceed."

Jason turned and peered behind the defense table, where Walt Cowan, his eyes bloodshot but otherwise looking presentable in a blue blazer, white shirt, and gray slacks, nodded back to him.

"The defense calls Mr. Walter Cowan," Jason said.

———

Walt Cowan's testimony took less than ten minutes. He testified that he'd never seen his son, Trey, shoot a firearm of any kind and that he'd never taught Trey to shoot. Jason sat down, having brought out the facts he'd told the jury about in his opening. Mission accomplished.

Shay's cross was brief but powerful. "Mr. Cowan, isn't it true that you've barely seen your son since your divorce from Ms. Cowan?"

"Uhhh, I seen him a lot less."

"Couple times a year?"

"That's close."

"And how long has that been the norm?"

"Like you said. Since the divorce, so . . . four years."

"Did you know that Trey had bought himself a shotgun last year?"

"No, I didn't."

Shay rolled her eyes at Walt and looked at the jury. "No further questions of this witness."

After Jason declined to redirect, Walt returned to his seat behind the defense table. Meanwhile, Judge Barber had endured enough.

"Members of the jury, we are adjourned for the day. We will resume at nine o'clock in the morning." He banged his gavel, and Jason and Shay stood while the jurors exited the courtroom. Once they were gone, Barber turned to Jason. "Will you be having any more witnesses, Mr. Rich?"

"Possibly, Your Honor. I'll be making a decision on that tonight."

Barber shook his head but said nothing. "All right. I'll see you both in the morning."

118

Jason walked out of the courthouse on shaky legs. He was exhausted. Physically. Emotionally. And there was still much to do and decisions to make.

He knew he needed to call Trudy Cowan to testify about Trey's depression, because he'd promised the jury they'd hear that in his opening. She'd be his first witness tomorrow. After that, all he had were questions.

Should Trey take the stand?

Should he call George Mitchell and force the issue? Jason had subpoenaed Mitchell, Hatty, and Sheriff Griffith ahead of trial. If Mitchell wasn't present, then a warrant would be issued for his arrest.

Should he call Jan Mitchell's private eye? The man's name was Doug Bolden, and he was from Albertville. He could testify to the pictures he'd taken of Sergeant Mitchell the night of April 8 at Trudy Cowan's house.

Finally, in closing, who was his best alternative suspect? Mitchell . . . or Colleen Maples? Or both? Regardless, he knew he had to give the jury another plausible option.

As he reached his Porsche, his phone dinged to indicate a text. He pulled out his device. It was Hatty Daniels.

Meet me at your office . . . NOW.

Feeling his heart flutter and his fatigue replaced with adrenaline, Jason jogged down the sidewalk to his office. He walked in the door and saw that his two assistants were gone for the day. He headed down the hall and entered the library where he'd studied as a child.

Detective Hatty Daniels sat at one end of the long rectangular table. On either side of her were Sergeant George Mitchell and . . . district attorney Shay Lankford.

"What's going on?" Jason asked, looking from Hatty to Shay to George.

"I got a text to be here coming out of the courtroom," Shay said, her voice tired.

"I wanted you both to hear it from the horse's mouth," Hatty said. "So neither of you think I'm playing favorites. I am an officer of the law, so my loyalties are with the State of Alabama. But I am also on the side of justice." She turned to Shay. "And Madame Prosecutor, you need to hear this as much as Mr. Rich does."

"Hear what?" Shay asked, scowling at George. "Why you've abandoned your post the last two days, Sergeant Mitchell?" She glared at Hatty. "That seems to be a theme in your department. Abandonment."

Hatty shook her head and gestured with her hand at George. "Tell them like you told me."

"Tell us what?" Jason asked. "Can we get on with it?"

George's shoulders drooped as he spoke. "Sheriff Griffith knew that Flowers was meeting our informant at twelve thirty on April 9. I told him after we both discussed the altercation that Flowers and Trey Cowan had been involved in at the Brick. I told the sheriff that Hatty and I were investigating Flowers and that he was supposed to meet with Chase Wittschen at just past midnight."

"*What?*" Shay said. "Are you saying Griff knew all along?"

"He knew when I broke the news to him, but he acted like he didn't know," Hatty said. "But that's not even the worst of it. Tell them, George."

George cleared his throat, but his voice was still scratchy and weak. "He told me that he was going to go to Branner's Place and handle things. With Kelly and with our informant, Wittschen."

"Handle things?" Jason asked, feeling the final piece to the puzzle sink into its slot. "But why were you seen at Trey Cowan's mother's house."

"The sheriff asked me to track down where Trey was. When he wasn't at his apartment, I tried Trudy's, and sure enough, he was there. Then I called the sheriff from Trudy's driveway, told him everything I knew, and he said he'd handle things."

"What did you think he meant by that?" Jason pressed.

"I didn't know." Mitchell paused. "That's why I waited down the street from Trudy's house until the sheriff pulled in."

"Oh my God," Shay said, her words mimicking Jason's thoughts. "He didn't."

George nodded, his face as white as cotton. "He did. He got out of his truck, opened Trey's vehicle . . . and pulled out the shotgun."

119

In the bank parking lot across from the Rich Law Firm, a man dressed in the uniform of Wilson Construction was repainting a parking place white. Or at least he seemed to be.

What he was really doing was watching the law office.

And waiting for instructions. Seconds later, his phone rang.

"We got a 911." Tyson Cade's voice. "You know the score."

"Yes, sir," Matty Dean said, walking back to his car and opening the driver's-side back door. Keeping the door open, Matty loaded the rifle.

Then he waited.

120

"Did you follow him to Branner's Place?!" Jason was yelling.

"No," George said. "I didn't. I was scared. I'd already seen too much. I went home.

"The next afternoon, after the murder, Griff came into my office. He told me that if I ever breathed a word of what happened the previous night, he'd make sure I never worked a day in law enforcement again. He said if I talked, he'd make sure I went down for being an accessory to murder. I thought it through, and I didn't see an out. Even if I wasn't charged with a crime, I knew I'd never wear the badge again. I was selfish, but the job was all I had. I'd lost my wife. I'd lost my kids in the custody battle. My parents were dead. I didn't have anything but the badge."

"Why are you coming forward now?" Jason challenged.

"Because, after Hatty was nearly killed, I started to feel different about things. And as we got closer to the trial, I just knew I couldn't perjure myself again. Regardless of whether I was ever able to be a cop again, I couldn't let Trey Cowan be framed for this murder. I couldn't let Griff get away with it."

"But why, George? Why would the sheriff do this?" Shay asked. "What in the world could have been his motive?"

"It's an election year," Hatty said, "and he figured an internal investigation against one of his officers for using his authority to coerce sex from unwilling women would bring him down and cost him his job."

She spoke with authority, and both Shay and Jason nodded. It made sense, but was that enough?

"That ain't it," George said, moving his eyes around the room. "Flowers had something else on Griff. Something worse than losing the election."

"What could that possibly be?" Shay asked.

"I went into Huntsville every so often. Sometimes I went with Kelly. Other times I went by myself. I ain't proud of it, but I used to go to skin clubs."

Jason had thought the last puzzle piece had fallen, but he was wrong. He felt an even bigger chunk slide into place. "Bella Flowers," he whispered.

George nodded. "I never saw them together, but Bella gave me a dance one night. She was on something. Probably meth."

Jason remembered his own interaction with Bella and didn't doubt the sergeant's story.

"She whispered into my ear that the sheriff was in love with her. That he was going to leave his wife and marry her."

"And you think Kelly got wind of it."

George nodded. "Kelly knew everything. He gathered up information like a sponge, especially if it was beneficial to him."

Shay stood and crossed her arms. "I'm going to puke."

"I'm sorry, Shay," Hatty said. "I really am, but I thought you . . . and Mr. Rich should know the truth."

"What if he's lying?" Shay asked. "George has been gone the last two days. He's been through his own divorce. What if . . ." She trailed off and shook her head. "No. Why would he lie about this?"

"Exactly," Jason said, also standing and turning to Shay. "What are you going to do?"

"I need some time to think." She forced a weary smile. "And maybe a cocktail."

"Shay, if you don't dismiss all charges against Trey Cowan by nine o'clock in the morning, I'm going to put George on the stand and let him tell the story he just told us to the jury. Do you want that?"

"No," she said, with no hesitation. "Just give me . . . a second, would you? This is hard to process."

They looked at each other, and then Jason glanced at Hatty, who nodded.

"All right," Jason said. "Call me later tonight . . . or in the morning."

"I will."

———

Five minutes later, the four of them walked out on the stoop of Jason's office. At just after 6:00 p.m., the sun was beginning to set in the west. Jason Rich smiled at Hatty, but she didn't return the gesture. "It's over," he said.

"This doesn't make me happy," Hatty said. "But I am satisfied that justice will be done."

"Hatty?" George Mitchell had paused at the bottom step. "Will you ever forgive—?"

But he never got the question out. The head of Sergeant George Mitchell exploded like a pumpkin dropped from the balcony of an apartment. Hatty ran to a nearby car for cover, and Jason lunged for Shay Lankford, covering her with his body. Shots splashed over their heads.

He heard the rapid patter of a different type of gun from above and looked over his shoulder. Hatty Daniels was perched on one knee and firing her pistol at a vehicle that was now swerving onto Gunter Avenue.

The detective began to run after the car and then took off across the street. Jason watched her reach into the nearest squad car and scream something into a radio microphone. Then she got behind the wheel and took off in pursuit.

Jason crawled toward the lifeless body of George Mitchell. Half the man's head was gone. He looked back at Shay. "Are you OK? Are you hit?"

She shook her head. "Not hit."

Jason's ears were buzzing, and he had to read her lips to understand her. He hadn't gotten a good look at the driver of the Honda, but he knew who was behind the attack.

Cade.

121

Judge Barber recessed the trial until Monday morning. Shay Lankford spent the weekend at Marshall Medical Center South, being treated for severe shock. Meanwhile, Hatty Daniels, who was not injured in the attack, went straight to work, leading the department's investigation of the shooting and the contemporaneous search for Sheriff Griffith, who had disappeared.

Jason Rich endured Friday, Saturday, and Sunday locked up at Mill Creek, the house being watched by all three Tonidandel brothers. Fully armed. Ready for anything.

He called Nola and Niecy in Birmingham and begged them to watch out for themselves. He also doubled security for both of them.

When he'd arrived home on Thursday, Chase had been gone.

No note this time. Just . . . gone.

Jason tried to spend the time productively, but it was no use. He was too tired to do anything but sleep.

And he couldn't sleep for the nightmares.

He wanted a drink so badly he couldn't stand it, and he had no doubt that he would have fallen off the wagon by now but for his forced solitude by the Tonidandels.

On Monday morning, at 8:15 a.m., he dressed for court. He'd not been able to talk with Shay since the shooting, and he had no idea what was going to happen. Without Mitchell's testimony, it was possible she might proceed with the case, but Jason didn't think she would do that. Besides, he had a backup plan.

As he walked out the front door of his house, he saw something that took his breath away. Colonel Satch Tonidandel stood against his black Ford Raptor with the tinted windows. He was dressed in his full army green service uniform. The silver insignia of an eagle was pinned on his lapel, and a white-and-gold peaked cap perched high on his head. Next to him, Captains Mickey and Chuck Tonidandel, also dressed in their uniforms, stood at attention.

"If you don't mind, Jason, you're going to be escorted to court today by the Screaming Eagles."

Jason felt a lump in his throat. Everyone in his life had abandoned him except the three brothers. "*The by God Tonidandels*," as his father had not-so-affectionately called them. "I'd be honored, sir."

"No, sir," Satch said. "The honor is ours."

——

Twenty-five minutes later, the door to the Raptor was opened, and Jason stepped out and into the waiting grasp of Detective Hatty Daniels. While Chuck parked the car, Satch and Mickey walked on either side of Jason, with Hatty out front leading the way. They entered the courtroom and took the elevator to the second floor. As the ancient machine creaked its way, Hatty smiled at Jason and then looked at Satch and Mickey. "You two are quite a sight."

"Yes, ma'am," Satch grunted.

As they entered the courtroom, Jason saw no spectators. No media. Not even Bella Flowers. The only people he saw between the double doors were the district attorney, Shay Lankford, Walt and Trudy Cowan, and his client, Trey Cowan.

Jason hadn't seen Trey since the shooting, but they'd talked on the phone. He'd told his client to be hopeful for a dismissal but not to expect it. They had to be ready to go.

As Jason crossed through the gate that separated the spectators from counsel, Mickey stayed behind to watch from the back while Satch continued on with Jason. "Colonel, you can't be here," Jason said.

"I can be any damn where I want. Shut up."

Jason shrugged and patted Trey on the back. Then he walked over to Shay. "How are you?"

The district attorney clasped her hands together and looked away from him, as if she were trying to gather herself. Then she leaned into Jason and put her arms around his neck. "Thank you." She pulled back and nodded her head several times, trying hard not to lose her composure. "You . . . saved my life."

"Anyone would have done the same."

"No," Shay whispered. "Not anyone."

"ALL RISE!" the bailiff's salvo startled them both, and Judge Barber walked with his head down to the bench.

When he looked up, he frowned at Satch. "Who are you, sir, and why are you dressed like a soldier and . . . armed with a weapon . . . in my courtroom? I should hold you in contempt."

When Satch spoke, his gravelly tone was so deep and ominous that Jason figured it would make Sam Elliott jealous. The voice gave him goose bumps, as did his words.

"I'm Colonel Satchel Shames Tonidandel. One Hundred and First Airborne Division. Screaming Eagles. I'm here to protect my friend Jason Rich from being attacked like he was the last time he was in downtown Guntersville. Outside of Detective Hatty Daniels, I don't have a great deal of faith in the sheriff's department of this county in light of the conduct of this trial and the attempt on my friend's life. So, if it's all the same with you, Judge, I don't think I'll let you hold me in contempt today. In fact, I think I'll just stand guard over everyone in this courtroom along with my brother Captain Mickey Tonidandel, who's in the back and dressed like me, and my other brother, Captain Chuck Tonidandel, who's guarding outside, also as conspicuous as myself." He paused, before giving the slightest of nods of his head. "Your Honor."

Barber stared in bewilderment at Satch and then Jason. Finally, he just shook his head. "Are we ready to proceed with trial?"

"No, Your Honor," Shay said, standing and straightening her suit. "The state hereby moves to dismiss all charges against the defendant, Trey Jerome Cowan."

Barber glared at her. "You're serious. You're just going to let him go."

"As a heart attack, Judge. Later today, I plan to file a new charge of murder." She paused. "Against Sheriff Richard Griffith."

Barber's face went pale, and then he scratched his ear. He scowled at Jason, who was now standing at the defense table. Trey Cowan was on his right. Satch Tonidandel his left.

"Mr. Cowan?" Barber said, his nasally southern accent sounding like chalk running down a chalkboard. "I have no choice but to grant the state's motion. All charges against you are dismissed." He hesitated. "You're free to go."

———

Trudy Cowan's squeal was so loud it would have broken the windows if there had been any inside the courtroom. She hopped over the barricade between the front row and her son and wrapped her arms around him. Then she did the same to Jason, lifting him off the ground. Finally, she looked at Satch and gave the colonel an awkward hug.

Jason shook Trey's hand, who mouthed a thank-you. He seemed too overcome with emotion to speak. Jason turned and saw Walt, still sitting on the row. Jason walked over and saw that the man's feet and hands were shaking.

"It's over, Walt," Jason said. "We won."

"I . . . can't believe it," he said, looking up at Jason. "I thought I was going to lose my son. Thank you, Mr. Rich."

Jason squeezed his shoulder. "You're welcome."

———

As Jason turned to go away, he heard the banging of Judge Barber's gavel. "Mr. Rich, I think you are forgetting something?"

Jason left Walt Cowan's side and approached the bench.

"If we aren't going to be trying the Trey Cowan case today," Barber began, "then the charges against you, Mr. Rich, will proceed. Trial was reset for October 21, remember?" He smiled. "That's today."

"You can't be serious."

"I can and I am."

"Madame Prosecutor, are you ready to try the case of State of Alabama versus Jason Rich?" Barber asked. "Or would you be requesting another continuance in light of . . ." He struggled for the right phrase. ". . . recent events?"

"Your Honor, there isn't going to be a trial against Mr. Rich," Shay began, her tone all business. "Our witness, Mr. Kevin Martin, has, for the second trial setting in a row, failed to show." She paused. "The state dismisses all remaining charges against Mr. Rich."

"Hoo-ah!" Satch said, his voice so loud and deep that Barber jumped in his seat.

Barber stared at Shay like a kid would glare at someone who'd stolen all his toys. Then he moved his gaze to Jason. "The state's motion is granted. Charges dismissed." He sighed. "Mr. Rich, you're free to leave as well."

122

Six hours later, at 3:00 p.m., after a press conference called by the Board of Marshall County, Shay Lankford huddled with the newly appointed high sheriff.

Ms. Hatty Daniels.

They were seated across from each other in the war room of the sheriff's department. "We have a lot of work to do, Hatty. Matthew Dean is missing and wanted for George Mitchell's murder and the attempt on all of our lives. Bull Branner remains missing and is presumed dead." She sighed. "And Griff . . ."

"AWOL," Hatty said, finishing her thought.

Shay nodded and then smiled. "Are you ready . . . Sheriff?"

Hatty returned the gesture. "I've been ready for this my whole life."

123

A week after the dual dismissals of the charges against Trey Cowan and himself, Jason Rich stood before the Alabama State Bar Disciplinary Commission.

Chairman Winthrop Brooks scowled down at him while the other commissioners avoided eye contact. Jason glanced at his friend Tony Dixon, the general counsel for the state bar, and Tony also averted his eyes.

Oh, shit . . .

"Mr. Rich, the commission has considered the recent events involving you, in particular the charges that were brought by the State of Alabama for harassing a minor, destruction of property, and trespassing, along with the volatile nature of your two criminal trials. You seem to have left a wake of dead bodies in both of them, sir."

"Mr. Chairman, the criminal charges against me were dismissed. And the deaths in the two criminal trials I've handled, while very tragic, weren't my fault."

"The bottom line, Mr. Rich . . ." Brooks removed his glasses. ". . . is that you were under a strict zero-tolerance policy, and you have tested our patience until we finally feel we have to do something."

"You have to be kidding," Jason said. "Tony, they can't do this."

"Mr. Rich, based on the power vested in me by the Alabama State Bar Disciplinary Commission, we hereby suspend your license to practice law for a period of two years. Any advertisements by you to solicit business from clients need to be removed within sixty days, or the commission will consider a stiffer penalty."

"This is retaliation, Win!" Jason yelled, losing all restraint. "The charges against me were dismissed. You heard what Ashley said." He pointed at the only person in the room, his mentor, Ashley Sullivan, looking right at him with a gaze that registered concern. "I've done everything you've asked. I took two criminal cases. I won them both. I won a civil case for $25 million . . . *against you, Win*."

"You will address me as Mr. Chairman, or we may reassess our decision."

"Fuck you!" Jason screamed. He walked around his table. "Fuck all of you. I'm going to sue every damn one of you."

"We'll look forward to it," Brooks said. "Make sure you retain a licensed lawyer."

Jason wanted to scream "Fuck you" again, but knew it was no use. He busted out of the doors and knew exactly what he was going to do.

———

Ashley caught up to him in the parking lot. When he started to protest to her, she reached forward for a hug. "I'm sorry, Jason. I don't agree with their decision. But don't prove them right."

"What do you mean?"

"Don't fall off the wagon."

"What am I supposed to do here?" Jason screamed. "I'm running out of trigger defusers here. I just somehow survived the most stressful case and situation in my life, did the best work I have ever done, and the bar just took my license away. I can't practice law anymore."

"You can in two years."

"Two years!"

Jason stormed to his Porsche, cranked the ignition, and backed the car up. When he tried to move forward, Ashley was blocking his path. She held up an index finger.

"I know how you feel," she said.

"How could you possibly—?"

"I lost my first three cases out of rehab. Two in Cullman and one I got homecooked over in Lawrence County by a local attorney who'd donated a bunch of money to the judge. I wanted to have a drink after that one. I wanted to badly. I even bought a bottle of vodka." She was breathless, and she leaned against the Porsche. "But I didn't."

"How'd you stop the urge?"

"I was like you. I was out of defusers. So I decided to do something crazy. Dangerous. So out of character for me that I wouldn't have time to take a drink."

Jason was finally curious. "What'd you do?"

She grinned. Then giggled. Then turned around to make sure no one else was in the parking lot.

Jason felt a warmth come over him as he looked into Ashley's green eyes and saw her genuine smile. "What?" Jason pressed.

"About halfway back to Cullman . . . I pulled down my skirt and took off my blouse." She burst into another fit of giggles. "And I drove the rest of the way in my bra and panties."

"Oh, no you didn't." Jason laughed out loud.

"Oh, yes I did. Once I was back home, the urge was gone. And I never had a desire to drink again as strong as that one. Doing something dangerous and risky cut the head off the snake for me."

"Are you telling me I need to drop my drawers and see how far I get on I-65?"

"Jason, you were investigated by the bar for streaking the Quad a few years ago with a federal judge's daughter. I don't think exhibitionism is as dangerous to you as it was to me." She punched his shoulder. "What's something you're afraid of? Something that you're more scared of than falling off the wagon?"

Jason nodded to himself and stared at his steering wheel. He felt a warm moistness on his cheek and then hot breath in his ear. "You can do this," she said, pulling away from him.

"Ashley . . . can I call you when I get home?"

"You're supposed to call me once a month, remember, silly?"

"Not like that, I mean . . ." He fumbled for the right words.

"I like you, Jason, but remember what I said about the passenger in the airplane when the plane is in trouble. You're still wrestling with your own oxygen mask." She paused, her face turning serious. "Until you get yours on, you aren't going to be good for anyone else."

124

Jason drove home with no music. The only sound was the wind blowing through his hair and the noises from other cars.

He made it almost forty-five minutes before he stopped. It was a gas station in Helena. He bought a six-pack of Lagunitas India Pale Ale, his absolute favorite during his drinking days. He opened a can and breathed in the citrusy hops.

But he didn't drink it. Just smelled it. When he finally made it into Marshall County, he rolled his window down and poured out the open beer.

Thirty minutes later, he pulled into his driveway. He didn't go in the door but instead walked down to the boathouse, still holding the remaining five beer cans. It was almost midnight, but he didn't care. He set the beer on the dock, opened up the doors, gassed up the Sea-Doo, and backed the watercraft out of the lift. It was freezing outside, and Jason didn't care.

Once he'd maneuvered the Sea-Doo out into the main channel, he squeezed his right hand all the way on the throttle as he hurtled toward Honeycomb Cove. When he reached the cliffs at Goat Island, he cut the ignition. *Kids make this jump every single day of the summer. I'm a grown-ass man, and I'm going to check this box. I don't care how cold or dark it is. I am going to do this.*

"Siri, play my theme music over and over again!" he yelled.

"I'll repeat the song," the monotone voice replied.

As the opening guitar riff of "Highway to Hell" blared out of the speaker, Jason James Rich tore off his shirt, ripped off his pants, and jumped into the ice-cold water wearing nothing but his boxer shorts.

Ten minutes later, he had climbed to the top of the cliffs.

"Ohhhhhhhhhhhh! Yeahhhhhhhhhhh!" Jason screamed, doing the "Macho Man." *The cream will always rise to the top!*

"Do you hear me, Cade?!" he screamed.

You've always been a goofy bastard. Jana's voice.

Helpful? Maybe.

"You know it, sister!" Then he took off his boxer shorts, slung them over the edge, and as the opening chord of "Highway to Hell" rang out again, he screamed his loudest Ric Flair.

"Wooooooooooooo!"

Then Jason Rich jumped from the top cliff at Goat Island.

EPILOGUE

Three weeks after the close of the trial of Trey Cowan, at 10:30 a.m. on a perfect mid-November day, Tyson Cade stepped out of the Alder Springs Grocery. He had a Twinkie in one hand and a Sun Drop in the other.

He glanced to his left and saw a car approaching. He began to walk toward the road as the car slowed its pace. As Tyson was about to get in, he heard a voice yell out from behind him.

"Tyson, wait!"

He turned and saw Dooby Darnell.

"You forgot your change."

He wrinkled up his face. Then, feeling his stomach tighten, he tried to duck.

He wasn't fast enough.

Gunfire erupted from behind the convenience store, and Tyson felt his chest explode. He dropped to his knees.

Dooby Darnell dropped the change she was holding to the ground and covered her mouth.

Tyson Cade blinked his eyes and fell over on his back. He touched his chest and looked at his bloody hand. Then, as his pulse slowed and he began to lose consciousness, he laughed.

And the cars continued to pass on Hustleville Road.

ACKNOWLEDGMENTS

My wife, Dixie, read the prologue of *The Professor* in 2002 and told me she thought I should chase my dream. Twenty years and nine books later, and we are still chasing. She is my first editor and my favorite person to run story ideas by. I love her so much.

Our children—Jimmy, Bobby, and Allie—are our greatest creations, and they inspire, motivate, and delight me every day.

My mom, Beth Bailey, is my biggest supporter. She is the steel magnolia of our family, and I don't know what any of us would do without her.

My agent, Liza Fleissig, is a force of nature, and her persistence and drive keep us moving forward. I am incredibly fortunate to have her as my wingman on this writing journey.

My developmental editor, Clarence Haynes, has now worked with me on seven novels. His insights and editorial prowess are a tremendous asset to me as a writer, and my favorite part of the process has become our annual check-in phone call to brainstorm ideas. Excelsior, Clarence!

To Megha Parekh, Gracie Doyle, Sarah Shaw, and my entire editing and marketing team at Thomas & Mercer, thank you for your support and encouragement. I am so proud and grateful to have you as my publisher.

My friend and law school classmate Judge Will Powell was a great bouncing board for criminal law and trial questions.

Thank you once again to my friends Bill Fowler, Rick Onkey, Mark Wittschen, and Steve Shames for their early reads of the story and for supporting my dream.

My brother, Bo Bailey, to whom I dedicated this novel, has supported my goal of being a writer from the beginning. I am grateful for his calm, well-reasoned, and steady advice along this journey.

My father-in-law, Dr. Jim Davis, continues to be my firearms expert for my stories. I am grateful for "Doc" and appreciate his support and positive energy.

My niece Bentley League answered pivotal questions regarding the Honeycomb Cove area of Lake Guntersville.

My friend Jonathan Lusk continues to provide key insights on his hometown of Guntersville and Marshall County.

To Judy Kennamer DeBlanc, who took the photograph of the boathouse on Lake Guntersville that was utilized for the cover of *Rich Blood*, thank you for capturing this wonderful image, which was perfect for the story.

To Shasti O'Leary Soudant, who provided the beautiful cover designs for *Rich Blood*, *The Wrong Side*, and *Legacy of Lies*, thank you for sharing your talent.

To Jarrod Taylor, who designed the cover of this book, thank you for capturing the haunting essence of this story with your work.

My friends Joe and Foncie Bullard from Point Clear, Alabama, were with me in the beginning and continue to provide incredible support. I treasure their friendship so much.

My friend Richi Reynolds was instrumental in setting up our book launch for *Rich Blood*. I appreciate her support and am honored to have been featured in her *Three Friends and a Fork* blog.

ABOUT THE AUTHOR

Photo © 2019 Erin Cobb

Robert Bailey is the *Wall Street Journal* bestselling author of *Rich Blood*; the Bocephus Haynes series, which includes *The Wrong Side* and *Legacy of Lies*; and the award-winning McMurtrie and Drake Legal Thrillers series, which includes *The Final Reckoning*, *The Last Trial*, *Between Black and White*, and *The Professor*. He is also the author of the inspirational novel *The Golfer's Carol*. *Rich Waters* is Bailey's ninth novel.

For the past twenty-three years, Bailey has been an attorney in Huntsville, Alabama, where he lives with his wife and three children. For more, please visit www.RobertBaileyBooks.com.